NOBODY'S
HERO

ALSO BY M. W. CRAVEN

The Ben Koenig Series

The Washington Poe Series

The Avison Fluke Series

NOBODY'S HERO

M. W. CRAVEN

FLATIRON
BOOKS
NEW YORK

NOBODY'S HERO. Copyright © 2024 by M. W. Craven. All rights reserved. Printed in the United States of America. For information, address Flatiron Books, 120 Broadway, New York, NY 10271.

www.flatironbooks.com

Library of Congress Cataloging-in-Publication Data

Names: Craven, M. W. (Mike W.), 1968– author.
Title: Nobody's hero / M.W. Craven.
Description: First U.S. edition. | New York : Flatiron Books, 2024. | Series:
    Ben Koenig series
Identifiers: LCCN 2023059366 | ISBN 9781250864598 (hardcover) |
    ISBN 9781250864611 (ebook)
Subjects: LCGFT: Thrillers (Fiction) | Novels.
Classification: LCC PR6103.R374 N63 2024 | DDC 823/.92—dc23/
    eng/20240117
LC record available at https://lccn.loc.gov/2023059366

Our books may be purchased in bulk for promotional, educational, or business use. Please contact your local bookseller or the Macmillan Corporate and Premium Sales Department at 1-800-221-7945, extension 5442, or by email at MacmillanSpecialMarkets@macmillan.com.

First published in the United Kingdom by Constable, a division of
Little, Brown Book Group

First U.S. Edition: 2024

10   9   8   7   6   5   4   3   2   1

To Jake Burns, for giving me the book's title,
and to Steve Harris, for giving me
the protocol's code name

NOBODY'S HERO

CHAPTER 1

When Stephen Williamson regained consciousness, when he figured out where he was, he wished he hadn't. He wished he had remained *unconscious*. Or, better yet, someplace else. Because, when he opened his eyes, Stephen saw he was strapped to an industrial workbench in an abandoned auto factory in Detroit. He knew it was a factory because the oil-stained concrete floor was pockmarked with the foundation holes of long-gone heavy machinery. He knew it was abandoned because the support pillars were covered in graffiti and he could smell urine. And he knew it had been an auto factory and that it was in Detroit because of what was on the redbrick wall. The first was an Oldsmobile sign, white on a black background. Kind of looked like a rectangular peace symbol. And although most Oldsmobile vehicles had been built in Lansing, the second sign was a United Auto Workers logo. A blue-and-white circle. "Local 35" was stamped underneath. Local 35 was a Detroit union.

It took Stephen a touch over four seconds to work this out. He had that kind of mind. It was analytical. He spent the next thirty seconds working out *why* he was strapped to a bench in an abandoned auto factory in Detroit. He ran through a series of scenarios and came up with only one that worked all the way to the end: His abduction was a case of mistaken identity. He must share similar characteristics with another Stephen Williamson. It was a common name, and he had no distinguishing features. He didn't have an eye patch or a crooked back. He was ordinary-looking. No one was going to say, "We must have the wrong Stephen Williamson. This one has a hump and a neck tattoo."

He studied the people who had taken him from his home in Hopewell, New Jersey. There were six of them. Four men and two women. They wore black jeans and heavy boots. All six had short hair. They were talking quietly among themselves. They weren't paying him any attention whatsoever. Having an elderly academic tied to a bench in an abandoned auto factory in Detroit was clearly not a big deal. Like it was the kind of thing they did every day. This was not a comforting thought.

Hopewell to Detroit was a six-hundred-mile drive. Nine hours in a car. Yet Stephen couldn't remember the journey. He wasn't in pain, but he did feel groggy. They'd drugged him. Which wasn't as easy to do as it looked in the movies. It needed expertise. That meant he was dealing with professionals. Yet they'd got the wrong person. Which meant he *wasn't* dealing with professionals. It was contradictory.

"You have the wrong person," he said. "My name is Stephen Williamson. *Stephen*. With a *P-H*, not a *V*."

"Good morning, Stephen with a *P-H*," one of the men said, walking over. He was tall, maybe six one. Blond-haired and blue-eyed. High cheekbones and an aerodynamically shaped head. Like a bird's. Possibly Slavic. His English was flawless but clipped. Like he'd learned it when he was an adult, not a child. "I am glad you're awake. My name is Jakob Tas."

Stephen didn't respond. The name meant nothing to him.

"A client hired us to put some questions to a very specific group of people," Tas continued. "Unfortunately, you *are* one of those people. So, I will ask you some questions. Hopefully, you will answer them. If you do not, then . . . well, let us say, it would be better for you if you did." He took a step back. A woman broke away from the group. "But before we get started, my colleague Miss Cora Pearl is going to conduct a rudimentary medical examination to ensure you have not suffered any ill effects."

Pearl was a wiry woman in her thirties. If Tas was Slavic, Pearl was pure West Coast. Light, tousled hair bleached by sun and salt. Tanned skin. A dusting of freckles across the bridge of her nose. Her face was makeup-free, and she wore no jewelry. She examined Stephen with fingers that were long, thin, and strong. She wasn't rough, but neither was she gentle. She lifted his eyelids and shone a penlight into his eyes.

"He's dehydrated," she said.

"Do we need to put him on a drip?"

"Drink of water will do."

Pearl reached into her bag and brought out a bottle. She unscrewed the lid, lifted Stephen's head, and helped him drink. Stephen hadn't realized how thirsty he was. He drank the whole bottle in one go.

"You have the wrong Stephen Williamson," he said again. "I'm a history professor at Princeton, not a . . . whatever it is you think I am."

"And what is your area of expertise, Stephen?"

"My area . . . ?"

"If you are a Princeton history professor, you must have a period of history that you specialize in. I would like to know what that specialization is, please."

"The Ottoman Empire. It was—"

"One of the largest empires in recorded history," Tas cut in. "It lasted six hundred years, controlled most of Southeast Europe, North Africa, and West Asia, and at its peak, it covered almost eight million square miles. We do not have the wrong Stephen with a *P-H*. We do not make mistakes."

As well as having an analytical mind, the kind of mind that could work out where he was based on a couple of old factory signs, Stephen had also been good at predicting outcomes by studying known facts. "An extraordinary gift for extrapolation," his professor had said when he submitted his thesis. Stephen had always thought it was a pity that Suleiman the Magnificent's advisers hadn't had the same gift. If they had, the Ottoman Empire might not have failed.

Right now, Stephen didn't like the future he'd predicted for himself. Tas and his colleagues weren't wearing masks. It suggested they weren't concerned about being identified later. And they knew who he was. That was clear now. Abducting him hadn't been a mistake. Which made no sense. To the best of his knowledge, he had never moved in the same circles as men like Jakob Tas, or the kind of people who hired men like Jakob Tas.

"You are an intelligent man, Stephen with a *P-H*," Tas said. "I think you have already worked out that your situation is precarious."

Stephen said nothing.

"Precarious, but not hopeless, I think," Tas continued. "If your answers stand up to scrutiny, in the fullness of time, you will leave here in one piece. If your answers *don't* stand up to scrutiny, you will leave here in small bags. Do you understand?"

"I understand," Stephen said.

"Good. Then let us be—"

"I understand your client has made a mistake. They must have. Because I do believe that you guys know what you're doing. You've grabbed who you were told to grab. But you must understand, you're working from flawed data. I'm not the person you want to talk to."

"But you do not know what I want to talk to you about yet, Ste—" He stopped to cough. A wet rattle, one from the bottom of his lungs. The others looked away, embarrassed. "Allergies," he said after he'd got it under control.

"There's nothing we *can* talk about," Stephen said. He used his head to gesture at his surroundings. "Nothing that makes any sense of this. I'm an academic. I'm not the man you—"

"Ten years ago, you attended a meeting at this address," Tas said. He unfolded a piece of paper. Showed it to Stephen. "I want to know everything that was discussed."

If Stephen had been standing, he'd have fallen over. It would be like the room had tilted. Tas hadn't made a mistake. Neither had his client. He wondered who'd talked. It wasn't him. He'd never mentioned the meeting to anyone, not even his wife.

There was no point denying it. That Tas and his client even knew about the meeting was proof enough that the thing that could never happen already had. The leakproof security arrangements had leaked. Despite the shock, he allowed himself a small smile. The fact he was strapped to a bench in an abandoned auto factory was proof that at least part of the security arrangements had held firm. They didn't know everything.

It was a comforting thought.

He was about to die. It was inevitable. Tas couldn't allow him to live, not with the stakes this high. But Stephen would be missed. He had a family. He had friends and colleagues. An employer. If he vanished, people would ask why. Tas knew this but had abducted him anyway. That meant he'd been forced to. It was a risk.

Stephen knew his life could be measured in minutes now, not hours. He had one job left: to provoke a reaction that ended with him dead and Tas no further forward.

"If you know anything about that meeting, you'll also know I'll die before I talk about it," he said.

Tas nodded. Like he'd expected him to say something like that. A seventh person came into view. He was a big man. Had so many scars on his face he looked like Frankenstein's monster. He wore a long-sleeved plastic gown, rubber gloves, and a face visor, like a doctor during the early days of COVID. He was holding a chain saw, casually, as if he used one all the time. Stephen's mouth went dry. He started to hyperventilate.

"This is Konstantin," Tas said. "My organization does not have a human resources department, per se, but we take employee welfare seriously nonetheless. When he was a child, Konstantin's brother died of AIDS. He is now terrified of contracting a blood-borne virus. But he also has an unmatched enthusiasm for this line of work. You academic types might call it a proclivity. Which is why we provide him with the personal protective equipment he is wearing now. It makes him feel safe." Tas paused a beat. "Does Konstantin's PPE make *you* feel safe, Stephen?"

Stephen shook his head. Didn't even realize he had.

"Tell me about the meeting," Tas said.

"Never."

"Never is an awfully long time, Stephen."

Stephen gulped. He wasn't a particularly brave man, but he had never considered himself a coward. "Do your worst," he said.

Tas sighed. "Mr. Konstantin, if you please?"

Konstantin stepped forward, emotionless. He revved the chain saw. A burst of noise. It sounded like an angry lion. Exhaust fumes filled the abandoned factory. Konstantin pressed the tip of the spitting blade against Stephen's bare ankle . . .

CHAPTER 2

TWO YEARS LATER. HYDE PARK, LONDON.
Speakers' Corner in Hyde Park is the oldest and most famous free speech platform in the world. Karl Marx, George Orwell, and Winston Churchill have all mounted soapboxes to debate the great issues of the day. So did Lenin, Vanessa Redgrave, and Harold Pinter. Noteworthy figures all.

The unhinged, foam-flecked ranter currently occupying the soapbox was *not* noteworthy. He was called Derek Bancroft, and he passionately believed that Denver International Airport was the secret headquarters of both the Illuminati and the New World Order. He claimed the artwork, sculptures, and engravings in the airport were secret messages to those in the know. And Derek was in the know. He was less clear on why the Illuminati and the New World Order had revealed their secrets to a chicken sexer from Brixton, but if you were searching for lucid, well-constructed arguments at Speakers' Corner on a Sunday morning, you were in for an unrewarding wait. Nonetheless, the enthusiastic Derek was being cheered on by a growing and not-a-little-hungover crowd. Enthusiasm was everything at Speakers' Corner.

Derek was the warm-up act, though. The person everyone was waiting for was a prominent flat-earther. Maybe it was the irony of someone asking you to not believe your own eyes in the very place the author of *Nineteen Eighty-Four* had spoken, but the flat-earthers always attracted a good crowd. People would heckle and challenge and argue and throw eggs, and that was as it should be in a healthy democracy.

One of the people watching Derek was a well-dressed woman called Margaret Wexmore. She was in her mid-sixties but looked older. She was as thin as a pencil and fish-belly pale. Her hair was gunmetal gray. Margaret watched Derek with enjoyment. She seemed glad to be outside, as if it had once been an everyday occurrence but wasn't anymore.

While Margaret watched Derek, two Romanian pickpockets watched her. London had a problem with Romanian gangs. It had started with the 2012 Olympics. Organized gangs had brought in pickpockets and prostitutes and beggars to take advantage of the massive influx of visitors. Now pickpockets worked Speakers' Corner all year round.

The Romanians watching Margaret were called Darius and Alexandru. They had been pickpockets their entire lives, but they weren't like the loveable scamps found in Dickens's novels. Darius and Alexandru were mean and aggressive and carried *douk-douks*, French-made pocketknives. They were usually assigned to Oxford Street. They hadn't worked a static crowd for a long time. They were used to fast-moving, inattentive shoppers. People in a hurry. A crowd like this made them nervous. That they'd been given counterintuitive instructions hadn't helped. Usually, they knew what they were looking for. People brandishing new iPhones. Men with Breitling watches, women with Prada handbags. Overt signs of money.

This time they had a photograph.

They were after a *who*, not a what.

Darius double-checked the photograph on his phone. The woman looked older and frailer now, but it was a good likeness. She was where they'd been told she would be, and she was alone. Darius deleted the photograph as instructed, then checked his watch. It was nearly time.

He glanced over his shoulder and checked if anyone was watching. Undercover cops sometimes prowled Speakers' Corner. There was no one there. Just a homeless woman. Darius frowned. He didn't like being watched. He glared at her, but she continued to stare. Her shoulders were stooped like a month-old daffodil, and she kind of shuffled without moving anywhere. She wore so much clothing she bulged. She could have been overweight, or she could have had the physique of a ballet dancer. It was impossible to tell. She wore a coat with a hood. The coat was stained with what looked like egg but was probably vomit. The bottom half of her face was covered with a surgical mask. It was blue and it was grubby. It looked like the kind of mask that *started* global pandemics rather than ended them. She held a carrier bag in each hand. Darius wasn't interested in what was inside them. Homeless people collected all kinds of shit and hung on to it like it was treasure.

The homeless woman continued to stare. Or maybe she was watching the crazy guy talking about the airport. It was hard to tell where she was looking underneath the mask and the hood. Darius put her to the back of his mind. Margaret Wexmore was important. The homeless woman wasn't. Even if she saw what was about to happen, she wouldn't go to the police. Homeless people never did.

It was nothing to worry about.

He turned back to Margaret Wexmore.

Underneath her mask, the homeless woman smiled. But not in a nice way. Resignation, not happiness. As if she'd decided to do something unpleasant.

And when Darius and Alexandru made their move, the homeless woman made a move of her own . . .

CHAPTER 3

The cold-blooded murder of two Romanian nationals was the lead in every British newspaper for days. That a homeless woman had committed the murder triggered emergency debates on housing and mental health. That she'd used a gun in a city more used to knife crime caused the mayor's approval rating to drop by ten points. That the homeless woman had subsequently abducted a retired academic and seemingly vanished meant the Metropolitan Police commissioner, the UK's senior police officer, was called to the Home Office for a chat without coffee.

The senior investigating officer in the Speakers' Corner murders was called Detective Chief Superintendent Danielle Brown. Her first task had been to send a team to the basement dwellers who monitored the city's CCTV cameras. London was one of the most surveilled cities on the planet. Despite that, her team had found nothing. A portal to a billion snatches of London life and not one workable lead. On the rare occasion the homeless woman had been captured on tape, she was still hooded and wearing the surgical mask. Danielle had cursed the pandemic that had made it acceptable for criminals to wear what were essentially Dick Turpin masks in broad daylight.

She gave up on CCTV and resorted to old-school policing: leaning on snitches and knocking on doors.

But deep underneath the streets and the sewage drains and the high-end restaurants was a basement dweller who hadn't given up. He was called Graham Hancox, and from his swivel seat he could access all of Westminster Council's static and mobile CCTV cameras. He'd taken it as a personal insult that the homeless woman had managed to evade him. Because Graham was exactly the kind of person who believed a multimillion-pound surveillance system belonged to him. In his spare time Graham trawled the streets of London, looking for private cameras the police might have missed. Doorbell cams, nanny cams, dash cams, shop security systems. When he found one, he had the raw footage sent to his work email.

So far, he had found nothing.

But that was about to change.

The paused footage on Graham's screen was of the homeless woman and Margaret Wexmore. The homeless woman was gripping Margaret's arm and dragging her along one of the few suburban streets that wasn't covered by CCTV.

"Where did you get this?"

Graham explained that the owners of a Greek deli had aimed a private CCTV camera at the cash register near the door, and because the gyro meat was cooking, the door had been wedged open to let in some air.

Danielle was disappointed. All the footage showed was the homeless woman in a different part of London. It added to what they knew of the journey she'd taken, but it didn't contribute to the wider story of who she was, or where she and Margaret Wexmore were now.

Graham saw her expression. He said, "Watch this."

He pressed play. Instead of walking out of shot, the homeless woman removed a fob from her pocket. She used it to unlock a Volkswagen Golf. She opened the passenger door for Margaret and helped her inside. She then walked to the driver's side and opened the door.

But before she got in, she took off her coat and removed her mask.

Three weeks after the Romanian pickpockets were shot in the back of their heads, Detective Chief Superintendent Danielle Brown finally saw the face of the woman who'd pulled the trigger. Graham took a screenshot and Danielle rushed it through the Metropolitan Police's facial-recognition program.

One hour later, the case was shut down.

Several things happened in that hour.

The first was the facial-recognition program returning a negative result. The homeless woman wasn't in the system. The second thing that happened was that a silent alert was triggered. It automatically sent an eyes-only email to the cultural attaché at the US embassy in Nine Elms, the biggest American embassy in Western Europe. The cultural attaché, a CIA veteran called Bernice Kopitz, opened the email, read it twice, then followed the instructions exactly. She called a number in Virginia, and when it was answered, she said "Acacia Avenue." Bernice didn't know what that meant, and she knew she never would. She deleted the email she'd been sent and cleared it from her trash. She then went back to work and forgot all about it.

They didn't forget all about it in Virginia. "Acacia Avenue" was passed up the chain of command until it found the one person with the right security clearance. That person used an eleven-digit code to open a safe in his office. It was only the second time it had been opened. The first was shortly after it had been installed. The man opening the safe now had no idea what was inside. He only knew that if the phrase "Acacia Avenue" was passed up the chain of command, he was to open the safe and follow the instructions he would find inside.

Inside the safe was a sealed envelope. He opened it and removed the single sheet of paper. It was a list of names. A list of names and a single sentence. It said he was to contact the person at the top of the list and tell them the Acacia Avenue Protocol had been initiated. If that person couldn't be contacted, he was to go on to the second name.

The list had four names. He recognized the first three. Knew them personally. He also knew they were dead. The big three: cancer, a stroke, and an old-fashioned heart attack. He'd gone to their funerals.

He didn't know the fourth name on the list, though.

He typed it into his computer. A single result came back. He frowned. It didn't make sense. The first three names had been serious people with serious jobs. The fourth name was a nobody. He pressed the intercom on his desk and summoned his aide.

The aide, an air force captain, was there immediately.

"Sir?"

"I need you to find someone for me."

"Who, sir?"

The man told him.

"Who the hell is Ben Koenig?" the aide said.

PART ONE

QUIS CUSTODIET IPSOS CUSTODES?

Who will guard the guards themselves?

CHAPTER 4

NEW YORK. HALLOWEEN.

"Who the hell are you?" Ben Koenig said to the woman who'd slid into the seat next to him.

She had the physique of a long-distance runner and looked twice as miserable. She wore her makeup harsh. Thick mascara and a powdered face. If she added a green wig, she could have joined the trick-or-treaters as a Batman villain. She looked like she'd have been a mean cheerleader, the kind who laughed when the quarterback busted up his knee.

"I'm your worst nightmare," she said.

"You're a dietician?" Koenig replied.

"Funny." She turned and faced a hipster at the computer opposite. Stared until he noticed, then kept staring. The hipster had intricate tattoos and a pubic beard. He wore a beanie hat and corduroy dungarees. Looked like every hipster everywhere. The kind of man who slept in a hammock. He'd been playing some sort of role-playing game, but he caved under the woman's withering glare. He picked up his canvas man-bag and left without speaking.

A man immediately took his place. He was so overweight he walked like a duck. He stared at Koenig like he was a day-old doughnut.

Koenig checked out the rest of the internet café. The dynamics had changed. He hadn't noticed, but no one new had entered for at least thirty minutes. It had been full a couple of hours ago. He'd had to wait for a computer terminal. Now it was almost empty.

Another guy was sitting at a terminal next to the door. A hulking, beetle-browed man with a flat nose and asymmetrical ears. Looked like he'd taken a few punches over the years. He hadn't even gone to the pretense of turning on the computer. If this were a movie, he'd have flipped the sign to CLOSED after the hipster had left. Made sure Koenig watched him do it. Koenig figured there was someone outside stopping new customers from entering. That made four. The three inside were wearing jeans. Not like a uniform, more like if you put any three Americans together, sure as milk on Mondays, most will be wearing jeans. Koenig was wearing a pair himself.

The woman twisted to show the Colt Detective Special she had in her right hand. She held it low and tucked in tight to her hip. Professional. No way to disarm her before she could put a couple into his liver. She gave Koenig an appraising look. "I thought you'd be bigger," she said.

"I get that a lot."

"Hand over your cell phone."

"Don't have one."

"Everybody has a cell phone."

"I don't."

"Stand up," she said.

Koenig did. Standing was better than sitting. It gave him more options.

Walks-like-a-duck guy waddled around and expertly patted him down. Pulled out Koenig's wallet and threw it on the table. It clattered against the keyboard.

"He wasn't shitting you," he said. "He don't have one."

"Check his backpack. Let's see what else he doesn't have."

They waited while Walks-Like-a-Duck rooted through Koenig's back-pack.

"Looks like he's going camping. There's a knife but no cell phone and no gun."

"Let's take this outside," the woman said. "You grab his bag, we'll bring him."

Koenig sat down and folded his arms. More to see what they did than for any tactical advantage.

"Stand up," she said.

"No."

She sighed, like she'd expected him to refuse. "Either you stand up and follow me out, or we drag you out after I've put a bullet in your hip. Choose now."

Koenig checked out what the other two were doing. They were watching him. The beetle-browed guy had his hand inside his jacket. Koenig could see the butt of a handgun. Looked like a SIG. Maybe a Browning. So far no one had gotten excited. No one had panicked. The internet café's solitary staff member hadn't noticed someone was being abducted right in front of her. She was wearing a She-Hulk costume. It bothered Koenig that adults wore costumes for Halloween. They hadn't when he was growing up in Boston. Maybe it was a New York thing.

He glanced at the woman. He believed her when she'd said she'd shoot him in the hip. And if she did that, they would have to kill She-Hulk too.

"Do you know why I'm here?" Koenig said.

"You were watching a film. Some old vampire movie."

"You've been watching me for a while then? That's interesting. But no, I meant do you know why I'm in this café *today*?"

"What the hell do I care?"

"You should care a great deal," Koenig said.

"And why's that?"

"You clearly know who I am."

"Obviously," she said.

"But did you know I'm kinda on an invisible leash? It's not a short leash and I can pretty much do what I want, but I'm on a leash nonetheless."

The woman said nothing. She frowned and glanced at Beetle-Brow. She wasn't in charge then. Useful to know. Beetle-Brow shrugged.

"Ah, this is new information," Koenig said. "Let me help you out. You were quite right, I was watching a movie. *Captain Kronos: Vampire Hunter*. Have you seen it? It's probably Horst Janson's most well-known English language film."

"No one's seen your stupid film, asshole."

"Oh, you really should. There's this cool scene in the local tavern where Kronos runs his sword across some thugs' throats before they even have time to move. There'll be a test on that bit later."

"Killing you will be a public service."

"Anyway," Koenig said with a polite smile, "I try not to spend a lot of time in the same place, you know, in case some bounty hunters find me, but occasionally I stop long enough to catch a movie. I suppose I was what you might call a buff. A movie buff. It's one of the things I had to give up when the Russians put five million bucks on my head."

"Can you *please* get to the point," the woman said. "We're getting old here."

"If you were watching me for as long as you claim, you'll know that I'd finished watching my movie, yet knowing I can't stay in the same place for too long, I didn't leave the second Kronos saves the village and rides off into the sunset. A more inquisitive group of bounty hunters might have asked themselves why that was."

"And what might this group be more inquisitive about?" Beetle-Brow said.

"I've got you guys in stereo now?" Koenig said. "I thought you might leave all the long words to the Joker."

"My name's Cunningham, asshole!" the woman snapped.

Koenig smiled. He loved it when people lost their cool. It meant they weren't thinking clearly. They were deviating from their plan. This wasn't the first time people had tried to claim the bounty, and it wouldn't be the last. "You guys want to tell me your names as well?" he said to Beetle-Brow and Walks-Like-a-Duck.

"Shut the hell up," Beetle-Brow said.

Koenig didn't.

"You see, this invisible leash I'm on means I'm required to send an email by five p.m. on the last day of every month. Today is Halloween, and Halloween is the last day of October." He paused. "Stop me if I'm going too fast."

No one stopped him.

"It's why I was watching the movie in an internet café instead of a cinema with a feed bag of popcorn and a gallon of Sprite," Koenig continued.

"So what?" Cunningham said.

Koenig moved his seat so she could see his screen. "I haven't sent my email yet. It's still in my draft folder. If it doesn't get sent, a bunch of people are going to get mad at me. Then they're going to *worry* about me. Then they're going to look for me. And then they're going to get mad at *you*."

The woman said "So what?" again.

"These are not the kind of people you want to upset."

"Let me guess," she said. "You think we should let you go. That we should walk away from the biggest payday we'll ever have. That what you think?"

"No. I think you should let me send my email."

"You think I'm an idiot? I'm not letting you write an email."

"I *know* you're an idiot," Koenig said. "I told you, it's already done. I wrote it before you came in. I haven't added to it since you sat beside me. It can't possibly have anything incriminating in it. Not unless you think I'm psychic. *Do* you think I'm psychic, Cunningham?"

Before she could reply, Koenig reached over and pressed enter. She jabbed the Colt into his ribs and twisted the barrel. "What the fuck have you done?"

"See for yourself. I assume you can read."

She turned the screen and found the email he'd sent. Her lips moved as she read it. Voicing, Koenig thought it was called. Had its roots in grade school when children were taught to read phonetically and out loud so the teacher could see they were saying the words right. Some kids never kicked the habit. Meant they could only read as fast as they could talk, around 150 words a minute. Cunningham was categorized as a slow reader.

And a slow thinker, as it turned out.

"Why would you risk a bullet in the gut to send that?" she said.

"What does it say?" Beetle-Brow asked.

"Just some bullshit to a woman called Jen. Says, and I quote, 'Everything fine. Just about to leave New York. Not telling you where I'm going next.'"

"Riveting."

"Why would you risk a bullet to send that?" Cunningham repeated.

"Guess I don't want anyone to worry about me," Koenig said.

"And now they won't. Perhaps you shouldn't have sent it. If I were in your shoes, I'd be desperate for someone to worry about me."

"You plan to kill me? Claim the five million?"

"Not us," she said. "We don't do that. We have a buyer lined up. Our organization gets fifty percent of whatever he gets. Nice little payday, and even better, there's one less asshole in the world."

"Why? Is he killing you as well?"

"You have a smart mouth. Wonder if it'll still be smart when our guy's peeling your skin off."

"That's not in the contract."

"It isn't," she admitted. "He just likes doing things like that. And for two and a half million bucks, who are we to say no?"

"Guess I made a mistake sending that email then," Koenig said.

"Guess you did," she said. "Now, on your feet. If you make a fuss, I'll pop one in your pelvis and my friend over there will drop the Incredible Hulk."

"*She*-Hulk," Koenig corrected.

"Whatever. The point is she'll be dead, you'll have a bullet in your hip, and we'll still get what we came for."

"I need to pay first. If I don't, She-Hulk is going to call the cops. I'm guessing you don't want that."

"We'll take care of the check," she said.

"Do you have a prepaid credit card?" Koenig said. "This is a cashless business. Post-COVID thing. Try to pay with cash in here and you're going to stand out. Which I'm guessing none of you want."

Cunningham frowned.

"I'm also guessing that none of you want your Amex getting pinged in the last place I was seen."

She didn't reply.

"Tell you what," Koenig sighed. "How about I pay? But next time you guys are picking up the tab. Deal?"

"What's fucking wrong with you?" Cunningham said.

"I don't follow."

"Sure you do. All this crazy 'I'm not scared' bullshit. Offering to pay the tab. Sending that email. You got a screw loose or something?"

"I'm in a good mood," Koenig said.

"Whatever. Pay the tab then. But try anything funny and—"

"Yeah, yeah. I get a bullet in the hip and She-Hulk gets one in the head. Did you have enough coffee this morning? You seem cranky."

Koenig picked up his wallet from the computer desk. He removed his credit card. It was an untraceable card from an IBC, an international business corporation. IBCs were like offshore companies, and that was where Koenig kept most of his assets. Meant he could confidentially access his money. Even the Supreme Court couldn't find out which ATM he'd used. He clicked the end-session button. *Captain Kronos: Vampire Hunter* was a ninety-minute film, and he'd been talking to his potential abductors for almost ten. He owed eight bucks. He swiped his credit card against the reader and settled the tab.

He stood. Quickly. Cunningham jerked back. The two men reached for their weapons. Koenig smiled.

"Outside," Cunningham hissed. "Slowly. Hands where we can see them."

Koenig did exactly that. He showed them his hands. There was nothing in them.

Which was odd. He should have been holding his credit card.

CHAPTER 5

"I want you to know, this isn't personal," Beetle-Brow said when they were in the parking lot. Koenig had been bustled to the rear of a cream Ford Taurus. A tall, rangy beanpole of a man was waiting for them. He unlocked the trunk. It opened slowly, like it understood the gravity of the situation. Walks-Like-a-Duck threw in Koenig's backpack.

"I thought you guys were an urban myth," Koenig said. "I'd heard rumors when I was in the Special Operations Group, of course, but this is quite the surprise. And not a nice surprise. Not like finding a nickel. This is more like finding blood in your urine."

Walks-Like-a-Duck said, "Jesus, does this asshole never shut up?"

"Oh, you do talk?" Koenig said. "I assumed you'd only be able to quack."

Walks-Like-a-Duck scowled. His nostrils flared. He bared his teeth.

"Easy, Ken," Beetle-Brow said.

"So, he's Ken and she's Cunningham," Koenig said. "The driver's seat is pushed all the way back, so that means it's Beanpole's car. That makes you the guy in charge. And collectively you're part of the East Coast Sweeney."

An uneasy silence. Then, "And what might that be?"

"It's a cabal of corrupt cops. Supposed to be active in the big East Coast cities. Boston, Philly, Baltimore. New York, obviously. They get paid to take down rival drug kingpins. The occasional hit. Safe passage for felons and high-value packages. It's named after the Flying Squad, the unit responsible for investigating robberies in London. In the seventies they were exposed as having close ties to the criminal fraternity. A lot of them were sent down for corruption."

"That a fact?"

"It is," Koenig said. "Like I said, until now the East Coast Sweeney was a rumor. Oh, and in case you don't understand the provenance of your name, in cockney rhyming slang, 'Flying Squad' is 'Sweeney Todd.' The villains shortened 'Sweeney Todd' to 'Sweeney.' They made a film and a TV series about them." He paused a beat. "None of you know what 'provenance' means, do you?"

"Let's get this asshole in the trunk so we can go and get paid," Cunningham said.

"Not yet," Beetle-Brow said. "Everybody keep cool. That includes you, Koenig." He nodded to the far end of the parking lot. A woman and two kids were using it as a shortcut. The woman looked harried, like she'd just left work and now had to take her boys trick-or-treating, instead of kicking back with a pinot grigio. The boys were dressed as Batman and Robin. Koenig figured they were twins. He wondered how they'd sorted out who would be who. All things being equal, no one wanted to be Robin. Batman was asking the woman why, if he had a booger in one nostril, he always had a booger in his other nostril. It didn't seem like it was something she wanted to discuss, though. She hurried the boys along, walked straight past them all. Didn't even glance in their direction.

"In the trunk, Koenig," Cunningham said after they'd cleared the parking lot.

"I want to know how he knew who we were, first," Beetle-Brow said.

"It's not import—"

"It *is* important. If we've slipped up, we need to know."

"Lucky I'm in a sharing mood then," Koenig said. "You guys are cops. Have to be. I've only been in New York a few hours. I haven't been followed, and no one's given me a second look. I check my email account once a month and never in the same state as the last time. Yet you guys found me. The only way that could have happened is by facial-recognition technology. New York is Orwellian; it has over fifteen thousand FRT cameras. Plus, you know how to hold guns, you know how to pat someone down, and you all have regulation haircuts. You're therefore serving NYPD officers. I imagine you uploaded one of the photographs of me that circulated after the incident last year. Probably never expected to get a hit."

"And that's exactly what's going to happen, my friend," Beetle-Brow said. "You're about to get hit, and we're about to get two and a half bricks richer."

"We call it retirement planning," Walks-Like-a-Duck said.

"Hey, do you guys think you could beat Batman in a fight?" Koenig said. He nodded at the woman. "I'm not talking about Cunningham here, of course. We *know* she thinks she can beat Batman in a fight. She'd probably use razor-tipped playing cards or an acid-squirting lapel flower. The Joker always used something wacky."

"What the hell are you talking about?" Beanpole said.

"Although I suppose it would depend on which Batman you were fighting. I kinda think Adam West's Batman could be taken down with an old-fashioned kick in the balls. The way he wore his underpants on the outside of his gray tights. It would give you something to aim for. And George Clooney smiled too much. Made him look dumb. I'm going to be controversial. I think Ben Affleck's Batman would be the hardest to beat. He had an edge the others didn't."

"Oh, to hell with this!" Cunningham snarled.

"Not here!" Beetle-Brow hissed.

But Cunningham was committed. She grabbed Koenig's arm and Beetle-Brow grabbed hers. Which was a bonus. Up until then, they'd been spread out. They were keeping their distance. None of them were within Koenig's strike range. From above it would have looked like a Venn diagram where none of the circles intersected. But when Cunningham grabbed him and Beetle-Brow grabbed her, their circles intersected with Koenig's. Became three-fifths of the Olympics logo. He'd hoped for one, but now he had two. Two was better than one. Two was half their number. Fighting four people at once was impossible. It wasn't like it was in the movies. They didn't come at you one at a time. They didn't take turns to punch and stomp. You can't fight four people. The numbers don't work. Koenig only had two legs and two arms; collectively, they had sixteen. The best he could do was block a quarter of their incoming blows. The East Coast Sweeney were four times heavier than he was. They had four times as many eyes. If he tried to fight them, he would lose. The only way to deal with multiple assailants was to flip a switch and go into full combat mode. Narrow the number quickly.

So, that's what Koenig did.

He palmed the credit card he'd slipped up his sleeve. He flipped it in his hand so the edge, the one he'd filed down until it was thinner than paper, was pointing forward. Without warning he reached out and slashed the credit card across Cunningham's forehead. Did it hard and fast, like he was striking a match. Her skin sprang apart like elastic. Hung down like the butt-flap on a prospector's long johns. Her own blood blinded her. Before she even had a chance to scream, he'd slashed at Beetle-Brow. Same trajectory. But Beetle-Brow was a couple of inches taller than Cunningham, and instead of his forehead, the credit card caught his left eye. Sliced it right open. Vitreous humor, the jellylike gunk that keeps the eyeball at the right pressure, burst out and hung there like egg white. Koenig followed it up with a punch, right in the soft part of Beetle-Brow's temple. Felt his knuckles go into his skull. Beetle-Brow groaned and hit the concrete like a wet sandbag. If he ever got up, he was going to need speech therapy. Koenig grabbed Cunningham. One arm around her neck, another around her waist. Her blood made his hand wet. Beanpole and Walks-Like-a-Duck drew their weapons, but neither had a clear shot. They would have to go through Cunningham. And Koenig reckoned they wouldn't want a gun going off. Not in this part of the city.

Cunningham began to struggle. Koenig increased the pressure on her neck, but all that did was make her panic. She kicked out and caught Walks-Like-a-Duck on the side of his knee. The knee is a load-bearing hinge, and Walks-Like-a-Duck was a big guy. There was a lot of load. His knee buckled. He staggered and tripped on the unconscious Beetle-Brow. Before he could get back up, Koenig stepped forward and kicked him in the head. Heard the crack as his neck broke. Walks-Like-a-Duck went bug-eyed, twitched once, then either died or went into a coma. Koenig didn't care which.

Koenig turned Cunningham so they were facing the last man with a gun: Beanpole. "I told you there was going to be a Captain Kronos test later," he said into her ear. "I don't have a sword, but a sharpened credit card will do in a pinch."

"You're a dead man!" Beanpole snarled. He raised his weapon.

"Actually, I'm fine," Koenig replied. "Can't say the same for your friends, though. If I were you, I'd call 9-1-1."

Instead of responding, Beanpole reached into his pocket for his shield. He held it and his weapon in the air. Koenig turned to see why. Eight uniformed NYPD cops had their weapons pointing at him. He let go of Cunningham, dropped to his knees, raised his hands.

This was going to take some explaining.

CHAPTER 6

The rib eyes were as big as a Bible and twice as bloody. Finely marbled and dry-aged, they'd been pan-seared by a chef who knew how to cook meat. The two men had ordered them rare. It didn't look as if they knew each other, just happened to be seated together as the restaurant had a single-diner policy on Saturday nights. Single diners sat at the grill, or they didn't sit at all. The maître d' lined them up like they were playing blackjack and the grill chef was the dealer. That they were sitting next to each other seemed like happenstance. A random encounter.

One of the men had gray hair, buzz-cut short, and a chiseled jaw. Strong arms and calloused hands. If you didn't know him, you might think he worked a physical job. And as they were in Coos County, Oregon, maybe he was in agriculture or timber. He was called Hank Reynolds, and if you thought he was in agriculture or timber, you'd be wrong. Hank had an indoor job.

The other man was his physical opposite. He was small and neat and fussy and pale. He looked like he might be an accountant or an auditor. A job that kept him out of the midday sun. One of those jobs that no one at school dreamed about doing. The fussy man's name was Stillwell Hobbs, and if you thought he was a cube dweller, you'd be wrong about that too.

Dead wrong.

The rib eyes came with a side of white asparagus and a scoop of mashed potato, loaded with butter and cream. All the steaks came with asparagus and mashed potato. The only choice was whether you wanted a fried egg on it or not. It didn't cost extra and almost everyone said yes. It felt like you were getting something for free. Reynolds had said yes to the egg. He asked for it over easy but got what everyone did—sunny-side up. The chef didn't have time to flip eggs. Hobbs said no to the free egg. Seemed like he couldn't even look at it. Reynolds figured his dining companion must have an allergy. He'd heard about egg allergies. They sounded like a pain in the ass.

"Don't like eggs, huh?" he asked.

"Not a fan, no," Hobbs replied.

Reynolds cut into the rich yellow yolk and spread it over his steak. Hobbs looked away.

"Allergy?"

"Something like that," Hobbs said, his gaze fixed on something in the distance.

"Too bad," Reynolds said. "Eggs are in a whole bunch of stuff."

"Yes, they are."

"Name's Hank Reynolds."

"Stillwell Hobbs."

"Pleased to meet you."

They shook hands.

"Damn shame about the eggs, Stillwell," Reynolds said. "I was about to ask if you'd join me in a whiskey sour. Heard this place does the best in the Northwest."

"They do, Hank," Hobbs said. "And I'm fine with egg whites, it's the yolks I have a problem with."

"Let's do it," Reynolds said. He held up his hand and caught the attention of a young server. "Two whiskey sours for me and my friend, ma'am," he said.

"Sure," the server said. She had random tattoos on her arms, like she'd been playing paintball while wearing a sleeveless top, and a lumpy birthmark on the side of her face. It was in the shape of Italy. "I guess you guys won't want to see the wine list?"

"Just the whiskey sour for me," Reynolds said.

"Same," Hobbs added.

"Can you pass me your wineglass, sir?" the server said to Reynolds. "Save me reaching across you."

Reynolds did as he was asked, and the server walked off to place their order at the bar.

"Apart from great steaks, what brings you to Coos County, Hank?" Hobbs asked.

"Work," Reynolds replied.

"And looking like you do, it must be agriculture or fishing?"

Reynolds shook his head. "Boring government job. But every now and then I'm allowed out of the office. I get to make sure everyone's doing what they're supposed to be doing. What about you, Stillwell?"

Hobbs paused. "I guess I'm a problem solver."

"And what problems do you solve?" Reynolds said, spearing an asparagus tip with the end of his fork.

"Whatever needs solving."

"Sounds interesting."

"It has its moments."

After five minutes their whiskey sours arrived, and the two men settled into an easy conversation. It was as if they'd known each other for years.

The server's name was Harper Nash, and she knew exactly who both men were. Stillwell Hobbs was her father, and Hank Reynolds was the problem they'd been hired to solve. She'd taken a server's job at the restaurant a fortnight earlier and her references were impeccable. They were also completely fabricated. That didn't matter, though. By the time anyone in the restaurant's HR department thought to check, she'd have handed in her notice and disappeared.

She held Reynolds's wineglass by its stem and placed it into a paper bag. She told her shift supervisor she was going on her break, then left the restaurant through the kitchen. Two minutes later she was in the lobby of the Gobblers Knob Hotel. It was the same hotel Reynolds was staying in. No one gave her a second look. She was a guest there as well. If anyone wondered how someone on a server's salary could afford to live in a hotel, they didn't ask. Harper was one of those people who fitted in.

"Yo, Harper," the concierge shouted. "You heading over to Sally's later?"

Sally's was the local bar. Its patrons called it a dive bar, although it was in a good neighborhood and didn't feel edgy like the best dive bars did. Harper had made herself a regular as it was where the bellboys and maids and concierges hung out after work.

"Maybe later," Harper said. "But I'm kinda beat tonight. Just going to head to my room and get some stuff."

Which was what Harper did. She went to her room and she got her stuff. She was on the same floor as Reynolds, and her stuff included a camera, a portable laser printer, an acetate sheet, a tube of wood glue, and a laptop.

She'd gotten a maid drunk at Sally's the night before and cloned her key card while she was throwing up in the bathroom. She used her clone to slip inside Reynolds's room. The floor's CCTV had been working, but at 9 p.m. it went down. It would stay down until the following day. Harper turned on the lights and examined Reynolds's wineglass. She had three prints to choose from. She selected the thumb. She thought the thumb was the most likely. She took a dozen photographs, selected the best one, and Bluetoothed it to her laptop. She opened an image-editing app and created a negative of the photograph. She sent this to the laser printer and printed it onto the acetate sheet. This created a 3D structure of the negative. She cut off the tip of the wood glue tube and spread a thin layer across the print. She took the acetate sheet to the bathroom, rested it on the heated towel rail, and waited for it to dry. She checked her watch. She figured her dad would have convinced Reynolds to order a dessert by now. After fifteen minutes she peeled off the slim thumbprint copy. It was an unsophisticated hack, but more than enough to unlock Reynolds's laptop. His government files had additional layers of security, but Harper had no interest in them. She opened a fresh Word document and began typing. It took her two minutes. She proofread it, then proofread it again. It was correct.

She rechecked her watch. It was time to leave.

But before she did, she had one last job. Maybe the most important job. She walked over to the fruit bowl and put the banana in her bag. She couldn't leave that there.

That wouldn't do at all.

Thirty minutes after leaving for her break, she was back on the restaurant floor. Hank Reynolds was just leaving.

Hank Reynolds stepped inside his hotel room. He rubbed his eyes and rolled his shoulders. He felt like he should go for a stroll. Walk off the meat and the liquor. Funny that Stillwell was allergic to egg yolks but could handle egg whites. He hadn't heard of that before. Come to think of it, he hadn't said he was allergic to eggs. He'd said, "Something like that." What the hell did that mean? The more Reynolds thought about it, the more he realized there was something a little off with Stillwell Hobbs. Talking to him was like watching a movie where the audio was slightly out of sync. Shouldn't spoil your enjoyment, but it did anyway. Reynolds didn't have an ego, but when someone tells you they have a government job, it's normal to ask what that job is. But Stillwell hadn't cared.

Reynolds sat at the room desk. "Stillwell Hobbs" was an unusual name. Maybe he was on a database somewhere. He lifted the laptop lid and pressed his thumb against the scanner. Reynolds stared at the screen in confusion. It should have opened on the desktop. A photo of his wife, his two-year-old daughter, and his labradoodle, Monty. The photo he'd taken on their trip to Montana. But instead of grinning faces and a panting dog, there was an open Word document. Reynolds rarely used Word. He communicated by email, departmental intranet, or Teams. He reached into his inside pocket for his reading glasses.

He read the first line out loud. "'I've been living a lie . . .'" He blinked in surprise. "What the hell?"

Which was when the cord from the dressing gown, the thick white toweling one that hung from the back of the bathroom door, was slipped around his neck. Stillwell Hobbs was too experienced a killer to pull the cord back. For sure it would have been easier to murder Reynolds that way, but he was staging a suicide, and even a first-year pathologist knew the difference between a hanging and a ligature strangulation. The wounds were different. Pulling back would leave a horizontal furrow on the neck. Instead, Hobbs yanked the cord up. Made sure the wound followed the underside of the jaw, all the way up to the ears. Reynolds scrambled back but only succeeded in falling off his chair. Hobbs had counted on that. Reynolds was now only being held up by the cord around his neck. As if he had hanged himself from a door handle.

Which was exactly where the maid found him twelve hours later.

Hanging from his bathroom door.

CHAPTER 7

"This goes to trial, you're coming in second," Detective Mallinson said. "There's no way a New York jury finds for you."

"My colleague's right, Mr. Koenig," Detective Wagstaff added. "Don't matter what fancy-ass trick your lawyer pulls, they're gonna find for the DA. Juries always do when a cop's been killed. Makes 'em feel safer. That usually means life without the possibility of parole. Come clean now, though, and you might get out before you're eighty."

Mallinson and Wagstaff had been interviewing Koenig for an hour. Mallinson was wearing a Brooks Brothers suit and a stained tie. Looked like coffee. Wasn't the worst cop Koenig had met, wasn't the best. Wagstaff had a Van Dyke beard, trimmed and dyed. He seemed the smarter of the two. Koenig got the impression neither he nor Mallinson liked Beetle-Brow and his crew. Probably didn't even know why. Corrupt cops gave off a vibe other cops could sense. Like when you knew which dog was going to bite and which one wasn't. They were still cops, though. The blue shield covered them all.

The interview room was small and boxy. Drab but functional. A table bolted to the floor, two light chairs on the cops' side, a welded bench on Koenig's. The bench had an eyebolt, and his handcuffs were threaded through it. They'd exchanged his rigid arrest cuffs for a pair with a longer chain. Meant he could take a drink from the beaker of dusty water they'd put in front of him. A dome camera stuck to the ceiling like a shiny wart. Koenig could see three microphones but assumed there'd be more he couldn't. Courts had ruled the NYPD were allowed covert mics in interview rooms.

"What time is it?" Koenig said.

"That's the third time you've asked what the goddamned time is," Mallinson said. "The time is whatever the hell I tell you it is. That's what time it is."

Koenig nodded. "I agree that time is an artificial construct," he said. "That it's just an illusion of memories. If the human brain didn't have memories, time as we know it wouldn't exist. We would live in a succession of nows." He took a sip of water. "Did you know there's a clock that's so accurate it only loses one second every fifteen billion years?"

Wagstaff sighed. "You may not believe me, Mr. Koenig, but we're trying to do you a favor. We know Cunningham and her crew are douchebags. Everyone in this *precinct* knows they're douchebags. And I have no doubt that they were up to something they shouldn't have been. No way do the four of them decide to meet for a coffee at an internet café. Not on their day off. Not unless those places pay you to drown cats."

He paused a couple of beats and, in a well-rehearsed move, Mallinson took over. "Maybe they ripped you off, maybe they did something else. But can we at least agree that what you did was a staggering overreaction?"

Koenig said, "What time is it, please?"

Wagstaff threw up his hands. "If I tell you the goddamned time, will you tell us what happened in that goddamned parking lot?"

"No," Koenig replied. "But I will tell you what's going to happen next."

CHAPTER 8

"Fine," Wagstaff said. He checked his watch. "It's coming up to five after seven. Happy?"

Koenig did some mental calculations. Decided he could give a little back. He said, "You've heard of the East Coast Sweeney?"

Wagstaff snorted. "Sure, I've heard of the East Coast Sweeney. Same way I've heard of the tooth fairy and the Easter Bunny. You're not supposed to believe that shit after kindergarten, though."

"Which was exactly what I thought when I was with the Special Operations Group."

Mallinson blinked in surprise. "You? *You* were with the SOG?"

"I was."

"You're a bum and a cop killer," Mallinson said. "You ain't never been a US Marshal. You don't have the self-control."

"Feel free to check," Koenig said. "But the point I'm trying to make is that when I was with the SOG, I didn't believe in the East Coast Sweeney either. I thought a cabal of corrupt police officers surviving all these years was about as likely as the 'birds aren't real' lunatics finding a robot pigeon."

"But you're claiming the cop you killed and the two you assaulted were both in this fantasy criminal organization?"

"I am."

"That's how it's going, is it?"

"I'm not following."

"Sure you do," Mallinson said. "You're going for a justifiable homicide defense. That it was either them or you."

Koenig said nothing.

"I guess it's the only play you have left," he continued. "Hope that if you throw enough shit at four highly decorated officers, you'll find a couple of gullible jurors to hang a jury? Might work. It's something you can't prove, but more importantly, it's something the DA can't *dis*prove. There were no cameras in the internet café and there were none in the parking lot. Pretty convenient, huh?"

"They're highly decorated officers now, are they? You were just calling them douchebags."

"What do you want?" Wagstaff said.

"Nothing."

"You must want something. This is a play. You know there ain't no East Coast Sweeney. *We* know there ain't no East Coast Sweeney. And if it comes to it, we'll get the most impressive experts ever assembled to dispute their existence to a jury. Despite your little game here, there'll be no hung jury. So, I'll ask you again—what do you want?"

"I want to know what time it is."

"It's five minutes after the last time you asked."

"Ten after seven?"

Wagstaff checked his watch and nodded.

"She'll be here soon then," Koenig said. "And you guys better watch out, she's gonna be mad as hell."

CHAPTER 9

"Who's coming?" Detective Mallinson asked.

"I'll tell you in a minute," Koenig replied. "First, I'm going to let you in on a few secrets."

"You are? Why?"

"Because soon you'll have signed form SF-312."

"What the hell is that?"

"Standard Form 312," Koenig said. "It's a nondisclosure agreement. And that means I can tell you things I probably shouldn't because I know you'll never be able to repeat anything. Not even to your wives."

Wagstaff and Mallinson shared a look. Wagstaff shrugged. "We're listening," he said.

"Despite what I look like now, I *was* in the Special Operations Group. I was one of its commanders. What do you know about them?"

"Our lieutenant occasionally calls on them," Wagstaff said. "Mainly when there's a high-value prisoner to move, or a fugitive to locate and apprehend."

Koenig nodded. "That's right," he said. "The SOG doesn't get called in because they're better or braver than you guys, they get called in because they're extensively trained in tactics and weaponry. They have specialist equipment and intelligence networks and a whole bunch of other stuff that I won't tell you about."

"Let's say I believe you were SOG, which I don't, what's this got to do with what happened this afternoon?"

"It's context."

"Context?"

"First, I need you to turn off your recording equipment," Koenig said.

"Why the hell would we do that?" Wagstaff said.

"Because you don't want what I'm about to tell you on tape. This is for your benefit, not mine. Every single person who hears this will be interviewed by the kind of people who don't use last names. They're going to have their lives turned upside down. Their families' lives are going to be turned upside down. I imagine you want to avoid that."

"Turn off the tape," Wagstaff said to Mallinson.

"But—"

"Just do it, Mal."

Mallinson left the room. A minute later the green lights turned red. He came back in and said, "Satisfied?"

"Like I said, it's for your benefit, not mine," Koenig said. "Soon every hard drive in this place is going to be seized. Now, where were—"

"Wait!" Mallinson cut in. He left the room again. Returned a minute later.

"You accidentally forget to turn off one of your covert mics?"

Mallinson nodded. Wasn't even embarrassed. Koenig didn't blame him. He'd sat on the other side of the table more times than he could remember.

"Can we start now?" Wagstaff said.

Koenig nodded. "My name is Ben Koenig, and there are four things you need to know about me, Detective Wagstaff." He held up his index finger. "Seven years ago, the Solntsevskaya Bratva Russian crime syndicate put a five-million-dollar bounty on my head. I'd killed the son of a boss during a raid. I've been living off the grid ever since. I had to. They threatened my family." He put up another finger. "The second thing is that I have a condition that makes it impossible for me to feel fear. It's called Urbach-Wiethe. My amygdala, the part of the brain that regulates the human fight-or-flight response, is compromised."

Wagstaff leaned forward. "You're saying you always choose fight?" he said.

"No, I'm saying I never choose *flight*. It wouldn't occur to me."

"That sounds way cooler than it probably is," Wagstaff said.

"You have no idea."

"What's the third thing?"

"A few years ago, I was shot in the head. A ricochet got under my tactical helmet. The neurologist did scans to make sure I was OK. That's when he spotted the Urbach-Wiethe."

"You got canned?" Wagstaff said.

"I didn't get canned."

"Desk job then?"

"The opposite. Instead of riding a desk, my director sent me on the most ridiculous program you can imagine. For two years I trained with every crazy-ass unit you can think of and a load more you won't even know about. Some don't officially exist. I practiced targeted killing techniques with the Israelis, which is a fancy way of saying assassination. I did LINE fighting with an ex-marine and CQB with Delta. I lived and worked with the British SAS. I trained with the Russians and Chinese. I became an expert in weapons and improvised weapons. A whole other bunch of stuff I'm embarrassed about."

"Might have been kinder to can you," Wagstaff said.

"It would *definitely* have been kinder to can me."

"So why agree to it?"

"Can I ask you a question?" Koenig said. "You both seem like good cops. Dedicated. If you got injured in the line and you were offered the choice of retirement with full benefits or the chance to go on training to make you an even better cop, what would you choose?"

"Fair point," Wagstaff said.

"Retirement," Mallinson said.

Wagstaff punched him on the shoulder. "Asshole."

"If this is true," Mallinson said. "If you *do* have all this specialist training, why didn't you put them on their asses? Wait for us to sort it out?"

Koenig explained how multiple assailants was a math problem, not a fighting problem. He said that one death out of four was a good result. He'd expected to kill them all. "They weren't putting me in the trunk of that car," he said. "It makes me sleepy."

"It's a nice story," Wagstaff said. "But at the end of the day, the DA has a dead cop, another in a coma, and two living ones who'll spin whatever story they've rehearsed until it ain't even funny. Cunningham is disfigured for life, and you can bet your ass the DA will put her on the stand. Let her cry crocodile tears. Ask her to show the jury what the nasty man did to her forehead. But you don't seem worried. And you told us there were four things we needed to know about you. You've told us about the Russian bounty, the Urbach-Wiethe, and your specialist training. I make that three. What's the fourth?"

"The fourth is why I keep asking you what time it is," Koenig said. "I wasn't naive enough to think my training program was altruism on behalf of my director, but I at least thought it was mutually beneficial. I got to return to work, and he got someone who'd walk through any door he pointed me toward."

"It was something else?"

Koenig nodded. "I believed it was my director who'd put together my training program. I thought he'd called in all the favors he'd collected from thirty-odd years in law enforcement. And I thought that because that's how it was sold to me."

"But?"

"But in hindsight I should have realized that even the director of the US Marshals doesn't have those kind of contacts. Like I said, some of these units don't officially exist."

"Who *does* have contacts like that?"

"The people behind everything. And those people didn't see a marshal who needed a helping hand."

"What *did* they see?"

"A guinea pig."

CHAPTER 10

"A guinea pig?" Wagstaff said.

"Have you heard of DARPA, Detective?" Koenig said. "The Defense Advanced Research Projects Agency?"

"Sure. I've seen *The X-Files*."

"Turns out, DARPA had been playing about with the amygdala for years. They claim it's to improve PTSD recovery rates, but I suspect their primary goal is getting our troops to react differently to effective enemy fire. Suppress that initial fear. I found out later that my training regime was a Department of Defense test program. They wanted to find out what someone who doesn't feel fear is capable of."

Wagstaff snorted. "You took out four cops with a fucking credit card. I'd say they got what they wanted."

"But they didn't," Koenig said. "Because of the Russian bounty, I disappeared before an in-depth assessment could be done. I didn't know it at the time, but they'd assigned a handler to me. Woman called Jen Draper, and if you think I have a complicated past, it's nothing compared to hers. She pretended to be a new member of the SOG. Really, she was there to evaluate me. Not just my skills. My decision-making was also important to the DoD. Someone who doesn't feel fear is useless if they're also reckless. They want soldiers, not berserkers."

"You've resurfaced now, though," Wagstaff said.

"I resurfaced last year too," Koenig said. "Friend of mine tracked me down.

Wanted help with something. I ended up killing a bunch of bad guys. And for my troubles I was given a choice: do what they asked or get convicted of murder. They had plenty of bodies to choose from."

"What did they want?"

"Nothing. Jen Draper was still my handler, and all I had to do was check in once a month via an email account they set up. We did it through the draft folder. Nothing was ever sent. That's why I know she's on her way. I sent my last email. Didn't save it to the draft folder. Cunningham didn't think there was anything in the message she needed to worry about, but she'd missed the point. Sending it *was* the message. It'll have set off all sorts of alarms. Jen will have called it in immediately, and they'll have sent her up here to get me. She'll have been in DC when all this happened. I figure with traffic to get out of DC and into New York, she'll have ditched her car and taken a helicopter instead. Half an hour to get to a DoD airfield, ten minutes to clear a flight plan and a ninety-minute flight. Another thirty minutes to get from the airfield to the precinct."

"She's late then."

"She is."

"But you still think she's coming."

"Oh, I *know* she's coming," Koenig said. "She won't miss the chance to gloat." He paused. "We have a hate-hate relationship."

"You keep mentioning 'they.' 'They' offered you a choice. 'They' will have sent her up here to get you. Who are 'they'?"

"That's the five-million-dollar question, isn't it, Detective Wagstaff? I have absolutely no idea who 'they' are."

The interview room door burst open. A tall blonde woman marched in. She glowered at Koenig.

He sighed. "But I suspect she does," he said.

CHAPTER 11

Jen Draper entered the room like she owned it. She turned everyone else into background. Koenig hadn't seen her for a year, but she hadn't changed. She was still tall and lithe and still looked capable of beating men twice her size to a bloody pulp. Even though she'd been on secondment from the CIA, she'd been the best marshal he'd ever worked with. She was the toughest in the unit, the best shot in the unit, and she was the most resourceful. They'd hated each other immediately. Koenig because he didn't think she was a team player, Draper because she'd been forced into a babysitting job she thought beneath her. To be fair, it *was* beneath her. Looking after Koenig was a punishment. She'd done some shady stuff while serving overseas. Enhanced interrogation, black sites, extraordinary rendition, probably more she hadn't told him about. She'd tried atoning. Became a whistleblower. All that achieved was the revocation of her overseas status and a stateside posting. Her superiors thought she would get bored and resign. They were wrong. She was too stubborn. But when Koenig disappeared, they were able to sack her for gross incompetence. She'd had one job: evaluate and monitor him. She couldn't even tell her boss where he was. But instead of sulking and becoming a pain in the butt, she founded a private intelligence company, and because most of the people she'd worked with knew what had *really* happened, a lot of Pentagon contracts were thrown her way.

Or that's what she'd thought.

The CIA weren't stupid. They didn't want to burn an asset like Draper.

Instead, they made sure she got a bunch of government contracts. Told her if she did a good job there'd be plenty more. But government contracts are like crack. Once she had them, she couldn't do without them. She had employees, and they had families and mortgages and school fees and medical bills. Turned out she was on the same leash as him, their futures tied together. Like conjoined twins who didn't get on.

Two men followed Draper into the room. They were both in suits. One was clearly a cop. He was too angry to be anything else. Wagstaff and Mallinson immediately looked to him for instructions. Probably their lieutenant. He wasn't happy. His chest was puffed out. He was breathing hard, like he was blowing out candles on a birthday cake. Koenig thought he was ready to hit someone, and he probably didn't care who.

"Lieutenant Glenister," Wagstaff said.

"I'll deal with you two clowns later," Glenister snapped. "What the hell were you thinking, turning off the sound like that?"

Wagstaff mumbled something, but Glenister wasn't interested in hearing from them right now. He would later, though. Koenig thought Wagstaff and Mallinson were going to wish they'd called in sick today.

The other guy wasn't a cop. He reminded Koenig of himself. He walked into the room, then became forgettable. A gray man. Koenig did it himself whenever he was somewhere new. He faded into the background. He could be in a diner all night, and if someone asked the waitress what he looked like, she wouldn't be able to remember. There was a skill to being the gray man, and the second guy had it in spades. Everything about him was nondescript. His clothes, his hair, the way he stood. It was all just . . . blah. Carefully cultivated blah. Koenig was impressed. He hadn't seen someone this good for a long time.

Koenig had expected Draper, and he'd expected her to be accompanied by a more senior cop. Someone trying to find out what the hell was happening. He hadn't expected a gray man.

Lieutenant Glenister wasn't interested in being the gray man. He wanted to be seen. He wanted everyone to know how angry he was. Koenig sympathized with him. But only a little. Glenister didn't know what Koenig knew. Didn't know what had happened in the internet café. All he knew was what Koenig had done to his guys. And instead of being charged with murder, a man and a woman had walked into his precinct like they had every right to be there.

"I have a dead cop, a cop who's gonna need round-the-clock care for the rest of his life, and another who looks like she's had an asshole carved into her forehead. And you got the balls to come in here and tell me that not only is this piece of shit not spending the rest of his life sucking dicks in Sing Sing, he's walking out of here like nothing even happened?"

"I think we all know something happened, Lieutenant Glenister," Draper said. "The question is, are you part of it?"

"Part of what, lady?"

Koenig winced. Draper didn't like being called "lady." Men who called Draper "lady" ended up with swollen testicles. How he knew this wasn't important.

But instead of punching Glenister in the balls, she said, "You were listening to the first part of Mr. Koenig's interview, Lieutenant. You know exactly what."

"If you believe that East Coast Sweeney crap, then I got a bridge to sell you," Glenister said. "Because the East Coast Sweeney is a bunch of bullshit. And this asshole ain't walking out of here because he says different."

Draper removed a laptop from a tan leather briefcase. It was a MacBook Air, all sleek and shiny. She opened it and said to Lieutenant Glenister, "Before I show you what's on here, there are a couple of things you need to understand."

CHAPTER 12

"The first thing you need to understand," Draper said, "is that Ben Koenig is an asshole. If he won a competition for being an asshole, Koenig would think he was too cool to collect the award. That's how much of an asshole he is."

Koenig rolled his eyes.

"On that we are in complete agreement, lady," Lieutenant Glenister said.

Draper pushed out a breath through gritted teeth. "Call me 'lady' again and see what happens," she said. "I dare you."

"I wouldn't," Koenig muttered.

Glenister scowled but said nothing.

"Good," Draper said. "The second thing you need to understand is that Koenig is an asset of the US government. He is required to check in with me on the last day of every month. We do this through a draft email folder. That way nothing is ever sent. And if nothing is ever sent, then nothing can be intercepted."

"Who the hell is this 'we' you keep referring to?" Glenister said.

"If *we* tell you, you'll wish *we* hadn't," the gray man said, the first time he'd opened his mouth. "It'll involve . . . paperwork."

"Now, because Koenig's such an asshole," Draper continued, "we can't trust him when he checks in. He always lies. Says he's in Athens when he's really in Alaska. Connecticut instead of Montana."

"I've never been to Montana," Koenig said.

"Yet that's exactly where you said you were last April."

Koenig shrugged.

"But I'm going to let Koenig in on a secret," Draper said. "Because we don't trust him, we've been cheating. The moment he logs in to our shared email account, his location is immediately made known to us. And as we need to ensure he's fit and healthy, we also activate the computer's camera and microphone. For as long as he's logged in, we can see and hear him."

"In other words," the gray man said, "the conversation between Mr. Koenig and Detective Cunningham was recorded in its entirety."

"And it turns out I'm not the only one who has to work with assholes," Draper said. "Shall I press play?"

CHAPTER 13

"What do you think Detective Cunningham meant when she said she wasn't walking away from the biggest payday she was ever going to have?" Draper said. "Or when she asked Mr. Koenig if he'd still have a smart mouth when her guy was peeling his skin off?"

Lieutenant Glenister, Detective Wagstaff, and Detective Mallinson had watched the video in silence. It had lasted twelve minutes and none of it was open to interpretation.

When Glenister didn't answer, the gray man said, "This video was taken under the umbrella of the Patriot Act. There was no entrapment. It's legal, and copies have already been lodged with the FBI and the US attorney for the Southern District of New York. The East Coast Sweeney exists, and your guys were caught red-handed."

"What the hell did he say when you turned off the cameras?" Glenister asked Wagstaff and Mallinson. He seemed to have aged in the last ten minutes.

"Nothing that contradicts that video," Mallinson said. "He said there's a Russian bounty on his head, and it does sound like those douchebags were trying to claim it."

"I'm aware things are moving extremely fast, Lieutenant Glenister," the gray man said. "I've arranged for the attorney general to call you in fifteen minutes. She'll answer any questions you have. She'll tell you how to proceed. But for the avoidance of doubt, we're leaving right now, and Mr. Koenig is coming with us. Please unfasten his handcuffs and return his possessions. If you don't do as I ask, the FBI will arrest you."

Koenig's hands were stinging with pins and needles. He rubbed them together to get the blood running again. His possessions had been returned, even his sharpened credit card. After checking his Fairbairn-Sykes fighting knife was still there—the only possession he had any emotional attachment to—he followed Draper and the gray man into the precinct parking lot.

"My photograph isn't supposed to be on any database," Koenig said. "How the hell did the NYPD find me via facial recognition?"

"We dropped the ball," the gray man admitted. "The woman who monitors everything has gone on maternity leave. Something must have got missed in the handover."

"I killed someone today," Koenig said. "I put someone else in a coma. I scarred Cunningham for life. None of that needed to happen."

"I'm sorry."

"Who are you?"

"Part of the team assigned to your case. I was here to make sure you didn't spend any longer in custody than you needed to."

"Bullshit," Koenig said. "Jen has the biggest pair of balls in any room she's in. She doesn't need help, not when she has video evidence as damning as that. I'll ask again: Who are you?"

The gray man looked around the precinct parking lot. A few cops were milling around, sharing a smoke before they either went on shift or went home. They were staring at them with suspicion. "Not here," he replied.

"Our car will be here soon," Draper said. "We'll explain everything then." She took a moment. "That was a stroke of luck annoying Detective Cunningham so much she incriminated herself in front of the computer. It was almost as if you *knew* you were being recorded."

Koenig shrugged. "You've heard the fable of the scorpion and frog?"

"The one where the scorpion promises not to sting the frog if it carries him across the river? The scorpion says if he did, the frog would die, but he'd drown. The frog agrees. Halfway across, the scorpion stings the frog anyway. He couldn't change his nature." She took a silent moment. "I guess in this story I'm the scorpion?"

"Once a spook, always a spook. You lie by default."

"That's enough," the gray man said. He held up his hand. A car drove toward them. It was big and black and looked like the Beast, the armored Cadillac the president was transported in. The car pulled up beside them. The driver got out and took up a defensive position.

"Ooh, scary," Koenig said.

"Inside, please," the gray man said.

Koenig did as he was asked. The interior of the car smelled fresh and clean. Much more pleasant than the interview room. There were two bench seats. One forward-facing, the other rear-facing. Like a diner booth. Koenig chose to face forward. The gray man sat opposite him. There was a minifridge in the center console. Koenig opened a bottle of sparkling mineral water and took a swig. Draper tried to get in beside him, but the gray man stopped her. "Sorry, Miss Draper, you don't have the clearance for this."

Draper didn't seem to mind. Koenig imagined that in the intelligence game, you got used to being excluded from things that didn't concern you. That sometimes it wasn't your turn on the merry-go-round.

"What's this about?" Koenig said. "Jen has higher clearance than me. And I know this because I don't have any."

The gray man turned to Koenig. He said, "I need you to tell me everything you know about the Acacia Avenue Protocol."

CHAPTER 14

"Tell me who you are first," Koenig said.

"Who I am is not important," the gray man said.

"You'll have no problem telling me then."

The gray man frowned. "Why do you need to know?"

"I don't need to know, I *want* to know."

The gray man looked at him shrewdly. Koenig wondered what it was he saw. Did he see a drifter, a man who spent his days Forrest Gumping across the towns and cities of America, never staying in the same place twice? Or did he see someone else? Did he see another gray man?

"My name's Andrew Smerconish," he said. "I work for the Department of Defense."

"The DoD is our biggest government agency. Would you care to narrow it down?"

"No."

"And if I were to insist, you'd quote all sorts of national security reasons why you can't tell me?"

"Something like that."

"Did you work with Jen?"

"I met her for the first time today."

"Not what I asked."

Smerconish smiled. "I knew *of* her."

"And did she know of you?"

"I make it my business that people don't know of me."

"Why are you here?"

"To ask you about the Acacia Avenue Protocol."

"No. Anyone could have done that. I want to know why a high-ranking DoD official, almost certainly Defense Intelligence Agency, has just escorted me out of a police interview room. In other words, why are *you* here?"

"There's been a shooting," Smerconish said. "In London. It triggered a chain of events, the culmination of which was a safe being opened that had never before been opened. That safe was in a serious building and belonged to a serious man. Even he didn't know what was inside until he opened it. *That's* why I'm here."

"What was inside the safe?"

"Four names and a sentence: 'The Acacia Avenue Protocol has been initiated.'"

"That's it?"

Smerconish nodded.

"I was one of the names?" Koenig asked.

"You were."

"Who else?"

"I'm not saying."

"But you've asked them what the Acacia Avenue Protocol is?"

"I can't."

"Why not?"

"Because they're dead," Smerconish said. Before Koenig could say anything, he held up his hand and added, "And it's not a conspiracy. It was an old list and they all died of natural causes."

"I'm the only one left."

"You can see why I want to talk to you."

"I have some bad news then."

"I don't like bad news, Mr. Koenig."

"Do you know anyone who does?"

"Fair point. What's the bad news?"

"I've never heard of the Acacia Avenue Protocol," Koenig said. "I have no idea what it is."

CHAPTER 15

Smerconish made a series of phone calls. Each one contained a variation of "But he says he *doesn't* know." The last call ended with "Fine, I'll ask him."

"Ask me what?" Koenig said.

"You have a condition the US government has no problem exploiting."

"So?"

"But you don't like being handled. You don't respond well to authority. You'll say something is black even when you know it's white. You'll say you're in Montana when you're in Wyoming. That you're in good health when in fact you've been stabbed in the arm during an altercation with a meth-dealing biker gang."

"You knew about that?"

"We know *everything*, Mr. Koenig."

Koenig frowned. He didn't like that. Not one bit. "I really haven't heard of the Acacia Avenue Protocol, though." He paused. "But if you let me, I *will* help you figure it out."

"We've had experts on this for days. How can you help?"

"First, you need to bring Jen inside," Koenig said.

"Inside the loop?"

"Inside the car. It's October and she's wearing a light jacket. But also inside the loop. Someone put me on that list for a reason, and I want her involved."

Smerconish opened his door and asked Draper to join them. Koenig thought that was interesting. He was clearly able to make decisions on who had access to information and who didn't. A mid-level DIA spook wouldn't have that much authority. He'd have needed permission. Koenig butt-shuffled across the bench seat to make room. Draper climbed in. Her face was red and her nose was running. She rubbed her hands together, then blew through them.

"It's like a meat locker out there," she said.

"There's no such thing as bad weather," Koenig said. "Just poor choices of clothing."

"Why don't you shut the fu—"

"Children, please," Smerconish said. He then brought Draper up to speed, right up to Koenig offering to help but only if Draper was brought on board.

When he'd finished, Koenig said, "Tell me about the other names on the list."

"Their names are unimportant."

"But they all held highly classified positions," Koenig said.

A pause. Then, "They did."

"Yet I'm on the list as well."

"You are."

"And I've never held a highly classified position."

"You can imagine our confusion."

"Maybe it was something he was supposed to be told, but he disappeared before they got to him," Draper said. "Keeping him on the list was an oversight."

Smerconish shook his head. "The safe was sealed while Mr. Koenig was still a marshal. Even if that wasn't the case, it doesn't explain why he was on the list in the first place. The other three worked in intelligence; Mr. Koenig has only ever worked in law enforcement."

"This started with a murder in London?" Draper said.

"A double murder. A homeless woman shot two Romanian nationals in broad daylight, then seemingly disappeared without a trace. The British cops were nowhere. London has more CCTV cameras than any other Western city, but the homeless woman avoided them all."

"You don't know what she looks like?"

"We do now, but it took a while. Some IT geek grabbed an image from a private camera. Brits put it through facial recognition, and it triggered all sorts of actions, one of which was an order to shut down the investigation."

"Do you know who she is?"

"We don't. She's not on any database and we have access to them all."

"If her face triggered all this, she must have been on one at some point," Koenig said. "Can you not start there and work backward?"

"We've tried. Dead end."

"You have a photograph?" Koenig said.

Smerconish pressed a button on the center console. A panel slid open to reveal a safe. He shielded the keypad and tapped in a bunch of numbers. They didn't beep like a regular safe. Didn't even click. He opened the metal door and retrieved a thin file. He handed it to Koenig.

Koenig removed a glossy photograph. The image was black and white and a little bit fuzzy. His mouth went dry. He studied it until he was sure.

"I know this woman," he said.

Smerconish leaned forward. "How?" he urged.

"Because ten years ago, I killed her," Koenig said.

CHAPTER 16

"You mean you *figuratively* killed her?" Smerconish said. "Otherwise, that doesn't make a whole lick of sense."

"No, I mean literally," Koenig said. "I *literally* killed her. But yes, I also figuratively killed her."

"I'm glad you've cleared that up," Draper snorted.

"Please explain," Smerconish said.

Koenig did. He explained that the US Marshals were occasionally required to protect a witness who simply couldn't be protected. Regardless of the precautions taken, their safety couldn't be guaranteed. The people hunting them were too motivated. They had unlimited resources. They would do anything to get at the witness protection list. Nothing was off-limits, including targeting a marshal's family.

A few years before he disappeared, Koenig had been tasked to come up with a way of faking someone's death. The ultimate way of hiding someone was making it seem like they no longer existed. He'd thought it was a theoretical exercise. The parameters were specific: what would convince *him* someone was dead. That ruled out burned corpses, shotgun blasts to the face, no-body drownings. Eventually he'd said that it might be possible, under desperate circumstances, to fake someone's death by shooting them in the back of the head. It involved a reduced-capacity round from a handgun, a section of false skull, a bag full of the intended victim's *actual* blood, and a public execution. He was asked how dangerous it would be. Koenig explained that a shot to the head powerful enough to penetrate a section of false skull and a blood bag would probably still have enough power to penetrate the person's actual skull. He couldn't recommend such a drastic option, but he'd been asked for his opinion. He was thanked for his work and asked to forget all about it.

And he had.

Until a man who never offered his name (but who had been vouched for by Mitch Burridge, Koenig's director and a man he trusted) said he had a situation. He needed a woman to disappear. He wanted Koenig to fake her death using the method he'd theorized the year before. Koenig refused. He said it was too dangerous. His method had been an intellectual exercise. Nothing more. The man said the woman understood and accepted the risks. Koenig said he wanted to meet her. He didn't think she *did* understand the risks. So, he met her. Once. He wasn't told her name and he didn't know who she'd pissed off, but the woman said death was her only option. If Koenig couldn't fake it, she'd have to die for real.

After two hours, Koenig finally agreed to kill her.

"You shot her in a New York park?" Smerconish said.

"I did."

"She obviously survived?"

Koenig nodded.

"And that's the last you ever saw of her?" Smerconish said.

"It was."

"You didn't ask around, try to find out why her death needed to be faked? Because if you did, I forgive you. I'd have been curious too."

"You're a spook, I'm not."

"Who set up the meeting?" Smerconish asked.

"Never found out," Koenig replied. "But five gets you six, he was one of the names on your list."

"Would you recognize him?"

"I would."

Smerconish pulled a standard letter-sized document from the car safe. "Their names and positions have been redacted, but these are photographs of everyone on the list." He handed it to Koenig.

The four photographs were laid out in a grid, like a yearbook page. Koenig's photograph was bottom right. It had been taken from his old SOG ID card. Koenig pointed at the guy next to him, his bottom-row buddy. "Him," he said. "He's the man who arranged it all."

Koenig didn't expect to be given a name, and Smerconish didn't disappoint him.

"OK," he said. "That's somewhere to start. Thank you for your help. We'll take it from here. Is there anywhere we can drop you off, Mr. Koenig?"

"This woman was the bravest person I've ever met," Koenig said. "If she had flinched when I pulled the trigger, she would have died. The fact she's reappeared in such a public way means she felt it worth the risk. That means we need to find her. Fast. I got the feeling it wasn't her safety she was trying to protect. I think she had a secret. That means we may not be the only ones looking for her."

"We'll find her," Smerconish said. "We have our best people on it."

Draper shook her head. "No, you don't. Koenig's the best you have. And he's met her, which means when he finds her, she might not kill him."

Smerconish went silent. Neither Koenig nor Draper broke it. After a minute he nodded, once, like he'd come to a decision. "There'll be diplomatic passports waiting for you at the airport," he said. "Go to London. Report to the embassy. A woman called Bernice Kopitz will be expecting the pair of you."

Koenig wondered if it had been Smerconish's plan all along. He guessed he'd never know.

"I can't go," Draper said. "I have far too much going on right now."

"And he's not going without you," Smerconish replied. "The UK is an important ally and I need you there to make sure we don't have another Gauntlet, Texas, on our hands."

"I'll need to go home first then," Draper said. "I wasn't expecting to be away for more than a few hours."

"Your bag is already at the airport, Miss Draper. We had someone contact your assistant. She's packed some hand luggage for you. If you need anything else, ask Bernice. She'll get it for you."

Which kind of answered Koenig's question about whether this had been Smerconish's plan all along. The DIA spook might not know what was going on, but he knew enough to know he needed boots on the ground in London. And if those boots were worn by a woman with her own intelligence agency and a man the New York mob used to call the Devil's Bloodhound, then all the better. Koenig was tempted to punch Smerconish in the bladder. He hated being manipulated.

Instead, he said, "How big is this diplomatic pouch I keep hearing about?"

CHAPTER 17

Michael Gibbs let out a gentle burp. He smiled as the *shot de sang béarnais*, the spiced pig's blood, repeated on him. The American palate didn't usually stretch to things like *sang béarnais*, but despite La Terrasse being in Maine, it was an unashamedly French restaurant. It had been an excellent meal. A succession of small plates, one after the other as if from a conveyor belt. Room-temperature asparagus drizzled with a mustard-and-dill sauce. *Coquilles Saint-Jacques*, a single scallop poached in white wine and topped with mushroom puree and grilled Gruyère. Soft-cooked egg with shaved truffle. Crispy pork belly with Corsican honey. *Blanquette de veau*, a rich, creamy stew of veal and carrots. A delightful tarte Tatin served with brown butter ice cream. Chocolate truffles to finish.

The kind of meal that stayed in the memory.

He'd even flirted with the girl mixing his martinis, the one with the birthmark on her face and the tattoos on her arms. She'd smiled when she'd taken his coat, and she'd smiled each time she'd mixed his drink. He'd never cheated on his wife, and he never would, but when a pretty girl is flirting with you, it's polite to flirt back. She even offered to bring his car around to the front of the restaurant. Gibbs thought that was the kind of touch people came back for.

Harper Nash's job that night was easy. Boring, really. All she had to do was ensure Gibbs's car wouldn't cause problems later. She'd already been out to the parking lot for a cigarette break—she didn't smoke, but it was a useful reason to go outside—and checked through the windows. There was a smiley-face air freshener that would need to be gotten rid of. Otherwise, the interior was good to go. When Gibbs agreed she could bring his car around, she got inside and made sure she hadn't missed anything. She hadn't. The smiley-face air freshener was hooked around the rearview mirror with white elastic string. She removed it and put it in her pocket. She then started the engine, put the car in drive, and took it to the front. Gibbs was waiting for her.

She smiled at him.

He smiled back.

Men.

Park Loop Road is the primary route through the Acadia National Park. It's twenty-seven miles long and has the coast on one side, mountains and forests on the other. Gibbs left La Terrasse and, after a couple of smaller roads, hit Park Loop Road. He always took this route. It wasn't the quickest way home, but it was the most scenic, and after a meal at La Terrasse, he was in no hurry. His wife would be asleep anyway.

Gibbs usually drove a BMW X5, but he was in his wife's old station wagon tonight. He enjoyed driving the Park Loop Road in the station wagon. It didn't have power steering, it didn't have airbags, and the windows had to be cranked up and down with a handle. It added spice to what could occasionally be a challenging drive. Parts of Park Loop ran alongside a sheer drop down to the ocean. Sometimes there were deer on the road. He'd stopped for a black bear once, although he knew his wife thought he was bullshitting. The Park Loop Road was like a fine French meal, there to be savored, not rushed. He brought the station wagon up to forty-five miles per hour, then eased back on the gas.

Forty-five was a good speed.

Something bad would have to happen to send him crashing through the barrier.

The "something bad" was a tripod-mounted Chinese ZM-87 portable laser disturber. It looked like the crew-served blasters the stormtroopers used in *The Empire Strikes Back*, but instead of firing energized particles, its neodymium laser discharged five pulses a second and was capable of temporarily blinding someone six miles away. It would cause permanent eye damage at the distance Stillwell Hobbs planned to fire it. Blinding weapons were banned by the Geneva Conventions in 1998, but by then, several ZM-87s had already entered the market. Hobbs had bought one from a Hungarian arms dealer in 2014, but he'd not yet used it. He was looking forward to seeing what damage it could do.

Park Loop Road was quiet at this time of year, particularly this late at night. Hobbs hadn't seen a car for five minutes. The next one would be the station wagon. Harper had called when Gibbs left the fancy restaurant he ate at once a month, and Hobbs had timed the route enough times to know exactly when to expect him. He checked his watch. Unless something had happened between La Terrasse and the bend in the road, Gibbs should arrive in the next couple of minutes.

Hobbs heard the station wagon before he saw it. He hunkered down behind the ZM-87 and stared through the sight. He smiled in satisfaction. Gibbs was right on schedule. The next part was all about timing. Too early, and Gibbs would panic and hit the brakes while on a straight stretch of the road, stopping before he went through the barrier. Too late, and he would already be committed to the bend. Those old cars were stubborn when it came to steering. When you let go of the steering wheel on a modern car, the power steering straightened the wheels. It wasn't a safety design; it was just the path of least resistance. Physics. But the old station wagon didn't have power steering. When Gibbs took his hands off the wheel, which he would when he suddenly went blind, the station wagon would take longer to straighten out. It would drive around the bend itself. The optimum time to pull the trigger would be a fraction of a second *before* he committed to the bend. That way, when he braked, he would go straight into the crash barrier. The barrier was made of a lightweight steel and wouldn't be enough to stop a station wagon traveling at forty-five miles per hour. But to be sure, Hobbs had loosened the bolts of the section he knew Gibbs would crash into. He didn't remove them. That would look suspicious. He just loosened them enough so they had some give. Maybe half an inch. When the station wagon crashed into the barrier, there'd be enough momentum to ensure the bolts would shear off, the barrier would come away, and the station wagon would tumble down the cliff.

When Gibbs was one hundred yards away, Hobbs smiled again. He couldn't help it. He loved his job.

One minute Michael Gibbs was tapping the steering wheel to the beat of "Fortunate Son," by Creedence Clearwater Revival; the next he was completely blind. His vision didn't blur. The road didn't go hazy, then fade away. He could see and then he couldn't see. His first thought was that the station wagon's lights had finally gone.

And then he felt the burning. It felt like his eyes had been filled with fire.

He screamed and tried to slam on the brakes. In his panic he hit the gas, and instead of slowing down, he went through the sabotaged barrier going faster, not slower.

It saved his life.

Instead of the station wagon going through the barrier slowly, then tumbling down the steep, rocky slope, flipping over and over until every bone in Gibbs's body had snapped and his internal organs had liquified, he left the Park Loop Road like he was in a James Bond film. He was airborne for three full seconds before gravity pulled the station wagon back to earth. He hit the slope like it was the down ramp at a stunt show. His spine shattered, but sheer terror made him keep hold of the steering wheel. It meant that, despite being newly blind, newly paralyzed, and having a car without wheels, he steered the station wagon to a safe stop.

The silence was sudden and awful. Just the *tink-tink* of a cooling engine.

Gibbs let go of the steering wheel. He started to sob. After a minute he composed himself. Took stock of the situation. Something had happened to make him go blind. Possibly he'd had a stroke. Or a tumor in his brain had chosen that moment to make itself known. Or maybe it was a blood clot. He was a deepwater port expert, not a doctor. He pulled his iPhone out of his pocket. He touched the glass screen. It felt unblemished, didn't seem to have cracked. He felt for the concave home sensor with his thumb. Pressed down gently. He was expecting to hear a click as his thumbprint unlocked it. Instead, it vibrated. A failed attempt. He tried again. It vibrated again.

His thumb was wet. It must be blood, he thought. He was about to wipe his hands on his shirt when he heard footsteps. More of a scramble. Someone was climbing down the slope.

"Are you OK?" a voice asked.

"I can't feel my legs," Gibbs replied.

"That was quite the fall," the stranger said. "Let's get you some help."

"I've tried to call 9-1-1, but I think my thumb must have blood on it. It isn't unlocking my phone."

The stranger reached in and gently took his cell. "I'll call them," he said. "Don't you worry."

Stillwell Hobbs glanced inside the station wagon and nodded in satisfaction. Harper had removed the smiley-face air freshener, like she'd said. He tossed the cell phone into the driver's footwell. He grabbed the back of Gibbs's head, held it at the right angle, then slammed his throat against the steering column. He only did it once. Gibbs was unconscious in three minutes, dead in eight. Hobbs waited fifteen to be sure.

Other, lesser contract killers might have been tempted to repeatedly bludgeon Gibbs. Kill him quickly. But that was for the two-grand-a-hit hoods the jails were full of. Hobbs knew that a single, devasting injury was far more convincing than a succession of blows. To an overworked pathologist, a single fatal blow looked like bad luck; a head beaten until it was the size of a pumpkin looked punitive. Turned an accidental death into a suspicious one. Made the cops get off their fat asses and start looking for alternative explanations. It was things like this that made Hobbs feel invincible. No other killers thought the way he did.

It was why he would never be caught.

CHAPTER 18

Koenig had hoped for a military flight, but Smerconish wanted them in London as soon as possible. That meant flying commercial. He'd gotten them the last two tickets on Red Velvet, a Virgin Atlantic Airbus. The flight would take seven hours, but because of the time difference, they'd land two hours after they'd taken off.

The Virgin Atlantic check-in officer told them he had one ticket in economy and one in Upper Class.

"I'll take the Upper Class," Koenig said.

The check-in officer hesitated.

"Problem?" Koenig asked.

"People pay thousands of dollars for Upper Class tickets, Koenig," Draper said. "They don't want to sit next to someone who looks like he owns a WILL WORK FOR FOOD sign."

"I need space to think. I won't get that in economy."

"Seat allocation is an airline decision, sir. I've already put Miss Draper in Upper Class," the check-in officer said.

Draper looked at Koenig then nodded. She planted her elbows on the counter. "Mr. Koenig has a diplomatic passport," she said. "How long do you think you'll have a job if you stick him in economy? Do the math."

The check-in officer did the math.

* * *

Koenig sat with Draper in the departures lounge. They had found an ice cream parlor. Draper was having a coffee. Black. Koenig was having a chocolate milkshake. He'd paid.

"Tell me about Jane Doe," Draper said, nibbling at the Italian biscuit that came with her drink.

"What's to tell?" Koenig said. "I met her once. I needed to make sure she understood the risks."

"And she did?"

"Honestly? I don't think she cared."

"She was suicidal?"

"More resigned to a course of action."

"How did she come across?"

"I thought she was very impressive."

"She murdered two men in cold blood."

"Apparently."

"She abducted an elderly academic."

"If you say."

"*I* don't say. Until they were slapped with a D-notice, the Brit tabloids ran with it for almost a week. There's a lot of information out there."

"We'll get a full briefing at the embassy."

"You aren't curious?"

"I'm *desperately* curious," Koenig said. "Jane Doe took an extraordinary risk when she faked her death. That she's reappeared like she has means something's gone wrong. I want to know what. But the SOG always worked best when we were briefed by the right people. In this case, our contact at the embassy is the right people. Anything else is white noise."

Twenty minutes later their flight was called. Draper called Koenig an asshole when Upper Class were invited to board first. He was shown to his seat, but only after his ticket had been checked by three different members of the cabin crew. He declined the complimentary Champagne but accepted an apple and a bag of pretzels. After he'd eaten, he removed his boots and wedged his jacket behind his head like a pillow. Sleep first, think later.

By the time Draper's seat was called, Koenig was asleep.

CHAPTER 19

Koenig was the second person off the plane. He'd slept the entire flight and had woken hungry. He waited for Draper to disembark. It was fifteen minutes before she was able to join him. She looked exhausted, like she needed matchsticks to keep her eyes open. Economy clearly hadn't agreed with her.

"Hey there, sleepyhead," he said.

She told him to perform a sex act on himself. Rude.

They made their way to passport control. The uniformed Brit behind the Perspex screen scanned their passports, then waved them through without playing twenty questions. Either he'd been expecting them, or the UK Border Agency were under instructions not to delay diplomats, however unkempt they looked. Neither of them had checked luggage, so they headed straight to the arrivals concourse.

A woman was holding a printed BK & JD sign. She was in her early fifties and was wearing it well. Wasn't trying to hide it. She was tall and graceful, sort of like Draper fifteen years down the line. A thin face, a straight nose, and little to no makeup. She wore cotton canvas trousers, and a plain white T-shirt underneath an unfastened trench coat. She held the sign in the air, like she was a ring girl in a title fight.

"That's Bernice Kopitz," Draper said.

Koenig didn't ask how she knew. Not only was she in the private intelligence game, Smerconish had taken her aside before they had checked in at JFK. They'd talked for fifteen minutes, and although it had seemed heated toward the end, Koenig assumed Draper was getting information he wasn't yet privy to.

"She's come herself?" Koenig said. "I'm impressed."

"Don't be," Draper said. "Bernice was a bit of a legend back in the day. The London posting will be a reward for services rendered somewhere inhospitable. The journey to the embassy will take half an hour; she won't want to waste that time."

Which she didn't. Instead of introducing herself, Bernice said, "The diplomatic pouch arrived three hours ago, Mr. Koenig. We'll talk in the car, and I have a briefing prepared back at Nine Elms."

She led them to a Mercedes in short-term parking and threw Draper's hand luggage in the trunk. She slipped into the London traffic and eased past a truck with SAINSBURY'S written on the side. It was a garish orange and yellow and white. Koenig couldn't tell if it was transporting groceries or circus animals. He glanced at the Merc's dash. The temperature gauge said it was below freezing. He'd have to buy more clothes at some point. He looked up at the low gray clouds and the perma-drizzle, at the early commuters and their umbrellas. And maybe a hat, he thought.

"Damn," Bernice said, glancing in the rearview mirror. "I've picked up a pigtail."

"I'm not familiar . . ." Draper said.

"Scotland Yard know about you. It's always a risk when I drive myself. They sometimes put a car on me, see if I'm going somewhere interesting. I thought I'd gotten away with it this morning. It's early and I'm in my assistant's car. Probably playing silly buggers because our guys got their guys to quash the Speakers' Corner investigation. They'll be running your photographs now."

"Can you sort that?" Koenig asked. "I can do without the distraction of bounty hunters right now."

"Leave it with me," Bernice said.

"They know who you really are then?"

"Everyone who needs to does. It's sort of a given that we keep an eye on each other. It's what allies do. Stops us falling out. And you can't come here as an official CIA asset, not if you want to get anything done. The cultural attaché role gives everyone the cover they need to let me get on with the job."

"Which is?" Koenig asked.

"Liaise with the British security services, mainly. Bit of other stuff I won't go into. Plus, as cultural attaché, I do get invited to some cool shit. I was in Stratford-upon-Avon last night. Guest of honor at the Royal Shakespeare Company's *All's Well*."

"I prefer movies."

"I know," Bernice said. "I believe you had quite the collection of Super 8s."

"I still do, I think," Koenig replied, unsurprised at the depth of Bernice's knowledge. "A friend of mine put them in storage for me. Who knows, maybe I'll get to go home and watch them one day."

"I gather there was some trouble stateside before you left," she said, changing the subject. "Had a run-in with some naughty cops."

"That's putting it mildly," Draper snorted. "He killed one, blinded one, and disfigured one."

"So I heard. The one you blinded is in an irreversible coma, I'm told. They'll be turning off the machine soon."

"I didn't know that," Koenig said. He thought about it, then decided he didn't care. They were going to take him to a man who skinned people alive. It was a pity he hadn't killed them all.

"And the East Coast Sweeney, long on rumor, short on facts, now officially exists. I understand the FBI are putting a task force together this week. Seems like you did some good yesterday."

Koenig looked out of the window, stared into the cold fog of a London dawn. "I just wanted to be left alone," he said.

CHAPTER 20

The new US embassy at Nine Elms opened in 2017. It was in Battersea, south-west London. It looked like a sugar cube, easily one of the least attractive build-ings in the city. And it was surrounded by a moat. A *moat*. When did America get so scared that they were resorting to medieval defensive systems? What was next? Trebuchets on the roof? A portcullis over the entrance? Murder holes? What was wrong with a bunch of marines and an "open to interpretation" rules-of-engagement policy? The embassy looked like a joke on the people of London. Revenge for Piers Morgan.

Bernice took them to a secure briefing room. It was boxy with high ceilings. Windows you could look out of but not see into. Probably covered with anti-eavesdropping film. No pictures on the walls, no knickknacks on the bookcase. This was a room for working, not entertaining. Coffee, pastries, and fresh fruit were on the conference table. Koenig took a Danish and filled an embassy-branded mug with piping hot coffee. Draper did the same.

"We'll sweep the room before we start," Bernice said.

"Is that necessary?" Koenig asked.

"It's protocol when the agenda includes items above a certain security classification. It won't take long."

A suited man entered the room. He had short hair and didn't speak. He removed a wand from a metal case and started running it over any obvious places a bug could have been hidden. Behind the wall monitor. The lights, the electrical sockets. Underneath the conference table. Bugs had gotten smaller and smaller since Koenig's SOG days. He thought they were probably undetectable to the human eye by now. He took his Danish to the window. The briefing room overlooked the Thames. It was sluggish and murky brown. It looked like the chocolate river in Willy Wonka's factory.

"Looks like an open sewer, doesn't it?" Bernice said, joining him at the window. "It was called the Great Stink until a cholera outbreak forced the Brits to build a new sewage system. It's now the cleanest river that flows through a major city."

"It's brown."

"It has a muddy bed and it's tidal. It's *always* brown." She blew on her coffee. "I understand your sister lives in London?"

"Zoe, yes."

"You making the time to see her?"

"Afterward, maybe," Koenig said. "This is my priority right now."

"All clear, ma'am," the man sweeping the room said.

"Thank you, Kevin," Bernice said.

They took a seat at the conference table. After they had refilled their drinks, Bernice said, "Before we start, I have something for you, Mr. Koenig."

She slid a bag across the table. He opened it and smiled. Inside was his Fairbairn-Sykes fighting knife. It was like being reunited with a limb.

"I could have gotten you one of those," Bernice said. "You didn't have to put it in the pouch."

Koenig closed the bag and placed it by his feet. He said, "I have a history with this one."

"Where do you want to start?" she asked.

"Tell me about the academic Jane Doe abducted."

Bernice opened a laptop and pressed a button. The wall monitor flickered into life. A stern-faced, gray-haired woman appeared on the screen. She was facing the camera and she wasn't smiling. The picture looked like it had been taken for a mug shot or a passport. One of those photographs that came with a whole bunch of instructions. Her eyes seemed kind, though, Koenig thought. They twinkled. Made her look as though she was in on the joke and you weren't. She looked like the type of person who'd own a cuckoo clock.

"Margaret Wexmore," Bernice said. "Sixty-three years old. British." Now she'd started her briefing, Bernice rattled off the facts like a machine gun. Short, economical sentences. No wasted words, no filler. "Spent most of her life at the LSE. That's the London School of Economics. This is her faculty ID photograph. I'm told she's not usually this austere."

"What does she teach?"

"Cultural anthropology," Bernice said. "She's considered one of the leading academics on what happens when culturally different groups come into contact with one another."

"Sounds riveting."

"It took me three attempts to get all the way through her latest book," Bernice admitted.

"Anything?"

"Nothing that explains why she was abducted. She didn't ruffle any feathers, didn't write anything controversial. Her ideas were slightly different, but it's cultural anthropology—most of what she talks about has already happened."

"Something in her personal life?"

"Never married. No children. Owns a modest house in Camden Town. That's in northwest London. Paid her mortgage off fifteen years ago and lives within her means. Holidays in Scotland twice a year. Occasionally gets offers to lecture abroad, but she turns down more than she accepts these days. No obvious vices."

"Health?"

"There, I *do* have new information. She has a rare cancer called thymic carcinoma. It was diagnosed four years ago, too late for a good prognosis. I did some digging, and it seems she's been exploring her palliative options."

"How much time does she have?"

"No clue," Bernice admitted. "But if she's looking at palliative care, it can't be long."

"Medication?" Koenig asked.

"She stopped taking it a couple of months ago. I think she's resigned herself to dying."

"We can't find her through her prescription then."

"You think she's still alive?"

"I do," Koenig said. "It looked like she got into Jane Doe's car willingly. And if that's the case, this wasn't an abduction."

"I'll show you the Speakers' Corner film in a minute," Bernice said. "It was *definitely* an abduction."

"Jane Doe was disguised as a homeless woman," Koenig said. "It's possible

Margaret only *thought* she was being abducted. It's why she initially struggled. But when Jane Doe identified herself, Margaret went with her of her own accord."

"Interesting theory," Bernice admitted after a beat. "Scotland Yard were working on the assumption that Margaret got into the car under duress. Regardless, I don't see how that helps you find them. Jane Doe avoided almost every camera in London, and that's no mean feat. She could be anywhere now."

Koenig reached for another Danish. "I think I'd like to see the Speakers' Corner video," he said.

CHAPTER 21

The video was a compilation of every CCTV camera that had caught the Speakers' Corner incident. Kinda like the highlights reel on Oscars night. Some cameras covered other areas of Hyde Park, and Speakers' Corner was on the periphery and out of focus. Other cameras were too far away. There was no aerial shot. And Jane Doe had avoided almost every camera in London until she'd been caught on the one at the Greek deli.

It came down to what one modern camera had caught. The picture was crystal clear, as high-def as any CCTV footage Koenig had seen. If he'd been shown it out of context, he'd have figured he was watching a "found footage" movie. Koenig thought movies like *The Blair Witch Project* or *Cloverfield* were an unwelcome trend. They restrained movies rather than liberated them. In any case, if Koenig wanted to watch a bunch of chuckleheads running around in circles, he'd go and see the Yankees.

But the Speakers' Corner video wasn't a found footage movie. It was a slice of life. And death. *Two* deaths. The camera must have been positioned at least twenty feet in the air as everyone in Speakers' Corner was visible.

They watched it three times, and each time Koenig saw it, the more convinced he became that something had been missed. Or rather misinterpreted. He asked to see the footage again, this time from the moment Margaret Wexmore had arrived, instead of when the Romanian pickpockets had. He set the timer on his watch. When Jane Doe arrived, he nodded.

Smerconish only had half the story. The same half the British tabloids had run with. That Jane Doe had murdered the two Romanians in cold blood. And while that was technically accurate, it lacked context. Because if Smerconish's interpretation of events was ketchup, Koenig's was tomato sauce. They looked the same, but they weren't. Koenig thought everyone had got it back to front. The wrong way around. They saw black. They should have been seeing white.

"Jane Doe wasn't abducting Margaret Wexmore," he said. "She was *protecting* her."

CHAPTER 22

"The sequence of events doesn't make sense," Koenig said. "Not when you stop looking through the Brit tabloid-tinted lens."

Draper said nothing. Koenig thought she'd probably seen it too. She'd spent enough time with the SOG to unshackle herself from some of her old instincts. The CIA were risk-averse. They had to be. They didn't see the world in the pastiche of grays that Koenig did. When your day job is protecting a nation, Occam's razor becomes the default position—when you have competing hypotheses, you select the one with the fewest assumptions. The CIA didn't give the benefit of the doubt. If something looked like a duck, swam like a duck, and quacked like a duck, the CIA were going to blow it up with a reaper drone. Because next time the duck might be wearing a suicide vest.

"Scotland Yard believe a woman, in the midst of a mental health crisis, shot two strangers in the back of the head," Koenig said. "She then abducted a stranger at gunpoint. And if you look at what happened as two distinct but unrelated events, that's not an unreasonable position to take."

"But that's not what happened here?" Bernice said.

"I don't think so. If you watch the whole tape, you'll see that Margaret Wexmore enters Speakers' Corner and starts watching the guy standing on the box. Scotland Yard say her routine was the same every Sunday. She had a coffee, she bought a newspaper, and she watched the speakers. Very little variation. Even now when we know she was ill. Exactly one minute after Margaret arrives, Jane Doe appears. One minute is an interesting length of time for people like us."

"And why is that?"

"Jen?"

"At a slow pace, it takes roughly a minute to walk one hundred yards," Draper explained. "And one hundred yards is the optimum distance if you've gone foxtrot on your own."

No one needed "gone foxtrot" explained. It was slang everywhere for mobile surveillance on foot. One hundred yards was the only distance manageable if you were forced to follow someone alone. Closer than that and you were vulnerable to rudimentary countersurveillance measures. Farther away and you risked losing your target.

"Jane Doe was following Margaret?" Bernice asked.

"She enters the park, then stops one hundred yards away from her," Koenig said. "She takes a position where she can see Margaret but not the idiot on the soapbox."

Koenig dragged the video's progress bar until the moment the Romanians entered the park. He pressed pause.

"Look at Jane Doe," he said. "She isn't moving, but I've been on enough stakeouts to know when someone is hyperalert. She's like a bird, watching everyone, missing nothing." He pressed play. "Watch what happens now."

"She closes the distance," Bernice said.

"Exactly. She makes sure she can reach the Romanians before they can reach Margaret."

Koenig left the footage running. They watched the Romanians scan the crowd. Scotland Yard believed they were selecting their victims. They were in a target-rich environment, and Margaret had a Louis Vuitton bag slung over her shoulder. She was also female, elderly, and alone. Easy pickings. Except Margaret wasn't the easiest target in Speakers' Corner that morning. There was a drunk, probably on his way home after a night on the town. He was staggering, oblivious to his surroundings. The pickpockets could have helped him into a cab, robbing him blind as they did. A trio of girls were sitting on the concrete, their handbags behind them. Easy pickings. Risk-free.

Yet Margaret Wexmore was who they had chosen. When they saw her, their expressions changed. Went from anxious to focused. Wavering to unwavering.

"And look," Koenig said, pointing at the screen, "the bigger Romanian even checks his phone. Sure as a juggler's box, he's checking he has the right person."

The Romanians conversed with each other, a couple of words only. Probably offering encouragement. Or reassurance. They marched toward Margaret Wexmore. They got within eighteen feet of her. Before they could get to seventeen, Jane Doe shot them both in the back of the head. Point-blank. No chance of survival. By the time they'd hit the concrete, Jane Doe had reached Margaret.

And by the time the screaming started, she'd dragged her away from Speakers' Corner.

"This wasn't a random double murder followed by a random abduction," Koenig said. "Jane Doe is a professional. She identified a threat, then she eliminated that threat."

CHAPTER 23

"What threat?" Draper said. "There *was* no threat. This was an execution, plain and simple. And while, on the face of it, it does look as though the Romanians chose Margaret Wexmore over easier targets, there could be myriad reasons for that. They could have been stealing to order and Louis Vuitton was on their list. They might have seen her earlier with an expensive cell phone. Or maybe they were assholes who got their kicks from beating on old ladies. My point is, Jane Doe had no way of gauging their intentions. She could have waited. She had a gun. She could have intervened before things got nasty. But she didn't. She went from not doing anything to . . . I'm sorry, Koenig, but that's murder. There's no other way to describe it. It was cold-blooded murder."

"I agree," Koenig said.

"You do?"

"Yes. It's irrational. To an observer it seems like the act of a crazy person. It's why the mental health angle played so well with the British press. Whatever the Romanians' intentions, this was, on the face of it, a staggering overreaction."

"But?"

"But the woman I met ten years ago wasn't irrational. She wasn't crazy. She was anything but. She was logical, measured, and very much in control of her thoughts and actions. There's a disconnect between the woman I knew then, albeit briefly, and the woman in that footage. So, when you say there was no threat, I say that's an assumption. I say there was no threat that we could *see*."

"We need to find her then," Draper said. "Fast."

"But how?" Bernice asked. "Scotland Yard had this for a week before we shut it down. They got nowhere."

Koenig walked up to the wall monitor and tapped Jane Doe's hand.

"That's how," he said.

CHAPTER 24

"Can you zoom in on her gun?" Koenig said.

"I can, but it'll lose definition," Bernice said. "I'll get tech to clean it up later, but even they won't get it clear enough to read a serial number."

"It'll have been removed anyway," Draper said. "Filed off with a grinder or burned off with acid."

"I'm not interested in the serial number," Koenig said.

Bernice fiddled with her laptop's trackpad and pressed a button. The gun now filled the monitor's screen.

Koenig studied the picture, then stepped back. Satisfied.

"This is where we start," he said. "That's a derringer. Probably a COP .357, judging by the mess it made of their heads. You can tell by the shape of the muzzle. It's square, not round. Bulky. And that's because it has four barrels. Stacked in a two-by-two block, like the holes on a button. It's an unusual weapon. I think I've only ever seen them in cowboy movies. Normally used to settle poker disputes. Some guy accuses another of having aces up his sleeve. Reaches into his boot, pulls out a derringer. Shoots the card cheat dead."

"So?"

"The Brits banned private ownership of handguns after a mass shooting in 1997. Get caught with a handgun over here and you go to jail for ten years. They're extremely rare, derringers even rarer. It's a signature weapon. I'd be surprised if there are more than two or three in the whole country."

"I'll do some digging," Bernice said. "See who's selling guns in London."

"She won't have bought it in London," Koenig said. "Scotland Yard has LFR capabilities. Live facial recognition. Similar system to the one in New York. They use it to keep a continuous lookout for anyone on a watch list."

"Where then?"

A familiar feeling washed over Koenig. Tracking people had been his thing in the SOG. He'd had a peculiar knack for it. He could get inside the heads of the people he was hunting. Think like them. Wear their shoes. And even though it felt voyeuristic, he found himself slipping inside Jane Doe's mind. She'd wanted a weapon. Probably didn't feel complete without one. But she was keeping a low profile in a country that hated handguns. So, it had had to be small enough to be permanently hidden. That was hugely limiting in the UK. The gangbangers didn't want small, easily concealable weapons. They wanted big shiny things with cool names like "Glock" and "MAC-10." They didn't want a boot pistol, even one as powerful as the COP .357.

That meant she hadn't gone to the guy who sold crap from the trunk of his 2011 Nissan. She'd gone to the kind of arms dealer who imported from Continental Europe or the States. Who had a select clientele. Only sold to people he knew. Hundreds of guys like that in the States, probably only one or two in the UK.

"I need a map and a marker pen," Koenig said.

CHAPTER 25

Bernice left the briefing room, returning two minutes later with a map of the UK. It was a pocket map, a flat sheet folded in a concertina pattern. She opened it and spread it out on the table, using embassy mugs to weigh down the sides. The table wasn't big enough. Parts of Wales, parts of Devon and Cornwall, and all of Northern Ireland hung over the edges. Koenig didn't care. Devon, Cornwall, and Wales didn't have major cities. You didn't go there for a specialist handgun. And while Northern Ireland was certainly somewhere firearms were sold, Koenig doubted Jane Doe would risk buying one over there. Despite the Good Friday Agreement, Brit security services maintained a watching brief in Belfast and beyond.

"If we discount London because of live facial recognition, there are only five cities our woman would have considered when it came to buying a black-market handgun," Koenig said. "Liverpool, Glasgow, Manchester, Birmingham, and Sheffield. There will be others, but you'd have to be in that life to know where. Jane Doe wasn't."

He flipped off the lid of a marker pen. Koenig circled the five cities, then rocked back on his heels and tried to think like a woman who'd faked her own death. Where would she have felt it was safe to live in the UK?

England was out. It had 85 percent of the population but only half the land mass. It was one of the most densely populated countries in Europe. Most people lived in London and the South East, but almost everywhere was full. And the places that weren't tended to be tourist traps. Northumberland and

Beatrix Potter's Lake District might look empty on paper, but the moment the sun came out, they were busier than Disneyland. He discounted Wales for similar reasons. Because of its proximity to London, it tended to fill up at weekends.

That left Scotland, and Koenig thought Scotland was perfect. It was the same size as South Carolina with the same size population. But whereas South Carolinians tended to be well spread out, most Scots lived in Glasgow, Edinburgh, and Aberdeen. Huge swathes had an Alaskan-like population density. And the Highlanders, Lowlanders, and Islanders who made their homes there were fiercely independent. They kept themselves to themselves. They were self-sufficient. They hated gossip. And the single malt flowed like running water. If Koenig had to hide in the UK, he'd choose Scotland. No question.

He didn't voice this. He didn't feel like sharing what was inside his head. It was like he didn't have permission. Telling Draper how Jane Doe thought would be a breach of trust. Instead, he took his marker and put a cross through Glasgow. Guns *were* for sale in Glasgow, but he didn't think she'd have wanted to buy one so close to home. It wouldn't have felt right. Like she was taking advantage of her adopted country's inner-city drug problem.

Draper and Bernice watched in silence.

That left four cities: Liverpool, Manchester, Birmingham, and Sheffield. Liverpool and Manchester were in the North West. Birmingham was in the Midlands, and Sheffield was on the other side of the country, in South Yorkshire. Koenig traced a line from Scotland coming down into England. Looked at the available routes. There were two north-south highways. The M6 serviced the west, and the A1 serviced the east. Neither was plumb-line straight. They both jigged about, connecting cities and bigger towns. On the map the highways looked like cloud-to-ground lightning strikes. The A1 began in Edinburgh, and the M6 began in Glasgow. Glasgow and Edinburgh were fifty miles from each other with good connecting roads. She could have taken either route into England without any difficulty.

In the end it came down to math. The M6 offered three chances, the A1 only one. Manchester and Liverpool were thirty miles apart, and the M6 bisected them. If you couldn't find what you needed in Manchester, it was a thirty-minute car ride to Liverpool. And if you left Manchester and Liverpool empty-handed, you were already on the right road to the UK's second largest city, Birmingham.

He crossed out Sheffield.

After that it was a simple case of logic. She would have tried the nearest city first. There was no point bypassing one in favor of another farther away. The longer she was in surveillance-happy England, the greater chance she would get picked up on some random camera.

Koenig circled Manchester.

CHAPTER 26

Koenig wanted to leave immediately. Manchester was in the north and London was in the south, but England was a small-ass country. The journey would only take four hours. Bernice arranged an embassy car for them.

"It's a stick, if that's OK?" she said. "The Brits seem weirdly attached to the inconvenience."

"Jen has a '73 Stingray," Koenig said.

"Which this asshole stole last year."

"Which I *borrowed* last year. So, yes, we can both drive sticks."

"The North West of England is an interesting place, don't you think?" Koenig said. "The UK's split by a great ridge of limestone that stretches from Dorset in the South West to Yorkshire in the North East. It's called the Jurassic Divide. Everywhere below has good agricultural land. Everything above is more suited to pastoral farming."

"Oh, my God," Draper said. "Do you *ever* shut up?"

The embassy car was a Jaguar XF, black as Guinness and just as smooth. When he saw it, Koenig had said, "Wasn't Chitty Chitty Bang Bang available?"

"Excuse me?" Bernice had replied.

"I was hoping for something less conspicuous."

"Face it, Koenig, you're an American abroad. You have to *own* that shit."

Koenig didn't like that idea at all.

He'd offered to drive so Draper could grab the sleep she'd missed on the flight over. He'd expected some kickback, but she'd accepted without comment. They were moving from intelligence gathering to fieldwork, and they both knew sleep mattered. It *counted*. She'd closed her eyes when they were still in London and hadn't opened them since. Koenig needed her awake now, though. There was a car in the Jag's rearview mirror. A black BMW. One of the sedans. It was two hundred yards behind them. Didn't matter if he dropped down to sixty or went up to ninety. The car stayed two hundred yards behind. He wanted Draper alert, not rubbing drool off her chin and asking what the time was.

"Because of the Jurassic Divide, the North West was an historically poor area," Koenig continued. "But that all changed with the Industrial Revolution. They had rivers to power their factories, they had soft water, and they had slave-grown cotton coming into Liverpool. They had a damp, cotton-friendly climate, and raw materials like coal and iron ore. The North West went from being one of the poorest areas to one of the richest. It's why it has so many big cities."

Draper yawned. "How do you know all this shit?"

"I spent time with the British SAS, and they spend longer on stakeouts than the SOG do. We had interesting conversations."

"You and I have very different definitions of 'interesting,'" she said. "Now, if you don't mind, some of us were in cattle class last night. I'm going back to sleep."

But Koenig was only half listening. The BMW had closed the gap to thirty yards. It had tucked in behind him, too close for another car to get between them. Now it was nearer, Koenig could see the telltale signs of an unmarked cop car. The gray panels on the grille that, at the touch of a button, would transform into police lights. It was a BMW 5 Series. A luxury car. Yet Koenig could see no optional extras. It looked like it had the basic package. Plain wheels. Nonmetallic paint. No spoilers. Not even a sunroof. This was a BMW bought with public money. But the biggest giveaway was that it was spotless. Koenig wondered if cops would ever catch on that their unmarked cars were always clean and sparkly. And perps knew that. When he was with the SOG, he never cleaned the cars they used for undercover work.

As if the driver had been reading his mind, a burst of blue light flashed from the grille and from behind the headrests. No alternating with red like in the States. The color for emergency lights in the UK was blue. There was no siren.

Draper saw him looking in the rearview mirror. She angled her neck and glanced in the passenger-door wing mirror.

"Were you speeding?" she asked.

"Probably," Koenig replied. "But that's not why we're being stopped. They've been tailing us for thirty miles."

"You never said."

"I didn't want to wake you."

"Why stop us now, though?"

"We've just passed a turnpike. The next one isn't for twenty miles. Nowhere for us to run. Or maybe we've crossed into a more friendly jurisdiction."

"You'd better pull over then."

"Guess I'd better."

"But as we don't know what this is, you'd better keep the engine running."

Koenig hadn't needed to be told that.

CHAPTER 27

Koenig pulled onto what the Brits called the hard shoulder. The BMW tucked in behind him. Koenig stopped. So did the BMW.

"If I say go, you go," Draper said. "You put your foot down and we get the hell out of here. I'm not getting whacked because you don't understand an asshole with a gun is dangerous."

"Cops here aren't armed," Koenig said.

"And cops back home aren't supposed to moonlight as bounty hunters."

"Fair point."

Koenig watched the BMW in the rearview mirror. There was a woman in the passenger seat. She was making a call. He couldn't tell if she was using a cell or a police radio. She said something to the man in the driver's seat, then opened the door. She approached Koenig's side of the Jag. Touched the trunk as she did. An old cop trick. Put her prints on the car in case something went wrong. Proved she'd been there.

She had shoulder-length black hair tied back in a ponytail. She wore black trousers, a white blouse, and a navy blue blazer. Her hands were empty. She wasn't carrying a bag. If she had a gun, it was tucked into her waist at the back. She knocked on the window. Koenig lowered it.

"How are you doing?" she said.

"Very well, thank you. Yourself?"

"Can't complain."

"We'll be on our way then," Koenig said.

The woman reached into her inside pocket and produced a thin black wallet. She flipped it open and held it out. "My name's Chief Superintendent Danielle Brown. Do you know why I've stopped you?"

"You've forgotten already?" Koenig said. "It was only thirty seconds ago. I'd see a brain doctor if I were you."

"Do you want to try again, sir?"

"Our Jag has a FREE DOUGHNUTS sign in the rear window?"

"You'd better tell him, Chief Superintendent Brown," Draper said. "He can keep this bullshit up all day."

"I have some questions for you both," she said. "How about we start with an easy one. What are your names? The truth, please."

"My name's Ben," Koenig said. "I'm an amateur bum, but I'm hoping to go professional next year. This is Jen. She used to torture people for the CIA but says she doesn't anymore."

Draper glowered at him.

"You won't get into heaven if you lie to police officers, Jen. It's in the rules. Anyway, she knows exactly who we are. Isn't that right, Chief Superintendent Brown?"

She nodded. No hesitation. "Please, call me Danielle," she said.

"Do you want to get in the back, Danielle? The seats are heated and it's cold outside."

"Thank you." Danielle put her thumb and forefinger together, flashed her driver the OK gesture. She climbed into the back of the Jag.

"How can we help you?" Koenig said.

"I want to know why my murder investigation was closed down," she said. "I want to know why someone dressed like a Victorian flower seller killed two people in cold blood. And I want to know how she managed to evade almost every camera in my city."

"Is that all?"

"For now."

"If you know who we are, then you also know that we can't tell you."

"Can't or won't?"

"Is there a difference?"

"There absolutely is a difference. 'Can't' means you don't know. 'Won't' means you're just a dickhead hiding behind some national security codswallop." She paused. "Are you a dickhead, Mr. Koenig?"

Which was low-hanging fruit to Draper. "Yes," she said. "God, yes."

"It's a 'can't,'" Koenig admitted. "We have absolutely no idea why she did anything. We don't even know her name."

"But you're here to find out?"

Koenig said nothing.

"I'll take that as a yes," Danielle said. "And because you came over on diplomatic passports, and because Miss Draper owns a private intelligence company, I'm going out on a limb and saying this is an unsanctioned operation. You're covert. You got material support from Bernice Kopitz and then she got rid of you as fast as possible."

"How'd you figure that?"

"I know Bernice. Met her a couple of times. She's incredibly competent. And if she's sent you out without support, it's because that's what she was told to do. Or she wanted no part of what's about to happen. Either way, you two are on your own. How am I doing?"

Koenig shared a look with Draper. She shrugged. "You have a suggestion?" he said.

"I do," Danielle said. "This is no longer a covert investigation. I know you're here and I know *why* you're here. And while you will both be given the courtesy that all our American guests get in the UK, none of the forty-five police forces will cooperate with you. Not from any sense of malice, you understand. We barely cooperate with each other. See what happens when you ask for assistance sounding like Joe Friday."

"I'm from Boston," Koenig said.

"I wasn't talking to you."

Draper smiled. Which was a relief. Koenig had seen her punch people for less. He came to a decision. A British cop *could* be an asset. They could call in favors. Lean on informants. Order beers that weren't warm. But only if she played at their level. He didn't have time for excess baggage.

"Why would we need cooperation?" he asked.

"Because we've watched the same movie," she said.

"I'll need a little more—"

"You're after a gun," she cut in. "Your mystery woman was holding a weapon our experts have identified as a COP .357 derringer. That's exotic. *All* handguns over here are exotic, of course, but this one especially so. I was ordered to shut down my investigation, which I did. I work in a command-and-control organization. I don't need to know the rationale behind every decision my superiors make. But they can't stop me thinking about it."

"And what is it you've been thinking about, Danielle?"

"That if I'd been allowed to continue, I'd have headed north looking for where she bought the gun."

"You work in one of the biggest cities in Europe," Koenig said. "Why not start there?"

"London has live facial recognition," she said. "And because the threat level hasn't been below 'substantial' for five years now, the LFR cameras are on permanent deployment. A woman this good would know that. She wouldn't risk London. Not when her face triggered the kind of response it did. That leaves half a dozen other cities. You're on the M6 and you've already passed Birmingham. That leaves Manchester, Liverpool, or Glasgow. All three have gang problems."

"Where *exactly* would you start looking?"

"Not in the cities themselves. The guy you're looking for will only sell to select clients. People he knows. The odd referral. He won't live in the city because he won't have to. But he'll have to live nearby. Somewhere rural or semirural. He won't want to make drops in an urban area. I think you plan to find someone with a gun and hit him until he tells you where he bought it. Then work your way up the food chain until you get to the big dog's kennel."

Koenig shared another glance with Draper. She nodded.

"Did I pass?" Danielle asked.

"You did," Koenig said. "I was going to find a street dealer tonight. Start there. Would that work?"

"It might," she said. "But if I were you, I'd skip a couple of the lower rungs by finding the right bar or club. The kind of place that sells punishment beatings. That type of place."

"You know anywhere like that?"

"I used to work for Greater Manchester Police. I haven't been back in almost ten years, but I still have contacts. By the time we get to where we're going, I'll have a name. Somewhere to start."

"You don't need to check in with anyone?" Koenig asked. "We may be a couple of days and I'm sure chief superintendents are kept busy in London."

"I'm on leave. Compassionate. Took it the moment Bernice collected you at Heathrow. Sick uncle."

"And your driver?"

"Won't say anything."

"He's not coming?"

"He *is* needed back in London. I'll get a lift with you guys. Reduce my carbon footprint. I'm good to go."

"You don't have an overnight bag in the trunk?"

"If I need something, I'll buy it."

Koenig slipped the Jag into first and eased back onto the M6. "Let's go and crack some skulls then."

"You know I'm a cop, right?" Danielle said. "No one is cracking skulls."

"Figure of speech," Koenig said. "And, just so you know, that whole personal-carbon-footprint thing is nothing but propaganda. The product of a one-hundred-million-dollar marketing campaign. BP wanted to deflect responsibility for climate change away from them and onto the individual. It's one of the most deceptive PR campaigns there has ever been."

Draper sighed. "Welcome to my world, Danielle," she said. "I've had to put up with this since we left New York."

CHAPTER 28

In the States, Big City Nights would have needed a lick of paint to get called a dive bar. In the UK, it was called a spit-and-sawdust pub. Or a shithole. Or, with the Brit tendency to understate things, "a bit rough." The kind of place that if you left with the same number of teeth you had entered with, you hadn't been enjoying yourself properly.

It was in Hulme, an inner-city area in Manchester. Danielle said "Hulme" was derived from the Old Norse word for a small island. Which was weird. As far as Koenig could tell, the only thing that surrounded this part of Manchester was more Manchester. They drove past tower blocks and derelict factories and rows and rows of public housing to get there. Danielle noticed Koenig looking at the gang tags painted on the walls and bridges and shuttered shop windows.

"It used to be really bad around here," she explained. "It may not look it, but it's a rapidly improving area. People want to live here now as it's so close to the city center. Lots of money being pumped into its regeneration."

Koenig, who'd switched his attention to a man walking a three-legged dog, said nothing.

Big City Nights was sandwiched between a bookmaker's that was full and a doughnut shop that wasn't. Koenig wasn't surprised. It only had one doughnut for sale and that was priced at five pounds. Six and a half bucks for a ring doughnut. Looked like it had been there for weeks. Koenig reckoned they should be honest and call the doughnut shop what it really was: a money-laundering outfit. It was so blatant it wouldn't have made any difference.

Koenig turned off the engine. He arranged the rearview mirror so he could see Big City Nights without turning his head. It looked shut. That meant nothing, though. Almost every business on the road looked shut. He watched the bar until a skinny guy lurched outside. He vomited on the road, wiped his mouth with his sleeve, then staggered back inside.

Danielle had called in a favor to get the name of a bar that might sell weapons. And although Koenig knew this wasn't the kind of place a COP .357 could be bought, he reckoned the people inside would know the name of a guy. Maybe that guy was the guy they wanted, or maybe he'd know the name of another guy. District attorneys called it flipping. Over here it was called turning Queen's evidence. Possibly *King's* evidence, now Charles had been promoted. It was the lure of the carrot. Much-reduced prison sentences for useful intelligence. That was a *big* carrot. Nice and orange and sweet and nutritious.

Koenig didn't have a carrot. But he did have a stick. A really pointy one.

"Let's do it," he said, unbuckling his seat belt and opening the door.

"We can't go in," Danielle said. "Not until I've called for backup."

"Why would we need backup?"

"Cops around here patrol in threes and only when they're wearing stab-proof vests."

"You wait for backup if you want," Koenig said. "I'm going inside." He paused, then turned so he faced Draper. "Unless this is one of those times when I haven't recognized a dangerous situation?"

"A bar full of assholes? Hell, I'm not scared, and my brain works just fine."

Koenig looked at Danielle. "Jen says it's fine."

Danielle shook her head, not fully understanding what had just happened.

"You'll stay with the car?" Koenig said to Draper.

She nodded.

Danielle said, "What about me?"

"You can stay here, or you can come with me. Your choice."

"I don't think I want to miss this," Danielle said, opening her door.

Koenig joined her on the damp pavement. His back was stiff from driving. He twisted it about a bit until it cracked like a glow stick. Rolled his shoulders and neck. Raised his arms and corkscrewed them. He reached back into the car and pulled his Fairbairn-Sykes from the driver's door pocket. He slipped it into the back of his jeans. Adjusted his jacket until it couldn't be seen.

Danielle raised an eyebrow.

"American Express," Koenig said. "Never leave home without it."

"You realize that simply carrying that in public will get you a four-year prison sentence?" Danielle said.

"Not me," Koenig said. "I have diplomatic immunity."

CHAPTER 29

Koenig and Danielle stood outside Big City Nights. The door was metal-framed. It was battleship gray. The paint was peeling like bark from a birch tree. It was tagged with graffiti and gang signs.

Danielle looked nervous. Koenig knew she was having second thoughts. He also knew she'd walk into Big City Nights with him and, if it came down to it, she'd have his back. He knew the type. The SOG had been full of them.

"Will she be OK?" Danielle said, pointing at Draper. She was lounging against the cooling hood of the Jag. Looked like she didn't have a care in the world. "That's an expensive car. Someone might want it for their chop shop."

Koenig considered how that might go down. "I think she'd enjoy that," he said.

"Did she really torture people for the CIA?"

"Of course not," Koenig said. "That would be illegal."

Now they'd stopped moving, they could hear noise. Muted talking, the occasional snort of laughter, commentary from a soccer game. Nothing that couldn't be heard outside any bar in any country. Koenig tried the door. It was locked. Yet the guy who'd come outside to puke hadn't kept his foot in the doorway. He'd let it shut on him. He hadn't needed a key to get back in and he hadn't knocked. Koenig studied the door frame. It was wood. Wood had natural fibers. It swelled when it got damp. Basic hygroscopic expansion. Metal didn't have the same properties. Metal expanded with heat, not moisture. When hot weather made the metal expand, the wood would shrink. When cold weather made the metal shrink, the damp climate of a British winter would make the wood swell. Koenig didn't know the scientific term for a simple machine made inefficient by its material's contradictory expansion properties, but he knew the nonscientific term: The door was stuck. He put his shoulder to it and pushed. Not wham, bam, like he was breaching a room and the whole point was to make noise and cause confusion. This was a gradual increase in pressure, like he was pushing a piano up a hill.

The door creaked, then swung open.

Big City Nights went silent. The soccer commentator shouted, "Goal!"

Someone muttered, "Bollocks."

CHAPTER 30

All eyes turned to Koenig and Danielle as they stepped into Big City Nights. The chatter stopped. Only the soccer commentator kept talking. Koenig studied the bar's clientele. Saw that "all eyes" wasn't the same amount as the number of people multiplied by two.

There was a guy at the bar who only had one.

Koenig wondered how he'd lost it. Not well, judging by the lumpy scar tissue in and around his eye socket. He'd replaced it with a ball bearing. Koenig was sure it was supposed to look menacing. Probably was in his social circle. All Koenig saw was someone with compromised vision. Monocular instead of binocular. Limited depth perception. A reduced ability to judge spatial distance. Probably why the bar didn't have a dartboard or a pool table. Games like that need two eyes. One-Eye looked like he was in charge, and that meant if he couldn't play, no one could.

One-Eye was a big man, bigger than the Jolly Green Giant. Six and a half foot in his bare feet. Bulky. Prison muscles, Koenig thought. The kind of man who found employment as someone else's blunt instrument. His face looked like it had been riveted together from scrap iron. Crudely shaved head. Looked like a badly plucked chicken. Lots of nicks, as if the razor had been blunt. He had the swollen knuckles of a brawler. He was probably effective against other brawlers. Put him up against a professional boxer, though, and he'd lose every time. He'd be too slow. Wild haymakers. No footwork, no balance. Just rage.

Nothing subtle.

Which as a metaphor for the bar was perfect.

Because Big City Nights was as subtle as a five-foot wrench. It didn't even have a bar. Not in the traditional sense. What Big City Nights had was scaffolding boards nailed onto stacked pallet crates. Three stacks. Two at each end, one in the middle to stop the boards sagging. The kind of hipster bullshit found in Greenwich Village. Where interior designers were paid thousands to get an edgy-but-safe look.

There was a metal bucket perched at one end of the makeshift bar. It was big and round and looked like the kind of thing farmers used to feed livestock. Pigs, not chickens. It was full of half-melted ice and cans of beer. Some cigarette butts. None of those woke ideas like fridges for Big City Nights. The floor was stickier than a flytrap.

There were no windows in Big City Nights. It was a square room. Like a holding cell. Or a drunk tank. It had probably been part of the bookmaker's or the doughnut shop before it was annexed. The metal door was the only way in and out. Big City Nights was less welcoming than a DO NOT STOP FOR HITCHHIKERS sign. It was the most unfriendly bar Koenig had ever been in, and he'd spent time in Paris.

Unless there was someone in the bathroom—which seemed unlikely; there wasn't one—there were five people in the bar. One-Eye, the bartender, and three men seated around a table that looked like it had come from a yard sale. They were playing three-card brag. Idiot's poker.

"What would you like to drink?" Koenig said to Danielle.

"What are my choices?"

Koenig cast his eyes behind the barman to the shelf where the whiskies and gins and vodkas were usually kept. All he saw was a bunch of dead flies and a mangy cat. It was either asleep or dead. It certainly wasn't moving.

"Beer or nothing, I think," he said.

"Beer's fine."

"Two," he said to the bartender. "And I don't suppose you have any Sam Adams cooling in the back?"

The bartender replied by pointing a remote at the TV on the wall and muting the soccer game. "We're closed," he said.

"That's a real shame," Koenig said. "This place looks so *kitsch*."

"We're closed," the bartender said again.

"And I say you're not. *I* say you're not being hospitable to strangers. I'm not sure I like how that makes me feel."

The bartender looked to One-Eye for instructions. One-Eye shrugged. The bartender reached across and fished two cans from the farmer's bucket. He slammed them on the makeshift bar.

"Not those two," Koenig said. "I'd like ones that aren't going to spurt everywhere. I'd hate to damage the wood."

"Who *are* you?" the bartender asked.

"Nobody," Koenig said. "I'm nobody, you're nobody, the three gentlemen playing cards are nobodies." He faced One-Eye. "But you, sir, I think you might be someone."

"Depends," One-Eye said.

"On?"

"On who's asking."

"I've told you," Koenig said. "I'm no one."

"And what do you want, Mr. No One? You might be a Yank, but you don't look like no tourist."

"I have a problem you might be able to help me with."

"How?"

"I need hardware."

"A gun?"

"*Guns,*" Koenig confirmed. "Plural. And I'm a cash buyer."

"Guns are illegal in this country."

"Which is why I'm not shopping at Walmart."

"Walmart is *definitely* illegal in this country."

"Can you help, or do I need to go elsewhere?"

One-Eye paused. Narrowed his eye until it was a slit. "You don't look like filth," he said.

"I have a wash every Sunday," Koenig said. "Even if I'm not dirty."

"Not *filthy*. Filth. A pig. Five-O, as you fucking Yanks say." He inclined his head toward Danielle. "She stinks of bacon, though. Stinks of bacon so much she's making me hungry."

"We're not cops," Koenig said.

"You sure? Cos you know you have to tell me if you are. Otherwise, it's entrapment."

"We're not cops," Koenig repeated.

"Let her answer," the brawler said. "That way it's all nice and legal."

"I'm not, and never have been, a cop," Danielle said without missing a beat.

She said it so convincingly even Koenig believed her. He reckoned she'd been undercover before. Lying like your life depended on it became second nature when you wore two hats. And it was surprising how many idiots believed the entrapment thing. Of course undercover cops were allowed to lie about not being cops.

"Something isn't adding up, though," One-Eye said. "My spidey senses are tingling."

Koenig sighed. Convincing a bunch of lowlifes to sell guns to a stranger was never the plan. Not in a gun-phobic country like the UK. Men like this were stupid, but they had animal-like cunning. If it were a choice between making a thousand bucks or going down for twenty years, well, that was no choice at all. Koenig knew that. Just like he knew that the men playing cards had stopped playing. They had gone from playing three-card brag to whispering excitedly. He'd said he was a cash buyer. It was possible they thought they had someone to rob. An easy mark for guys like them. Take the money, leave him in the gutter, bleeding. Do the same to the woman. Equal opportunity assholes.

But it could have been something else. One of the men at the table, a man with a pockmarked face and hair that stuck up like a toilet brush, was staring at Koenig, but trying to make it look like he wasn't. He then tapped something into his cell phone. Koenig heard a whoosh as he pressed send.

A fraction of a second later, One-Eye's phone beeped. Koenig didn't carry a cell phone, but he knew what an incoming SMS alert sounded like. A bunch of 1s and 0s had gone from the pockmarked guy's phone to One-Eye's phone. Unless it was a coincidence. Koenig knew coincidences happened all the time. Mark Twain's birth and death dates coincided with Halley's Comet. Without any planning, the first and last British soldiers to die in World War I were buried next to each other. But Koenig had been a federal agent. Coincidences were a lazy explanation. He reached behind and lifted his jacket free of his Fairbairn-Sykes.

One-Eye glanced at the screen, then frowned. He then looked at Koenig. His expression changed. Went from suspicious to welcoming. Which was the most suspicious thing he could have done. Koenig readied himself.

"My name's Stan," he said. "*Steeleye* Stan."

He said it like he was James Bond, then waited. Clearly, Koenig was supposed to ask a question. Koenig didn't.

"For obvious reasons," Stan added.

"Oh, you have a ball bearing instead of an eye," Koenig said. "I hadn't noticed."

CHAPTER 31

"OK, let's do some business," Steeleye said. "What do you need?"

"What can you get?" Koenig replied.

"Most things."

"I want a Lawgiver Mk. II. Two DL-44s. And, if you can get one, a Westinghouse M-27."

"Exotic," Steeleye said. "Not been asked to get these for a while." He pulled a crumpled notebook from his jacket pocket. It looked like one of the complimentary notebooks the hotel chains dished out like candy. Each page would have the hotel logo on the bottom. Free advertising and they traveled far beyond the local catchment area. Steeleye's was small, about the size of a dollar bill folded in half. It didn't have a protective cardboard cover. Scribble pads, Koenig thought they were called.

The barman handed Steeleye a half pencil, probably from the bookmaker's next door. He licked the end as if he were a 1920s newspaperman. He started writing down Koenig's order. He held the pencil awkwardly, like a monkey would.

Koenig looked over Steeleye's shoulder as he wrote. "The 'house' in 'Westinghouse' is spelled with an *S*, not a *Z*," he said. "And 'Lawgiver' only has one *V*."

Steeleye frowned but made the corrections.

"That all?" he said.

"It is. How long?"

"We have these in stock. As soon as we see your money, we'll place the order."

"And as soon as *we* see the hardware, you'll see the money. You know how this works."

"I'll make some calls," Steeleye said.

He got up and walked out of the bar.

CHAPTER 32

Steeleye walked back into Big City Nights like he owned the place. Which he probably did. Probably owned the bookmaker's and the doughnut shop as well. He sat on the stool he'd just vacated.

"We have everything you want," he said. "Not going to be cheap, though."

"How much."

"Eight grand."

"That's steep."

"This isn't the States; it's a seller's market here. The price is the price."

Koenig looked at Danielle. She nodded, like she was the money and he was the muscle.

"Fine," Koenig said. "But tell me, how'd you manage to get hold of everything so quickly?"

"We know people, if you know what I mean?"

"And do these people work in the movie business?"

Steeleye's brow furrowed.

"The Lawgiver Mk. II is Judge Dredd's handgun," Koenig said. "The DL-44 is the heavy blaster Han Solo used in *Star Wars*. And the Westinghouse M-27 is the plasma rifle Skynet's hunter-killer droids used in the Terminator franchise. A cynical man might think he was being exploited. But I'm a *reasonable* man, Stan. I prefer to think this has simply been an unfortunate breakdown in communication. That instead of offering the impossible, you were merely opening negotiations. Do I have that right, Stan?"

Instead of answering, Steeleye nodded at the guy with the pincushion face. He got to his feet and slouched to the door. Koenig assumed he was going for reinforcements. He was wrong. Instead of leaving, he slipped a key from his pocket and locked the door. He smirked at Koenig and rejoined his friends at the card table. They moved their seats and spread out. Leaned forward, ready and waiting.

Steeleye reached into his jacket pocket and came out with a handgun. He placed it on the bar, just out of Koenig's reach. It was a Glock 46. New. Probably stolen in Germany. The Glock 46 was designed specifically for the German police when they were upgrading from their SIG Sauer P6s. It was rare everywhere else. Externally it was the same as the Glock 17, law enforcement's weapon of choice the world over. The differences were mainly internal. It was reliable and robust. A deadly weapon.

"How about this, wanker?" Steeleye said. "Is *this* fictional?"

Koenig turned to Danielle. "Is this guy for real?" he said. He then reached behind his back and came out with his Fairbairn-Sykes. "Looks like I've brought a knife to a gunfight." He rolled his eyes and added, "I'm always doing that."

CHAPTER 33

"You're that guy," Steeleye said. "The one those Russian gangsters will pay five million dollars for."

"I am?" Koenig said.

"No question. Spax over there"—he tilted his head at the pockmarked guy, the one who'd sent the SMS—"likes to trawl the dark web. See if there are any jobs we can do for pocket money. He sent me a link. I went outside to check."

"And to collect your Glock."

"Er, what's this about a five-million-dollar bounty, Koenig?" Danielle said. "Because if it's true, that's the type of thing you mention *before* we step into the roughest pub in Manchester. Not afterwards. Not after some one-eyed arsehole has pulled a gun from his pocket."

"Yes, that *was* a stroke of luck," Koenig said.

"Luck?" Danielle said. "You think that was lucky?"

"If Stan had pulled a Saturday night special, we'd have had to go some-place else. But Stan *didn't* pull a Saturday night special. Stan pulled a Glock 46. And the Glock 46 is a rare beast. I've never even seen one before. No way does this pinhead have the connections to bring in guns like these from mainland Europe. Any arms dealer capable of getting his hands on a Glock 46 would run a mile from these clowns. That means Stan has a local supplier. An intermediary. Someone who can deal with the street thugs *and* the guys who import high-quality guns. It's *this* guy we want. And Stan's going to tell us. That's why it was a stroke of luck. It's lucky for Stan as well. Because even though he's pulled a gun on me, he gets to live. So, yay for him."

Stan's brow furrowed. "*We* sell the guns around here," he said.

"You guys couldn't pour piss out of a boot if the instructions were on the heel," Koenig said. "But here's the deal—tell me who you bought the Glock from, and I'll pretend you didn't point it at me. This offer expires soon."

"You're a cocky bastard, aren't you?" Steeleye said. "Especially for someone locked in a room with five armed men."

"*One* armed man," Koenig said. "And you've got it the wrong way around, Stan. I'm not locked in here with the five of you. You're locked in here with *me*."

Steeleye's right hand was still resting on top of the Glock. His index finger was inside the trigger guard. But because they were seated at the bar facing each other, the Glock's barrel wasn't pointing at Koenig. For that to happen, Steeleye would have had to hold it at an unnatural angle. Or rest it on his knee. Or hold it in his left hand. Koenig had trained on CQB ranges and could shoot right- or left-handed. He doubted a low-rate thug like Stan could say the same. Which was why the Glock was pointing between Koenig and the barman. If the barman was twelve o'clock and Koenig was three o'clock, the Glock would be pointing at two o'clock. Maybe one thirty.

It would only take Steeleye a fraction of a second to move the Glock 46 to three o'clock. And then he would shoot Koenig. Probably in the stomach. Then he'd shoot Danielle.

A fraction of a second. That's how long it would take.

More than enough time.

CHAPTER 34

Koenig struck with the Fairbairn-Sykes.

Overhand, like he was karate-chopping a brick. Came up from Steeleye's blind side. His ball bearing side. Meant that by the time he saw Koenig's shoulder move, it was too late.

Much too late.

By then the Fairbairn-Sykes had already staked his wrist to the bar. The handle vibrated like a twanged ruler. Koenig had aimed the acutely tapered, sharply pointed blade at the gap between the radius and ulna, the long bones that made up Steeleye's forearm. It had sliced through skin, tendons, muscles, and blood vessels like they were made of water. Stan instinctively tried to pull away. The knife held him at the bar as if he were anchored. He screamed in pain, then went very still.

Another shockingly violent event in Koenig's increasingly violent life.

Spax, the pockmarked thug, lurched to his feet. His two friends paused, then did the same. The bartender reached under the middle pallet stack. Came out with a claw hammer. Probably figured it was safe enough. Koenig wasn't a big guy, and his knife was stuck in Steeleye's wrist. If he pulled it out, Steeleye and the Glock would be back in play. If he left Steeleye pinned to the bar, like a moth in a natural history collection, he was unarmed. And it was four against one. Koenig reckoned they liked odds like that. And although these asshats didn't worry Koenig, beating on some hapless thugs wasn't why he was there.

"Sit down," Koenig said. "All of you. Let's not make this worse than it needs to be."

Spax advanced a step.

"If they don't get back in their seats, Stan, I'll twist this knife like a screw-driver," Koenig said. "Up to you."

He turned the Fairbairn-Sykes. Maybe two or three degrees. Not enough to cause damage, but enough for fresh waves of pain to course through Steeleye's arm.

"Sit the fuck down!" he hollered.

"The bartender too, please," Koenig said.

The bartender put down his hammer and joined the card-playing fools. He perched on the yard sale table. It wobbled.

Blood had pooled under Steeleye's wrist. It was dark red, not frothy and pink. Koenig had severed veins, not arteries. Meant they had time. There was no need to rush.

Sweat dotted Steeleye's brow. He paled. His eye began to water. He didn't yell out, though. Didn't scream empty threats. Instead, his breathing sped up. Became a fast snort. In and out, like a bull getting ready to charge. He frowned. Looked at the gun and concentrated.

Nothing happened.

"You can't pull the trigger because your flexor tendons have been severed, Stan," Koenig said. "You'll need complicated surgery if you ever want to bend your fingers again."

Koenig put one hand on Steeleye's forearm, the other on the Glock 46. He said, "This is going to nip a bit, I'm afraid."

He put his finger on the Glock's muzzle and started to push. Steeleye grit-ted his teeth and hissed. The Glock and Steeleye's trigger finger had formed a simple machine. The Glock was a wheel, the trigger guard was the hub, Steel-eye's trigger finger was the axle. When Koenig pushed the end of the muzzle, it rotated. As if he were changing the time on an old clock. He pushed until the muzzle had moved 180 degrees. It was now pointing at Steeleye's sternum. Underneath the tenth rib but above the stomach. Lots of important stuff in that part of the torso. The liver. The pancreas. The celiac artery.

"Who supplied you with this, Stan?" Koenig said.

"I told you, we move the guns around here."

"You're bottom-feeders, Stan. The people who import Glock 46s don't go near people like you. They sell in bulk and they sell to people who know how to keep a low profile." Koenig looked around Big City Nights. "This is not keeping a low profile, Stan. Ergo, you don't supply weapons like these. You're the end user. The customer. Nothing more."

"Fuck you."

"Let me explain what's about to happen. The human body responds to trauma with an inflammatory response. The injured area goes red, and it gets hot, and it hurts. This is caused by increased blood flow. As you can see, this is already happening. Your wrist is red. We've already established that it hurts like a bitch. It's how the body protects itself from further injuries. It's a warning not to use the injured area. The same way a flashing red sign on your dashboard tells you to get your car fixed up. Maybe put some oil in the engine. Or some gas in the tank."

Steeleye said nothing.

"Now, I imagine a big old bruiser like you has taken a punch or two," Koenig continued. "Which means you know exactly what happens next."

Steeleye grunted, "Swells."

"That's right, doc," Koenig said. "The injured area begins to swell. This is because the body sends white blood cells and proteins to the tissue damage."

Koenig took a break. He picked up the can of beer the barman had passed him. It was a brand he didn't recognize. It had Germanic-style lettering on the side but had way too many chemicals in it to be German. Germany had a purity law. Only four ingredients were permitted in German beer: barley, hops, yeast, and water. He popped the tab anyway. Took a sip. He grimaced and put the can down on the bar. It was like he'd put toilet cleaner in his mouth.

"The other thing that's no doubt dawning on you is that the Glock 46 doesn't have a safety catch. It has a small tab on the trigger that must be pressed before the trigger can be pulled. It's part of the Glock's Safe Action System."

Koenig leaned over and examined Steeleye's injury. The swelling had already spread to his hand.

"You ever been in a hospital when someone has broken their wrist, Stan? The first thing they do in the emergency room is cut off the rings on the patient's fingers. Wedding bands, engagement rings. Doesn't matter, they're coming off. It's such a common occurrence they have a specific tool for it. Unsurprisingly, it's called a ring cutter. Looks a bit like a tin opener. If they don't remove the ring, it acts like a torniquet. The finger swells until the ring stops it. The ring would be like a butcher's knot in a link of sausages. You see, there are no weak points on a ring. External force is distributed equally across the entire surface. When it comes to a swelling finger and the strength of a ring, the ring wins every time. If you don't get the ring off, the finger bursts like an overcooked hotdog. I've seen it happen, and it isn't pretty."

Koenig paused a beat. Let what he'd said sink in.

"Now, I don't want to be the wasp at the picnic, but the trigger guard is kinda like a ring," he said. "And your finger is swelling rapidly. The trigger pull on a Glock is five pounds. When the pressure caused by your swelling finger gets to five pounds and one ounce, the trigger will be pressed and the Glock will discharge. This is not open to interpretation. The Glock *is* going to fire."

Steeleye looked at his swelling finger. He looked at Koenig.

"What do you want to know?" he said.

CHAPTER 35

The Arctic Bridge is the polar shipping route that links the Russian port of Murmansk to the Port of Churchill on Hudson Bay. It's 3,600 nautical miles long and, when it's ice-free, acts as the geostrategic bridge between northern Russia and the Canadian heartland. It's not a route for the fainthearted. It's only open for four months of the year. Even then, the extreme Arctic weather and the unpredictable, ship-crushing ice floes make each journey a test of nerves and skill. Only the Cape Horn shipping lane, where the Atlantic meets the Pacific, is considered more dangerous.

The Danish-registered Merchant Vessel *Swan Hunter* had been delivering grain from the Canadian Prairies to Europe, and fertilizers from Russia to North America, for ten incident-free years. MV *Swan Hunter* was a handymax bulk carrier. She had five holds and four cranes. She was 190 meters long and had a maximum deadweight of fifty thousand tons. The holds were huge, cavernous. Floating grain silos, deeper than the Hollywood sign is tall.

But for the last two years *Swan Hunter* had been dry-docked in Murmansk. Officially, it was for a much-needed refit. The peeling and blistering paint had been blasted off and a new coat applied. Navigation and communication systems were upgraded. Crew quarters had been refreshed. The galley got new ovens and freezers. A modern cargo-management system was installed.

The cost ran into millions, the lost revenue even more. But the ship's owner had been asked to do this by the kind of people who wouldn't take no for an answer. Say no to these people and you might fall out of your hotel window.

And then, like nothing unusual had happened, MV *Swan Hunter* had resumed her route along the Arctic Bridge.

But something unusual *had* happened. The updated navigation and cargo-management systems, the 4K television for the crew, the new equipment in the galley, were smoke and mirrors. Deception. A way to explain *Swan Hunter*'s two-year absence.

The *real* reason for the refit was so that hold number five could be fitted with a false bottom. A twelve-inch lip had been welded to the inside of the hold, two meters from the hatch. The false bottom sat on the lip like the top tray in a jewelry box. It resembled a giant drip tray and was filled with the same bulk cargo as holds one through four. The rest of hold five was a smuggler's dream. Two hundred cubic meters of stale air. Bigger than three large shipping containers.

Three people on MV *Swan Hunter* knew about the false bottom. The captain and the first mate—who would both be involved in off-loading the cargo mid-sea—and an Australian called Simon Jenkins. Jenkins wasn't crew. He wouldn't appear on any manifest. He was a smuggler. His job was to transport the cargo to its next destination.

Until that time, he was supposed to stay hidden in his cabin.

Which was fine in theory. For ten days, Jenkins had done exactly that. He'd not seen or spoken to anyone. His meals were left outside his door by Gregor, the first mate. Other than Gregor and the captain, no one knew who he was. And that was fine. It was how it was supposed to be. It was what he'd signed up for.

Except he'd overheard one of the crew mention the northern lights. The aurora borealis. The natural light display caused by electrically charged space particles getting trapped by Earth's magnetic field.

Jenkins waited until the crew had retired for the night. He figured that if he didn't turn on any deck lights, it was unlikely whoever was on the bridge would see him. He would stay in the shadows and spend an hour watching the light show. Get some fresh air.

He was a heavyset man, running to fat, but he'd been a smuggler all his life. He knew how to move quietly. He made his way along the corridor and opened one of the watertight doors that led to the deck. The Arctic air hit him in the face like a blast-chilled sledgehammer. It literally took his breath away.

He was about to give it up as a stupid idea when he saw them. The northern lights. Dancing rivers of green and blue. Curtains of light, the edges tinged with crimson. Swooping and swirling like a murmuration of starlings. He stood and stared, his freezing face temporarily forgotten. It was mesmerizing.

Hypnotic.

Which was why he didn't hear the bosun.

Andrei Belyaev had been on the MV *Swan Hunter* for seven years. He'd started on the deck crew as an ordinary seaman, had quickly been promoted to able-bodied seaman, and had taken up the role of bosun during the refit. The bosun oversaw all deck operations, and he was keen to do a good job. Which was why he was on deck at 3 a.m. when everyone else was in bed. Strong winds were expected in the morning. He wanted to double-check everything loose was lashed down.

At first, he thought the big man was a trick of the shadows. The same way manipulating your hands could make a bunny hop across the wall. He didn't know why he thought that. It was clearly a man. But it was so unexpected his mind had provided a more plausible explanation. In all his years on the MV *Swan Hunter*, they'd never had a stowaway. Murmansk was the asshole of Russia, but Churchill in Canada was even worse. The northern tip of an Arctic wasteland. The nearest town was two hundred miles away; the province capital, a thousand. Churchill was supposed to be the polar bear capital of the world, like that was anything to brag about. Any town where there were as many polar bears as people, and the locals had to keep their doors unlocked so people could run into their house if a bear was chasing them, wasn't a real town as far as he was concerned.

Andrei didn't need to tiptoe up to the man. His eyes were fixed on the northern lights, and even if they hadn't been, the wind masked his approach. He pulled a wrench from his tool bag and tapped him on the shoulder.

Then he bashed him over the temple.

The captain of the MV *Swan Hunter* was called Dominik Volkov, and he wasn't a happy man. He blew into his hands and stomped his feet as he stared at the Australian. Jenkins was trussed up like a November Christmas tree. The bosun had restrained him with deck ropes, then alerted Volkov. Volkov had asked him to fetch the first mate.

"I only wanted to see the lights," Jenkins tried to say. His teeth were chattering so much it was hard to talk.

Volkov ignored him. He waited for the bosun to return with his first mate. They weren't long. No one got undressed on this trip. Even with the heating on, it was too cold to get naked.

The first mate and Volkov shared a glance.

"Show me where he was standing," Volkov said to the bosun.

The three left the shivering Jenkins and walked over to the edge of the boat. The deck was icy, and even with their rubber boots, it was treacherous underfoot.

"Just here, Captain," the bosun said.

"And he wasn't doing anything?"

"Just watching the lights."

"Did anyone else see him?"

"No, Captain."

"And have you told anyone about this?"

"Only you."

"That's a shame, Andrei," Volkov said. He nodded at the first mate.

The first mate was a squat man with weight-lifter arms. He crouched behind the bosun, wrapped his arms around his lower legs, and heaved him over the side of the ship. The bosun might have screamed on his way down, but if he did, the wind stole his voice.

The captain and the first mate walked back to Jenkins.

"Andrei was my friend," Volkov said. He let that sink in. "He was my friend and now the crabs have him."

"I'm sorry," Jenkins said. "I only wanted to see—"

"Do you wear spectacles, Mr. Jenkins," Volkov cut in.

"Excuse me?"

"You heard me. Are you near- or long-sighted? And if you are, do you correct your vision with spectacles?"

"I wear sunnies in the summer," Jenkins said. "But I don't need glasses."

"Then you won't miss an ear," Volkov said. He unfolded a clasp knife that Jenkins hadn't even known he was holding, bent down, and sliced his left ear clean off. Like he was pruning a rose bush. He threw it over the side as if it were fish guts. "Now you too are feeding the crabs." He leaned down and whispered into Jenkins's remaining ear: "If I see you out of your cabin again, I'll fucking keelhaul you."

CHAPTER 36

Big City Nights was in Hulme. The guy Koenig wanted lived in Hale. The two parts of Manchester were twenty-five miles apart but could have been in different countries. Hulme was urban. Parts of it were decaying, like it had cancer. Other parts reminded Koenig of Soviet-era East Berlin. But Hale was leafy and green. Koenig thought it looked like the set of a Richard Curtis film. A utopian, but depressingly bland, vision of England. Danielle explained Hale was the perfect balance of city and village life. A lot of soccer players lived there, she said. They only ventured into Manchester to play soccer or to film themselves committing sex crimes.

The address Steeleye had given Koenig was a shop. The embassy Jag had an intuitive satnav, and Koenig had found the shop easily enough.

Danielle had agreed to wait two hours before she called it in. Koenig had asked for six, but she was a cop and there was a gun on the premises. It wasn't something she could ignore. Two hours was the best she could do.

Draper had wanted to go to Hale as well, but Koenig didn't want Steeleye's goons trying to redeem themselves by sending a warning. She needed to stay in Big City Nights. Make sure they didn't do anything dumb.

He'd maneuvered Steeleye's swollen finger from the Glock 46's trigger guard. Steeleye had passed out, which Koenig had thought was probably for the best. He'd popped the Glock's magazine. It wasn't full, but it wasn't empty. He'd slid out the top round. Checked it for flaws. Bullets were as illegal as guns in the UK. A lot of rounds were recycled or old. Words for unreliable in Koenig's world. But these had looked fine. Fat and shiny and deadly. He'd pushed the magazine back into the Glock. Racked it. Handed it to Draper. Knives were OK for crowd control. But guns were better.

"A word of warning, guys," he'd said to Steeleye's Z-list henchmen. "If you think I'm bad, try something with my colleague here. She has a diplomatic passport and no conscience whatsoever."

Koenig didn't like the Jag. He thought it was a strange choice. It was too conspicuous for an unsanctioned job. It stood out. Koenig wondered why Bernice hadn't just hired them a car. Something boring. Boring was good in Koenig's world. Boring didn't stand out. But Bernice had insisted they take the embassy Jag.

And for some reason Draper had been reluctant to leave him alone with it.

Which made Koenig wonder if there might be something different about this Jag. Something not found in the owner's manual. Something off-spec. And because he'd once been a federal agent, he stopped wondering and decided to find out what it was.

So, before arriving in Hale, he'd driven to an industrial park and found somewhere quiet to search the car. He found what Draper hadn't wanted him to find in under a minute. A concealed button that opened a compartment under the dashboard. He removed what had been hidden and sighed. He made a few adjustments, then put it back where he'd found it.

The shop Koenig wanted was called This Is My Hollywood. It was an upmarket movie memorabilia store. The website listed a 1956 *Forbidden Planet* poster, an original Emperor Ming costume from the second *Flash Gordon* serial, and a skateboard from *Back to the Future*. Good stuff if it was genuine.

A man called Marion Summers owned the shop. Steeleye assumed Marion wasn't his real name. It was a girl's name, he'd said. And it was. Mainly. But it hadn't always been. It used to be a unisex name. John Wayne was born Marion Robert Morrison. Before he entered witness protection, the spree killer Charles "Sonny" Pearson was called Marion Pruett. Given the store Summers owned, Koenig guessed his given name had come from his parents' love of Westerns rather than men executed by the state of Arkansas. A lot of John

Wayne fans had subjected their sons to a lifetime of bullying by naming them Marion.

This Is My Hollywood was a redbrick building with an understated sign. Marion Summers had just flipped the OPEN sign to CLOSED. Koenig recognized him from the store's website. He was a forgettable-looking man. Thin, balding, a bit nerdy. But not so nerdy he'd stand out. He wore steel-rimmed spectacles and a REBEL SCUM SINCE 1977 *Star Wars* T-shirt.

Koenig glanced at his watch. It was 5 p.m. He guessed when you owned your own business you opened and closed when you wanted to. He knocked on the glass door.

Summers shook his head and pointed at the sign.

Koenig knocked harder.

CHAPTER 37

Summers frowned. He pointed at his watch, then pointed at the CLOSED sign again. "I'm shut, mate," he said through the glass door. "Come back tomorrow."

"Come on, man," Koenig replied. "I've come all the way from Boston. I'm not here tomorrow. Got some bullshit meeting in London."

Summers checked his watch again. Like he had somewhere else to be and time was an issue.

"I won't be long," Koenig said. "I'm only interested in the good stuff."

After he'd checked his watch one more time, Summers flipped the sign to OPEN and unlocked the door. "I can give you twenty minutes," he said.

Koenig stepped inside, flipped the sign back to CLOSED as he did. If Summers noticed, he didn't say anything. Instead, he walked around to the other side of the store counter and planted his elbows on the polished wood.

Like all memorabilia stores, it was half museum, half shop. Some of the items on display had NOT FOR SALE stickers on them. Every inch of wall space was taken up with movie posters. Old posters, new posters, signed posters. Tables filled to the brim with props, cabinets full of curiosities, and clothes racks packed with costumes. There were even old flip-down cinema seats to sit on while you took in the cinematic history on display.

It was the kind of place Koenig would have visited five or six times a month in Boston. He'd have been on first-name terms with the owner and friends with the regulars. Stores like this were more than just places to indulge your passion. They were places to hang out. Somewhere to discuss, debate, even vehemently argue about old movies, new movies, upcoming movies. Movies never made; movies that shouldn't have been made. Actors who were hopelessly miscast; actors who'd turned down iconic roles. In his old life Koenig would have held strong opinions on all of it, and he'd have spent hours talking with like-minded people. He'd been a movie buff all his life. Sure, he loved to read, but his love of cinema was ingrained. He could no more stop loving movies than he could grow a rat tail.

"Are you after anything in particular?" Summers said. "The website was updated last night, but a couple of nice pieces came in this morning. I haven't had a chance to put them on yet. Happy to do a cash deal if we can agree a price."

Koenig would have liked to discuss the *A Clockwork Orange* clapper board Summers had behind his counter. It hadn't been on his website, and he couldn't see a NOT FOR SALE sticker. In ordinary times, Koenig would have spent every buck he had to take it home with him. But these were not ordinary times.

And he no longer had a home.

So instead of asking how much Summers wanted for the clapper board, he said, "I'm a generic collector, but I've made this trip as I heard you have some cool Tom Derringer memorabilia."

"Derringer? You mean *Berenger*?"

"I do?"

"I think so. Tom Berenger was in *Platoon* and *Inception*. *Looking for Mr. Goodbar*."

"So, who's Tom Derringer?"

"I don't think he exists, mate." Summers frowned. "I thought you said you were a serious collector?"

"I can't imagine how I got that wrong," Koenig said. "Must be because I recently saw a movie where a derringer was used to commit a double murder. You probably saw it on the news."

"You a cop?"

"I'm not a cop."

"Who are you then?" Summers said.

"Just a guy interested in the derringer that the woman at Speakers' Corner used."

"I sell movie memorabilia," Summers said. "Why would I know anything about a gun?"

Koenig reached behind his back and grabbed his Fairbairn-Sykes. Held it up so Summers could see the blood on the tapered blade.

"That one-eyed idiot gave you up, Marion," he said. "And we need to talk."

CHAPTER 38

"I have no idea what you're talking about, Mr. . . . ?" Summers said.

Koenig didn't fill the gap.

"What's your name?" Summers said after a beat.

"My name? That's just the noise people make to get my attention. If I were you, Marion, I'd stop focusing on who I am and think about *what* I am. But to move things along, you can call me Ben."

"And what are you, Ben?" Summers said after a pause.

"I guess I'm a stick."

"A stick?"

"Or a carrot."

Summers didn't respond, but Koenig could tell he was thinking hard. Eventually he said, "I have no idea who this one-eyed idiot is. I sell movie memorabilia, I don't know anything about guns. Now, I'd like you to leave, please."

"Do you want me to tell you how I know you're lying, Marion?"

"I doubt I could stop you."

"I pulled out a knife. It has wet blood on the blade. Yet you didn't bat an eyelid. You didn't panic. You didn't scramble for your cell or yell out in fear. You saw a Fairbairn-Sykes, *I* saw someone who was unafraid. Someone used to being around weapons."

"I'm from Manchester, mate. This isn't the first knife I've seen."

"But do you want to know what *really* gave you away?"

Summers shrugged.

"You did," Koenig said.

"Me?"

"I've spent seven years as a gray man. I understand how to hide in plain sight. How to blend in. To be unmemorable."

"You're making a point, I take it?" Summers removed his elbows from the counter and put his arms down by his side. Out of sight.

"I see you, Marion. Not only that, I see *through* you. The unthreatening way you dress yourself can't hide your physique. It's toned, it's sinewy, and although I would advise you not to try anything, you'll undoubtedly be proficient in one of the more aggressive fighting techniques. The way you dress can't hide the way you looked me up and down when I entered your store, the way you immediately understood I was a threat. It's why you're behind your counter. I suspect you have a weapon under there. You may even be tempted to use it. If you do, I'll use mine and I'm not going to lie, I've been trained by the best. If I see a weapon in your hands, you'll never use them again."

Summers brought his hands out from behind the counter. They were empty.

"And there's the shop," Koenig continued. "The location is perfect to meet the needs of both Liverpool *and* Manchester. It's within a ninety-minute drive of a dozen ports, some of them lightly regulated. Easy to get guns into the country. And the nature of the shop itself is perfect to meet potential customers in a safe environment. No one's going to bat an eyelid if it's open at midnight— you're stocktaking or meeting an out-of-town collector, like I claimed to be."

Summers smiled. "So, you think I know something about that . . . what was it you called it, a derringer?"

"I think you sold it to her, or you know who sold it to her. And ever since Speakers' Corner, I think you've been dreading a guy like me turning up. *Especially* a guy like me."

"A guy like you?"

Koenig showed him the commando dagger again. "A guy comfortable using Fairbairn-Sykes diplomacy."

Summers smiled. Didn't look the slightest bit worried. They might as well have been talking about Stanley Kubrick.

"Let's pretend what you say is true," he said. "That I am this big bad arms dealer. Surely I'd be a fool to keep anything on any premises that could be linked to me? I'd probably have cutout after cutout. A whole team of mules who had no idea who was paying them." He paused. "Do you think I'm a fool, Ben?"

"I don't think you're a fool, Marion."

"Then we have nothing more to discuss. I'm sorry I couldn't sell you a movie poster, but you have nothing to threaten me with. No carrot, no stick. Just a rumor and a knife we both know you won't use."

"I don't think you're a fool, Marion, but I do think you're wrong. Because I *do* have something to threaten you with." He reached into the back pocket of his jeans and threw his passport on the counter. "Do you know what that is?"

"Is this a trick question? It's a passport."

"Wrong. This is a *diplomatic* passport."

Summers leaned forward and checked. The word "diplomatic" was front and center on the black cover.

"You say I have nothing to threaten you with, Marion," Koenig said. "How about the US government?"

Koenig pushed the passport across the counter.

"I've been sent to the UK with one purpose: to track down the woman who bought that derringer," he said. "I'm here on behalf of the kind of people who discuss things like wet work over breakfast. You've now been sucked into their gravity well. That leaves you with a simple binary choice: You either become an ally of the United States, or you become an enemy of the United States."

"But I'm neith—"

"If you choose the latter, the Brits will arrest you pending an extradition request."

"My country won't extradite me on unsubstantiated rumors," Summers said. "I have rights."

"Supplying weapons to enemies of the United States? I think the Brits will do *exactly* what we ask them to do. Otherwise, we might turn off Netflix. Or stop giving them the codes to their own submarines." Koenig paused. "Or maybe you're right. Maybe my no-name colleagues will extraordinary-rendition your limey ass to a black site in Eastern Europe."

Summers deflated like he'd been punctured. He picked up Koenig's passport and flicked through the pages. He reached under his desk and brought out a magnifying glass. Koenig figured he was always being offered memorabilia and a large part of maintaining the store as a viable front was identifying fakes.

A magnifying glass would be a tool of the trade. He bent down and examined the signature page and the data page. "This is real," he said.

"I'm afraid so."

"But it was only issued yesterday."

"I'm on the clock," Koenig said. "And now, so are you. If I step out of this shop without getting what I want, you'll be indefinitely detained as an enemy combatant at Guantanamo Bay."

"And if I cooperate?"

"Then you have options. The arms business is over for you, though. You know that, right? Steeleye Stan gave you to me, and I'm giving you to the cops. Way it has to be. But who knows? Maybe you're right, maybe there *is* enough separation between you and the guns that they can't get the main charges to stick. When we're finished here, your first call is to retain the meanest lawyer you can afford. I'm talking the Brit equivalent of Johnnie Lee Cochran Jr."

"Who?"

"The guy who got O. J. acquitted."

Summers nodded, like he'd made a decision. "What do you want to know?"

"Tell me about the woman who bought the derringer."

Summers sighed. "She said she hoped she'd never have to use it," he said.

CHAPTER 39

"She's coming back in three days," Koenig said to Draper. She was on her cell phone, and he was using the landline in Marion Summers's shop. It wasn't ideal—anyone with a touch of technical know-how could eavesdrop on them— but Koenig didn't want to let Summers out of his sight.

"You've found her?" Draper replied.

"I haven't found her. I said she's coming back in three days."

"For another gun?"

"And for a passport. Turns out Marion supplies those as well. I thought as much when he spent so long examining mine."

"Why the hell did you show him your passport?"

"It was either that or stab him in the liver," Koenig said. "He sold her the derringer a month ago. He's been preparing for the inevitable knock on the door ever since he saw the news."

"Where is he now?"

"Tied to a radiator, although he knows he has nowhere to run."

"I'll come right over," Draper said. "We can start planning something."

"Take a cab," Koenig said. "But first make sure Danielle knows that as soon as Steeleye Stan's been patched up, he's to be put in a dark cell. His pin-head friends too. No phone calls, no visits. The Brit Terrorism Act should give her enough power. Get Bernice involved if you think it'll help."

* * *

Draper arrived an hour later. She confirmed that Steeleye Stan and his crew were in custody. Danielle would play police station ping-pong with them. A couple of hours here, a couple of hours there. Even if they somehow managed to get a message out, the chances of a solicitor being at the right police station at the right time were negligible. It was an old but effective trick.

"Our mystery woman is after a passport?" she said.

"*Two* passports," Koenig said. "One for her, one for Margaret. She provided photographs, and Marion recognized Margaret from the news. She's also getting another gun. Whatever she's gotten herself involved in, the derringer clearly isn't enough firepower."

"The heat must be getting too much for her. She thinks she'll be safer in the States. More places to lie low."

"Maybe," Koenig said.

"Spit it out, Koenig. What do you think that I don't?"

"I don't know yet."

"I'll call Bernice and get one of our tactical teams over. We'll grab her when she comes for the passports."

"No outside help," Koenig said.

"Can you *please* check your ego for one second? We can't do this on our own; it's too important."

"It's got nothing to do with ego," Koenig replied. "The woman I knew was tactically aware and braver than a honey badger. If we try to take her on the street, she'll disappear like butter on crumpets."

"Not if we do it right."

"I know this woman, Jen, and I'm telling you—if there's a tactical team on-site, we *will* lose her."

"She won't be expecting us."

"She'll *absolutely* be expecting us."

"It doesn't matter. Once she's inside the net, she won't get back out."

Koenig took a moment, then said, "How would you manage a dead drop in a denied area of operation?"

Draper considered this in silence. "Damn," she said. "I wouldn't turn up in person. I'd pay someone a couple of hundred bucks to dress up like me. Send them in my place."

"Then what?"

"Well . . . if I was being uber-cautious, I'd have at least one more cutout.

Have the parcel handed off to another mule. Get the package handed over in some place she's in control of. Might be a hundred yards away from the store, might be a hundred miles. If she knows what she's doing, there are half a dozen ways of getting those passports safely."

"Exactly."

"What do you suggest?"

"I have an idea," Koenig said.

He told her what it was.

She said, "And you're sure this will work?"

"No. But I can't think of any other way of doing it."

"I guess you'd better make that phone call then."

CHAPTER 40

A lot can happen in three days, and on the other side of the Atlantic, Stillwell Hobbs and Harper Nash, the father-and-daughter contract killers, had a new target, a woman called Louise Durose. Louise was a senior sanitation engineer for the city of San Diego but advised departments up and down the West Coast. Her specialty was landfill construction and management. She was currently in New Jersey, having delivered a series of well-attended lectures on the most modern and innovative ways of layering and venting landfills.

Hobbs and Nash planned a variation of the Hank Reynolds murder, the guy whose suicide-by-hanging they'd staged in Coos County, Oregon. This time they were aiming for an overdose. Prescription pills. Louise had lost a vicious custody battle over the dog she and her ex jointly owned. Dexter, a chocolate Labrador, had been the love of Louise's life. She'd fed Dexter, she'd walked Dexter, and she'd taken care of Dexter's veterinary bills. Her ex hadn't given a rat's ass about the dog, but as is the case in many breakups, the object of custody disputes was more about hurting your ex than protecting your own interests. And somehow, her ex, a dull-eyed wannabe actor from Delaware, had convinced the family court judge that shared custody of Dexter was only fair. Hobbs thought Louise's friends would be shocked but not surprised by her suicide. People were weird about their pets.

But for the first time in a while, they'd made a mistake.

Harper had slipped into Louise's hotel room while she was lecturing and readied it for her father. There was no fruit bowl, so no bananas to worry about this time. But there *was* a mass-production print on the hotel wall: *Van Gogh's Chair*. That couldn't stay. The painting was of a rustic chair with a simple woven rush seat. The floor was tiled, and Van Gogh had painted a pipe and tobacco pouch on the seat. He didn't always sign his work, but in this painting an onion box in the background had the word "Vincent" stenciled on the side. Like it was the firm's name. Harper wasn't sure what to do with it. She couldn't turn it around. It would be suspicious—to Louise, but more importantly to the investigators as well. She could try replacing it with a more suitable print, but that would mean breaking into another room. She dismissed that option immediately. It was likely the hotel had bought *Van Gogh's Chair* in bulk. It might be in every room. In the end she decided to remove it completely. Hope neither Louise nor the investigating officers noticed it was missing.

She took it off the wall and removed the print from the cheap frame. She folded it up and put it into her bag. Next, she pushed out the glass and tapped it with the butt of her Ruger LCP II pocket pistol. The glass broke into six pieces, all small enough to fit into the bag. The frame came apart easily, and the backboard snapped in two without much effort.

Harper left the room as quietly as she'd entered. When she was out of the hotel grounds, she sent her father an encrypted message: "ROOM CLEAR." Hobbs had been in the conference center lobby, ready to warn his daughter if Louise left early. He waited for her, and without exchanging so much as a look, they swapped places. Harper would wait at the conference center and send Hobbs a message when Louise left. She would then trail her back to her hotel. Hobbs would be waiting for her in her room. And fifteen minutes later Louise Durose would be dead.

But as Hobbs would tell his daughter afterward, the only thing they could control was how much they prepared. After that they were dealing with that most unpredictable of things: human nature. Everything they knew about Louise Durose indicated she was a quiet, studious woman. She would deliver her talk, eat a meal at a decent restaurant, then go back to her hotel. Nothing in the exhaustive checks they'd completed indicated that Louise would hook up with a colleague.

But that's what she did.

Staging Louise's suicide only worked if she was alone. Harper sent her father the abort code. He wouldn't ask why; he trusted her judgment. They had a problem, though. The next name on the list was already lined up, and delays in New Jersey would have knock-on effects. Louise had to die tonight. Simple as that.

Harper trailed Louise and her new friend for a block and a half before she had an idea. She entered a pharmacy and made some purchases. If the woman behind the counter had questions, she kept them to herself. By the time Harper was back on the street, Louise was out of sight. That was OK. Harper knew where she was headed.

She also knew a shortcut.

Louise Durose was having second thoughts. She never hooked up with random guys, and she didn't think it was a good idea to start now. She was in her forties. It wasn't dignified. And she still had to prepare the next day's workshop. Landfill management was becoming increasingly complex, and unless some of her ideas were taken on board, garbage was going to become a big problem. When a hole is full, it's full.

She was figuring out how to say good night when a young girl staggered out of an alley. She was a skinny thing. Covered in tattoos with a weird birthmark on her face. Her eyes were wet, and her vest was ripped. For some reason she was wearing disposable nitrile gloves.

"You OK, honey?" Louise asked.

The girl didn't answer. She pointed into the alley, then burst into tears.

Louise never knew if the guy she'd hooked up with acted out of genuine concern, or through a misguided attempt at increasing his chances later, when he marched into the alley. But that's what he did. Louise followed him and the skinny girl followed her. The guy got to the end. There was no one there. He looked at Louise and shrugged.

"Boy, did you get horny at the wrong time," the skinny girl said to the man.

She then brought out a brick from behind her back and smashed it into Louise's mouth. Louise collapsed like her strings had been cut. Her teeth scattered like cheap pearls. She gurgled. The guy stared in horror, his brain failing to comprehend what had just happened. By the time he realized the danger he was in, it was too late. The skinny girl was on him. She swung the brick and caved in his skull. She hit him again. And again. She hit him until his skull was softer than warm ice cream.

She jogged over to Louise and checked her pulse. It was weak and fast. She raised the brick again and brought it down onto her temple. She did it a couple more times to be safe.

After throwing the brick behind a dumpster, somewhere she knew it would be found, she removed the nitrile gloves and put them in her pocket. She slipped on another pair, then took a roll of condoms and a packet of over-the-counter erectile dysfunction pills from a different pocket. She put them both in Louise's purse, then left the alley without a backward glance.

Ten minutes later, after Harper had told her father what she'd done, he said, "I don't think I've ever been prouder."

PART TWO

A TODDLER WITH A MACHINE GUN

CHAPTER 41

Koenig wasn't in a good place.

It was called the Trafford Centre. It was a shopping mall in Manchester. Koenig hadn't been in a mall for years. Malls had CCTV. They had security guards who didn't like people who looked the way Koenig did. More important, they had nothing he wanted. But his contact had said to meet in the Trafford Centre.

He chose a coffee shop, one of the smaller chains. The sign outside said, "Piping Hot Coffee's." It was written in paint, the kind that was supposed to look like chalk. Koenig ignored the misplaced apostrophe and went inside. He was curious to see why piping hot coffee was a big deal. Maybe everywhere else sold warm coffee. Or tepid coffee. Maybe piping hot coffee wasn't the norm. He ordered a large Americano, black, and a Reuben sandwich. He asked the barista about the piping hot coffee. She stared at him, then said, "I hate working here."

He took a seat near the rear exit and waited for his food. The same barista brought it over. He lifted the lid and grimaced. The sandwich was made with British corned beef, a fatty sludgy mess sold in cans. Looked like cat chow. Nothing like the paper-thin slices of salt-cured brisket they had in Boston. He ate it anyway.

His contact was called Rob Miller, and unsurprisingly, given what he did for a living, he was on time. To the second. He slipped into the seat opposite Koenig, picked up a sachet of sugar, and shook it. He tore off the end and emptied it into the black coffee Koenig had waiting for him. He repeated this four times. He had always liked his coffee sweet.

"You in trouble?" he said.

"Not this time."

"Heard about that banjo in Texas."

"Banjo" was SAS slang for a fight, used to describe anything from a bar-room brawl to a brigade-sized assault. Koenig had met Miller when he'd trained with an SAS saber squadron. Two months learning breach techniques, two months in the Horn of Africa shadowing radicalized Brits.

"You did, huh?" Koenig said.

"We *all* did," Miller said. "Some ex-regiment work for that boss of yours. Jen Draper. They say you went all in."

"She's not my boss."

"What is she then?"

"It's complicated."

Miller formed a circle with his left index finger and thumb. Poked his right index finger through it. "That kind of complicated?"

"Worse."

Miller checked his watch. "The missus is getting a present for her sister's birthday. Says she'll be ten minutes. Means I have an hour to kill." He reached inside his jacket and removed a bulky package. "Plenty of time for you to tell me what happened. I'll talk you through how this thing works afterward. The tech has improved since you were last involved."

Koenig smiled. Special forces soldiers were the same the world over. Everything had value, nothing was given away. He signaled for two more coffees, then said, "It all started when I made the US Marshals' Most Wanted list . . ."

CHAPTER 42

THREE DAYS LATER. THE SCOTTISH HIGHLANDS.

Koenig was cold and damp. An invasive cold that had gotten in his bones and stayed there. It hadn't rained since they'd arrived in Scotland, but it hadn't needed to. Not when the air itself was wet. It felt like he was taking a sauna in a meat locker. He took another bite out of a sickly sweet block of candy called Kendal Mint Cake. It was popular among mountaineers. Supposed to be a good source of energy. It would have to be. No one would eat it for pleasure.

He shivered but kept his eyes on the woman's cottage. Judging by the slate roof, it was one of the newer cottages in the *clachan*, a small settlement in the heart of the Scottish Highlands, one of the last great European wildernesses. Age was all relative, though—at five hundred years old, her cottage still pre-existed any building in the US.

Overhead, gulls pinwheeled and screeched like banshees. Koenig thought gulls sounded like angry birds. Like they always had a beef about something. Guess that's what happens when you stop eating fish and start eating trash.

"Anything?" Draper said in his earpiece. "It's been six hours."

As well as the equipment Miller had provided, Draper had gotten hold of some state-of-the-art surveillance and communication equipment. It was a pity neither of them had thought to ask for tactical sleeping bags. The kind used by snipers and close target reconnaissance experts. Koenig had always been told that any idiot could be cold and any idiot could be hungry. And now he was both.

"Nothing," he replied.

They were both three hundred yards away, but the military-grade thermal monoculars they were using had 4× magnification. It meant they could see everything. Koenig was watching the front door of the cottage; Draper was covering the rear. Her view also covered the approaches; all Koenig could see was the cottage and the misty Atlantic Ocean. It was a spectacular backdrop.

But they had a problem. They'd followed Jane Doe all the way to her front door, then switched to thermal imaging. They had expected to see two heat signatures. Instead, they saw one. Jane Doe was alone.

"Where the hell is Margaret Wexmore?" Draper said for the tenth time.

"Perhaps she's dead. Dead bodies don't give off heat."

"Then why collect a passport for her?"

"She had thymic carcinoma," Koenig said. "She'd been looking into palliative care. Maybe she died yesterday. Or this morning." He paused five heartbeats. "No, I'm not buying that either," he added. "Something doesn't add up. I feel like we're bluebottles, and the cottage is a Venus flytrap."

"We should go in anyway," Draper said.

Koenig thought it through. Could see no reason to put it off. Venus flytrap or not, they had to move on the cottage. The only thing waiting would achieve was trench foot. He checked his watch. It would be dark soon. He weighed up the advantages and disadvantages of getting into position now. Decided the boggy ground would be easier to navigate while there was still some light.

"There's a dip twenty yards in front of the door," he said. "It's hidden by a gorse bush and it's in dead ground. I'll see you there in thirty minutes."

CHAPTER 43

"Fuck's sake, Koenig," Draper said, sucking her thumb. "Sleeping Beauty's castle had less thorns than this asshole bush."

Koenig ignored her. "She still hasn't moved," he said, one eye fixed to his monocular. "Now we're at ground level, it looks like she's sitting down."

"How do you want to do this?"

That was the problem, Koenig thought. How *did* he want to do this? Draper had delivered a long and tedious lecture on the risks of knocking on the door. She said Jane Doe was armed. They knew she was prepared to kill. She would be nervous. Draper had said knocking on the door was dangerous. Kept on saying it until she was sure Koenig understood.

There was no obvious play. Not without specialist breaching equipment. The homes in this part of Scotland were designed to have their backs to the wind. The only way in was through the front door. He'd been eyeing it up. From his previous observation point he thought he might use Newton's Third Law of Motion—two interacting objects exert equal and opposite forces on each other. In layman's terms, he'd planned to run as fast as he could, then smash into the door with his shoulder. Shock it off its hinges. Draper could jump over him and disable Jane Doe before she had time to reach for her guns. Up close, he realized it wouldn't work. The door was bank-vault thick. The hinges were as big as anchors. He'd bounce off it like a rubber ball. The only thing he'd smash would be his collarbone.

"We could smoke her out," Draper said. "Smash a window and throw in some burning wood."

Koenig glanced at her. "Why not call in a drone strike while you're at it?" he said. "Plus, everything around here is wetter than an otter's pocket." He turned back to his monocular. "Anyway, this is her home, I'm not setting fire to it."

"OK, smart-ass, what's your idea?"

Koenig didn't immediately answer. For the last two minutes he'd been staring at the door. To be more accurate, he was staring at the keyhole. It was a big one. Wouldn't have looked out of place on a church door. He could see light shining through it, which meant the key wasn't in the other side. If he could get up to the door without being seen, he'd be able to see inside. Find out why Jane Doe hadn't moved in six hours.

"I'm going to look through the keyhole," he said.

"I'll do it."

"Why?"

"Because you're a clumsy asshole and I'm not. She'll hear you. Anyway, I'm always point."

Koenig nodded. Draper was right. Back in their SOG days, she *had* always been the first person in when they'd breached a room. She'd insisted on it. Back then it had seemed like she had a death wish. It was only later that Koenig discovered she'd been seeking redemption.

"OK," he agreed. "You go first, and I'll watch the heat signature. Make sure it doesn't move. If it does, I'll tell you to abort."

"Make sure you do," she replied. "I don't want a knitting needle in the eye because you were staring at my butt instead of the target."

She crawled out of the gorse bush, giving him a filthy look as she got scratched on the face. As carefully as she could, she made her way to the front of the cottage. Koenig tried not to look at her butt. She reached the door and put her eye to the keyhole. She turned to face Koenig. She was frowning. She gestured for him to join her. When he did, she stepped back so he could see for himself what was on the other side of the door. Koenig bent down and put his eye to it. The room was well lit. The door was so thick it was as if he were looking through the wrong end of a telescope.

He saw what had alarmed Draper so much. He turned to stare at her. She shrugged.

"I have no fucking idea what's going on," she whispered.

Koenig looked through the keyhole again. He didn't know either. Because the heat signature they'd been watching all afternoon wasn't the person they'd seen walk through the door of the cottage.

It was Margaret Wexmore, the academic abducted from Speakers' Corner. And Margaret wasn't dead; she was very much alive. She was also tied up. Jane Doe had vanished into thin air.

CHAPTER 44

It didn't add up. They had followed Jane Doe all the way from Manchester to her cottage. They had seen her face. The only way in and out of the cottage was via the front door or one of the two windows and Koenig hadn't taken his eyes off them. He *knew* she hadn't left. But heat signatures didn't lie. Jane Doe wasn't in there. Not unless she was ectothermic. Like a lizard. Or a fish.

"She's not sitting underneath her, is she?" Draper said, not bothering to keep her voice down anymore. "Using Margaret to hide her heat signature."

"For six hours?"

Nevertheless, Koenig bent down and looked through the keyhole again. Margaret wasn't a sturdy woman, looked like she weighed no more than ninety pounds. Maybe she'd always been like that; maybe it was the cancer. She was gagged with duct tape, and her gray hair was in a bun but coming loose. Disheveled. Otherwise, she looked unharmed. No one was hiding underneath her. He told Draper.

"She wasn't being rescued from Speakers' Corner then," Draper said. "The Brits were right all along; she *was* being abducted."

Koenig didn't respond. He couldn't get his head around it. Everything he knew about Jane Doe said she was one of the good guys. But the evidence was overwhelming. The evidence was also old and frail and no doubt very cold.

"We can't leave her like this," Koenig said. "She's going to need medical attention."

Draper scowled. Koenig knew she'd have preferred to sit on the cottage and wait. To use Margaret Wexmore like a tethered goat. But he was in charge, and he was going inside. He reached for the door handle.

"Wait!" Draper whispered.

"What?"

"How do we know this isn't a trap?"

He turned to check his back. Nothing. A rabbit hopped into view. It looked at them curiously, then began to nibble the wet grass.

"I guess there's only one way to find out," Koenig said.

"Koenig, there are *fifty* ways of finding out and none of them involve walking into this cottage blind. Come back to the bush; we'll have a rethink."

Koenig tried the handle. It turned.

"Asshole!" Draper hissed, scrambling to her feet.

He pushed the door open with his foot. Margaret Wexmore stared at them in astonishment.

Koenig marched in and knelt behind Margaret. He quickly untied her. She was trying to say something through the gag. Koenig reached up and peeled it off.

"Thank you, dear," she said. "That was quite uncomfortable."

"Do you need to go to hospital, Ms. Wexmore?" Draper asked.

"I'm not a Ms., I don't own a bordello. Call me Margaret."

"Do you need to go to hospital, Margaret?"

"I have a message to pass on first."

"A message?"

"Yes, dear."

"What message?" Draper asked.

Margaret smiled sweetly. "You're to put your hands in the air and turn around slowly."

They both heard the unmistakable sound of a gun being cocked. They did as they were asked.

Jane Doe was standing in the doorway. In her left hand she held her derringer; in her right she held the gun she'd just collected from Marion Summers, a Chinese-made Makarov. The derringer was pointed at Koenig's chest, the Makarov at Draper's. Both hands were steady.

"Hello, Mr. Koenig," Jane Doe said. "It's been a while. Who's your little friend?" She paused, then added, "And *did* you look at her butt?"

CHAPTER 45

Jane Doe was maybe five ten and lithe. She looked like the comedian Sarah Silverman, but without a lifetime of laughter. Her hair had been military-short the last time Koenig had seen her, but she'd grown it out. It had a few more gray strands but still looked healthy. Same with her eyes. A few more lines. Made her look wiser rather than older. Koenig thought she'd done a better job of living off the grid than he had.

"You're a little outside of your jurisdiction, aren't you, Mr. Koenig?" she said.

"I'm not a marshal anymore," Koenig said.

"And your friend? Although if my hands were free, I'd wrap 'friend' with air quotes. I was listening as you hid in the gorse bush like Br'er Rabbit. I don't think you like each other very much."

"You've got that right," Draper muttered.

"Who is she, Mr. Koenig?" Jane Doe said.

"Jen Draper," Koenig said. "Ex-CIA, current private intelligence company CEO. Due to a hilarious twist of fate, we're both at the whim of the kind of people I imagine you used to work for."

"And now you're both here. May I ask why?"

"The Speakers' Corner . . . incident set off a chain of instructions that culminated in a safe in Langley being opened. There was a single sheet of paper inside. On it was a list of names and a message: 'The Acacia Avenue Protocol has been initiated.' My name was on the list as I was the person who faked your death. I was asked to track you down. Find out what the hell is going on."

"And how *did* you track me down?"

Koenig didn't immediately respond. He thought he was being tested. He ran through the sequence of events—everything from the meeting at This Is My Hollywood to this remote cottage in the Scottish Highlands.

"You know how," he said eventually.

CHAPTER 46

"We thought you'd asked Marion Summers to get you a second weapon as you'd ditched the derringer somewhere in London," Koenig said. "But, as you're pointing it at my chest, that's clearly not the case."

"Clearly not," Jane Doe said.

"I think when the British press stopped reporting on Speakers' Corner, you figured out the murder investigation had been shut down at the request of the US government. You knew they would send over a covert team to find out why you'd reappeared after all this time."

"Go on."

"For some reason you need to get out of the country. You'd already gotten the derringer from Marion Summers, and you knew he did passports as well. But as a precaution, you asked for another gun—the Makarov you're currently pointing at Jen. You didn't need it, but you knew if someone was onto you, collecting the finished passports from Marion Summers would be a problem. It would be like the pinch point in an egg timer. Surveillance techniques are increasingly sophisticated these days, and you knew you couldn't be sure to spot them all—some of it can be done via satellite. But you knew about jarking."

"Jarking?" Jane Doe asked.

"The term originated in Northern Ireland," Koenig explained. "The SAS would sometimes find an IRA weapons cache. If they thought they hadn't been seen, they would 'jark' the weapons by putting tiny tracking devices inside them. That way they could track their movements, identify the IRA quartermasters, the shooters, the key players in the active service units. I think you asked for another gun hoping I'd accept the low-hanging fruit."

"Which this tactical genius did," Draper said.

"Which I did," Koenig agreed. "I got the tracking device from a Brit I used to work with and I jarked the Makarov."

"Go on," Jane Doe said.

"You figured it was better to know now if we were onto you," Koenig said. "That way you'd know what anti-surveillance techniques to employ when you tried to leave the country." He studied the cottage floor. "Where is it?"

"Where's what?"

"There's obviously another way out of here. You must have walked straight back out. By the time we'd switched to thermal imaging we assumed the heat signature was you, not Margaret."

Jane Doe smiled. "There's a root cellar in the pantry," she said. "All the homes here have them. The first thing I did was extend it and add a hidden exit. While you were untying Margaret, I got out and came at you from behind."

"Clever," Koenig admitted.

"So, here we are," Jane Doe said. "What happens now?"

"How about you lower your guns?" Koenig said. "You're making Jen nervous."

"But not you?"

"Guns don't scare me."

"What *does* scare you, Mr. Koenig?"

He took a silent moment. "That's a whole different conversation," he said.

Jane Doe stepped into the cottage and walked past Koenig. She put her guns on the kitchen table, then filled the kettle. She leaned against the counter. "I imagine you have many questions," she said.

Which was when Draper pulled a SIG Sauer P229 from her jacket pocket and pointed it at Jane Doe's head.

CHAPTER 47

Koenig sighed. "What are you doing, Jen?"

"My job," Draper replied. "Your orders were to track her down. I have *different* orders."

"Which are?"

"To evaluate the threat, then eliminate that threat."

"And what's your code name—Double-O Dork? License to overreact."

"Back off, Koenig," Draper said. "I'm in charge now."

"Put the gun down, Jen."

Draper ignored him. "What's the Acacia Avenue Protocol?" she said.

"It's classified," Jane Doe said.

"I have clearance."

"Not for this. No one does."

Draper thumbed back the hammer. Cocked it. Unnecessary on any modern semiautomatic. More a statement of escalation. "What's the Acacia Avenue Protocol?" she said again.

Jane Doe ignored her. "You're being remarkably calm, Mr. Koenig," she said.

"That's because I know she's not going to shoot."

"You don't know shit, Koenig!" Draper snapped. "Some of the stuff I've done in the past, this'll barely register."

"Take it from someone who doesn't like you," Koenig said. "You're not that person anymore."

"It's all right for you," she said, her voice suddenly flat and cold. "You and your white-knight syndrome, floating through life having your little adventures. You're a toddler with a machine gun, Koenig. You don't answer to anyone. But I answer to someone. I answer to my country, and I answer to my employees."

"You were never a goose-stepping jackboot, Jen. It's why the CIA booted you out." He took a moment, then added, "So please, put down the gun."

Draper didn't.

"You're not going to shoot her, Jen," Koenig said.

"If she doesn't tell me what I need to know, then you bet your ass I'm going to shoot her."

Still Jane Doe said nothing. And still Draper didn't fire.

Margaret cleared her throat. "Yoo-hoo," she said. "This appears to be an equation without a solution. Miss Draper has her instructions, but so does my friend. Neither seem able to budge."

"But you *do* have a solution?" Koenig said.

Margaret turned to Jane Doe. "Do you trust this man?"

After a beat, Jane Doe nodded. "I do."

"Then tell him," Margaret said. "Not everything, but enough so Mrs. Angry doesn't shoot you. The protocol's become a festering wound; we need to get some sunlight on it. And quite frankly, we could do with the help."

"Take the win, Jen," Koenig said. "Lower the SIG."

Draper did. She looked relieved.

"Talk," Koenig said to Jane Doe.

She nodded. Decision made. "My name is Elizabeth Carlyle," she said. "And I took an oath to protect my country from all enemies, foreign and domestic."

"So did we," Koenig said.

"But what do you do when the enemy is within? What do you do when you become the very thing you've spent your entire life fighting?"

CHAPTER 48

"That was all so very . . . American," Margaret said. "Dramatic and unnecessary. Now, if you don't mind, that kettle has boiled and my throat is parched. I'm making a pot of tea." She pulled a hairpin from her bun, refastened it, then got to her feet. Before anyone could stop her, she was reaching for mugs and getting milk out of the refrigerator. It was in a glass bottle. Foil top. Old school.

As she fussed around the kitchen area, Koenig, Draper, and Carlyle sat around the small dining table.

"We'll wait for Margaret," Carlyle said. "She can explain parts better than I can. She'll be exactly four minutes. That's how long her tea takes to steep."

Draper exhaled. "Jesus," she muttered.

"I won't be rushed, dear," Margaret called over.

"Ignore her, Margaret," Koenig said. "Four minutes is fine. Jen's in a bad mood because she hasn't waterboarded anyone today. She'll be fine once we get some warm milk and cookies into her."

"Oh, put a pin in it, Koenig," Draper said. "I'm not an assassin. I was never going to shoot her."

"I know you weren't."

"You need to do some FOG training then. You clearly don't understand the difference between fact, opinion, and guess."

"I understand the difference fine," Koenig said. "It was my *opinion* you wouldn't squeeze the trigger, but it was a *fact* you wouldn't shoot her."

"You see what I'm dealing with, Elizabeth?" Draper said.

"Please, call me Bess," Carlyle said. She frowned. "And you were remarkably calm during that whole thing, Mr. Koenig."

"Maybe it's a good cop/bad cop thing," Margaret called from the kitchen.

Koenig reached into his pocket and pulled out a small metal object. It was thin, precision-milled, and had a rounded point. Like a pen nib. Or the end of a dental probe. He put it on the table. "Do you know what that is, Bess?"

Carlyle picked it up. She held it to the light. "It's a firing pin."

"That's exactly what it is," Koenig said. "To be precise, it's the firing pin from a SIG Sauer P229. Do you happen to know anyone who's currently using a SIG, Bess? Do *you*, Jen?"

Draper ignored him. Instead, she picked up the SIG, pointed it at the ceiling, and squeezed the trigger. In the enclosed room the bang was deafening. Plaster floated down like icing sugar. The air smelled of cordite. Smoke twirled and rose from the SIG's muzzle.

"That's your firing pin, not mine," she said.

CHAPTER 49

"There were *two* SIGs in the Jag?" Koenig said woodenly. He felt very foolish. He was also aware he'd just gambled with someone else's life. It was the Urbach-Wiethe. Had to be. Fifteen years ago he'd never have done anything so reckless. He wondered if it was getting worse.

"One each," Draper confirmed. "Bernice thought we might need them. I retrieved mine while you were sticking your knife in that one-eyed asshole's wrist. I left yours in the concealed compartment."

Margaret brought the tea tray over. "Shall I be mother?" she said, lifting the ceramic teapot. Koenig reached for a cookie. Biscuits, they were called in the UK. These were custard creams. They were pretty gross. Koenig ate five. He never turned down free calories.

"In medieval Germany, married couples legally settled disputes by fighting a duel," Margaret said. "The man was inside a hole with one arm tied behind his back and the woman was given a sack of rocks."

"I don't need a sack of rocks," Draper said. "*My* gun has a firing pin."

Margaret picked up her cup of tea and took a sip. She sighed appreciatively, then said, "Where do you want to start, Bess?"

"At the beginning," Carlyle replied. "What do either of you know about the Future Threat Disruption Program?"

"Ah," Draper said. "It's about *that*, is it?"

CHAPTER 50

"'Future threat' refers to identifying the things that might bite us on the ass in the next few years?" Koenig said. "And the 'disruption' part refers to what can be done to *stop* said future threats from biting us on the ass?"

"In a nutshell," Carlyle confirmed. "It's an ongoing process, and part of it is that once a year a think tank is convened. An up-and-coming officer chooses around twenty individuals to spend a week doing blue-sky thinking. A no-idea-too-stupid kinda thing."

Carlyle drained her tea and took a cookie. She bit into it without grimacing. Koenig thought she'd been in the UK for too long if she'd gotten used to custard creams.

"Young officers traditionally use this week as a springboard. A chance to network with the men and women who might influence their careers. It takes place off base, usually a private residence." She took another custard cream. Looked at it like she didn't know what it was. "The problem is, when you gather the usual people, you discuss the usual threats. They rely on their intelligence briefings to cast their minds forward. China and Russia. Pandemics and cyberwar. Rogue states, or non-state bad actors, getting hold of weapons of mass destruction."

"The known knowns," Draper said.

"People ridiculed Rumsfeld at the time," Carlyle said. "But I didn't. For all the tortured language, Rumsfeld made a valid point. In the concept of future threats, there *are* known knowns. China, for example, *is* a known threat. Iran getting hold of nukes *is* a known threat. Even hypothetical threats like ethnic bioweapons are known knowns. He was also correct when he said there are known *unknowns*. COVID-19 is an obvious example. We knew a pandemic could threaten our interests, but we didn't know what form it would take. It was a known unknown."

She stopped and refilled her cup.

"Two months before Mr. Koenig faked my death, I'd arranged that year's Future Threat Disruption think tank," she continued. "As they did every year, lobbyists and defense contractors were falling over themselves to host it. I was offered beachfront houses in the Hamptons, chalets in Aspen, superyachts, even a private island. In the end, I chose a French Colonial in a small town in New Hampshire."

She looked at Koenig. She looked at Draper.

"It was on a street called Acacia Avenue," she said.

CHAPTER 51

"Acacia Avenue was the code name for your Future Threat Disruption think tank?" Koenig said.

"It was," Carlyle confirmed. "I don't know why, but each year's event was code-named after the address at which it was going to take place."

"And two months later you faked your own death."

"I did."

"I won't ask why. I *know* why."

"I'm not sure I do," Draper said.

"Bess grabbed the third rail," Koenig said. "She mentioned Rumsfeld's known knowns and his known unknowns, but she didn't mention the one that keeps everyone awake at night: the *unknown* unknowns. The threats we don't even know exist. Bess's think tank identified a threat so terrifying it immediately became a threat to our national security. She found Pandora's box."

"Yes, thanks for the mansplaining," Draper said. "I'm ex-CIA, and more importantly I'm not a fucking moron. I understood that part."

"What then?"

"She faked her death to protect this monstrous knowledge, this Pandora's box, she'd unwittingly come into possession of, yes? Yet despite there being twenty people at this think tank, she was the only one who had to disappear. Why was that?"

Koenig frowned. Draper was right. Either everyone disappeared or no one disappeared. It didn't matter if it was one black sock or twenty in with the whites; the result was still gray laundry. They were missing something.

"I was a lieutenant commander in the navy's Irregular Warfare Center," Carlyle said. "But I was never ambitious in the way some of my colleagues were. Getting promoted out of my current job was never more important than *doing* my current job." She took a moment, then added, "Do you know what undirected research is?"

"Research that doesn't have a preordained result," Koenig said. "The research itself dictates the direction it takes."

"I studied counterterrorism at college. Did you know that until the 1970s, the IRA was conventionally structured in companies, battalions, and brigades? But because they were easy for the Brits to infiltrate, they moved to clandestine cells called active service units."

Draper and Koenig both nodded. The SAS guys Koenig knew all had tales about what they had done in Northern Ireland. Koenig thought they'd rather enjoyed it. And he figured that Draper, as ex-CIA, probably had a working knowledge of all major terrorist organizations.

"Because I didn't know what threat we would identify, if any, I was sure as hell going to take security precautions," Carlyle continued. "The people at my think tank weren't military. Some, like Margaret, weren't even US citizens. They were a brilliant, eclectic bunch, each with a different area of expertise, but they were also eccentric and scatterbrained. In other words, they were a security nightmare. So, I put them in silos. Time slots, really. Some were there for a day or two, some only an hour. No one attended the full event. I kept it compartmentalized. At the end of the week, only I had the full picture. Some knew the broad strokes; others were intimately involved in specific parts without knowing what they were working on. I was the only one who understood that the whole was so much greater than the sum of its parts." She held their eyes. "*That's* why I had to die."

CHAPTER 52

"That seems extreme," Draper said. "The kind of staggering overreaction I'd expect from Koenig, rather than a presumably levelheaded naval intelligence officer. If you *were* the only person who knew what was inside Pandora's box, why not keep it to yourself? Lodge a nil report that year?"

"The Future Threat think tanks were routine," Carlyle said. "And because everyone knew about them, lodging a nil report would have raised eyebrows. People would have wondered what we'd *really* uncovered. I might have ended up in a shipping container with electrodes attached to my nipples."

"A false report then? Rustle up some bullshit about next-generation killer robots."

"I didn't submit a false report. A false report would have shone a bigger spotlight than a nil report. The report has a wide circulation list. Eventually it would have been read by people who had *attended* the think tank. They'd have known the report was bogus and they'd have asked why. Not out of malice, just a natural curiosity. They would have asked questions, and those questions could have found unfriendly ears. And we're back to the nipple electrodes again."

"OK," Koenig said. "We aren't here to second-guess a decision made almost a decade ago. It was done. Your death was faked. Pandora's box was protected. Yet a few days ago you very publicly murdered two men. I may not be the tactician you are, but for someone who has to stay hidden, you're going about it all wrong. If you're the only person who knows what this future threat is, why not live out your life in peace?"

"That's just the point," Carlyle said. "I'm *not* the only person who knows. Not anymore. As impossible as it sounds, there's someone out there who knows what I know. They know about the Acacia Avenue Protocol."

"Ah," Koenig said. "That's bad."

"It's worse than bad, Mr. Koenig," she said. "They've initiated it."

CHAPTER 53

Outside Carlyle's cottage, a gull screamed. Something else howled. Sounded like a wolf but probably wasn't. Some corduroy-wearing conservationists had proposed reintroducing wolves to Scotland but had been told to hightail it back to England, where that kind of bullshit was tolerated.

Inside, Draper said, "I think it's time you told us exactly what the Acacia Avenue Protocol is. Let us get the information to the right people."

Koenig said nothing. Carlyle said nothing. Margaret smiled and poured everyone more tea. The pot must have been bottomless.

"A burden shared?" Carlyle said.

"We can help," Draper said. "I hate Koenig, but the asshole does have skills. I'm the CEO of a private intelligence company. We're here on behalf of the Defense Intelligence Agency. You're not on your own anymore."

"Oh, but she is," Margaret said. "She's been on her own since Mr. Koenig shot her. She won't tell you what the protocol is. She won't even tell me, and I was part of it."

"We'll park that for now," Draper said. "You say someone else knows about the protocol, that they've initiated it?"

"I do," Carlyle confirmed.

"Yet I was briefed about current threats before we left the US. The alert level hasn't been elevated. The official line is that the DIA has no intelligence."

"On that we're in complete agreement," Koenig said. "We should get T-shirts printed."

Draper shot him a glance. Carlyle smiled politely.

Margaret said, "Well, this is awkward." She snapped a custard cream in half and popped a piece into her mouth. She chewed noisily, in that uninhibited way only people who didn't care what others thought could pull off. Koenig wondered if she'd always been like that, or if her terminal illness made not giving a rat's ass easier. She dabbed at her lips with a paper napkin, blew her nose on it, then said, "You have to give them something, Elizabeth. Enough for context. I don't think that's unreasonable. Tell them about the people who attended the think tank."

"Naming them is the same as naming their areas of expertise," Carlyle said.

"No offense to Jennifer and Benjamin," Margaret said, "but I don't think the world will end because they know you brought in an expert in Oriental studies."

"Fine," Carlyle sighed. "We'll start with Stephen. He was one of the academics I invited. He's a tenured history professor. His field of expertise is the Ottoman Empire."

Koenig glanced at Draper, confused. He hadn't expected that. The Ottoman Empire's decline began in the sixteenth century, two full centuries before the United States even existed.

"What about Stephen?" he asked.

"He's missing," she replied. "They're all missing."

CHAPTER 54

Draper gestured toward Margaret. "Not all," she said.

"Margaret is here today because of my intervention," Carlyle said. "But yes, I was using hyperbole—not everyone is missing. Some were present only to provide ancillary information, others weren't able to contribute. But enough have disappeared to confirm the pattern. The Acacia Avenue Protocol *has* been initiated."

A heavy silence hung in the air. Koenig broke it.

"OK," he said. "You say more of your attendees have disappeared than can be explained away as a coincidence—that someone has been hoovering them up. Presumably to extract their part of the puzzle. And whoever is behind this is extrapolating from the information your guys are being forced to tell them. And now they're *acting* on said extrapolation?"

"I didn't think it would be possible," she said. "But yes."

"Something else has happened then," Koenig said. "People disappearing is one thing. But you seem very sure that A has led to B. Why?"

"Do you play chess, Mr. Koenig?"

"I used to. Not so much these days."

"Miss Draper?"

"Same as Koenig. I used to."

"Well, imagine the protocol is a game of chess. A complex, multidimensional game of chess. If you wanted to play this version, what would you need first?"

"The rules," Koenig said.

"Exactly," Carlyle said. "You would make sure you understood how to play the game. That's what they were doing when they abducted my attendees. They were learning the rules. What would you need next?"

Koenig considered the question carefully. Chess was a beautiful game. A minute to learn, a lifetime to master. He'd been OK at it. Draper had been better. She'd been able to see the entire board. On the rare occasion they'd played each other, she'd always been five steps ahead of him. She had a better middle and endgame. She instinctively knew which pieces to protect and which pieces to . . .

And like that, he knew what had gotten Carlyle so spooked.

"Someone is removing key pieces," he said.

Carlyle winced. Then she nodded.

CHAPTER 55

"I can't tell you what the protocol is—" Carlyle said.

"I think you—" Draper started to say.

"—but I *can* tell you that for it to achieve maximum impact, certain people had to die first. Their deaths would amplify what followed."

"And these people have disappeared too?" Draper asked.

"No, but they are dead. At least three that I know of. Undoubtedly more that I don't."

"Murdered?"

Carlyle didn't respond. Instead, she looked uncomfortable. Like she didn't want to answer. Or she hadn't quite squared the circle.

"Bess?" Koenig said. "*Were* they murdered?"

"Hank Reynolds hanged himself in his hotel room," she replied. "His suicide note said he was tired of living his life as a closeted homosexual. Louise Durose was beaten to death with a brick. Cops think she and a man she'd picked up had a run-in with the wrong pimp. Michael Gibbs drove his wife's station wagon off Park Loop Road."

"Did they know each other?"

"Almost certainly not."

"Did *you* know them?"

"The first time I saw their names was when I read their obituaries."

"Then how—"

"Because I was looking for their deaths, Mr. Koenig. No, that's not quite right. Ever since Stephen disappeared, I was *expecting* their deaths."

"You were buying fake passports," Draper said to Carlyle while Margaret was taking a bathroom break. "Was that to travel back to the States?"

"Yes."

"Koenig?"

He shrugged. "Bess's academics disappearing is of concern."

"The other deaths?"

"We'd have to look for ourselves. It's possible to make a murder look like an accident, but three? That's tougher to buy."

"Gut feeling?"

"We take this seriously."

Draper nodded. "That's what I think. I'll call Smerconish. Tell him we're coming back."

"No," Koenig said. "We keep this to ourselves."

"Why?"

"Because we have no idea who's behind this. It's possible someone in the intelligence world is involved. It might even be Smerconish himself."

"That's ridiculous. He's the one who sent us here."

"He also gave you a kill order."

Which kinda took the wind out of her sails.

"What do you suggest?" she said.

"Bess is right. We need to get back to the States. And we can't fly commercial. Our passports will have been flagged."

"How *do* we get back then?" Carlyle said.

Koenig pretended to think about it. "Gee, I wish I knew the CEO of a private intelligence company. If I knew someone like that, I might be tempted to borrow their plane."

Draper sighed. "I'll make the phone call."

CHAPTER 56

"Did you know any of the missing academics, Margaret?" Koenig asked.

Draper was outside making her call. Carlyle had gone to the village shop to stock up on eggs. She wanted to make omelets. She said it was brain food. Draper had said Koenig would need six eggs in his, not three. It had been the first time they'd all laughed at the same time.

"I knew Stephen," Margaret said. "He occasionally guest-lectured at the London School of Economics. And as my expertise in cultural anthropology overlapped with his expertise in history, we sometimes had dinner together. He was a lovely man. Teeth like a witch doctor's necklace. Breath so bad you looked forward to him breaking wind."

Koenig chuckled. The way the British insulted each other as a mark of affection was very un-American. Taking the piss, they called it. As a rule of thumb, the politer they were, the more they disliked you.

"Do you think he's dead? You referred to him in the past tense."

The rims of her eyes filled. She blinked away the tears. "I do," she said. "And I don't think he died well."

"Why do you say that?"

"They're disguising murders as suicides and accidental deaths," she said. "But not one of the missing academics has been found. You seem like a thinker, Mr. Koenig. Why might that be?"

He didn't have to think for long. "Because you can't disguise a murder if their fingernails have been pulled out. Even the precinct drunk is going to ask questions."

Margaret winced. "There by the grace of God," she muttered.

Koenig patted her on the knee. "I won't let anything happen to you, Margaret," he said. "You have my word."

She smiled, then said, "Stephen was cranky and he was misanthropic. He wouldn't have told them anything on point of principle. They'd have had to tear it out of him." She paused a beat. "I'm going to miss the old fool."

"But maybe not for long?"

Margaret raised her eyebrows.

"We were told you've been exploring your palliative care options. How long do you have?"

"Put it this way, I've stopped buying green bananas," she said. Then she smiled and added, "Empathy isn't your strong point, is it, Mr. Koenig?"

Koenig said nothing. The DARPA guys monitoring his Urbach-Wiethe had explained that, alongside his own inability to experience fear, his ability to empathize might become compromised as well. He didn't think he was there yet, though. He thought it was his lifestyle. Seven years without meaningful human contact had blunted his people skills. Turned him into a social hand grenade. He said, "Sorry."

"Don't worry about it," Margaret said. "I don't. Not anymore. By the time it was caught, it was too late to operate. The damn thing had spread faster than Prince Andrew paying off someone he's never met."

"There was no more treatment?"

"Not if I wanted to die wearing Marks and Spencer knickers."

"That the Brit equivalent of dying with your boots on?"

"No one should meet their maker wearing nappies," she said. "Not children, not adults. At some point the choice is about dignity—do you want it or not. Anyway, the gadolinium gave me headaches."

"Gadolinium?"

"The contrast agent they used in their MRIs. Almost as bad for me as the damn tumor. It doesn't matter. I'm old. I would have died soon anyway."

"You're not that old, Margaret."

"That's very kind of you," she said. "But if I was milk, you'd sniff me first."

Koenig was spared more social blunders by the door opening. Draper walked in.

"The plane will be ten hours," she said. "There's a private airstrip near the Cairngorms National Park that's big enough for the G6. And it has refueling facilities."

The G6 was a Gulfstream G650. It was sleek and fast with a good range. A nonstop transatlantic flight wouldn't be a problem.

"What were you guys talking about?" Draper asked.

"I don't think so, dear," Margaret said. "Mr. Koenig may struggle with empathy, but you *feign* it."

"You don't know anything about me."

"I know you were prepared to shoot my friend. Everything you said to justify it was tinsel. Shiny, but as much use as tits on a flatfish." She struggled to her feet. "Now, if you'll excuse me, Mr. Koenig, I'm going to see what's keeping Elizabeth."

"I like her," Koenig said after she'd left.

Draper scowled.

CHAPTER 57

"Is it your plane or a lease?" Koenig asked Draper.

"Long-term lease."

"Bells and whistles?"

"It has everything."

"Can you arrange for the missing person reports on Bess's academics to be emailed to the plane? And try to get the police files on the people she thinks were murdered."

"I thought you said staging three murders was a tall order."

"Until I can rule it out, I'm ruling it in."

"I assume you don't want me going through Smerconish for this?"

"We keep the circle as small as we can."

Draper nodded. "I'll call my operations manager. He's been with me from the start, and I trust him completely. He'll get us everything there is."

The door opened. Carlyle walked in. A gust of wind followed her. It rattled a newspaper and blew Draper's hair into her eyes.

"Did you see Margaret?" Koenig said. "She went looking for you."

"I must have missed her."

Carlyle took a seat. She drained the teapot. Managed to get half a cup of lukewarm tea. She threw it down her neck like a shot of Jack. The door opened again. More wind. Margaret stepped in. She shut the door. The wind stopped.

"Ah, there you are, Elizabeth," she said. "You must have taken the scenic route back."

"I needed to think."

Margaret glanced at Koenig and Draper. "She does that sometimes," she said. "I've told her, self-indulgence is not at all British. Imagine if Churchill had taken scenic walks instead of bullying you Yanks into joining the war. We'd all be speaking German. So please, less of that nonsense, Elizabeth. And I bet you've forgotten the eggs."

"The store was shut. We'll have to make do."

"We're wheels up in ten hours," Koenig said. "We'll eat on the plane."

Draper passed Koenig his SIG. The weapon he'd thought was Draper's. He put the firing pin back in. He grabbed the empty shell casing from the bullet Draper had fired into the ceiling. He filled the base with candle wax, slotted it into the SIG's chamber, and dry-fired it. The impression in the wax was deep and true. It was the next best thing to firing the weapon.

Koenig preferred Glocks to SIGs. They were both good weapons. Accurate and reliable. Decent magazine capacity. He preferred Glocks because they were smaller, lighter, and easier to conceal. The Glock's boxy shape wasn't as aesthetically pleasing as the SIG, but who the hell cared what a tool looked like? He still liked SIGs, though, and had trained extensively with them. Like the Glock, the SIG had no safety to disengage. It was ready to fire. All you had to do was point it at the bad guy and squeeze the trigger.

CHAPTER 58

The airstrip was one hundred miles from Carlyle's cottage. A ninety-minute drive on normal roads, but the Scottish Highlands didn't have normal roads. If you thought of the UK's transport network as being like the body's circulatory system, the highways would be the arteries. The A, B, and C roads would be major and minor veins. And roads in the Highlands would be capillaries. The thinnest blood vessels in the body. Like the ones in the whites of the eyes.

Koenig figured it would take three hours to get there. Carlyle said it would be closer to six. She said progress would be slow. There would be animals on the roads. Sheep and cattle. Wild animals like deer and feral goats. And worst of all, tourists. Thousands of them, crawling over the Cairngorms like a fungal rash.

The airstrip had sheep on it. That was Koenig's first thought. His second was that as these were *living* sheep, they must know when to get off the grass and onto the heather. Plane versus ruminant would end badly for both. Like a ground-zero bird strike. If the bird was the size of a large woolly suitcase. And if the plane was at the statistically most vulnerable part of the flight.

He and Draper had tucked themselves into a crevice on one of the Cairngorms foothills. The airstrip was below them. It looked as flat as a road. It was surrounded by gorse, as thick as a hedge and twice as tall. It had been cut back at each end of the airstrip, probably in case of overruns. The only things moving were the sheep and a solitary guy manning the fuel station. The wind sock was as limp as a patched sock. The ground was dry. It was quiet.

So far, so good.

"It's a grass airstrip," Koenig said. "Can the G6 land on grass?"

"I guess," Draper replied, her eyes fixed to her monocular. "I've never been in one that has, but my pilot knows what he's doing. He wouldn't have chosen an airstrip he couldn't use." Her phone buzzed. She reached into her pocket and read the message. "We're on," she said.

They backed out of the crevice and made their way to where they'd left the Jag. Carlyle was watching out for them. She seemed anxious. Margaret was asleep.

"It's been a tiring few days," Carlyle explained. "She puts on a brave face, but she's in a lot of pain now."

"We'll try not to wake her, but the pilot's on his approach," Draper said. "And I want to get there before he lands."

CHAPTER 59

With few exceptions, runways are aligned with the most common prevailing wind. In Scotland that was southwest. The wind blows over the North Atlantic and is warmed by the North Atlantic Current. It's why Scotland is milder and wetter than countries of a similar latitude. Common sense would suggest the pilot would approach from the northeast. Land against the wind to help with the shorter runway. But the air was still. The moon had more atmosphere. Koenig figured it wouldn't matter which way he came in.

Draper pointed at the sky. "There he is," she said.

The Gulfstream was seagull white against the gray sky. Sleek and fast like a dart. Air-crash investigators called the three minutes after takeoff and the eight minutes before landing the Plus 3/Minus 8 time frame. Eighty percent of crashes occur during that eleven-minute window. But Draper's pilot knew what he was doing. The Gulfstream descended, lined up the runway, and gently kissed the grass. It bounced once, then used air brakes and reverse thrust to slow and stop. A perfect landing. It began taxiing toward the fuel station. Koenig put the Jag into gear and met it there.

The Gulfstream's door opened. The stairs and collapsible handrail folded out until they rested on the landing strip. The pilot skipped down the steps and shook Draper's hand. He was a tall man. Confident. Koenig thought he was probably ex-military.

"You made good time, Pete," Draper said.

"Had a decent headwind, ma'am," he said. "We won't need to take on as much fuel as planned, so we'll have a quicker turnaround. I assume you want to get in the air ASAP?"

Draper nodded. "You get the stuff I asked for?"

"Laptops are in the cabin."

They finished up; then Pete the pilot walked over to the fuel station. The guy was already unreeling the hose. Pete escorted him to the Gulfstream and opened the access panel underneath the wing. He said something Koenig didn't catch, but it sounded like he was telling the fuel guy to fill her up. About 4500 gallons on a plane this size, Koenig figured. Minus what Pete had saved by following the headwind. He watched the fuel guy attach the hose and start pumping in the jet fuel. He didn't know how long it would take. He knew that passengers weren't allowed on a plane while it was refueling, but it looked like Margaret really needed to lie down. He would ask Pete if he could make an exception. He probably would. Ordinary dynamics where the pilot's word was law—literally—didn't apply here. Pete reported to Draper, and Draper reported to no one.

"How long?" Koenig shouted over the noise of the pump.

"We're almost finished here, right?" Pete said to the fuel guy.

The fuel guy looked at his watch and said, "Two minutes."

He had an Eastern European accent. Polish. Maybe Lithuanian.

"Can I put Margaret on the plane now?" Koenig asked.

"Two minutes," the fuel guy repeated.

Koenig looked him up and down. He was a big man. Stocky. Short hair, tough and wiry, thinning on top. He wore bulky, fire-retardant coveralls. His gloves were tucked into the back of his belt. His boots were leather and well-worn.

Koenig saw all this.

He then took his SIG from his jacket pocket and shot the fuel guy in the stomach.

CHAPTER 60

"Get down!" Koenig yelled to Carlyle and Margaret. They were still in the Jag. They both dipped from sight. He quickly knelt and searched the wounded fuel guy. He was unarmed. He stood and kicked him in the face. Put him to sleep. "Get ready to take off," he said to Pete.

But Pete didn't move. He seemed rooted to the airstrip. Like a big dumb fence post. His eyes were glued to the fuel guy. They were wide and horrified. Scared. "What have you done?" he shrieked.

Koenig ignored him. He saw that Draper had taken out her SIG and was scanning the horizon. She hadn't hesitated. She'd gone from relaxed to tactical in a split second. She said, "What have you seen?"

"Wrong boots," Koenig replied. "Leather, not rubber. Leather boots would rot in this line of work."

"That it?"

"He checked his watch when I asked how long left to refuel. He should have checked the gauge. He's waiting for something, and I doubt we'll want to be here when it happens. We have less than two minutes."

"Get in the plane, Pete," Draper said. "Start the engine. Essential preflight checks only. Leave everything else until we're in the air."

"Are you crazy?" Pete hollered back. "We can't take off. We need to call the cops. Get this psychopath arrested."

"That's an order."

"I fucking quit then!"

Koenig saw Pete's head explode before he heard the crack of a supersonic bullet. Pete's head was on his shoulders and then it wasn't. All that was left was a bit of jawbone. Koenig could see his windpipe, all pink and wet. To cause that much damage it had to have been a dumdum bullet. Nasty. Designed to expand on impact and inflict maximum damage.

Pete hit the floor like a bag of wet towels. He was so dead he didn't even bother to twitch. Draper hunkered down behind the corpse. Used him as cover.

Sentimental.

"Koenig, will you please get behind something!" she shouted.

"Not yet," he said. "We need to know where they are. If they have nothing to shoot at, they'll stop shooting. We'll be here all day."

But to stop her moaning, he took a step to his left. As if to prove her point, a bullet pinged over his right shoulder. Right where his head had just been. Stroke of luck really. The bullet clipped the Gulfstream's undercarriage. Koenig heard the supersonic crack; then, half a second later, he heard the pop of the gunshot. Sound travels through the air at roughly 332 meters a second. Half a second meant the gun was about 150 meters away. Which meant it had come from the gorse thicket. No wonder they couldn't see the shooter. Gorse was perfect cover. If he was going to ambush someone here, it's where he'd have laid up.

Draper had reached the same conclusion. "Well done, Koenig," she said. "Now, get behind that fucking guy you shot."

Koenig lay next to the unconscious fuel guy. The blood from his stomach wound had started to soak into his pants. He could smell shit. He must have tagged the guy's bowel as well.

"Ideas?" Draper said as a three-round burst made her flinch. She immediately bobbed back up. She wasn't cowed; she was looking for a way out.

"We can't stay here," Koenig said.

"No shit, Sherlock."

"But I didn't hear the supersonic crack just then. Means they've switched to low-velocity weapons. Their plans have changed."

"Probably when you punched a hole in their guy's stomach."

"Almost certainly," he said. "The fuel guy knew what time the ambush was due to go down, but they panicked when I shot him. Went too early. And now I'm behind the fuel guy, you're behind Pete. Bess and Margaret have an engine block between them and the shooters."

"A stalemate then," Draper said. "We can't move from cover, and because the gorse has been cut down at the end of the airstrip, they can't flank us."

"They can't take potshots at us all day, though. Someone'll call the cops. I think they're considering a frontal assault. It's why they've switched to low-velocity weapons. Easier to use up close."

"But there's no cover and they know we're armed."

"With handguns. They have automatic weapons."

"Handguns we know how to use."

"They don't know that, though. Average handgun user can't hit a car at twenty yards. But automatic weapons are idiot-proof. You point, you shoot. The barrel's just long enough for the bullet to go where you want it."

Right on cue, another burst strafed the grass in front of the Gulfstream. It kicked up clods of earth, but it was ten yards short. And then nothing. No guns, no shouted orders. No assault. Just sheep munching on the tough, springy grass. Nothing else moved; nothing else made any noise. The sheep seemed oblivious to the sound of gunfire. Probably used to it. There were a lot of grouse moors in the Cairngorms.

"What's happening?" Carlyle shouted from the Jag. She'd lowered the window and had been listening to them. "They've stopped shooting."

"They have, haven't they?" Draper said. "You still think they're coming, Koenig?"

He thought it through. While a frontal assault was their attackers' only viable option, it was a high-risk strategy. Draper was right; handguns or not, the two of them *were* armed. And the fuel guy's gaping stomach wound was proof they weren't gun-shy. Even with the overwhelming firepower of modern submachine guns, their attackers would still be running toward people shooting from cover. They'd suffer casualties.

"I think they've withdrawn," he said. "They can't launch an assault while we're in cover. Our SIGs would be enough to hold them off. Unless they're bulletproof, of course."

Which was when three black-clad figures rose from the gorse. Ominous, like fins in a swimming pool.

"You had to fucking say it, didn't you?" Draper said.

CHAPTER 61

The black-clad figures approaching them didn't need cover. They *were* cover. Even from one hundred yards, Koenig could see they were wearing prototype integrated body armor. All futuristic and menacing. Looked like matte-black Iron Man suits. Full-face protective masks with built-in anti-flare goggles. Tactical helmets with slots for mounted accessories. Burn-proof coveralls. Armored plates covering the torso, thighs, shins, and arms. Thick boots. Hinged knee and elbow guards. Clunky to walk in, like an unsaddled medieval knight. But against the 9-millimeter Parabellums from Koenig's and Draper's SIGs, they were literally bulletproof. Koenig had known armored suits like this were in development with a dozen defense contractors, but he'd never seen them used in the field.

"Great," Draper muttered. "We're about to be killed by Darth Vader."

Their gait was exaggerated and ponderous. Slow but relentless. Like an incoming tide when you were stranded.

Koenig snapped off a couple of shots. He didn't expect to hit them; he wanted to see how they'd react to incoming fire. Whether they trusted their armor. They did. They ignored him. Continued walking toward them. Confident of the inevitable.

They were carrying Spectre submachine guns. Italian-made. To the casual observer, Spectres looked like their famous cousin, the Mini Uzi. They had similar rates of fire, around nine hundred rounds per minute, and a similar effective range, a little over fifty yards, but it was magazine capacity that made the Spectre the better weapon, Koenig had always thought. Fifty rounds compared with the Mini Uzi's thirty-two. A third more. When you were using weapons like Spectres and Mini Uzis, magazine capacity counted. You weren't bothered about accuracy. It was all about the firepower and the noise. They were a reassuringly odd choice. Professionals avoided Spectres and Mini Uzis like the pox.

Stupid weapons and stupid armor. That was good.

But they weren't firing yet. Hadn't even raised their weapons. As it was with Uzis, conserving ammunition was important with Spectres. One undisciplined burst and you were empty. Not firing while they weren't in effective range indicated they weren't as stupid as he'd thought. That *wasn't* good.

Koenig couldn't see a way out. The men in body armor would walk right up to where they were taking cover. Lay down suppressing fire, then shoot them like they were pigs in a poke.

"I don't suppose you have anything bigger on the plane?" he said. He waved his SIG in the air. "I kinda feel outmatched with this."

"If we can make it onto the plane, we're taking off," Draper said.

"They shot your pilot in the head," Koenig reminded her. "Unless you know how to fly a—"

"This is a transatlantic flight, dickhead," she snapped. "There's a copilot onboard. He's probably locked himself in the can, but he's in there somewhere."

"You have another pilot?"

"Of course I have another pilot. It's the law."

Koenig thought for a moment. "Well, this changes everything," he said. He stood up.

CHAPTER 62

Koenig jogged over to the Jag. One of the men in black stopped, raised his Spectre, and loosed off a burst. The bullets missed him by a good five yards. Fell between the car and the now groaning fuel guy. Which was interesting. Koenig was a big enough target, and he hadn't been sprinting. Perhaps the suits weren't all mashed potato and gravy. Maybe the anti-flash goggles restricted the field of vision. Maybe the heavy armor reduced maneuverability. Slowed reaction time. It was something to think about.

He knelt by the open window. Margaret was lying on the back seat. Carlyle was hunkered in the footwell. They seemed alert. Margaret looked terrified. Carlyle looked angry.

"You guys OK?" he said.

"We are, dear," Margaret said. "You?"

"Having a great day, thanks."

"And your vexatious friend?"

"In her element."

"What's happening?" Carlyle asked.

"They've killed the pilot," Koenig replied. "Jen's using him as a sandbag."

"I meant what's happening *now*?"

"We have men in advanced body armor about to start spraying us with bullets from vastly superior weapons."

"What's the plan?"

"I'm going to annoy them," Koenig said. "As soon as they start shooting at me, I need you to get Margaret on the plane. Jen will lay down as much cover as she can."

"Leave me behind, dear," Margaret said.

"Not a chance, Grandma. I gave you my word."

"Is there help coming?" Carlyle asked.

"Not unless Jen's called in an air strike."

"Then why do you want us on the plane?" Margaret asked. "The pilot's dead."

"Ha! That's what I said. But apparently transatlantic flights require *two* pilots."

She took a moment, then said, "Gosh. Who'd have thought?"

"You could have just shouted this, Ben," Carlyle said. "There was no need to expose yourself like that."

"I need your gun. The Makarov, not the derringer."

He thought she'd argue. Tell him she'd seen active service too. That she could handle a weapon. But she didn't. Instead, she handed over the Makarov without comment. Koenig knew she'd triaged their situation. He was expendable; she wasn't. It was cold, but he admired her for it.

Koenig press-checked the Makarov. There was a round in the chamber. It was an unfamiliar weapon, so he'd use the SIG first. He tucked the Makarov into his waistband. Cowboy thing to do, but he had no choice.

He stood and walked away from the Jag.

Time to see how good these guys were.

CHAPTER 63

Koenig had trained with the Rangers, one of the world's elite units when it came to ambush and counter-ambush tactics. The first thing he'd been told was that there were only two types of ambush: deliberate and snap. Everything else was a variation. The second thing he'd been told was that a deliberate ambush was largely unsurvivable. It was rehearsed, and it had security and designated kill zones. A deliberate ambush made use of mines and obstacles, and was only triggered when it met the unit's tactical objective.

Snap ambushes were different. By definition, they were put together quickly. The drills were rehearsed, but the specifics were dictated by the terrain. Nothing was prepared in advance. They predominantly relied on surprise. Snap ambushes were vulnerable to counter-ambush tactics.

His Ranger training instructor, a wiry Kentuckian with a scar running from nose to ear, had said, "If you got the balls, you charge them muthafuckas. You don't stop to think. You don't get down in the dirt and scratch about for a firing position. You charge, you scream like a stuck pig, and you get in among 'em. You think them muthafuckas gonna be nice and calm, thinking about keeping their breathing steady if a Ranger is charging toward them, screaming his head off? No, they fucking ain't. You make 'em regret the day they thought about ambushing a Ranger patrol."

Koenig didn't want to run. He thought that would be the wrong thing to do. A running target elicits a snap response from professional soldiers, which almost all mercenaries had been at some point. A running target is like the white tail on a startled cottontail. It draws the eye, lets muscle memory take over. Koenig didn't want the men in body armor using muscle memory when he stepped away from the Jag.

He wanted them thinking.

He wanted them *over*thinking.

He press-checked his SIG, then winked at Margaret. "See you on the plane," he said.

"I'll have a cold beer waiting for you."

"Good luck, Ben," Carlyle said.

Koenig stood.

Draper started firing. Tried to give him as much covering fire as her SIG would allow.

The men in body armor ignored her.

As one, they turned their Spectres on Koenig.

CHAPTER 64

Koenig couldn't see their expressions, but it didn't take an expert in body language to know the men in body armor were confused. Anxious even. He could sense doubt. Like when a sheepdog is confronted by a ewe with lambs. Ewes with lambs came with a whole bunch of attitude. Belligerent, not docile.

He had stepped out from behind the Jag, and the three men had opened fire. Short, controlled bursts. Disciplined. But despite him now being within the Spectres' effective range, none of the bullets hit him. The grass airstrip was hurting them. Only direct hits counted. The bullets were kicking up puffs of dirt, but they weren't bouncing up like they would if the Gulfstream had landed on a blacktop. Koenig didn't have to think about ricochets.

The men in armor glanced at each other. Koenig wasn't playing the game. He was supposed to cower behind whatever cover he could find. He wasn't supposed to walk toward them like *he* was the one wearing body armor. Koenig didn't think he needed it. Not yet. Despite it being a machine gun, the Spectre's barrel was only slightly longer than the SIG's. There was less than an inch in it. And the Spectre was heavier, and the men's vision was compromised. If Koenig could have designed a perfect opponent to walk toward, he'd have had them wearing cumbersome, impracticable body armor, firing one of the most inaccurate machine guns in production.

If they knew what they were doing—or were being led by someone who knew what they were doing—they'd have stood still, taken the best aim they could, then kept their triggers pressed until they'd emptied their magazines.

One hundred and fifty 9-millimeter Parabellums, the same ammo Koenig was using, all headed his way. The law of large numbers said at least one bullet would have hit him.

But they *didn't* know what they were doing. They were using the Spectres like scalpels when they should have been using them like sledgehammers.

One of them got lucky. A bullet slammed into the front of Koenig's boot. Right into the thick rubber tread. Stuck in it. Made his boot look like it had a small metal nose. Koenig stumbled but stayed on his feet.

"You ready, Koenig?" Draper yelled.

"Not yet."

His first shot had to count. He had to put one of them on the ground. Make them understand that up close, their body armor was a liability, not an asset. He wanted their hearts beating faster than a hamster's. He needed to be the only thing they were looking at. Only then would Draper have a chance of getting Margaret and Carlyle on the Gulfstream.

So Koenig kept walking toward them. SIG held at his side. Not brave, not stupid. Just doing what had to be done. They slowed down. Didn't want him closing the distance. Their adrenaline making them jittery and erratic.

"Aim for the pelvis!" Draper shouted. "There's no armor there, just padding!"

She was right. Koenig had hoped to get in close enough to put two rounds into the torso of the guy on his left. His bullets wouldn't penetrate the armor, but the kinetic energy would knock him on his ass. It would feel like a circus strongman had hit him with a tiny hammer. But the pelvis was a better target. The pelvis was the basin-shaped bone that connected the spine to the legs. Pelvic trauma turned a biped into a monoped. It put you down.

Koenig stopped, pointed his SIG at the guy to his left. Aimed for his hip. He snapped off a single round. Saw a puff of blood exactly where he'd aimed. The guy spun round, then slammed into the dirt. Began thrashing about like a landed fish. He screamed. High-pitched, childlike.

Koenig moved on to the guy in the middle. Aimed for the hip again but missed. Hit him in the lower abdomen instead. The guy staggered backward, then tripped. Ended up on his ass, legs in the air. Like an upended turtle. He tried to rock himself into a shooting position. Koenig shot him in the balls. The balls were an even better target than the pelvis. The guy dropped his weapon, clutched his groin, and gurgled something. It sounded like "Ah, man, not cool," but probably wasn't. He then either died or lost consciousness. Didn't matter to Koenig.

The guy to the right had seen enough. He dropped his weapon and ripped off his mask and tactical helmet. Threw his hands in the air. "I surrender!" he screamed.

Koenig said, "Good for you," and shot him in the face.

He walked toward the guy he'd shot in the pelvis, aware that stuff was happening behind him. Draper was shouting for Margaret and Carlyle to get on the plane. She was also shouting someone's name. Sounded like "Alan" but could have been "Alain." The copilot. Koenig wondered if he was still cowering in the Gulfstream's toilet.

Pelvis guy was writhing on the grass airstrip. It was clear he'd forgotten all about the Spectre he was holding. Koenig stood on his wrist anyway. He reached down and pulled off his mask. Saw a woman, not a man. There was no reason why a woman couldn't be a mercenary asshole, but it took him aback anyway. She was about thirty-five and had hard eyes.

"Who do you work for?" Koenig said.

"Go to hell!"

She had an accent he couldn't place. The *H* in "hell" had been throaty and breathy. Not Russian, but that part of the world. Estonia maybe. Possibly Ukraine.

"Last chance."

"Fu—"

Koenig shot her in the mouth.

He jogged over and checked on the guy he'd shot in the balls. He was unconscious. Lots of blood on the airstrip. Too much blood for him to survive. Koenig removed the guy's mask. His face was swarthy and stubbled. His fillings were cheap. Koenig committed his face to memory, then stomped on his windpipe. No point wasting bullets.

He checked them for ID but found nothing. Lots of cash, which Koenig pocketed, but no credit or debit cards. He gathered up their Spectres. He wasn't interested in keeping them, but he didn't want them lying around where kids might find them.

"Let's get the hell out of here, Koenig!" Draper hollered. "The cops are coming. I can see the blue lights."

He looked up. Saw the lights too. At least two cars. Probably a mile away.

Five minutes on these roads. He ran to the Gulfstream. The engine had already started. The plane was vibrating with energy. Draper was waiting at the door, ready to pull up the steps.

Time to go.

CHAPTER 65

Koenig used his Fairbairn-Sykes to dig the bullet from the tip of his boot. If it had been a TV show, he'd have said something like "Get this to the lab." But it wasn't a TV show, so he threw it in the trash. He knew who'd fired it.

They were already over the Atlantic. Alan the copilot had wanted to fly to the nearest commercial airport, but Draper wasn't in the mood. She told him that he was flying them to DC, and if he quit bitching, there'd be a six-figure bonus in his next paycheck.

The Gulfstream was a lease, but it had been retrofitted for Draper's private intelligence company. There were three main compartments. The front was the seating area. Four luxurious leather seats, cream-colored. Two on each side, facing each other opposite elegant teak tables. Each seat had its own oval-shaped porthole. They were flying through the night, so the shutters were down. The middle section was the intelligence hub. It was on the other side of a soundproofed door. Computers, a printer, a wall-mounted TV screen, high-tech communication equipment. A narrow table. Bunch of other stuff Koenig didn't recognize. The third section was the smallest. It contained the galley, the bathroom, a basket stretcher and defibrillator (seemed Draper's guys occasionally got into the odd scrape), a safe, and a secure equipment locker.

Margaret handed Koenig a frosty bottle of Blue Moon. "That was a very brave thing you did, young man," she said. She had paled in the last thirty minutes, and she had already been whiter than salt.

Koenig drained half the bottle. It felt good. He said, "I got lucky."

"It was more than luck," Carlyle said. "There was something unsettling about the way you walked toward those men, Ben. They had body armor and machine pistols. You had nothing, yet you didn't seem concerned. Your calmness made them panic. What am I missing?"

"I guess you're not the only one with secrets," Draper said, taking the seat beside him. She was carrying a laptop. "And the Pentagon won't commit to full body armor for the exact reason Koenig exploited. Until the mobility issues have been resolved, it isn't combat-ready."

Draper opened her laptop. "Now, I have to tell Pete's parents their son is dead." She glanced at Koenig. "What are you going to do?"

He touched an imaginary cap. "Police work, ma'am," he said.

"Police work, Benjamin?" Margaret said.

"I'll go through the reports on the men and women who Bess thinks have been murdered. I used to be part of the oldest law enforcement agency in the country. Crime detection is in my DNA, Margaret."

"So is arrogance," Draper said.

CHAPTER 66

Koenig grabbed another beer and made his way to the Gulfstream's intelligence hub. He closed the door behind him. He set up a laptop on the narrow table and opened the police files Draper's guys had uploaded.

He started with Hank Reynolds, the man who'd hanged himself with the cord from his hotel dressing gown. A suicide note had been found on his open laptop. It hinted, but didn't explicitly say, that he was tired of living as a straight man. Koenig thought this death would be the easiest to confirm one way or the other. Hangings and strangulations left different wounds. He would know if someone had staged a hanging. The ligature furrow would be horizontal. He scrolled through to the autopsy photographs. Sure enough, the wound was where he'd have expected it to be—underneath the jaw.

He read the suicide note, but it offered nothing. It was vague, but the language was consistent with other documents he'd written. The investigating cop's report stated that Reynolds had dinner with an unidentified male and had seemed in good spirits. He'd had half a dozen whiskey sours, then returned to his room. He was discovered in the morning by the maid. The police report didn't offer an opinion as to why Reynolds had chosen to kill himself in Coos County, Oregon, but suicidal people were rarely thinking clearly.

Koenig read about Louise Durose next. She was a sanitation engineer from San Diego. She and the man she'd hooked up with at a convention had been beaten to death in a New Jersey alley. Carlyle believed Louise was the target, and the man was collateral damage. She refused to explain why. Condoms and erectile dysfunction pills had been found in Louise's purse. The detective investigating the double murder concluded they'd been looking for a third person to turn a twosome into a threesome—his words, not Koenig's—and had crossed the wrong pimp. Koenig thought that was a jump. Pimps lived under near constant threat, and they habitually carried firearms. He didn't think a pimp would use a brick. He thought a mugging gone wrong was more likely. That someone had used a weapon of convenience. Other than that, Koenig couldn't see anything to suggest their deaths were anything other than a tragic case of wrong place, wrong time.

He read the statement from the cop who'd delivered the death knock to her ex-partner, the man who was battling Louise Durose for custody of their chocolate Labrador, Dexter. On hearing about her murder, he'd said, "Does this mean I can sell this asshole dog now?" Nice guy.

The last file belonged to Michael Gibbs, the guy who'd driven his wife's station wagon off Park Loop Road in Acadia National Park. Koenig spent the least amount of time on this one. The accident investigation unit report was unequivocal. It had been an accident. The officer in charge said it was likely Gibbs had fallen asleep at the wheel after a heavy meal. It was why there were no skid marks on the bend in the road. The barriers had been no match for the heavy station wagon.

Koenig shut the laptop and sighed. Reading reports like these had been part of the job in his SOG days. He hadn't missed them.

The soundproof door opened. Draper stepped through. She shut it behind her.

"Smerconish has called. He wants to know what happened in Scotland."

"How did he know it was us?"

"We left the embassy Jag."

"Of course. What did you tell him?"

"Not as much as he wanted."

Koenig grunted. He didn't trust Smerconish. The firefight at the airstrip meant someone had accessed the Gulfstream's flight plan. That kind of information wasn't readily available.

"Anything?" Draper asked, tilting her head at the laptop.

He shook his head. "A suicide, a mugging, and an accident, as far as I can tell. With the same information, I'd have reached the same conclusions." He paused a beat. Opened the laptop again. "But I'm going to keep looking."

CHAPTER 67

Koenig fixed himself a pot of coffee, then figured out how to wirelessly connect the laptop to the printer. He printed hard copies of every photograph in the reports. There were 164 in total. He had to refill the printer's ink twice. He then printed a bunch of documents.

When he was done, he gathered the untidy stack and carried it to the conference table. Instead of sorting them into three case-related piles, he arranged them in evidence types. When you're looking for connections, you don't look at things in isolation; you look at them together.

He started with where the bodies were found—Oregon, Maine, and New Jersey. Oregon was in the Pacific Northwest. Maine was in New England. Neither state had flourishing organized crime, certainly nothing big enough to collaborate across the three thousand miles that separated them. New Jersey *did* have organized crime, but their collaborations and feuds tended to be with New York, Chicago, and Philly. Sometimes Boston and Pittsburgh. Koenig shuffled the location pile together and set it to one side.

He moved on to the victim biographies. Where they lived. What they did for a living. What they got up to in their spare time. That kind of thing. Louise Durose had been a sanitation engineer with an expertise in landfill management. Hank Reynolds worked in cybersecurity. Michael Gibbs had something to do with deepwater port productivity. Important jobs, but not the kind of thing that got you murdered. He jotted down a note to find out exactly what Reynolds's work had entailed. Cybersecurity was Draper's area of expertise, not his.

The photographs taken at the scene were next. All 164 of them. Most were of Louise Durose and the man she'd been with. Homicides generated more paperwork than suicides and accidents. The CSI guys had photographed the bodies, the alley they'd been found in, the murder weapon. They'd documented the blood spatter on the walls and the alley debris. The empty liquor bottles, the cigarette butts, the broken glass. They'd gone to her hotel room and photographed her possessions.

Koenig reread the autopsy reports. He flicked through the cause-of-death sections. Cause of death was never as useful as the movies made out. Pathologists rarely provided the golden bullet. Their role was mainly confirming what the cops already suspected, and gathering the evidence that would convict the perpetrator. Cause of death was about facts. It was black and white. It was *manner* of death that was interesting. Manner of death wasn't black and white. It fooled around in the gray areas. Cause of death was the specific injury that began a lethal chain of events that resulted in death. Manner of death was *how* the injury happened. Cerebral hypoxia, where the brain is cut off from its supply of oxygen, caused the death of Hank Reynolds. The *manner* of his death was that he was hanged.

If you knew what pathologists looked for, it was possible to stage a hanging. Koenig hadn't seen it for himself, but he'd once spoken to a detective who had. The sergeant, a barrel-chested Irishman from Boston, was called to a suicide. A woman had jumped through her loft hatch with a towrope around her neck. The detective said he only caught it as the drop was long enough to have snapped the woman's neck. Instead, she'd died by strangulation. They'd arrested the victim's brother, and he eventually admitted to lying in wait in the loft, slipping the noose over her head, then yanking her up like the rope was a spring-loaded snare.

A staged hanging was an overly elaborate way of disguising a murder, though. There were easier ways to stage a suicide. Disposing of the victim, then leaving their car and clothes at the beach. Forcing a gun into their mouth and blowing the back of their head off. Pushing them off a cliff and claiming they jumped. Koenig thought the investigating cops had gotten it right. He thought Hank Reynolds *had* hanged himself.

It was more likely they'd got it wrong with Michael Gibbs. The lack of skid marks on Park Loop Road meant they should have at least considered suicide. Yes, Gibbs had just eaten a heavy meal, but he wasn't a six-week-old puppy.

Food didn't immediately send healthy adults to sleep. Excessive alcohol, maybe, but not food. And the extravagant feast Gibbs had spent a small fortune on did have the whiff of a last meal. A blowout before he pulled the plug.

Potentially *two* suicides then.

Louise Durose hadn't killed herself, though. She'd had her face smashed in with a brick. Koenig wasn't convinced by the death-by-pimp conclusion the responding New Jersey cops had jumped to. He thought it was a lazy reach. But regardless of who'd wielded the brick, Durose *had* been murdered. The homicide cops were working it hard. They were taking it seriously. They'd canvassed for witnesses. They'd studied thousands of hours of CCTV footage. They'd spent most of their annual budget on lab tests. They'd even done a reconstruction. Nothing. Not a thing. It was as if Louise Durose had been alive and then dead, and the world had missed the bit in the middle.

There was only one, probably easily explained, chink in the armor of Koenig's mugging-gone-wrong theory: the *Van Gogh's Chair* print in Durose's hotel room. The maid had reported it missing. Koenig studied the CSI photograph, and if you knew the print was supposed to be there, you *did* notice the slightly darker rectangle of paint. A patch the sun hadn't gotten to. A New Jersey detective had taken the hotel manager's statement. He'd explained that the hotel bought the prints in bulk from a company that specialized in supplying artwork to the hospitality sector. They'd cost three bucks a unit.

Still, Durose hadn't checked out, and the print wasn't found in her luggage or her rental. Unless the guest before her had taken it, it was a mystery. One that would likely never be solved. Certainly not by the New Jersey homicide unit. They had NFA'd it. No further action.

Koenig poured himself a fresh coffee. The cups on the plane were bone china. Thin as paper. Nothing so crass as mugs with corporate logos for Draper.

He found an image of *Van Gogh's Chair* on a website about Postimpressionists. He'd never really appreciated art. Had always felt undereducated in the company of people who did.

At first glance, *Van Gogh's Chair* looked like any other still life. A ratty yellow chair and a box of onions. Pale blue walls and a dark blue door. Terracotta tiles on the floor. Famous because of who had painted it. No narrative. Nothing to see that hadn't been painted. But as he read how Van Gogh had painted it just before his breakdown, how he'd used it to send a coded message to his onetime friend, the French symbolist Paul Gauguin, he saw what Van

Gogh had been trying to say. That every item on the canvas was a story about Van Gogh's life. About his philosophy. His hopes and his fears. The despair he felt as his friendship with Gauguin disintegrated.

None of that explained why Durose had stolen the print, though. It had no monetary value. If she'd taken a fancy to it, better-quality prints could be ordered almost anywhere.

Koenig sighed. He rubbed his eyes and rolled his shoulders, as his body reminded him he wasn't as young as he used to be. He didn't want to go to sleep, though. Not until he'd exhausted everything. Turned over every stone.

The printer whirred. Draper must have been printing something from her laptop. Koenig waited for the document to appear, but all that happened was the OUT OF INK light flashed. Again. Koenig opened the cupboard and pulled out another box of ink cartridges. He slotted in the cyan. He slotted in the magenta.

But when it came to the yellow cartridge, he paused.

He turned the ink cartridge over in his hand and studied it. He didn't know why, but the part of his brain that worked silently in the background was trying to grab his attention. Higher-order thinking, he thought it was called. And HOT went beyond memorizing facts. HOT asked the brain to do something *with* those facts. Things like idea generation and critical thinking. Problem-solving and big picture visualization.

Making connections.

And right now, Koenig's higher-order thinking was telling him the ink cartridge was important. That it would help him understand what was happening. Maybe not the cartridge exactly. But something to do with the cartridge. A feature of the cartridge that was present in all three deaths.

Koenig cleared away all but a dozen of the CSI photographs. He pored over them until his eyes began to blur. He rearranged them. He added photographs and he took others away. He rocked back on his heels and took them all in at once. He crouched over the table and studied each photograph individually.

He couldn't see anything. There was nothing there.

Except that wasn't quite right. There *was* something in one of the photographs. Something that wasn't in any of the others. And it should have been. It was a smiley-face air freshener. It was in the photograph taken when Michael Gibbs had driven his wife's station wagon into the parking lot at La Terrasse, the restaurant in Maine. The restaurant recorded all cars as they entered in case there was a malicious valet-parking claim later. Company policy. The smiley face was hanging from the rearview mirror's mounting bracket. All yellow and happy. But it wasn't in the photographs taken at the bottom of the ravine.

Which was strange.

What had happened to it? Had the elastic string snapped? In Koenig's experience, the string on air fresheners was thin but durable. And if it had snapped, where was it? It wasn't in the station wagon's interior. He supposed it could have snapped and been tossed out as the station wagon bounced down the ravine, but that seemed unlikely.

Had Gibbs removed it before he headed home? Had he gotten sick of an air freshener that had run its course? Koenig thought back to the time when he'd owned a vehicle. He'd never bought an air freshener, but auto dealers always had new ones in their cars, and all his personal cars had had air fresheners. And he'd never thrown one out. Not once. Throwing out an air freshener seemed like more effort than leaving it there. He figured if he were ever going to throw one out, it would be if he'd bought a replacement. A like-for-like, one-in, one-out kinda deal.

He picked up the photograph with the smiley face. Held it next to the ink cartridge. Saw what it was that connected them. And then, like a Magic Eye picture coming into focus, everything dissolved until all that remained was the answer.

The answer to what was there.

And what *wasn't* there.

He picked up a satellite phone. While he waited for it to power up, he searched for the telephone number he needed. When the light turned green, Koenig tapped in the number for the Gobblers Knob Hotel in Coos County, Oregon. It was answered immediately.

"Can you put me through to housekeeping?" he said.

CHAPTER 68

It was crowded in the Gulfstream's central compartment, but Koenig wanted Draper, Carlyle, and Margaret to see everything the way he had—together. He laid out seven photographs on the table. Arranged them so they were visible to everyone. He placed the yellow ink cartridge next to the photographs. That was all he needed.

Three photographs were from the Hank Reynolds file. The fruit bowl, a photograph of the trash can under the dressing table, and a photograph of the trash can in his bathroom.

The fourth photograph was the gap on the wall in Louise Durose's hotel room where the missing print should have been. The fifth wasn't a CSI photograph; it was a picture of *Van Gogh's Chair* that Koenig had printed off the internet.

The sixth and seventh photographs were of Michael Gibbs's station wagon. One with the smiley-face air freshener, the other without it.

"Tell me what you see," Koenig said.

"We were due to land in DC in three hours," Draper said. "Now you're saying we're going to JFK. If that's the case, I need to tell the pilot now. Stop dicking around and tell us what you've found."

"I'm not being a jerk," he said. "I need to know I haven't made a connection that isn't there."

"We don't have time—"

"Is it a puzzle, Benjamin?" Margaret cut in.

"Sort of, Margaret," Koenig replied.

She readjusted her hairpin, then said, "In that case, I'll need a pot of tea and some biscuits."

"Why did you include a picture of *Van Gogh's Chair* among these police photographs?" Margaret asked.

It was the first time in five minutes that anyone had spoken. Draper, after huffing and puffing and moaning about changing flight plans at the last minute and a bunch of other stuff Koenig didn't listen to, had settled down and studied the photographs the same as everyone else.

"It was the print that was stolen from Louise Durose's hotel room," Koenig explained.

"Was it valuable?" she asked.

"About three bucks."

"Did Louise steal it?"

"I don't think so."

"Then who?"

Koenig didn't answer.

"Yellow," Draper said. "That's what connects everything—the color yellow."

"Explain," Koenig said.

"The smiley-face air freshener is missing from the wrecked station wagon," she said. "It wasn't missing when Gibbs arrived at the restaurant. The dominant color in *Van Gogh's Chair* is yellow. It should have been hanging in Durose's hotel room, but it wasn't. Like you said, someone removed it."

She picked up the three photographs taken in Hank Reynolds's hotel room: the fruit bowl, the bedroom trash can, and the bathroom trash can. She studied them, blowing a wisp of hair out of her eyes as she did. She barely paused before she said, "Bananas. There's no banana in his fruit bowl. You included the trash cans to show he didn't eat it when he got back to his room?"

Koenig nodded.

"Perhaps he took it with him?" Carlyle said.

"I rang housekeeping, and the room was serviced while he was out," Koenig said. "Each fruit bowl gets one red apple, one green apple, one orange, and one banana."

"OK," Draper said. "If we accept that for reasons unknown, everything yellow has been removed from Hank Reynolds's hotel room and Michael

Gibbs's station wagon, why did *Van Gogh's Chair* need to be removed from Louise Durose's hotel room? How does that fit? She wasn't murdered in her room; she was murdered in an alleyway."

"I'm guessing now," Koenig said. "But I think whoever is behind this planned to kill her in her room. Probably another staged suicide. Pills, not hanging. Statistically, that's how women kill themselves. But Louise went off script. She hooked up with someone. Was on her way back to her hotel room with him. I think one of the killers improvised. Beat Louise to death with a brick. I think Bess is right; the man she hooked up with was collateral damage."

"You said *one* of them improvised? You think it's a team?"

"I do."

"Why?"

"I've heard of them."

"And removing yellow from the crime scene is kinda their calling card?" Carlyle said. "A way to taunt the cops? Like the Beltway snipers leaving tarot cards and the Night Stalker leaving pentagrams?"

"Nothing like that," Koenig said, shaking his head.

"I don't understand then."

"No reason you would, Bess. You were military. Jen was CIA, then private intelligence. And Margaret's an academic. But I was law enforcement. I was tuned in to a different kind of rumor mill. One that was fed at both ends—by the cops *and* the robbers. And during my last few months with the SOG, there was a rumor about a father-and-daughter contract-killing team. High-end. Referrals only. Most of us dismissed it. But it was persistent. Kept cropping up when perps were trying to make deals."

"And the yellow?"

"Way I heard it, the dad has xanthophobia," Koenig said.

"Which is?"

"For the dad it's a debilitating condition that makes it impossible for him to be near the color yellow. For the daughter it's employment. She goes on ahead and cleans the kill zone of anything yellow like—"

"Bananas, Van Gogh prints, and smiley-face air fresheners?"

"Exactly, Bess," Koenig said. "She cleans the kill zone, then he moves in and does the actual deed."

"Do you know how to find them?" Draper said.

"I'm not even sure they exist."

"But you want to go to New York anyway? What's your plan? Stand on the corner of 53rd and 3rd with a caged canary, see who pukes?"

"We're not going to New York to stand on a street corner," Koenig said. "We're going to New York to offer someone the deal of a lifetime." He paused. "If she's still speaking to me, that is," he added.

"If who's still speaking to you?"

Koenig told her.

"Oh, you've got to be fucking kidding," she said.

CHAPTER 69

MV *SWAN HUNTER*. THE ARCTIC BRIDGE.

It was the Devil's Hour, 3 a.m. The time of night when ghosts, witches, and demons were at their most powerful. For superstitious Russian sailors, 3 a.m. was the wrong time to be out on deck.

But it was the right time for Captain Volkov.

MV *Swan Hunter* would soon enter Canada's exclusive economic zone and the Royal Canadian Navy regularly patrolled their waters. And although the RCN was more concerned with protecting one of the world's richest fishing resources than boarding a grain ship they'd seen a hundred times before, it was a risk Captain Volkov didn't need to take.

Anyway, Volkov was sick of the Australian. He hadn't seen him since he'd cut off his ear, but he could feel his presence. He knew he'd be in his cabin, wishing ill on everyone on board. It was like having Jonah as a passenger. The Australian was bad news. The sooner he was off his ship, the better for everyone.

Volkov sent a message to the first mate. Told him the crew were in their cabins and that he was ready. The first mate replied immediately. Said he would collect the Australian and lock everyone else inside just in case. It wouldn't be necessary. Volkov had plied the crew with vodka all night. He said it was to celebrate leaving Russian waters after the two-year refit. Really, it was to ensure they were sleeping like the drunks that, given the chance, Volkov knew them to be. By the time they woke, they would be able to see Canada.

Jenkins, the now one-eared Australian, had wrapped a bandage around his head. A crude job made from strips of pillowcase. He glared at Volkov but lowered his eyes when the Russian showed him his clasp knife. Jenkins knew he wouldn't be thrown overboard like the bosun. He was mission critical. He was the only one who could navigate the smuggled cargo around Nova Scotia and on to Maine. But he also knew he still had lots of appendages Captain Volkov could cut off. So, instead of pushing his luck, Jenkins swallowed his pride and thought of what he would do when the job was over, and he had a million bucks in an offshore account and nothing to do but get fat.

Volkov and Jenkins made their way to hold five—the one with the false bottom. The first mate unlocked the controls to the crane. They had rehearsed this once in Murmansk, and that had been once too much. It wasn't rocket science. Volkov pressed the button that opened hold five's cargo hatch. The hatch cover was two large panels. They were on wheels. Hydraulic rams pushed them along their tracks until they hung over the edge of the ship like stubby wings. When the hold was open, the Australian jumped into the false bottom. His feet sank into the animal feed. The first mate lowered the crane's jib. Four chains were fitted to the hook. The Australian fastened a chain to each corner of the false bottom and climbed back out. The first mate raised the jib. The false bottom, animal feed and all, lifted into the frigid air. When it was clear of the hold, the first mate rotated the jib until the load was over the water. He then lowered it into the sea and unhooked it. The false bottom and the chains disappeared into the depths of the Arctic. The Australian leaned over the side, but it was too dark to see anything.

The first mate switched on the hold lights, and Jenkins and Volkov climbed down the hold ladder. For a moment, neither of them spoke. They just stared at what it was they were being paid to smuggle.

It was a boat. A four-year-old NorseBoat 21.5 called *Lady Sybil* to be precise. The open model with a fiberglass hull. The kind of boat you'd expect to see sailing the Miami coast. It had an easy-to-handle sloop rig. Sailed well. Not that the Australian would use the rig. Nor would he use the four-horsepower outboard engine that came standard with the NorseBoat. This one had been fitted with a pair of twenty-fives.

"What's inside this thing, mate?" Jenkins said.

Volkov didn't answer. He didn't want to know what was hidden in the NorseBoat. He couldn't imagine what was so valuable it warranted such an extraordinary operation. Two years in a dry dock would cost the company tens of millions of dollars. A solid-gold NorseBoat wouldn't cost that much. Instead, he said, "Just do your fucking job."

The NorseBoat was in a padded iron cradle. More air than metal. Sturdy. It served two purposes: to protect the boat in transit, and to lift the boat out of the hold and onto the sea. Volkov and Jenkins fixed chains to each corner of the cradle. The first mate lowered the jib, and Volkov fixed the chains to the crane's hook.

Jenkins climbed on board and fitted the two outboards. He checked every one of the jerry cans to make sure none of them had leaked. There were twenty in total. Every bit of stowage on the NorseBoat was carrying spare fuel. He opened his provisions box. It was full of jerky and nuts and chocolate and other high-energy food. Nothing that needed cooking. He tapped his water container. It was full. He opened his duffel bag and pulled out the clothing he'd have to wear when he was on the open water. He'd asked an Alaskan trawlerman what he would need and written down everything the cranky old man had told him. You didn't get to be an *old* Alaskan trawlerman without learning how to stay warm and dry. He pulled on a dry suit, face mask and goggles, an alpaca-wool sweater, and some padded trousers. Thick gloves. Few more items.

"Are you ready?" Volkov asked.

"I'm ready," Jenkins replied.

Volkov made a circling motion above his head, and the cradle, the Norse-Boat, and the Australian began to rise out of the hold. It reminded Volkov of an elephant in a sling he'd seen on the Discovery Channel. It was being relocated after a run-in with poachers. Volkov climbed back out and watched the first mate maneuver the boat. It wasn't a difficult task. Unloading cargo was what they did. Admittedly, it was the first time they'd done it at sea. Or during the Devil's Hour. Or with someone *in* the cargo. But they were just details. It was still an unloading job.

The crane's jib pivoted until the NorseBoat was over the Arctic. The first mate then lowered the cradle and boat onto the sea. Volkov held his breath. In his worst nightmares he'd thought that the cradle might drag the boat down. Something would catch. Or some weird salt-air alchemy would fuse the boat and the cradle together during transit and they'd both sink like a stone. But it went as planned. The boat floated; the cradle didn't. The Australian waited until the cradle had cleared the bottom of the NorseBoat's hull, then started one of the outboard motors. He moved the boat until it was clear of the chains. The first mate released the cradle. It silently joined the false bottom on the seabed. In two years, a load of cod and skate and king crabs would call the cradle and the false bottom their home. In ten thousand years, a bunch of archaeologists would ponder its use. *Good luck*, the first mate thought.

Jenkins chugged a hundred yards from the MV *Swan Hunter*, then killed the engine. He turned to wave off the captain and the first mate. They hadn't seen eye-to-eye on this trip, but they'd achieved all their objectives.

But the deck was empty.

It was like they'd never been there.

Jenkins was alone.

CHAPTER 70

Metropolitan Detention Center, Brooklyn—better known as MDC Brooklyn—was the federal prison that served the Eastern District of New York. It was a boxy, low-rise building in Sunset Park. A cube-shaped warning of what awaited anyone who slipped on the criminal-justice banana skin. Originally a warehouse, it was converted into a federal prison in the mid-nineties. It now warehoused human beings.

Koenig was no prison abolitionist, but even he thought MDC Brooklyn was grim. It was smelly, it was cold, and it was damper than a puddle. It looked like it was held together with black mold.

Draper had wanted to call Smerconish. Let him know they were back on US soil. Koenig hadn't wanted her to call anyone—"Trust no one" seemed a good maxim right now—but in the end it was moot. They needed his connections. When Draper told him what they needed, he'd asked one question: "Is it necessary?"

"Yes," Draper had replied.

"Consider it done then."

They were met at MDC Brooklyn by five FBI agents. Special Agent in Charge Isaacs and four lackeys. Isaacs was a doughy man with deep-set eyes. He looked like a cartoon toad. He checked their passports, raised an eyebrow at Koenig's and Draper's diplomatic status, paid special attention to the forged passports of Margaret and Carlyle, then took them through security. The guard asked Margaret to remove the hairpin that kept her bun together. She pulled it out and handed it over. It was long and smooth with a ribbed collar.

"Be careful with that, please," she said. "It's Roman."

"Nice," Koenig said.

She shrugged. "I wasn't always old, dear," she said. "I used to have suitors."

Isaacs led them into an interview room. It had been set up with a camera and recording equipment. A steel table was bolted to the floor.

"We only need a speakerphone," Draper said. "No camera, no recording equipment."

Isaacs scowled. "We'll get you a phone," he said, "but everything else stays. Including me. That's nonnegotiable."

"I'm not negotiating."

"Miss Draper, I've been ordered to facilitate this meeting, but the prisoner is in *my* custody. We have a lawful reason to—"

"You don't have the security clearance, Agent Isaacs," Draper said. "No one here does."

"Don't blow smoke up my ass," he said. "*None* of you have security clearance. Mr. Koenig looks like he sleeps in a dumpster, you used to carry a badge but don't anymore, and your friends presented counterfeit passports to a federal agent. That's a crime. As far as I'm concerned, you've *all* committed a crime. And your diplomatic passports don't mean shit stateside. We either arrest you or we cooperate—the choice is yours. Don't take long. I'm a reasonable man, but my IBS is acting up. It's making me crabby."

"Agent Isaacs, in fifteen minutes the attorney general will call the speakerphone you're going to get me. You can explain to her then why you've gatecrashed a matter of national security. No skin off my ass. Either way, you'll be leaving this room."

Which stopped Special Agent in Charge Isaacs in his tracks. The AG was Isaacs's boss in the same theoretical way the president was his boss. You expected to go your entire career without meeting either. Unless you were getting an award, you didn't even want them knowing your name.

"Don't leave this room," Isaacs said. "I need to make a call." He got a phone out of his belt holster and used his thumb to flick it open. He left the room. The four other agents left with him. The one at the back turned and winked. Koenig got the impression that Isaacs was a bit of an asshole.

"Who the hell still has a flip phone?" Draper said when the room was empty. "Although he *was* right about one thing."

"What's that, dear?" Margaret said.

"Koenig does look like he sleeps in a dumpster."

Five minutes later, the camera and recording equipment had been removed. Five minutes after that, the person they'd come to see shackle-shuffled into the interview room.

She took one look at them, screamed, and launched herself at Koenig. The prison officers with her held her back as best they could, but it was like they were wrestling a greased pig. Eventually, and after much cursing, they got her to the floor. Even then, the woman managed to twist her heavily bandaged head so she was facing Koenig. She shrieked and spat and hollered and panted until foam formed at the corners of her mouth and snot hung from her nose. Koenig didn't think he'd ever seen anyone look so angry.

"Hi, Cunningham," he said. "How's your forehead?"

CHAPTER 71

While they waited for the prison staff to secure Cunningham to the table's eyebolt, Draper explained what they were doing at MDC Brooklyn.

"Before this started, Koenig had a run-in with four corrupt police officers," she said. "They were going to deliver him to a man who planned to skin him alive."

"Why?" Carlyle asked.

"Why did someone want to skin Koenig alive, or why did the cops want to take him there?"

"Both, I guess."

"You're looking for something more nuanced than they'd met him?"

Carlyle's lips stayed pressed together. Koenig got the impression she didn't laugh much.

"I have no idea about the first, other than there are some sick assholes with some even sicker predilections out there," Draper said. "The second is easier to explain: Koenig has a five-mil bounty on his head. The cops planned to get half of it."

"Gosh," Margaret said. "What happened?"

"Koenig killed one, put another in an irreversible coma, and swiped a credit card across Miss Cunningham's forehead like he was paying for dinner."

"Psycho asshole split my head open!" Cunningham yelled.

"Oh, stop complaining," Draper said. "You had guns, he was unarmed."

"Stop complaining?" she said. "Are you fucking kidding?" She reached up and pulled up her bandage to reveal an ugly welt across her forehead. It was red and livid and thicker than lipstick. The surrounding skin was as bruised as a dropped apple. "Look what he did to my face. They had to take skin off my ass to patch it together. You got any idea what it's like in here for a cop with an asshole grafted to her head? As if I don't have enough shit to deal with right now."

One of the guards tugged her restraints. "The prisoner's secure," he said.

They left the room. Draper locked the door and put her ear to it. Koenig doubted Isaacs was stupid enough to have a glass pressed up against the other side, but Draper was an ex-spy; suspicion was her default position.

"What happened to the fourth police officer?" Carlyle asked.

"The NYPD arrived," Draper said. "Otherwise, he'd have gone the same way as the others. Unfortunately for Miss Cunningham, she's carrying the can for the whole thing. The fourth cop was waiting in the parking lot. He claims he had no idea what his friends were doing. The FBI have him on a bunch of conspiracy stuff with more charges to follow, but right now, Miss Cunningham's only play is to make a deal."

"A deal?" she said. "With that asshole? I'd rather do my time."

"All of it?"

"Yes, all of it. What do you think I'm gonna do? Dig a tunnel?"

"You don't know this yet," Koenig said, "but the feds are going full RICO on your ass. Even the part that's stitched to your face. Conspiracy to murder. Kidnapping. Murder for hire. Money laundering. Tax evasion. A smorgasbord of offenses, enough to feed even the hungriest US attorney. So, when my colleague said, 'All of it?,' she wasn't talking about your sentence; she was talking about your life." He let that sink in. "How old are you, Cunningham? Sixty-five, Sixty-six?"

"I'm thirty-one, asshole!"

"So, if you can avoid getting shanked, you might reasonably expect to spend another fifty years in here. I'm no somnologist, but that's bound to keep you awake at night."

Koenig hadn't told Cunningham anything she hadn't already worked out for herself. Prosecuting dirty cops was the gift that kept on giving. It restored public confidence in the police. It showed a prosecutor's independence from their institutional allies in law enforcement. And the voters loved it.

"Best you can offer is where I serve my time," she said. "My own lawyer says I ain't never getting out."

"You were a cop once, Cunningham," Koenig said. "Try being one again. What's different about this room? What do you see?"

She looked around. "I don't see shit."

"That's good. At least your face-ass isn't leaking."

"Screw you."

Koenig waited.

Cunningham shrugged. "There ain't no Liberty."

The Liberty Interview Recorder was the NYPD's interview room recording system. It had three cameras, two fixed and one with pan-tilt-zoom capabilities. Koenig doubted MDC Brooklyn used anything as advanced, but at least Cunningham understood the room was clean.

"That's right," he said. "There are no cameras, no microphones, and no FBI agents. What does that tell you?"

"You're going to beat a confession out of me."

"There are no cameras or feds in here, Cunningham, because what we're about to do will make Special Agent in Charge Isaacs lose his mind."

CHAPTER 72

"Full immunity?" Cunningham said. "You're offering full immunity?"

"The attorney general will confirm it shortly," Draper said.

"Even though you know some of the shit I done?"

Draper nodded.

"I ain't no rat," she said after a few beats. "And even if I was, my life wouldn't be worth spit if I flip on those guys. And don't give me that 'We can protect you' bullshit because you can't. You have no idea who you're dealing with."

"We don't care about the East Coast Sweeney," Koenig said. "And Special Agent in Charge Isaacs doesn't need you to flip. He has your bank accounts, and he has your friends' bank accounts. I used to hunt people like you, and the one thing you all have in common is that you don't understand how money works. How much of an auditable trail it leaves. But the FBI understands. The FBI understands that once it has one bank account, it has them all. It won't be long before Special Agent in Charge Isaacs has unraveled the whole sordid affair. He'll get everyone."

Cunningham swallowed. Hard. It was obvious she hadn't considered that. "They'll think I ratted them out," she said.

"Way I see it, you only have one option: take the deal and get the hell out of Dodge before the rest of the East Coast Sweeney are hoovered up."

The phone rang, shrill and loud in the enclosed interview room. Cunningham flinched. Draper reached over and hit the answer button.

"This is Arianna Dowd, Miss Cunningham," a voice said. No preamble. "Do you know who I am?"

The United States attorney general wasn't one for wasting her words.

Cunningham stared at the phone in astonishment. After a moment she said, "For real?"

"Sure as gravity."

"Well, I guess I've heard of you then."

Koenig wasn't surprised that Cunningham knew the AG. Arianna Dowd was that rare thing in DC: a political appointment liked by both sides of the aisle. She grew up in Rockaway Beach, cut her teeth prosecuting Cosa Nostra families in the 1980s, hammered white-collar pension fund raiders in the 1990s, and was called to the bench in 2001. She was as tough as a bobcat and twice as mean.

"And what have you heard, Miss Cunningham?"

"That you're fair."

"What else?"

"You hate dirty cops."

"Goes without saying. What else?"

"You don't like repeating yourself."

"And I'm not about to start with a piece of shit like you," the AG said. "This is a onetime deal. Full immunity in exchange for verified information. I have an hourglass on my desk, Miss Cunningham. Only I know how much time it measures, but I'll give you this for free—it isn't an hour. I've just turned it over. When there's no sand in the upper globe, I'm hanging up. You have until then to tell Mr. Koenig what he needs to know."

Cunningham blew out her breath like a horse whinny.

"Ask your questions," she said.

CHAPTER 73

"There's a murder-for-hire team we need to find," Koenig said to Cunningham. "Help us, you walk out of here with a bleached record. Don't, and you spend the rest of your life in this rat hole. Somewhere worse if we can find it."

"How the hell am I supposed to know—"

"Rumor is it's a father and daughter. The father has xanthophobia."

"What's that?"

"The color yellow makes him puke like a supermodel."

Cunningham's eyes narrowed. Her face went hard. She either knew them or she knew of them. Looked like she was figuring out the best way to play this. She had information and they needed it. Koenig could see her cogs turning.

"I want access to my bank accounts, and I want a new identity," she said. "And I want to be relocated. Somewhere warm."

"Are you fucking high?" the AG said. "The deal is the deal is the deal. You either talk or you don't. Believe me when I say I don't give a rat's ass what you choose. But if I were you, I'd choose quick 'cause there ain't much sand left."

"I heard of 'em," Cunningham admitted. Beaten.

"Anything you tell me now is covered by the agreement, Miss Cunningham. Anything we find out afterward is not."

"They lived under our umbrella," she said.

"You let them operate?" Koenig said. "In return you took a cut of their take?"

Cunningham nodded. "What do you want to know?"

"Start with their names."

"The dude's called Stillwell Hobbs," Cunningham said. "I don't know if it's legit, but it's the name he used when we met with him."

"His daughter?"

"Harper Nash."

Draper snorted. "Harper Nash and Stillwell Hobbs? Are you shitting me?"

"Like I said, I ain't sure they were their real names."

"Tell me about Stillwell Hobbs," Koenig said. "What does he look like? Where does he live? How do you contact him?"

Cunningham shrugged.

"White. About five ten. Mid-forties. Balding. Normal-looking, I guess. Type of guy you wouldn't look twice at. Which would be a mistake as he's one of the most dangerous men in the world. I know when we met with him no one ran their mouth. You don't disrespect a dude who knows a hundred and one ways to stop your clock."

"Distinguishing features?"

Cunningham looked at the table. Seemed like she was concentrating. "His teeth," she said eventually.

"What about them?"

"They're rotten. All brown and uneven and chipped. Looked like he went to a Brit dentist."

"Hey," Margaret said.

Koenig didn't respond. Bad teeth weren't uncommon with people serious about protecting their privacy. Dentists took X-rays. Photographs. They occasionally took blood. Koenig had once used a half-bitten apple to confirm a perp's identity. Took it from him in a diner, had it checked against his dental records, and arrested the guy that night.

"And the girl?" he said.

"Skinny coldhearted bitch," Cunningham replied. "Bunch of tattoos on her arms. Look real, not fake."

"What kind of tattoos?" he asked. "Tribal? Portraits? Japanese? Black and gray or color? Professional or the kind done in prison?"

"Like the old ones sailors used to get," Cunningham said.

Koenig thought she meant traditional tattoos. Bold black lines and bright primary colors. Lots of anchors and women wearing oyster-shell bikinis. Roses and playing cards. They'd gone out of fashion in the 1950s but had seen a surge in popularity recently. Retro.

"Are they covering scars?"

"Not that I saw."

"Anything else?"

"A brown birthmark." She touched her left cheek. Pushed her fingers up to her temple to show where it was. "It's gross, like someone's flung mud at her face. Shaped like Italy. Didn't seem self-conscious about it, though. Guess no one was gonna laugh at her. Not twice, anyway." She paused. "I know it's Hobbs who does the wet work, but that Harper Nash was scary as hell. A real psycho. When you find her, look in her eyes and tell me I'm wrong."

"That bad?"

"When I was a kid, I wanted to be an artist," Cunningham said. "Problem was I couldn't draw for shit. I kinda fell into the NYPD. They were recruiting and I didn't have a job. But that girl . . . you just know killing people is what she's always wanted to do."

"If you do what you love for a living, you'll never work a day in your life?"

"Exactly."

"How do people make contact with them?"

"They don't. Strictly by referral. And if you think they'll accept one now, you must be stupider than you look. They'll know we've been picked up, and they'll assume we'll be looking for things to trade. Anyway, I heard they hadn't taken on a job in two years. Big contract."

Draper and Koenig exchanged a glance. Carlyle looked worried. Margaret yawned. It ended with a small hiccup.

"OK," Koenig said. "How do *you* make contact with them?"

"We had set times. Two of us would go to a bar and wait."

"Which bar?"

"It changed, but it was always here."

"New York?"

"Well, it ain't in the MDC. Of course New York."

"Talk me through it."

"We'd sit in a bar that was set the last time. Someone would come by our booth and drop us a note telling us where the new bar was."

"Why the subterfuge?"

"We were cops, they were contract killers. I assume they wanted to make sure it wasn't a trap."

Koenig nodded. Hobbs and Nash were right to be cautious. Corrupt cops couldn't be trusted. It was kind of the point.

"But?" Koenig said.

"But what?"

"The East Coast Sweeney operated for years without anyone knowing they existed. You were bad fiction."

"Yet here I am."

"You got greedy," Koenig said. "Saw an easy payday and moved before you'd done your research. Most of the time you'd have been even more careful than Hobbs and Nash. And that means, despite what they thought, you were controlling the meeting, not them. You might not have known which bar it was going to be in, but that didn't matter, did it?"

Cunningham shook her head.

"Because you knew where they lived. People like you don't take chances. You can't risk it being a setup. At the very first meeting you'll have followed them home. Had them checked out. Maybe even surveilled them for a while. Made sure they were who they claimed to be. That about right?"

"Who the hell are you?"

"Answer the question," the AG said.

"We followed them home," Cunningham admitted. "Watched them for a few weeks. Saw him walking that cat of his."

"He has a cat?"

Cunningham nodded. "One of those creepy-ass breeds. Bald as an egg. More wrinkles than Yoda. He follows it around the block on a leash. Looks like he's taking his balls for a walk."

"Where do they live?" Draper asked.

Cunningham told them.

"Well, isn't that handy," Koenig said.

CHAPTER 74

Koenig enjoyed stakeouts. Always had. Which was just as well as he'd been on thousands. He'd always considered a good stakeout mentality to be the single most important attribute a SOG marshal could have. The kind of perps they'd hunted were rarely at home waiting to be arrested. They dodged and they dived and they hid. But, with few exceptions, they eventually visited their old haunts. Their mom, their girlfriend or boyfriend, wife or husband. The family dog. Their bookie or their local bar. Koenig had even staked out one guy's favorite wet-shave joint. Waited for him to tire of his stubble. Which he did. Still had shaving cream on his face when Koenig had led him out in cuffs. Stakeouts took patience. They took discipline. Getting bored doing something boring wasn't an option. Falling asleep wasn't an option. Drinking so much coffee you constantly needed the bathroom wasn't an option.

But Koenig enjoyed them. He'd found a way to concentrate while his mind wandered. He'd pondered the big things in life. Like how much honey would cost if bees were paid minimum wage—190,000 bucks a jar the last time he'd checked. Or what he'd wear on HD 189733 b, an exoplanet that rained molten glass. Probably a thick overcoat. Maybe a hat.

And he could let his mind wander like this while he was in a freezing loft, rats crawling over his feet and legs, with his eyes fixed to a pair of tactical binoculars.

Zen.

He wasn't going to enjoy this stakeout, though.

Not one bit. Surveillance was a team effort. Had to be. It could go on for weeks or months. Years even. But there was no team here. Just the four of them. And they didn't know what Hobbs and Nash looked like. All they had were the descriptions Cunningham had given them. Nash had a birthmark on her face and tattoos on her arms. There was nothing distinctive about Hobbs. Cunningham had pressed that point. Like his anonymity was remarkable.

To make matters worse, the address Cunningham had given them was a converted warehouse on the intersection of the Lower East Side, Chinatown, and SoHo. It was a busy, bustling part of New York. Packed sidewalks during the day. Bars and restaurants and bodegas after lights-out.

There was nowhere to set up indoor surveillance. Not without being noticed. Not without people talking. Talk that Hobbs and Nash would no doubt be tuned in to.

That left *outdoor* surveillance. In New York that meant hiding in plain sight. To stay near the target building they needed a reason to be on the sidewalk for extended periods of time. A plausible one. To be a rock in the river of commuters. In this part of the Lower East Side there wasn't a lot of choice. The homeless and professional-beggar guises, both of which Koenig had used in the past, wouldn't work in this neighborhood. The NYPD moved them on. Handing out flyers for the nearby clubs and bars would work, but only at night. They needed to be on the sidewalk at all hours.

"You're still set against bringing in Smerconish?" Draper had said. "We could have eyes and ears inside their apartment within two hours. Commandeer every camera in a ten-block radius."

"Nothing's changed," he'd replied. "Someone sent a kill squad to that airstrip, and that means your pilot's flight plan was hacked. And Smerconish was one of a handful of people who knew we were in the UK at all. So, no, we'll use him only when we have absolutely no choice."

"I have an idea then."

"I'm not doing it," Koenig had replied.

"I haven't told you what it is yet."

"You don't have to, you're smiling."

"You are smiling, dear," Margaret had chipped in.

Draper explained her idea.

And after much complaining, Koenig eventually sighed and said, "Fine."

He couldn't see any other way.

CHAPTER 75

Draper had paid cash for a room in a hotel two blocks away. Nothing flash, but it had twin beds and a hot shower. They would use it as a base. Somewhere to rest.

"Ready?" Draper asked.

Koenig scowled at the human billboard leaning against the bathroom door. It was going to be as humiliating as he'd feared. But Draper was right. When it came to hiding in plain sight, it was the perfect disguise. It was absurd, but it would make him invisible. Human-billboard guys were out in the street at all hours. They were never moved on. And no one looked at their faces. You didn't want to catch their eye. You didn't want to see their "how did it come to this?" look.

With Chinatown a block over, Koenig had taken a job with Gurkha Spicy, an up-and-coming Nepalese restaurant. Thirty bucks a day, cash in hand. The front board promoted Gurkha Spicy's lunchtime special; the back board was their full evening menu. Koenig slipped the billboard over his shoulders and adjusted the straps until they fit tight and snug.

Draper said, "I'm hungry."

"Funny," Koenig said.

"Quit pouting. We'll take turns. You take the first shift, then I'll take over."

"You can't. It pains me to say this, but you're a good-looking woman. If you wear this, people are going to wonder why. They're going to stare."

"I can do a shift," Carlyle said.

"No," Koenig and Draper said together.

"We need you safe and out of the way," Draper explained. "Same goes for you, Margaret."

"I didn't offer, dear."

"It's just me then," Koenig said.

"Looks like it," Draper said. "But there's a bar on their block. If I can get a window seat, I'll have a decent view of their apartment and sidewalk. I'll do the night shift from there. Let you come back here for some rest."

"You'll get hit on all night."

"Let me worry about that. Anyway, it'll help me blend in. We'll figure something out for the small hours."

Koenig didn't like it, but he was out of options. "What do we know about their address?" he said.

"They have the loft apartment. Registered to an offshore company. My guys will run it down, but it'll take time."

"Schematics?"

"Four floors. Two apartments on floors one to three. Just the loft on the fourth. There's an old elevator—a converted manual—and switchback stairs if you prefer the cardio."

Koenig nodded. Switchback stairs were split-level, U-shaped staircases with two flights per floor, facing 180 degrees from each other with a small landing platform in between. They saved space compared with more sweeping staircases.

"Fire escape?" he asked.

"Wrought iron. External. We won't need to cover it, though; it goes down into the alleyway, and that comes out on the same sidewalk we'll be on."

"We'll check it out anyway," he said.

The alley was clean by New York standards, but it was still an alley. It wasn't a thoroughfare. You couldn't walk into it and come out at the other end. It was closed. And that meant trash and city debris had nowhere to go. Once it was in, it stayed in. Swirling and dancing in the air, obeying the laws of aerodynamics. The alley was wide enough for a horse and cart but not a modern garbage truck. It was why the dumpsters were nearer the entrance than the back wall. If every dumpster in New York had to be dragged thirty yards to get emptied, the city would grind to a halt.

The alley separated two converted warehouses. The fire escape was the usual iron structure. A sharp-edged urban jungle gym. Ugly and clunky. Put up to comply with industrial building code with no thought to aesthetics. It clung to the bricks like metal ivy, fixed there by rusty iron bolts.

Satisfied the alley held no surprises, Koenig rejoined Draper on the side-walk.

"Can you see the alley entrance from the bar?" he asked.

"I think so."

"OK, I'll do from now until around ten p.m. You take over while I get some sleep, and when the bar closes, we'll do walk-pasts until the morning. It's the best we can do." He paused. "But I hope these morons don't take too long. I already feel like an idiot."

PART THREE

OUT OF LEFT FIELD

CHAPTER 76

While Koenig prowled the Lower East Side, Chinatown, and SoHo, Jakob Tas, Cora Pearl, and Konstantin were doing some prowling of their own. They were in New Silloth, a fishing village in Maine. It had a thriving arts community, but the tourists hadn't yet found it. Not in the kind of numbers that turned villages into amusement parks. New Silloth's primary source of income was still the lobster and haddock they pulled out of the gin-clear water, not ice cream and "I ♥ Maine" T-shirts.

They'd just eaten fried-haddock sandwiches, extra pickle, extra tartar, in a café that stayed open for the whiting and cod fishermen. One cold beer each. The fish was delicious, caught that morning and perfectly cooked, but Tas hadn't enjoyed his. He was anxious, and his meal wasn't sitting right. It was heavy in his stomach. Like cement.

Or a tumor.

Which was ironic, he thought. It was a tumor that had started all this. Lit the blue touchpaper. And it was the tumor that made him uniquely qualified for this job. His *last* job. He winced. Thinking about what was in his stomach made him think about the pain. It was back. The last of the fentanyl had leached from the patch on his arm. He had two patches left but didn't want to use a fresh one yet. They made him drowsy, and this was a critical part of the operation. He needed to be alert for the boat.

Except there was no boat. It was late. It was late and he didn't know why.

If there was a problem, the Australian was supposed to call. Tas checked his cell again. Made sure he had a signal.

"Don't worry, boss," Pearl said. "He'll be here."

Tas frowned. He didn't like relying on others at the best of times. The Australian had come highly recommended, but Tas hadn't worked with him before. He was untested. And until proven otherwise, untested meant unreliable. But nor did he like looking weak. And he'd caught Pearl sneaking glances lately. Like she knew there was something wrong. Maybe she'd seen the patch. She'd only ever looked at him with fear. Now he thought he could see pity. He didn't like that either.

He slipped his phone back in his pocket. "Let's get some fresh air," he said.

Konstantin and Pearl finished their beers while he paid the check. He left a large tip. Large enough to be remembered.

As soon as they were away from the lights of the café, he grabbed Pearl by her hair. Pulled her head back and pressed a punch-dagger into the soft part of her lower jaw. He pressed until he drew blood. The punch-dagger was short-bladed with a T-shaped handle, designed to be held in a closed fist with the blade protruding between the middle and ring fingers. When it wasn't being used, it was concealed in his belt buckle. A custom job, not off the shelf. Good enough to fool airport security. Tas kept it sharper than an obsidian scalpel.

"Do I look worried, Cora?" he said quietly.

She gulped. Carefully. "No, Jakob," she whispered.

"Then why did you tell me to stop? Are you giving orders now?"

Pearl recognized a rhetorical question when she heard one. She didn't respond.

"What about you, Konstantin? Do *you* think I look worried?"

Konstantin, who rarely spoke, was saved when Tas's cell rang.

The punch-dagger was out of Pearl's throat and into Tas's belt buckle faster than the eye could see. It fitted with a barely audible *snick*. Tas grabbed his cell and pressed the answer icon.

"Yes?" he said. The Australian talked. Tas listened. He ended the call and said, "ETA thirty minutes. Apparently, he had to cut his speed. The engine prop was vibrating, whatever that means."

Pearl had grown up near the ocean. She knew what a vibrating engine prop meant, but she wasn't saying. Not while blood dripped from her chin.

She had seen Tas kill people for talking back. Instead, she said, "He couldn't let us know?"

Tas ignored her. He checked his watch. "I want the truck here in exactly twenty minutes."

Tas had chosen New Silloth because it was a working fishing village. It had a slipway big enough to haul trawlers out of the sea. More than big enough for the truck. Tas heard it before he saw the lights. A low rumble, like a sleeping bear.

Pearl rounded the corner in the truck, then reversed down the slipway. The commercial boat trailer she towed was fully submergible. She backed up until only the bow stop and winch were above the water. She put the truck in park and waited.

Tas ignored the truck and stared out to sea. He didn't look away until he could see the boat's tricolored mast headlight, the single fixture that did the work of the port, starboard, and stern lights. Garish, but commonplace in a village like New Silloth.

The Australian turned on the dock LEDs and slowed the boat. By the time he nudged up against the trailer's bow stop, he'd all but stopped. He leaped onto the bow, reached down for the trailer winch, and hooked it on to the tow eye. He turned the winch handle until the boat was pressed tight against the bow stop, then attached the safety latch. With the boat secure, he raised the engines so the propellers wouldn't catch on the slipway. Judging by the scars on the concrete, not everyone remembered. Pearl put the truck in drive and slowly hauled the trailer and boat out of the water. The NorseBoat stank of the ocean it had been pulled from.

The Australian banged the side of the cab while the trailer was still on the inclined slipway. The truck stopped. The Australian grabbed a wrench from his tool bag and walked to the stern of the NorseBoat.

"What are you doing?" Tas asked. He needed to be seen, but he also needed to be on the road before the town woke up.

"Removing the drain plug," the Australian explained. "Gets the water out of the bilge."

He was a fleshy man. Had an accent like that asshole from *Crocodile Dundee*. The one with the stupid knife. He had sun-bleached hair. A dimple in his chin that looked like a butt crack. And he only had one ear. He'd definitely had two when Tas had hired him. He'd counted them.

"What happened to your ear?" Tas said.

"What?" the Australian replied.

A man wandered out of the shadows. He was carrying a bait box and three fishing rods. He was bowlegged and walked like a croquet hoop. He had a wind-beaten face and calloused hands. If you cut him in half, you'd see the word "local."

"Fine-looking boat," the man said.

Konstantin glanced at Tas. He ran a finger across his throat. Tas shook his head. It was important he gave them someplace to start looking for him, but he wanted to leave breadcrumbs, not bodies.

"Not mine," Tas said. "Belongs to the person I work for."

"Ain't it the way," the man said. "Working stiffs do the work, the boss gets the boat. But hey, I bet he hardly uses it. I reckon you guys have got a bit of fishing done, though. Am I right? Take it out for a test drive. Make sure everything's working right. Maybe take some beers and some live bait at the same time. What he don't know don't hurt him. Am I right? Shame to see a girl like this tied up all year."

Tas smiled. "Well . . ." he said. "We *did* land a couple of swordfish last year."

The man whooped. He put down his bait box and high-fived Tas and Konstantin. Konstantin didn't know whether to smile or set him on fire. He went for a smile. It looked like he was laying an egg. Smiling didn't come naturally to Konstantin. Not unless he was holding his chain saw.

"What's up with her?" the bowlegged man said, pointing at the Norse-Boat. "We have fine marine engineers around here. Boys who piss seawater and crap oysters."

"She's getting a refit over in Denver," Tas said. "Then the owner wants to spend some time in the Pacific. Think it's got too cold for him around here."

"The Pacific," the man sneered. "What a pussy. The Atlantic's the only real ocean. A *man's* ocean. Any ocean you can fish while wearing a grass skirt ain't no ocean. Am I right?"

Tas offered him his hand. It acted like a full stop on the conversation. "We need to get going," he said. "Good fishing, my friend."

The bowlegged man trundled off. Tas waited, hoping he would slink into the darkness, then turn to watch them leave. The man did exactly that. He thought the shadows hid him. They didn't. The shadows were where Tas lived. He knew when they didn't look right.

"Cells," he said.

Konstantin and the Australian handed Tas their cell phones. Pearl threw hers out of the cab window. Tas made a show of removing the SIM cards and bending them in half. He did the same with his own cell. He walked to the end of the town's pier and dropped everything in the sea.

Breadcrumbs.

Tas had other cell phones, but he was glad to be rid of this one. The connection between him and Stillwell Hobbs was finally severed.

He wiped away the sweat that had beaded on his forehead and thought about his next fentanyl patch. He'd slap one on as soon as they were on the road.

They had a long journey ahead of them.

CHAPTER 77

FOUR DAYS LATER.

New York embodied America's past, present, and future. That's what Koenig thought. The city's history was in plain sight, and it was hidden. No doubt some of it was still to be discovered. Parts seemed utopian in their ambition and vision. They filled him with hope. Other parts were bleak. More *Blade Runner* than *Metropolis*. Run-down and driven by crime and despair. Rudy Giuliani's "broken windows" policy hadn't cleaned up the city. Not really. All it had done was push the undesirable to the fringes. Or force them into wearing suits and neckties. Play the game properly.

Koenig was sure he'd met most of these suit-wearing undesirables in the four days he'd spent around the intersection of the Lower East Side, Chinatown, and SoHo. And that's because the human billboard promoting Gurkha Spicy, New York's premier Nepalese restaurant, was an asshole magnet. People seemed to think it was fine to treat human billboards as less than human. They sneered and they hurled insults. He was there for anyone trying to impress a date, and he was a punching bag for the bad-tempered and the angry. If he'd heard "Get a real job, asshole" once, he'd heard it a hundred times. It was very disappointing.

But other than that, the surveillance had gone exactly as he'd expected: a whole load of nothing. No sign of Hobbs or his daughter. Just assholes being assholey. But that was surveillance. Boring as hell until it wasn't.

Koenig and Draper had settled into an easy routine. He would collect his sandwich board and patrol the sidewalk opposite Stillwell Hobbs's apartment.

He started around 9 a.m. and kept going until mid-afternoon. Draper would then relieve him by taking a window seat in the bar on the street corner. Koenig would grab something to eat and check in with Carlyle and Margaret. Margaret was usually asleep. Carlyle spent her time on the internet. She wouldn't say what she was looking for.

After an hour, Koenig would head back out and spend the rest of the evening on the street. Draper would relieve him at ten p.m. Ten p.m. was the last sitting at Gurkha Spicy, and a suspicious person might wonder why he was still promoting something they couldn't have. And Koenig knew Hobbs would be suspicious. It was the only way he and his daughter could have practiced their trade for so long.

Depending on who was in, the bar closed between three and four in the morning. Koenig had assumed he and Draper would have to improvise some mobile surveillance, walking past every thirty minutes or so. It would have been imperfect, and susceptible to rudimentary countersurveillance moves, but it was all they had. In the end, though, there'd been no need. A Korean-run bodega wedged between two apartment blocks opened when the bar shut. Within minutes it was full of happy barflies eating hot and spicy rice cakes, twisted doughnuts, and mung bean pancakes. Draper simply switched one seat for another. She sat on a stool by the window, drank coffee. Chatted to the bar's regulars and Mr. Sun, the bodega's owner. Within a day she was on first-name terms with twenty people, and Koenig was reminded that Draper was ex-CIA. Infiltrating groups was second nature.

At 9 a.m. Draper would say goodbye to Mr. Sun, and Koenig would take over.

It was working well.

Until it wasn't.

CHAPTER 78

Koenig was taking a break. He had removed his sandwich board and was eating takeout *chasa momo*, Himalayan-style chicken dumplings, on the stoop of a brownstone. He'd gotten them from Gurkha Spicy. Free. Perks of the job. They were delicious. Just the right amount of chili heat. The dumplings had come with a fortune cookie. It said, "Enjoy yourself while you can," which Koenig thought sounded more threatening than inspirational.

When he saw the three men, he thought "Enjoy yourself while you can" was the kind of thing they might say. It was early evening and they were drunk. Not falling-over drunk, but they'd clearly been drinking all afternoon. Probably had a successful morning doing whatever it was men like them did on Wall Street. Government-approved theft. They wore fitted suits and pink shirts, like a uniform for douchebags. They were glassy-eyed and sweating. People were crossing the street to avoid them.

They were heading directly for him.

The middle one, a squabby man with fat hands, grinned, but it was nasty and mean. He nudged the others and nodded in Koenig's direction. They spread out and sped up. Their intention couldn't have been clearer if they'd been wearing *Bumfights* T-shirts.

Koenig was carrying his Fairbairn-Sykes and his SIG. He wouldn't need them. These idiots were softer than pudding. He wiped the grease off his hands with a paper napkin. Rolled his shoulders. Mentally rehearsed his first move.

Crushing the squabby man's nose with a headbutt seemed the right thing to do. Put him on the ground, see what the others were made of.

Which was when they saw the girl.

She was a waif of a thing, as thin as a heron's leg. About five nine with short black hair. She was on the other side of the street and looked like she was heading home after a day's work. Her head was down and she wore wireless headphones. She walked gracefully, like a ballerina.

The change in the men's demeanor was immediate. They looked like a cackle of hyenas that had stumbled upon a limping wildebeest. As one they crossed the road. A cab screeched to a halt, but they ignored it.

The girl didn't notice. She was near the alley by Stillwell Hobbs's apartment, the one Koenig had worried they didn't have eyes on. They were going to reach her before he could. If they got her into the alley, by the time he arrived, she'd already have been through something horrific.

Koenig started to run but knew he wouldn't make it. By the time he'd crossed the street, the men had already reached the girl. The squabby one dragged her into the alley. One of the others pulled two of the dumpsters together and blocked the alley entrance.

Koenig put his head down and sprinted even harder.

CHAPTER 79

A minute wasn't a long time. Sixty seconds. Not long enough to read a page in a book. Or boil an egg. Wasn't even long enough to watch "Fresh Guacamole," the shortest film ever nominated for an Oscar.

But for someone being sexually assaulted, a minute is a lifetime.

Koenig reached the alley at a run. He yanked the dumpster away from the entrance. He blinked in surprise. He didn't see what he'd expected. He'd expected to see three bare-assed men. Men who were about to add rape to their résumé. "Consensual intercourse," their high-priced attorneys would no doubt call it. He'd expected them to turn around and look sheepish for a moment. Then bullish and indignant as self-preservation kicked in.

But that wasn't what Koenig saw.

Instead, he saw three men lying on the oil-stained concrete, blood pooling by their heads. The squabby man was clutching his throat and gurgling. The other two weren't making any sound at all.

The girl looked unharmed and unworried. Her left hand was wet with blood. Koenig could see a ring on her index finger. It had a hooked bevel tip that looked like a raptor's beak. They were called single-point self-defense rings, and they were weapons designed to be worn as everyday jewelry. In the right hands, they were deadly. It seemed like the girl had the right hands. She'd torn out her would-be assailants' throats like she were a werewolf.

"Who are you?" she said.

"My name's Ben," Koenig said. "I saw them drag you into the alley. I came to help."

"Thanks," the girl said.

"You're welcome."

Koenig then took his SIG from his jacket pocket and shot her in the ankle. She screamed and collapsed on top of the gurgling man. Koenig hurried over. The girl reached for her bag. Koenig kicked it away, then stomped on her hands. He bent down and studied the birthmark on her face.

It *did* look like Italy.

"Hello, Harper," he said. "Where's your dad?"

CHAPTER 80

Draper skidded around the corner as if she were in a Tom and Jerry cartoon. She took in the scene in a single glance.

"Jesus, what happened to them?" she asked, gesturing toward the men on the ground. The squabby man had stopped gurgling.

"She did," Koenig replied.

"And who's . . . ?" It took a beat for it to register. "That's Nash."

"It is."

"Why'd she kill them?"

"They were about to rape her."

"Boy, talk about picking on the wrong psychopath. You shot her?"

"Broke her fingers too."

Draper nodded in approval. "We'd better move her before the NYPD arrive. Her being unconscious is useful. We'll pretend she's passed-out drunk and we're helping her back to her apartment."

"She's not going to talk," Draper said to Koenig. "Look at her. She should be scared, but she's not."

Draper was right. Nash *didn't* look scared. She was in pain, but other than that, it seemed like having a bullet in her ankle and a bunch of broken fingers was an inconvenience. Other than saying Stillwell Hobbs was still away on business, she hadn't said a thing.

Nash was an odd-looking contract killer. With her ripped jeans, short spiky hair, and colorful tattoos, she looked like she'd be more at home in a second-hand record shop. Flicking through the crates for rare Black Sabbath LPs. She certainly didn't look like the kind of girl who could rip the throats out of three men in less than a minute. Until you looked into her eyes. They were deader than leather. And they missed nothing. Koenig could see how she was actively checking they hadn't made mistakes with her restraints. How she ignored the pain she must have been feeling and was testing them by flexing the muscles in her forearms and legs.

"Smerconish has people who'll make her talk, though," Draper continued softly.

"People like you?"

"Worse than me, Koenig. Much, much worse."

It looked like it had been a difficult thing for her to admit. Koenig wished he'd not said anything.

They were in the apartment Nash shared with her father. They'd carried her from the alley like she was a deadbeat drunk, through the front door and into the small lobby. They waited for the elderly elevator to clunk and bang its way to the first floor. They saw no one, which had been a relief as the blood from Nash's ankle had puddled on the tiled floor. Koenig used the rest of his paper napkins to mop it up.

When Nash was secure, Koenig went back down to the alley and hid the three dead men in the dumpsters. Covered their corpses with garbage. Kicked dust over the blood. A rush job, but the best he could do. He then collected Carlyle and Margaret. By the time he returned, Draper had packed and patched Nash's bullet wound and taped her broken fingers together. It was agricultural, but better than nothing. Professional medical attention would have to wait.

The loft apartment was modern and minimalist. Sterile. In direct contrast to Koenig's old townhouse, which had been a riot of movie posters, albums, DVDs, and books, it was fifty shades of black and white. Like you were inside a crossword puzzle. Just what a man with a phobia of the color yellow needed, Koenig imagined. The most colorful thing in the loft was Nash's blood. And even that was turning black. The loft had two bedrooms, a home office, some closets, a kitchen area, and a sunken living room. Probably cost over a million bucks.

Carlyle was in the sunken living room, scrolling through a laptop she'd found. She was deep-diving into C-SPAN, Reuters, and the BBC. She didn't look happy. Margaret was resting in Hobbs's bedroom. Koenig went to check on her. She was lying down but awake. Didn't seem to be in too much pain.

"Can I get you anything?" he asked.

"A cup of tea would be nice, dear." She reached into her handbag and pulled out some tea bags. "Like your American Express, never leave home without it."

"I'll rustle one up."

"Boiling water please, dear. A little milk. The way you Americans make tea is sacrilegious."

"Margaret wants a drink," Koenig said to Draper when he returned to the living area. "You want anything?"

"I could use a soda," Draper replied. "Better get some water for this asshole. She's lost a lot of blood."

The refrigerator was stainless steel and taller than Koenig. It had an ice dispenser and double doors. Expensive. He opened the door on the left, looked inside. He closed it and opened the other. There was nothing in the refrigerator apart from a six-pack of Classic Coke. Full fat, not diet. The iconic "hobble skirt" bottle. The one Andy Warhol came up with when he wanted a shape to represent mass culture. So distinctive it could be identified when shattered on the ground. But that was all there was in there. No cheese. No cooked meats. No milk. Nothing perishable. Just the Coke. He frowned and checked the cupboards. He then picked up his SIG and press-checked. Pulled the working parts back a fraction to make sure there was a round in the chamber. Instinctive.

"Gag Nash," he said. "Hobbs will be here soon."

Draper didn't hesitate. She ripped off a strip of the duct tape and covered Nash's mouth. Tugged it to make sure it was on tight. Koenig got the impression she'd done that before. Draper collected her own SIG and said, "How'd you know?"

"The refrigerator's empty bar a six-pack of Coke," he said. "Nothing in the cupboards either. They haven't been home for days, and there's no food in the apartment. Only cat chow."

Cunningham had mentioned Hobbs doted on his cat, and the chow was the gourmet stuff. Line-caught Scottish salmon. Air-dried lamb. Herring and orange. No horsemeat in sight.

"Hobbs must be getting takeout. Nash probably came home to put the oven on. Maybe warm the plates. Or maybe she doesn't like waiting in line."

Nash rolled her eyes. Like she was embarrassed by him.

"There's definitely no blood on the lobby floor?" Draper asked.

"I got most of it. Not enough to fool the *CSI: Miami* guys, but there's nothing to see with the naked eye." He turned to Carlyle. "Can you join Margaret, please, Bess?"

Carlyle obviously understood the problems with an overcrowded room. She picked up the laptop and left the living area. Without saying anything, Koenig and Draper took up tactical positions. Draper got on the floor with a line of sight straight down the hallway. Koenig stood behind the apartment door and kept his eye glued to the peephole. When Hobbs arrived, he would step to the side and allow him to enter the apartment. With luck, Koenig could take him unawares. If he was cautious and didn't step over the apartment threshold, Draper would shoot out his knees. They'd done this a hundred times when they were with the Special Operations Group. Apart from the shooting-out-the-knees bit.

Koenig needn't have worried. He heard Hobbs before he saw him. He was holding two takeout bags. He put them down while he got his keys. Koenig stood to the side. The door opened and Hobbs entered his apartment.

"How's Chairman Meow, honey?" he said, closing the door with his foot. "Did Mrs. Benowitz give him his medicine? And I hope the fryer's on—I've bought enough tempura to feed the imperial court."

"Yum," Koenig said, stepping out behind him and crunching the SIG onto the back of his head.

CHAPTER 81

Hobbs had a head wound. It was bleeding heavily, even more than the bullet hole in Nash's ankle. Koenig had cracked him on the skull way harder than he'd intended. Although in his defense, he explained, Hobbs was a dangerous man.

"It's not *much* of a defense," Draper said. "Look at him."

She had a point. Hobbs was round-jawed and droopy-eyed. He had male-pattern baldness and a stooped neck. The bad teeth that Cunningham had mentioned looked like popcorn. In direct contrast to his punky daughter, Hobbs wore a three-piece suit. Turd brown. He looked like the kind of person who clapped when the plane landed. Cunningham had been right; he was kinda breathtaking in his blandness.

"I can't get the bleeding to stop," Carlyle said, discarding a sodden kitchen towel and pressing a fresh one to Hobbs's head wound.

"There's some superglue under the sink," Koenig said. "I'll get it." It was in a box of miscellaneous crap. The kind of stuff that didn't naturally belong in any one room. He unscrewed the top, pierced the foil cap, and said, "Ready?"

Carlyle nodded. She pinched the wound together while Koenig drizzled a generous glob all along his handiwork. Simple, but effective. Superglue was used to stop bleeding in Vietnam. Saved a lot of lives. The FDA didn't approve it stateside, due to its unknown toxicity and because the exothermic reaction could cause tissue damage.

Hobbs's eyes fluttered open. He took in his surroundings in silence. It wasn't until he glanced to his left and saw his daughter on the stool next to him that he groaned.

Koenig sidled over to Draper. "You're the interrogation expert," he whispered into her ear. "How do you want to play this?"

"Do we have a carrot?"

He considered it for a couple of beats. Decided they didn't. "Nothing I can think of."

"Stick it is."

"Unless not using the stick *is* the carrot."

"In my experience, that never works. But go for it."

"You have information we need," Koenig said to Hobbs. "Unfortunately, there is no way for you to pass on this information without confirming what we already know: that you and your daughter are high-end contract killers."

"I have no idea what you're talking about, Mr. . . . ?"

"Koenig. My name is Ben Koenig."

Which at least got a reaction, even if it was just a widening of the eyes.

"The fact you've heard of me confirms you are who we think you are," Koenig said. "And even if you hadn't, your friends in the East Coast Sweeney gave you up. Here's what's going to hap—"

"If you think we're killers for hire, search our apartment." He smiled, some of his swagger back. "I assure you, there are no weapons here. No incriminating evidence. And in case you're recording this, that's because my daughter and I have committed no crimes. I've never had so much as a parking ticket." He took an exaggerated pause. "But you're going to prison for a long time. All of you. Someone shot my daughter. Broke her fingers. Struck me on the head with a weapon. That's aggravated battery times three. You tied us up. That's abduction. We're respected members of the community. I'm a businessman. My daughter's a businesswoman. We're not killers."

"She is," Koenig said, pointing at Nash. "She killed three men not thirty minutes ago."

"You did?" Hobbs said to his daughter. "Why?"

Nash shrugged. "They put their hands on me."

Hobbs's lips tightened. His breathing sped up. The tips of his nostrils whitened. "Then there's not a court in the—"

"Exactly what *is* your business, Mr. Hobbs?" Draper cut in.

"Excuse me?"

"You claim you and Miss Nash are in business. If it's not murder for hire, what is it?"

"That's confidential."

"It must be lucrative," Draper said. "This is an expensive apartment."

Hobbs snorted. Didn't bother hiding his contempt. This was getting them nowhere, Koenig thought. He needed Hobbs to understand he wasn't in Kansas anymore. "Can I have a word?" he said to Draper.

They moved to the hall. Stood by the front door, out of earshot. Not out of sight, though. Hobbs and Nash were too dangerous for that.

"I need you to do something."

"What?"

Koenig didn't answer. He didn't need to. The realization of what he was asking hit Draper like a sledgehammer.

"You've got to be fucking kidding!" she snapped. "All the shit you give me, and now, when it's something *you* need, all of a sudden it's OK."

"It's not OK," he said. "It's never OK. But it has to be done and it has to be you. Nash looks like she doesn't have a care in the world, and we have to assume that Hobbs's appearance is a carefully cultivated disguise. That underneath his shit-brown suit, he wears a second skin, one that's just as insane as his daughter's. We need something more nuanced than no-frills pain."

"Don't ask me to do this, Koenig," she said. "I'm not sure I'll get over it again. I witnessed this and *did* nothing. I did this and *said* nothing. There must be another way."

"I'm all ears."

Draper said nothing. Eventually she slumped, like an inflatable tube man with a puncture. After a few more moments, she said, "Which one?"

"Her," he replied. "Definitely her. He's thinking like a parent right now, not a killer."

"OK, Koenig," she said. Her spine stiffened. Her face grew hard, her eyes distant. Koenig wondered how many people had seen that expression before. And how many had seen it and wished they hadn't. "But if we're doing this, we're doing it properly. That means I talk, you don't. There's only one interrogator, and that's me. You'll do what I say, when I say it. No exceptions. It doesn't matter if they want to talk. This isn't just a case of threatening his daughter; he needs to believe we'll kill her. That means I'll have to hurt her. Are you OK with this?"

Koenig wasn't. But he nodded anyway.

They walked back into the living area.

"I hope the pair of you are insured for water damage," Draper said. "Things are about to get very wet."

CHAPTER 82

In 1947 the United States charged Yukio Asano, a Japanese officer, with war crimes for waterboarding a US citizen. Sixty years later it was official US policy. Which was five hundred years after it had been the official policy of the Inquisitors. Spain's Tribunal of the Holy Office of the Inquisition used the "water cure," under strictly controlled conditions, when all other methods of getting a confession had failed. It polarized Spaniards in the fifteenth century just as it polarizes Americans now.

Its champions claim that compared with what the myriad enemies of the US are prepared to do, waterboarding is a mild inconvenience. It's a high-intensity, kinetic interrogation, but it leaves the detainee unmarked and undamaged. It's as effective at extracting information as electric shocks, amputations, and burning.

To its detractors, waterboarding is torture. There is no gray area. It's controlled drowning, and it opens a door that cannot be closed. It's also an ineffective vengeance-based fantasy, as likely to extract junk information as anything useable. They point to a Cambodian man who was tortured by the Khmer Rouge. During his interrogation he confessed to being a Catholic bishop, a CIA spy, a Buddhist monk, the son of the king of Cambodia, and a hermaphrodite. He was actually a schoolteacher who happened to speak French. Their point is that people will say anything to make torture stop. A more practical argument is that if the US allows waterboarding, it can't complain when other regimes use it on captive US citizens.

Koenig fell somewhere in the middle. There were two sides to the argument, and he didn't trust the people who refused to acknowledge that. He'd been through waterboarding when he'd undertaken Survival, Evasion, Resistance, and Escape training with Marine Recon. All US special forces go through SERE. It's worst-case scenario training, and he'd gotten himself added to one of the programs. And the one thing he'd taken from his time in the chair was that waterboarding was torture. Even for someone who couldn't experience fear, it was a horrific experience. It didn't simulate drowning; you *were* drowning. Waterboarding was torture and torture was wrong. It was immoral and it spat out information that couldn't be trusted. It had to be verified. And if you had the capabilities to verify information, why bother using torture in the first place?

But on incredibly rare occasions, time simply didn't permit anything else. The threat was imminent, and the fallout so catastrophic that to do nothing was to be complicit.

They carried Nash, still strapped to the kitchen stool, to the white leather couch in the sunken living room. Draper positioned the stool so its legs were on the cushions and the back rest was on the raised arm. The stool and the couch arm formed a simple machine. The stool was the rigid beam, and the couch's arm was the fulcrum. When the time came, Koenig would lift the stool's legs, which would put Nash's feet above her head.

Nash didn't react. Not everyone did when it came to waterboarding. It was a strange kind of torture. Compared to the pliers and the blowtorches, it seemed cerebral. Like you could manage it by staying calm. That it would only work if you allowed it to work. That changed when the hypothetical met with reality. Even with a prearranged stop signal, Koenig had seen twenty-year veterans of the Marine Corps refuse to strap themselves to the board. But Nash was serene and calm.

They went back for Hobbs and turned his stool so he faced his daughter. It was as if the sunken living room were the stage and the kitchen were the dress circle. The tier above the stalls. Best seats in the house. Close enough to be immersed in the action, not so close you missed anything.

"If so much as a single hair on her head gets wet, I'll kill you," Hobbs said. His voice was flat and cold, but his eyes told a different story. They burned hot and angry. "I'll kill you all."

"I thought you weren't a killer?" Draper said.

"Don't test me on this. You have no idea what I'm capable of."

"Oh, I think we do."

"You look scared, Mr. Hobbs," Koenig said.

"If that bitch hurts my baby, you'll be looking over your shoulder for the rest of your life. You think *I'm* scared? I swear you don't know the meaning of the word."

"You're right there, Mr. Hobbs," Draper said. "He doesn't."

CHAPTER 83

"Gag him," Draper said, nodding toward Hobbs. Her voice was emotionless. Ominous, like welded razor wire.

Koenig had never met this version of Draper. This was the Draper who'd worked behind the curtains. Who knew where the black sites were. Who'd been involved in extraordinary renditions. The Draper who'd tortured enemy combatants. Koenig hated himself for forcing her to become the person she'd struggled for so long to escape.

So, Koenig did as he was asked and gagged Hobbs. Tore off a strip of duct tape and stuck it over his mouth. Smoothed it out but lifted a corner and folded it in on itself. It would make it easier to rip off. Like the crocodile tear strip on a FedEx parcel. Or a grip tab on a pack of sliced turkey. He gagged Hobbs not just because it was what Draper had ordered; he did it so he shared culpability for what was about to happen. He wanted Draper to know that if it came down to it, he'd be standing by her side when the Monday morning quarterbacks judged their course of action.

"Here's how this is going to work," Draper called out to Hobbs. "In a minute, I'm going to remove the tape from your daughter's mouth and replace it with a towel. Mr. Koenig will lift her legs so they're above her head and I will start pouring water over the towel using the two-gallon container you considerately had in your closet. Harper will keep her mouth closed, but she can't shut her nose and sinus cavities. They will quickly fill with water. Her immediate reaction will be to hold her breath. It's *everyone's* first reaction and it's quite natural. In fact, it'll be her only option. But this is a high-pressure situation, not a controlled test. In all my years doing this, I never saw anyone last more than thirty seconds. I've never *heard* of anyone lasting more than thirty seconds. Harper's gag reflex will make her expel the air from her lungs. This will clear the water from her nose, but then what? She's already held her breath. She's in an oxygen deficit. She'll do the only thing she can: She'll inhale. But she won't be inhaling air, she'll be inhaling water. This water won't stay in her mouth and nose, though. She'll suck it into her lungs. And when that happens, the simulated drowning stops and the *actual* drowning starts." She paused. "Nod if you understand."

Hobbs nodded, defeated.

"Now, you might wonder why I've gagged you," Draper continued. "The answer is simple. I'm not interested in anything you have to say. Not yet. If I ask you questions under the threat of hurting your daughter, you might be tempted to tell me a lie. Or a half-truth. Or you might think you'll get away with the sin of omission. This is why you're gagged. I'm about to hurt your daughter and I need you to understand that there is nothing you can do to stop me."

Hobbs started to buck and thrash on his stool. His eyes bulged. His scalp wound burst open. Koenig made no move to close it. He now understood why Draper was doing this the way she was. It was psyops. Psychological operations. Influencing emotion and behavior by conveying information in a certain way. Draper was in Hobbs's head now. And so far, she hadn't done anything. Koenig was impressed, the same way a stranded surfer might be impressed by how, in that moment, in that environment, the great white circling their longboard was the perfect killing machine. He'd asked her to do this, but he was still appalled.

Hobbs began to weep.

"I'm going to keep pouring the water until I decide to stop," she said. "It might be twenty seconds; it might be three minutes. I'll keep pouring the water until you're begging to tell me what we want to know. Again, nod if you understand."

Hobbs didn't this time. He seemed stunned. Like he couldn't believe what was happening. It seemed like even though he dealt in death, he'd never believed it would happen to him. That karma was for other people. Ten minutes ago, he'd been talking about tempura. Now he was tied to a stool and his daughter was about to be drowned like kittens in a sack.

"Lift her legs, please," Draper said.

Koenig didn't ask if she was sure. He lifted Nash's legs.

And Draper began to pour.

CHAPTER 84

The effect was immediate. The second the towel became waterlogged was the second she started to buck and thrash. Koenig thought that was unusual. There was normally a period, ten seconds or so, when the person being waterboarded tried to wait it out. When they thought that waterboarding wouldn't work on them.

But Nash didn't even try to hold her breath. As soon as her nose and throat filled with water, she expelled it like she'd accidentally swallowed bleach. It sounded like a whale's blowhole. Came through the towel in a fine mist. She looked at Hobbs, her eyes wider than Bambi's. Pleading.

To the untrained eye, it looked like she'd panicked. Hadn't even *considered* holding her breath. That's certainly what Hobbs thought. He was definitely panicking. He was thrashing about more than his daughter. The veins on his head were popping. He was trying to scream through his gag. Koenig didn't think Nash was panicking, though. He thought she was being pragmatic. She couldn't stop the waterboarding from happening. It wasn't in her wheelhouse. She was completely at Draper's mercy. And right now, Draper seemed fresh out. There was no safety word she could use. She couldn't tap the floor in submission. The only person who could stop the waterboarding was her father. Koenig thought that, far from panicking, she'd decided to amplify the effects. Bring her father around as quickly as possible.

Draper didn't stop, though. She kept pouring.

Now Nash had a problem. Blowing out the water in her nose and throat had left a vacuum in her lungs. They were empty. They needed to be filled. She looked at Koenig and winked. It was little more than a flutter, an almost imperceptible movement of her left eyelid. But Koenig saw it. She was letting him know that he was in on the joke. He was in on the joke and her father wasn't. It was their little secret.

After exactly ten seconds—Koenig counted them—Nash decided to take the hit. She breathed in and inhaled Draper's water. The towel clamped tight across her face. Looked like a death mask. Nash started to convulse.

And still Draper kept pouring. She kept pouring until Nash went limp and Hobbs was apoplectic.

"Your daughter is now dying, Mr. Hobbs." She said it so matter-of-factly she might as well have been telling him the clock on his microwave was two minutes fast. "Do you want me to stop?"

He frantically nodded. It looked as if he would agree to anything.

"Lift her up, Koenig," Draper said.

Koenig did. The towel fell from Nash's face and she started to spasm. Koenig thumped her back, and after a moment she expelled a load of water and snot. She took in huge rasping breaths. Then vomited. Her fear might have been exaggerated, but the drowning was real.

"Are you ready to talk?" Draper asked Hobbs. "Because I barely washed her face that time."

Koenig peeled off the gag.

"Yes!"

"So talk."

Hobbs hesitated, only for a second, but Draper was playing a zero-sum game.

"Put his gag back on, Koenig."

"Daddy!" Nash screeched. "Make them stop! Please!"

Hobbs seemed stunned, unable to process what had happened. What was still happening.

"The gag!" Draper snapped.

Koenig fixed the duct tape over Hobbs's mouth again.

"Lift her feet."

He did.

Nash winked again.

Draper placed the sodden towel over Nash's face and started to pour. The waterboarding was shorter this time but seemed much longer. Hobbs certainly thought so. He didn't struggle. Just quietly wept as he watched his daughter drown. Shoulders hunched. He was ready to talk. Everyone in the room knew it. Koenig had never seen anyone so utterly defeated.

Draper stopped pouring. Koenig lowered Nash's feet.

This time Hobbs didn't hesitate. The instant his gag was removed he screamed, "Jakob Tas!"

CHAPTER 85

The quickest way to verify the information was to split up Hobbs and Nash and ask them the same questions. They carried Nash, still secured to the kitchen stool, to the room Margaret wasn't using. They put her on the bed.

It was clearly Nash's room. It had a younger vibe than the one Margaret was resting in. Maybe too young. Like she played on being daddy's little girl. Got what she wanted that way. There were stuffed toys on a chair and Spice Girls posters on the walls. A pair of brown Dr. Martens under her dressing table. A mug with "Girl Power!" written on the side. Stained with tannin. If Koenig had gone into this bedroom blind, he'd have figured it belonged to a fifteen-year-old in the '90s.

But it wasn't *all* teddy bears and Baby Spice. There was also a complete set of first edition James Bond novels on a display shelf. A serious collection. And *Moonraker*, *The Man with the Golden Gun*, *Goldfinger*, and a couple of others had yellow spines. Probably served two purposes. The yellow would keep Hobbs out of her room. Ensured her privacy. More important, first edition Bonds were a shrewd investment. They were finite. A first edition *Casino Royale* went for over sixty thousand bucks in 2019. And unlike portable assets like gold and jewelry, books didn't attract scrutiny at international borders. Koenig doubted an underpaid and overfed customs agent would know the difference between a highly collectible *Dr. No* and a mass-produced *Live and Let Die*. Even the scholars couldn't agree. A couple of these in her hand luggage and she'd be walking around with six figures' worth of undeclared currency.

They returned to the living area. Draper leaned against the kitchen island. She studied Hobbs the same way a vivisectionist studies a squirrel monkey.

"I need to tell you two things," she said eventually. "The first is that Koenig and I don't exist. Koenig shot your daughter and I waterboarded her, but no one will look for us. We won't have to explain our actions to anyone. Koenig's a ghost, and I'm so well protected there's more chance of the president having to answer for this. Do you believe me?"

Hobbs nodded.

"The second thing is that you and Harper will need to work hard to stay alive. My default position is that I want to kill you. Now, I'm the first to admit that I've got a somewhat checkered past, but compared to you I'm a fucking saint. You and your daughter are monsters. I'd be doing the world a favor if the last thing I do today is open your throats with Koenig's knife."

This was the Jen Draper show. Koenig kept his mouth shut. He couldn't have added anything that would have scared Hobbs any more than he already was. Draper had delivered her monologue in such a casual, singsong way that her tone didn't match her message. But Koenig knew Hobbs believed her. Hell, *he* believed her. If Draper didn't get what she needed, Hobbs would die tonight. His daughter would die tonight. And then Draper would walk away.

"Here's what's going to happen," Draper said. "You're going to tell us about every job you've been hired to do in the last five years. Every single one. We decide if it's relevant, not you. We're then going to question you. And then we're going to question your daughter. If her answers don't match yours, you both die. You don't get a chance to confer, you won't be allowed to amend your answers. These are the rules of the game—do you want to play?"

"On one condition," Hobbs said. "Harper gets immunity."

Draper snorted. "This isn't the Make-a-Wish Foundation, asshole. Five minutes after we leave, some people are going to arrive. They won't be the cops and they won't be feds. They won't even tell you who they work for. You'll be transported to a place that isn't on any map, where you'll be questioned under the banner of the Patriot Act. For as long as they fucking want. Unwittingly or not, you've threatened this country's national security. You and your daughter are now enemy combatants. So, no, Mr. Hobbs—even if you know who the Zodiac Killer is, Harper is not getting immunity."

She said, "Now, why don't you start by telling me who Jakob Tas is?"

CHAPTER 86

"It's over," Carlyle said. "They don't know anything."

It was true. Although Hobbs had told them everything, it was clear he and Harper were subcontractors. Bit players. They didn't know why their targets had to die, only that they did. Jakob Tas had contacted them through a trusted intermediary, and they'd met in the bar of a Holiday Inn in North Dakota. They'd negotiated a fee, although Hobbs got the impression Tas would have agreed with whatever he'd asked for. Money didn't seem to be in short supply. Hobbs was given a burner phone and a list of people to kill. The "how" was up to them, but their deaths were to look accidental or self-inflicted. Nothing that raised suspicion. A payment of $250,000 landed in their offshore account within twenty-four hours of each death. In two years, they'd killed nineteen people. Koenig did the math: $250,000 multiplied by nineteen was $4,750,000, almost as much as he was worth to the Russians.

Carlyle checked each name against criteria known only to her and nodded every time. As the interrogation went on, her expression grew darker. She didn't know the people Hobbs and Nash had murdered, but they meant something to her anyway. She could see a pattern they couldn't.

Chuck Hiatt from Arizona had been their most recent murder. According to Hobbs, seven days ago he'd had a nasty accident. He'd fallen out of the window he was cleaning and snapped his neck. Clumsy. Hobbs and Nash had spent a week in El Cuyo, a quiet beach town on Mexico's Yucatan coast, before heading back to New York and into their waiting arms. If they'd gone straight home after the Chuck Hiatt job, things might have turned out differently.

"Who's next?" Koenig asked.

"We were done," Hobbs said. "Chuck Hiatt was the last name. It's why we had a vacation."

"I need you to call Jakob Tas," Koenig said. "Tell him you need to meet. Say there's a problem with one of the jobs. That you left evidence behind that might identify him."

"I can't. I don't have the burner anymore. Getting rid of it was a condition of the job."

"Use another phone. In fact, because you were doing as you'd been asked, you'd *have* to use a different cell."

Hobbs shook his head. "Won't work," he said. "Tas only answers numbers he recognizes."

Koenig frowned.

"What's his number?" Draper said. "I'll get my guys on it."

"It's no longer in service," Draper said, reading from her own phone. "My tech guy ran the number; it went dead four days ago. Hasn't been used since."

"*Four* days?" Koenig said. "Not seven?"

Draper checked her phone. "That's what the email says. Why?"

"Because unless Tas is better at this than me, he's made a mistake."

Carlyle looked up. Koenig saw something in her face he hadn't seen before. Hope. "He has?" she said.

"I think so," Koenig said. "Hobbs claims his last job was seven days ago. Yet Tas turned his phone off *four* days ago. That means Hobbs's last job and Tas turning off his phone are unrelated. Otherwise, he'd have gotten rid of his phone immediately after Hobbs rang. He'd have gotten rid of it seven days ago, not four. Why risk carrying it an extra three days?"

"I'm not following."

"It's something you said, Bess. You said, 'It's over.' And I think it is, just not in the way you meant it. You were referring to our search for whoever is behind this."

"I was."

"But what if Tas turned off his phone because the part of the operation when he needed to be contactable is over?"

Draper didn't respond. Carlyle looked thoughtful.

Margaret snored and woke herself up. "Sorry," she said. She stood and stretched. "I'll make a pot of tea. We've no milk so we're having it without, I'm afraid." She moved toward the kitchen area and turned on the kettle. She leaned against the counter and looked out of the window. Koenig didn't blame her. He didn't want to look at Hobbs either.

"This is an operation with several moving parts," Koenig continued. "It has to be. Hobbs and Nash have been killing seemingly unconnected civilians. Your think tank academics have been disappearing. We were attacked at a remote Scottish airfield. And right in the middle is the mysterious Jakob Tas. He might be the organ grinder; he might be the monkey. We have no way of knowing. But four days ago, he turned off his phone. Why?"

"You have a theory?" Draper said.

"What if there are no parts left to move? What if Tas turned off his phone because he doesn't need it anymore? That he's incommunicado because the end-game has started?"

"If that's the case, turning off his phone would be the sensible thing to do," Carlyle said. "Yet you seem to think he's made a mistake."

"I do," Koenig said. "Because as far as Tas knows, everything is going to plan. Turning off his cell was a precaution, not a necessity. He wasn't forced to turn it off, he *chose* to."

"He's proceeding as planned," Draper said, looking thoughtful.

"He is. And if we can find out when and where his cell was turned off, we'll know when and where that last part stopped moving. The trail hasn't gone cold; it's red-hot."

Draper picked up her cell phone. She pressed redial and put it on speaker-phone. It was answered immediately.

"Ma'am?" a man said.

"I need the last known location of that number I gave you," Draper said. "I also need the exact time it was turned off. And then I want a breakdown of every tower it pinged. I want to know exactly where it's been. I want the breakdown within twenty-four hours; I want the last known location in the next fifteen minutes."

"On it," the man said.

Draper ended the call and made another. Again, it was answered imme-diately.

"Get the Gulfstream ready," Draper said.

"Where are we headed, ma'am?"

"I'll let you know when I know." She ended the call and slipped her cell back in her pocket. She pointed at Hobbs and Nash. "What are we going to do with these two?" she asked Koenig.

"No idea," Koenig said. "We can't take them with us, and we can't hand them over to Smerconish. Not until we know who's leaking our actions. I say we wrap them in duct tape and leave them here."

"They're not fucking Sea-Monkeys, Koenig," Draper said. "They'll need food and water. I won't have someone starving to death on the wrong side of my ledger."

Koenig thought for a moment, then said, "Whatever happens next, it's likely to be fast-moving. Agreed?"

"Probably."

"Why don't we leave Margaret? If she restricts herself to spoon-feeding them, she should be safe enough."

"What if she collapses?"

"She's an adult and we're out of options."

"You know her best, Bess," Draper said. "What do you think? Will she do it? And if she says yes, is she even up to it?"

Carlyle considered the question carefully. "She's a tough old bird, but she's very ill." She paused a beat. "But we don't have a choice. Ben's right: We can't take them with us and we can't hand them over. But you're right as well: We can't let them starve to death. Someone has to stay with them. It can't be either of you, and it can't be me. That leaves Margaret. I say we ask her."

"Margaret," Koenig called out. "Grab your tea and pop over here. We have a favor to ask."

But Margaret didn't answer. She was staring out of the window. She seemed transfixed by something happening outside.

"What is it, Margaret?" Carlyle asked.

She didn't answer.

Carlyle joined her friend at the window. She peered out as well. She turned, her face paling. "There are men on the street," she said. "Men with guns."

CHAPTER 87

Koenig and Draper double-timed to the kitchen area. They peered out of the window. Carlyle was right. There *were* men with guns outside. They had them under their coats. Koenig caught a glimpse when a blast from a street vent lifted one guy's coat like it was Marilyn Monroe's white dress. Submachine guns. Perfect weapons for an urban assault. They were on the sidewalk opposite Hobbs's apartment. A black van pulled up beside them. The panel door slid open. Three men climbed out and joined their colleagues on the sidewalk. That made seven. They made no move to enter the apartment. They were standing around, like office workers after a fire alarm.

"They must have been on the apartment," Koenig said. "They were watching it, just like we were watching."

"Why didn't we see them?" Draper asked. Annoyed.

"We were improvising; they had time to do it right."

One of the men reached into the van and hauled out a briefcase-sized box. It was black. Looked like the president's nuclear football. Koenig recognized it immediately. It was a military-grade jammer. Expensive, best part of a hundred thousand bucks.

Draper pulled out her cell phone. "I still have a signal," she said. "I wonder why they didn't arrive with it powered up."

"That thing will knock out every phone in a ten-block radius," Koenig said. "And no matter which route they took to get here, they'd have had to pass an NYPD precinct. And if a precinct's comms goes down without warning, they don't mess around. They assume it's terrorism. Everyone with a badge gets out on the street. Last thing these guys want."

Draper stared at her cell like a teenager checking their Instagram likes. "Losing my signal will be their starter pistol then," she said. "I'm too far away to see what model they're using, but military jammers don't take long to warm up. Five minutes, tops."

"If that."

Her cell phone chirped a song Koenig neither knew nor liked. Draper answered it.

"Yes? . . . Where the hell is that? . . . OK, tell her she can have anything she needs . . . I'm about to lose my signal, but I'll reestablish comms as soon as I can."

She ended the call.

"Jakob Tas's phone went dead in Maine," she told Koenig. "A fishing village called New Silloth."

"That mean anything to you, Bess?" Koenig asked.

Carlyle shook her head. "I don't know anyone there."

"As luck would have it," Draper said, "a woman on my payroll has a hunting cabin less than an hour away. She's already on her way. Rachel's ex-FBI, so if there's anything to find, she'll find it."

"First bit of luck we've had," Koenig grunted.

"Feels that way, doesn't it? Anyway, assaulting a building is your area of expertise, not mine. How do you want to do this?"

"We have the stairs; they have the numbers," Koenig said. He watched two of the group outside split off and head to the alley. "Must be relegated to covering the fire escape. That leaves five for me to deal with." His SIG was tucked uncomfortably into his waistband. He reached for it and ejected the magazine. Pulled back the slide and held it to the rear. Checked the working parts weren't clogged with threads of denim. He'd seen it happen. It was clean. He released the slide and pressed home the magazine. "We can't let them reach the apartment. How about I go downstairs while they're all standing together?"

"No," Draper said firmly. "We won't get away with that again. They aren't like the goofballs at the airstrip. There are more of them. They aren't wearing stupid armor. They have the right weapons. And if they know what went down in Scotland, they'll be expecting you to come straight at them."

"We call 9-1-1 then. Wait for the NYPD, then hit them from both ends."

"Even if we *were* prepared to sacrifice a bunch of cops, which I'm not, best-case scenario is we all get arrested. And if you're right about Tas entering the endgame, we don't have time to wait for Smerconish to bail us out."

"Assuming it wasn't Smerconish who sent these assholes."

Hobbs turned on his stool. "I can help," he said. He seemed frightened. Which, for a man about to be rescued, seemed counterintuitive. He should have been looking relieved.

"How?" Draper said.

"Give me a gun. Even the odds."

"What a marvelous idea," she said. "You want *me*, the person who's just tortured your daughter, to give *you*, a professional killer, a gun? Not even Koenig is stupid enough to fall for that bullshit."

"You don't know these guys!" Hobbs said, frantic now. "I do. They're butchers, not surgeons. Mr. Koenig was right—you can't sit back and let them reach our apartment. They aren't interested in letting anyone live. They'll blow the door off its hinges, then lob in grenades until they've turned us into ground beef. Our only way out of this, the only way *Harper* gets out of this, is if we engage them on the stairs."

"I'm not giving you a fucking gun."

"Your cell still has a signal?" Koenig asked Draper.

She nodded. "It does."

"They can't stay there forever, though; they're standing out like pepper in salt." He turned to Carlyle. "Bess, when this starts, can you cover the fire escape? Make sure they don't come at us from the rear. I doubt they'd be so stupid, but we can't ignore the possibility."

"I will."

"I can tell you what the plan is," Hobbs said quietly.

"I know what the plan is," Koenig said. "They'll do exactly what you said—they'll blow the door off and throw in grenades. Stun or fragmentation. Maybe white phosphorus."

Margaret stepped away from the window. It looked like she was pressing ahead with her tea. Brits, Koenig thought. Think there's nothing that can't be fixed with a cuppa. When he'd trained in the UK, he'd been told that during the Falklands War, Royal Marines Commandos took cover and stopped fighting the Argentineans so they could brew up.

"Don't get too close to Hobbs, Margaret," he warned.

"I won't, dear."

"I don't mean their plan now," Hobbs said. "I mean Jakob Tas's plan."

It was a good ten seconds before anyone spoke.

"You know what Jakob Tas is planning?" Draper said.

"Some of it."

"And you're only remembering now? How convenient."

Hobbs sighed in frustration. "You might not like what we do, but we *are* good at it," he said. "And that means even when we get a referral from a trusted source, we don't go into the meeting blind. When Jakob Tas arrived at the Holiday Inn in North Dakota, a venue he'd chosen, he assumed it was neutral."

"But it wasn't."

"No. I arrived late, and that allowed Harper to subdue one of the servers. She took their uniform and bused Tas's table. She did this to make sure I wasn't walking into an ambush."

"And she overheard them discussing their master plan?" Draper said skeptically.

"No, Tas is no James Bond villain," Hobbs said. "But she did hear a phrase, a phrase I think might be important. It wasn't something Tas said, it was the Russian guy who travels everywhere with him. A monosyllabic brute called Konstantin. He said it and Tas shushed him."

"Bullshit," Draper said. "We asked Harper the same questions we asked you, remember? She didn't mention overhearing anything."

"That's because she didn't understand the significance of what Konstantin said. I did. She thought it was a throwaway comment, a bit of nonsense, but I spent time in Russia when I was a young man and—"

"I don't think you should be bothering everyone with this twaddle, dear," Margaret said. She then took the Roman hairpin from her bun and pressed it into Hobbs's ear, all the way in like she was skewering a baked potato.

Hobbs slumped over as much as the duct tape allowed. Margaret checked his carotid pulse and smiled at everyone.

"Whoopsie," she said.

CHAPTER 88

Three things happened simultaneously.

Carlyle lunged for Margaret, Koenig grabbed Carlyle, and Draper knocked Margaret on her ass with a right hook to the jaw that would have felled a stevedore.

"We need her alive, Bess," Koenig said.

"I trusted her with my life!" Carlyle shrieked, struggling to get out of his bear hug, clawing at the air. She looked like a boxer who thought his corner had stopped the fight too early. "I told her everything! EVERYTHING!"

"Perhaps you shouldn't have, dear," Margaret said before her eyes rolled into the back of her head and she lost consciousness.

"Oh, this is fucking perfect," Draper said. She knelt and began wrapping Margaret's wrists with duct tape. They were going through so much they should have bought stock in the company. Draper tore the tape with her teeth, then said, "She's been reporting to them in real time. No wonder they always knew where we were."

"We can discuss our catastrophic security failure later," Koenig said. "Right now, we need to get Nash ready. We're getting out of here, and she's coming with us. They're both coming with us."

"*How* are they coming with us?" Draper asked, not looking up. "There are seven armed assholes outside."

She had a point. Seven was too many now they had prisoners to manage. Koenig needed to reduce the odds. But how? Their SIGs weren't enough.

They needed something heavier. There was nothing in the apartment, though. Hobbs had intentionally kept it free of weapons. No guns, no grenades, not even an ornamental sword on the wall. The apartment was virtually empty. Just pots and pans and some gourmet cat food. Some Classic Coke, some takeout tempura, and three bags of non-clump kitty litter. A James Bond collection. Perhaps he could throw books at them.

Koenig closed his eyes and visualized the stairway Tas's men would have to navigate. The switchback stairs were as steep and as narrow as the spiral staircases in medieval castles. Most staircases were in cities where space was at a premium. New York especially so. It had polished teak banisters and a black-and-white-tiled floor. Ten steps per flight, twenty steps per floor.

There was the elevator too, but Koenig wasn't worried about that. Any hired goon who took an elevator to work deserved a Darwin Award. But to be safe, he'd call it to the top floor when they left the loft apartment. Give them something to think about. Maybe they'd keep someone at the bottom, just in case. Might work, probably wouldn't.

Hobbs had been right earlier; Koenig needed the firefight to take place on the stairs. It was the only chance they had. Even with superior firepower, you were vulnerable when assaulting a stairway. Incoming fire could come from myriad angles. Far more than horizontal areas like hallways and rooms. The assaulters were exposed from the landing above, from the triangular gap between the split-level stairs, and from anything the people defending the stairs threw down. Back in his SOG days, he'd assaulted a three-story Colonial in New Hampshire, and the perp had thrown a live pig at them. He hadn't asked why the perp had one on the top floor with him. He doubted it was anything nice. The terrified animal had torn down the stairs like the boulder in *Raiders of the Lost Ark*. Everything's a weapon when you're desperate.

"I've lost my cell phone signal, Koenig," Draper called out.

"You don't have a spare pig, do you?" he replied.

"Excuse me?"

But Koenig didn't answer. He was staring at the boxes of takeout tempura Hobbs had brought in with him. Koenig loved Japanese food, and tempura, when done right, was a particular favorite. The batter, which used sparkling water rather than still, was delicate, light, and crispy. But it didn't travel well. It was better eaten fresh.

And after he'd asked after his cat, the first thing Hobbs had said to his daughter was that he hoped she'd put the fryer on. Not the oven, the *fryer*. Which meant he'd bought cook-at-home tempura. Probably a tub of premade batter and a bunch of vegetables like carrot batons, sliced eggplant, and shii-take mushrooms. Maybe some seafood. Shrimp worked well. So did whitefish and squid.

Which gave him an idea.

He ran to the kitchen area and opened the floor-level cupboards. He hadn't really checked them before. Food was always stored in eye-level cupboards. Floor-level cupboards were for detergent and dishwasher tablets and other cleaning products. Some of the bigger pots and pans. Seldom-used kitchen equipment. He found everything he needed and set it all on the kitchen work-top. He then got the six-pack of Classic Coke from the fridge.

"Anyone thirsty?" he said.

CHAPTER 89

Dwight Snow had done some nasty shit during his time with Jakob Tas. He'd been to Yemen, Nigeria, and Kurdistan. He'd protected oil fields in Syria and terbium mines in Myanmar. He'd spent time in Ukraine, fighting either a "war" or a "special military operation," depending on who was paying his check that week.

And now he was in New York. About to assault a building on the Lower East Side. But for the first time since he'd started working for Tas, something wasn't sitting right. He felt queasy, like he'd eaten warm oysters. It wasn't the task. Assaulting a building with stairs was something he could do by muscle memory. It was working stateside that he didn't like. Killing Americans on American soil was wrong. It wasn't something he could shrug off. But their instructions were clear. They were to go inside and kill everyone in the loft apartment. Even the old lady, and she was supposed to be one of theirs. When he'd joined the marines all those years ago, he'd sworn an oath to protect the Constitution from all enemies, foreign and domestic. And sure, he'd joined Tas's crew because he found civilian life meaningless, but he'd still thought his moral compass pointed true north. He'd even squared the circle of fighting both sides of the Ukrainian conflict by telling himself that if it hadn't been him, it would have been an untrained Russian conscript facing Western weapons.

He wasn't the only one who felt this way. The other two Americans on the squad had expressed the same doubts. For a while the op was in doubt. They were civilians. They weren't subject to military law. They could walk away. They wouldn't be going AWOL. There wouldn't even be a breach of contract dispute. Not for a job like this. The worst that could happen was getting black-listed. Big deal. If Tas was operating on US soil now, it was time to go anyway. He didn't want to break his Marine Corps oath.

That was the way it was going. It looked like the squad would be reduced to four: the Polack; the two Samoans, Big Sam and Little Sam; and Lester French, their squad leader. Cotton Pope, a big guy from Minnesota, had even gotten halfway out of the briefing room door when French stopped him in his tracks with, "There's a five-million-buck bonus in it."

Which kinda refocused everyone.

French went on to explain that one of the people in the apartment was a man called Ben Koenig. Apparently, Koenig had had a run-in with the Russian mob some years earlier. They'd placed a bounty on his head. Five million bucks, dead or alive. French was clear: If everyone in the apartment died, Koenig's corpse was theirs. He proposed an almost equal split. A million for him, the remaining $4 million being divided between the six squad members. If some-one didn't make it—and on an op like this there were always casualties—the survivors got a bigger slice of the pie.

The squad had whooped and hollered and high-fived each other. Even Cotton Pope. They were already spending their share. Boats or Vegas hookers, sometimes both. Lots of laughter. Snow hadn't joined in. He had the nagging feeling that someone with five million bucks on his head had to get very good at killing just to stay alive. The way Snow saw it, Koenig might be worth five million bucks, but no one had managed to claim it so far.

But so far, the assault had gone to plan. The jammer had turned everyone's cell phones into bricks, and they'd entered the building in well-rehearsed moves. Four members of the squad ahead of him, Snow was covering the rear. Tail-End Charlie. The remaining two on the street watching the fire escape.

Cotton Pope was point. He'd gotten all the way to the third-floor landing when it started to go wrong. And all it had taken was the sound of glass breaking. It wasn't an uncommon sound, not in New York. Along with yelling, car horns, and sirens, the sound of breaking glass was part of the city's soundtrack. If Snow had been in a bar, he'd have cheered. Laughed at whoever had dropped their drink. But in the silence of a covert assault, it was eerily out of place. Like giggling at a funeral.

The broken glass was followed by someone falling down a flight of stairs. It was an unmistakable sound. *Thud. Thud. Thud.* Sounded like a muffled bass drum. Snow heard Pope cry out, "Shit, I've broken my damn—"

Two gunshots rang out. A double tap. Fired so closely together it sounded like a single shot. Snow would have bet every dollar he'd ever earned it was Koenig.

A lesser squad might have panicked. They'd have selected automatic fire and let rip. But this wasn't a lesser squad. This squad was well trained and highly motivated. All they'd lost was the element of surprise, and they could only lose that once. They'd also lost Cotton Pope, but as French said when he spoke into their earpieces a fraction of a second after the double tap, "More candy for us when this is over. Stick to the plan."

Snow held his position.

"Move," he heard French say.

Little Sam was the bigger of the two Samoans. Military humor. He was the fourth guy in the assault team and the guy directly in front of Snow. Little Sam moved onto the second-floor landing. He gave Snow the all-clear sign. Snow followed him up, then turned to face the way he'd come. His job was to protect the rear. If he saw Koenig, things had gone terribly wrong. His eyes occasionally swiveled to the second-floor apartments, but the doors stayed shut. The occupants were either out or pretending they were out. New York was a safe city, but not safe enough to get all curious when you heard gunshots on the other side of your front door.

Glass broke again. Then a curse.

"He's throwing bottles of oil!" Big Sam, the shorter Samoan, hollered. Big Sam was now point. "Can't stay on my goddamned feet."

Snow understood why the assault was stalling. Koenig—and it could only be Koenig—was using oil to slow them down. Snow had studied military history in college. He knew hot oil had rarely been used as a defensive weapon. It took too long to heat. It was unwieldy and it was expensive. It was also a fire hazard. What the besieged *had* used oil for was making vulnerable approaches too slippery to walk on. Even on stone, oil was hazardous.

And the squad was standing on polished tile. They were wearing rubber-soled combat boots. Oil, rubber, nonporous porcelain tiles. No wonder they were falling over themselves. Someone else fell down a flight of stairs. Big Sam. Another scream, then another double tap. Chaos.

And then there were three, Snow thought. He ignored the rear and turned to face the action. He couldn't help himself. It was what marines did.

Semper fi, motherfucker.

Samoa has no standing army, so Little Sam had served his time with the Royal New Zealand Infantry Regiment. Tough unit. Snow knew Little Sam would stand his post. He signaled that the Samoan should advance. The big guy nodded and turned the corner.

Nothing happened.

"Stairs clear," Little Sam said.

He advanced up the stairs carefully, weapon pointing up. Snow followed him. Little Sam stopped on the landing platform. They were now between the second and third floor.

"What is it?" Snow asked.

"The boss," he replied. "I can see his ass, but he isn't moving. Looks like he don't like being promoted to point."

That's because he ain't a marine, Snow thought. He waited for French to decide what to do. Koenig had evened the odds. Maybe he even held the upper hand. A tactical retreat would be sensible. Lick their wounds and go after him on the street.

"To hell with this," French said. "That's five million bucks up there. We have automatic weapons. All he has is bottles of oil. Cover me."

Little Sam rolled his eyes and crossed himself. He raised his weapon and covered his squad leader as best he could. But the floor was now slippery with oil, and Little Sam couldn't keep up with French.

Which saved his life.

Another crash-bang-wallop, another double tap. No million bucks for Lester French.

Little Sam stepped back down the stairs, carefully. He joined Snow on the landing.

"Now what?" he said. "Just the two of us left in here. Two more outside. That's nearly a million and a half each, but I don't know about you, I'm getting the feeling we'll never get to spend it. Whoever this Koenig is, he's better than us."

Snow nodded. "I feel like one of the *Home Alone* burglars."

"Let's get out of here. I've had enough working for these assholes."

Snow nodded again.

Which was when something shattered at his feet. *That looks like a Classic Coke bottle*, he thought. Oil and broken glass spilled everywhere. Covered the landing. Smelled of sesame. Kinda reminded him of Japanese food. He lurched and grabbed the banister to steady himself. Saw Little Sam had done the same. They looked like newbie ice skaters.

Might be safer to shuffle down on my ass, he thought. He looked at the broken glass. Changed his mind.

Snow was still thinking about that when the body of Lester French pinwheeled down the flight of stairs like a crash test dummy. It slammed into him and Little Sam. Knocked them both on their asses. Something cracked that wasn't supposed to crack. Snow thought it might have been his wrist. The H&K fell from his hands. Clattered down the stairs he'd just walked up. Made a hell of a noise. Little Sam had lost his weapon too. Seemed he'd also lost the use of his legs. He was scrabbling about on the oily floor as if he had spinal shock. Helpless.

Snow couldn't help himself. He looked at Lester French. His squad leader's neck was at right angles, like his ear was glued to his shoulder, but it wasn't the initial slip that had killed him. He'd been shot in the bridge of his nose and his eye socket, and then, it seemed, he'd been thrown down the stairs. Koenig was using the bodies of the dudes he'd killed to knock the living ones off their feet. It took Snow two seconds to work that out. Another two to realize the terrible danger he was in.

He looked up.

And saw Koenig. He wasn't hurrying. His expression was monstrously calm. He held a semiautomatic pistol in one hand and had a bag of kitty litter tied around his neck. Looked like a hipster's papoose. Koenig reached into the bag and threw down a handful of kitty litter as if he were seeding a lawn. It covered the tiles like Spill-Sorb, the absorbent granules orderlies used to clean blood in hospitals. So *that* was how he had managed to stay on his feet when no one else could, Snow thought. Very clever. Badass. Koenig double-tapped Little Sam in the head, then moved toward him.

And then Koenig was standing over him. He looked at Snow without emotion, like he was studying the cheese trolley at a restaurant. He wasn't even breathing hard. He pointed his gun at Snow's head. It was a SIG.

"Please," Snow pleaded.

Koenig squeezed the trigger. Twice.

And that was the end of Dwight Snow, oath-breaker.

CHAPTER 90

Koenig rapped on the apartment door. Draper opened it immediately. Koenig hurried in and closed the door behind him.

"I can't believe you MacGyvered us out of this," Draper said.

"They should have withdrawn and regrouped when the first bottle of oil smashed, but they knew about the bounty. All they could see was five million bucks."

"Bess says you got the two watching the fire escape as well."

"They had their backs to me. Are we ready? Jammer or not, the cops will be here soon."

"Margaret's only just regained consciousness," Draper said. "She's a bit groggy, but she'll be able to walk if I help her."

"I need you on Nash," Koenig said. "That's where the danger is. It's not ideal, but Bess will have to help Margaret."

"Let's go then. My pilot's waiting."

Koenig led them out of the apartment. Five steps behind, an incensed Carlyle propped up an unsteady Margaret. Five steps behind them, an alert Draper held an equally alert Nash by the scruff of her neck, her SIG pressed against the base of her spine.

"It gets oily lower down," Koenig said. "I'll throw some more kitty litter, but watch your feet."

When he reached the third floor, one of the apartment doors opened.

Koenig spun round, SIG at the ready. It was an old lady. Half blind and three-quarters deaf, judging by the thick spectacles and hearing aids. Her hair was cobweb-thin and grayer than ash. She had a mole on her chin the size and color of a blueberry. She wore a ratty yellow cardigan, the buttons in the wrong holes giving her a lopsided appearance. She held something pink and wrinkled in her arms. Looked like a cross between a small pig and a large blobfish. Hobbs's cat, presumably.

The old lady seemed oblivious to what was going on. "Hello, Harper," she said. "Are you here for your father's cat?"

Her voice was so dry Koenig was surprised dust didn't come out of her mouth. He said, "Please go back inside your apartment, ma'am."

"You can keep Chairman Meow, Mrs. Benowitz," Nash said loudly. "I'm going away for a bit."

It took longer than Koenig would have liked, but eventually woman and cat were coaxed back into the apartment.

"I hate that fucking cat," Nash said when Mrs. Benowitz had finally shut her apartment door.

"Come on," Koenig said, keen to keep moving.

The next obstacle, the only one he'd thought might be a problem, was what Nash would see on the half-landing between the third and second floor. Koenig hadn't moved any of the bodies. There was one coming up: the body he'd thrown to knock their point guy off his feet. Stillwell Hobbs.

Nash looked at her dead father without emotion. She shrugged and said, "It's what I'd have done."

CHAPTER 91

They left the jammer in the apartment lobby. It was a traceable piece of equipment. It would give the NYPD somewhere to start. Draper had turned it off and called her pilot.

"ETA thirty minutes," she said. A pause, then, "Five—two are hostiles, so get some restraints ready."

They commandeered the van that the guys who'd assaulted the building had used. Draper took the wheel while Koenig and Carlyle sat in the back with Margaret and Nash. Margaret was smiling like they were going to the Ritz for afternoon tea. Nash was clammy but calm.

"I'm briefing Smerconish, Koenig," Draper said when she stopped for a red light. She didn't wait for permission. When the light turned green, she jammed her cell between her ear and her shoulder so she could drive and talk. "Andrew, we have a problem," she said without preamble.

She told Smerconish what had happened. Explained how Margaret had been their snake in the woodpile. That Hobbs had given them the name Jakob Tas, and his cell phone had gone dead in a fishing village in Maine. That they had narrowly survived an attack at Hobbs's apartment and were now on their way to the airport. And no, Carlyle still hadn't told them what the Acacia Avenue Protocol involved.

Koenig listened to Draper but kept his eyes fixed on Nash. He had never come across anyone like her. She was wrapped in so much duct tape she resembled an Egyptian mummy, but she still looked ruthless. Willing to do anything to escape. If he didn't need to know what she'd overheard Konstantin say to Jakob Tas, Koenig would have put a bullet in her head. Same way he would a rabid fox. Safer for everyone.

"Smerconish is worried," Draper said when she'd finished her call. "He wants us to fly to Maine."

"What did you tell him?"

"That Maine was where Jakob Tas *was*. We need to fly to where he *is*."

"Which is?"

"Let's find out." She made another call. "I need an update," she said when it was answered. She listened for a few seconds, then added, "I need you to call this cell phone"—she rattled off Smerconish's number—"and tell the person who answers *exactly* what you've just told me. He's a friendly, so if he has follow-ups, help him."

She threw the cell phone onto the dashboard.

"I hope you like surfing, Koenig," she said. "We're going to San Diego."

CHAPTER 92

Rachel, Draper's ex-FBI special agent, had arrived in New Silloth shortly after they'd identified it as the location where Jakob Tas had ditched his phone. Rachel didn't know what she was looking for, but she knew that a fishing village in Maine was a different beast from a megacity like New York. The first rule of New York was that you minded your own business; the first rule of a Maine fishing village was that you minded *everyone's* business. Not in a nosy-needs-to-know way, more like they watched out for each other.

And that meant strangers stood out. They were watched. Not like Edward Woodward was watched in *The Wicker Man*. They weren't sacrificed because the harvest had failed. Rachel knew if she wandered around looking a little bit lost, it wouldn't be long before someone asked if she needed help.

The residential streets were dark and sleepy, so she'd headed to the docks where the fishermen and -women were making an early start. She stood and watched the boats. Made sure people saw her. Sure enough, it wasn't long before someone sidled up to her. A bowlegged man in his fifties. He offered her a coffee in a chipped mug.

"You a cop?" he'd asked.

Direct.

"Who's asking?"

"You look like a cop."

She'd flashed her old FBI credentials. Covered the RETIRED stamp with her thumb. Tricksy.

He'd grinned. "Seen that too many times to be fooled, *ex*–Special Agent . . . ?"

"You can call me Rachel. You're ex-job?"

"Willy Deeker, Baltimore PD. Mainly worked narcotics."

"Like *The Wire?*"

"I get that a lot."

"Sorry."

"What are you doing in New Silloth, Rachel?"

"There's a guy we're keen to find. His last known location was here."

"When?"

"When what?"

"*When* was his last location known? If you know the where, you also know the when."

Rachel had told him. Willy Deeker nodded. As if he'd been expecting it.

"There were three of them. They were hanging around not far from where we are now. Looked like they wanted to be noticed. They were waiting for something."

"Did you see what?"

"A NorseBoat 21.5. Good condition. Soon as it appeared, a truck turned up. They trailered it right out of the water. Seemed like an odd time to be doing something like that, so I went over for a look. Acted the fool so they wouldn't worry."

"And?"

"The story they cooked up about moving the boat from the Atlantic to the Pacific was a crock of shit. The Australian who piloted the NorseBoat was the only one who knew what he was doing. The guy in charge didn't even know what the drain plug was for. The others didn't speak. The big guy didn't even look like he *could* speak. Anyway, they were breaking no laws I could see, so I went on my merry way."

Rachel doubted that. If Deeker was ex-BPD, there was no way he'd have left it like that. "I sense a 'but' coming . . ."

"But not before I saw the guy in charge take everyone's cell phones and drop them in the sea."

"That was . . . suspicious."

"Yes, ma'am."

"I don't suppose you happened to get the truck's license plate, Willy?"

"I went one better than that, Rachel," Willy Deeker had replied. "I got a photo."

Rachel called in what she'd discovered. Draper's tech guy had back-doored his way into Maine's automatic license plate recognition database and tracked the truck to the New Hampshire border. New Hampshire only allowed license plate data to be retained for three minutes, so he'd bypassed the Granite State and headed straight to Vermont, where he picked it up again. As soon as he'd figured out the truck's general direction, he cast ahead until he'd found them in Kansas and plotted out their journey, interstate by interstate, until he lost them in California, fifty miles outside San Diego.

He'd then waited for the boss to get a signal.

CHAPTER 93

Koenig took charge when they got to JFK. Securing prisoners was bread and butter to an ex-marshal. There would be no *Con Air* escapades on this flight.

He wanted to talk to Margaret first. It was the right play. Nash was a subcontractor. A hired gun. She hadn't seen the bigger picture. Margaret seemed more involved. She could add color to Tas's operation. Context. And Koenig thought context would be important when it came to questioning Nash. Hobbs had said she hadn't understood the significance of what she'd overheard. That it had meant nothing to her. But it was important enough for Margaret to break cover and stop him stone-dead. Literally. So when Nash told him what it was she'd overheard, he needed to already know what Margaret knew.

He pushed Nash to the rear of the plane, where he fitted her with leg cuffs and rigid handcuffs, which he fitted to a belly chain. Hannibal Lecter had fewer restraints. Koenig then strapped her to the table. It looked like she was on a gurney.

He returned to the front of the Gulfstream. He didn't close the door that separated the two sections. He trusted the restraints, but he didn't want to take his eyes off Nash. Not for a second. He'd hunted the worst America had to offer, but he hadn't seen anything like her before.

Margaret was in the same seat she'd used on the flight to New York.

"You want her cuffed, Koenig?" Draper asked.

"Have you checked her for another hairpin?"

"She's clean."

"Then I don't want her cuffed."

The pilot stepped out from the cockpit. He gave Draper a thumbs-up. "We're cleared for takeoff, ma'am," he said.

Draper said, "Let's go."

They waited for the Gulfstream to get into the air. It didn't take long. They didn't have to wait in line for a slot on the runway. Koenig suspected Smerconish had prioritized their flight. The Gulfstream climbed until it reached its cruising altitude, then leveled off. The pilot turned off the FASTEN SEAT BELTS sign. Nobody had been wearing one. Koenig guessed it was regulations.

"Do you want a drink, Margaret?" Draper said. "This is a six-hour flight and I suspect you'll be talking for most of it."

"I'd better take a coffee then."

Koenig walked over to the drinks station and poured her a cup. Filled it with cream and sugar. Lots of quick-release energy. He placed it on the table in front of Margaret. Some of it slopped over the rim. "Sorry," he said, but made no move to clean it.

"Thank you, dear," she said. She took a sip and sighed in appreciation. "You Americans might not be able to make tea, but your coffee has always been excellent."

"How were you recruited, Margaret?" Koenig said.

"The usual way. I was approached while I was lecturing abroad. We all were. It wasn't uncommon, and as long as we reported it, it wasn't a problem."

"Approached by who?"

"By *whom*, dear."

"Sorry. Approached by whom?"

"They never said, but I imagine it was the intelligence service of whatever country I was in at the time."

"Countries hostile to the US?"

"Not always, dear. I'm told spying on our friends is just as much fun."

Koenig glanced at Draper.

She shrugged. "We need to know what *everyone* is thinking."

"Which of these agents was the one . . ." He trailed off.

"What is it?" Draper asked.

Koenig didn't answer. Something in the back of his mind was trying to grab his attention. It had been there since Margaret stuck a hairpin in Hobbs, growing slowly and insidiously, like her cancer. He wondered what had prompted it. He tried to remember every conversation they'd had, but this time he put everything through the filter of someone living a lie. He thought she'd made a mistake, although he couldn't put his finger on what it was. He broke down the problem. Margaret had her cover story, and it would have been well rehearsed. But inevitably, a large part of it was improvisation. She couldn't predict everything. At some point she would encounter something she hadn't planned for. Good agents, even ones with impeccable legends, had to be able to think on their feet. Then they had to remember what they'd said. Sometimes for the rest of their lives.

He mentally backed up. He'd stumbled over something again. Not something he'd said. Something he'd *thought*.

A word.

It was "agent."

For some reason the word "agent" was bothering him. He didn't know why, only that it was. Margaret must have mentioned it. Probably in passing, and without the current context it hadn't meant anything. And she'd said it freely, hadn't tried to correct herself. Hadn't realized she'd made a mistake. He cast his mind way back, ended up in the middle of a conversation they'd had in the Scottish Highlands. They'd been talking about her illness. She'd used "agent" when discussing her cancer.

And then, like he'd swept his hands across a cluttered desk, everything became clear. He knew what was bothering him. Trusting Margaret had been a terrible mistake. They were making another one now. He removed his Fairbairn-Sykes and placed it on the table. Spun it round until the blade was facing Margaret.

"What is it?" Draper asked again.

"Her cancer's a lie," he said. "Margaret isn't dying." He took a few beats to let that register. "And because she faked her diagnosis two years before Bess's guys started to go missing, it means she wasn't recruited for a role in all of this. She *is* all of this."

Margaret grinned. "Fuck-a-doodle-do," she said.

CHAPTER 94

While Koenig was busting Margaret, Cora Pearl was backing up the truck and boat trailer through the open door of an empty warehouse in San Diego. Tas was pleased. The journey from Maine to California had been incident-free. The Australian had been sullen, but Tas didn't care. His role was over.

Almost.

When Pearl had parked the truck, Konstantin pushed the button that closed the roller door. As soon as it had clunked its way down the oiled chain and touched the crumbling concrete floor, Tas climbed out of the cab. Pearl and the Australian followed him.

Tas checked the warehouse to make sure everything was how he'd left it. It was. No one had been in since he'd taken on the short-term lease. The warehouse had once belonged to a paint wholesaler. The kind of place that sold to the trade. The business had gone bust two years ago. Another victim of the pandemic.

It was a shell of a building now. The owner had stripped out everything of value. The only things left were towering metal shelves that looked like an out-of-hand Erector Set project and a bunch of vintage paint posters: "Well done! with Walpamur Paints" and "Carter White Lead," which apparently lasted longer than "Old Dutch" white lead. The warehouse floor had so many paint spills, in so many colors, it looked like it had been set up for a communal game of Twister.

The Lincoln Navigator was where he'd left it. It was parked in the warehouse's other vehicle bay. It was white and brand-new. Four-wheel drive with a twin turbocharged V6 engine. Tas had opted for the long-wheelbase configuration. He figured it looked the part. The Lincoln Navigator was able to tow 8,700 pounds. The combined weight of the NorseBoat and trailer was less than 2,000. The Australian unhitched the boat trailer from the truck, and he and Konstantin manhandled it to the rear of the Lincoln. When the trailer hitch was secured to the tow ball, the Australian connected the electrics.

"Good?" Tas asked.

"We're good, mate," the Australian replied.

Tas walked to the back of the truck. He aimed a reverse nod Konstantin's way. The big Russian followed him.

"How long have we known each other, Kostya?" Tas said.

"Long time," Konstantin grunted back.

Tas nodded. "And how long have I known Cora?"

Konstantin shrugged. "I think maybe five years."

"So why do you think she's doing that?" Tas asked, pointing toward the Lincoln.

Konstantin's head turned to follow Tas's finger. As soon as it did, Tas pulled a PSS silent pistol from his pocket, pressed it against the base of Konstantin's skull, and pulled the trigger. The PSS was a compact pistol. Easily concealable. It used noiseless ammunition instead of a suppressor, and the inside of Konstantin's skull absorbed what little sound there was. Some of his brain hit the wall like a splat of chopped liver. Tas grabbed Konstantin under the arms and controlled his fall. He pushed his finger into the side of his neck. There was no pulse.

"Sorry, my friend," he whispered. He then stood, removed the concealed punch-dagger from his belt buckle, and called for Pearl.

The ex–bounty hunter came immediately. Her eyes widened when she saw Konstantin lying in an expanding pool of blood. They widened even further when Tas slashed her across the throat. Three times. Forehand, backhand, forehand. Like he was Zorro. He controlled her fall too. Rested her head against Konstantin's shoulder. He waited for her to die. It didn't take long.

The Australian must have seen something in the wing mirror; he was already sprinting for the door. Tas's bullet entered the back of his knee. Punched out his kneecap like it was a Champagne cork. The Australian fell and skidded into the metal roller door. Tas shot at him again. Went for the headshot, but the fall saved the Australian's life. Instead of turning his brain to mush, the bullet removed his remaining ear. He shook himself. Sprayed blood. He attempted to stand, realized he couldn't. He grabbed the chain that controlled the door. Tried to haul himself upright. By the time he was on his feet, Tas was standing next to him with the PSS raised.

"I'm not even sorry about this," Tas said.

He then shot him in the eye.

Tas breathed a sigh of relief. He had been mentally rehearsing the last thirty seconds for two years. In his wildest dreams it hadn't gone as smoothly. He was almost disappointed. He pressed the button and opened the roller door. It went up at the same speed it had gone down. Annoyingly slow. He checked he had everything he needed, then climbed into the Lincoln. It started immediately. A throaty purr, like a well-fed dog. He pulled out of the bay and left the paint warehouse. When he was clear, he jumped out of the Lincoln. Put a key into the control pad next to the door. Turned it ninety degrees, then pressed the button that lowered the door. When it was eighteen inches from the concrete, he stopped it. Turned the key and locked it in position. He figured eighteen inches was about right. A normal-sized person could crawl under a gap like that. And they would. They'd want to know why the door wasn't closed. They would investigate.

They would find the bodies.

Which was good.

It was part of the plan.

CHAPTER 95

"What gave me away, dear?" Margaret said.

"You did."

For someone who'd been caught faking cancer, she didn't seem the least bit embarrassed. The people who pulled these scams usually ended up being led into court with blankets over their heads. Ashamed. Their families mortified. Margaret was smiling, though. Like she'd been caught cheating at charades.

"May I ask how?" she asked.

"Something you said in Scotland, right after you told me you no longer bought green bananas."

Margaret raised a single, perfectly sculpted eyebrow. She looked like Roger Moore's mom. "I've said a lot of things."

"About how the gadolinium was giving you a headache," Koenig said.

"Ah. I assume it is no longer in use?"

"The EU severely restricted its use as a contrast agent in 2018," Koenig said. "Something to do with deposits being left on the brain. It's mainly used for scans of the liver now. You claimed to have thymic carcinoma, which is a cancer of the upper chest. You would have been injected with something else."

"You seem annoyingly overeducated regarding MRI contrast agents, Benjamin."

"I get scanned every six months. And because I trust my doctors even less than I trust Jen, I question everything. So, yes, I *do* know a lot about contrast agents."

"Well, wasn't I Little Miss Over-Egging the Pudding?" Margaret said. "It's almost as if I've had no training whatsoever for this kind of thing."

"So why bother?" Carlyle asked woodenly. She looked defeated. Withdrawn. "I've been involved with military intelligence most of my adult life, and one of the most important lessons I learned is that the simplest cover story is the *best* cover story."

"Because of the freedom a cancer diagnosis gave her," Koenig said. "An operation this size needed a sponsor. She needed cash and she needed access to resources. Her cancer gave her the space to go and *seek* that sponsor."

"No one questions requests for time off when you have cancer," Margaret confirmed. "Colleagues give you a wide berth; friends find reasons not to visit. And traveling wasn't a problem. The university's HR department accepted I was exploring treatments abroad without asking for evidence. Bless their gullible souls." She paused a beat. "I'm surprised everyone isn't at it, to be honest. A cancer diagnosis is the ultimate hall pass."

"You approached the same people that had approached you all those years ago?"

She nodded. "I did."

"It's a big risk for a country, though," Carlyle said. "The think tank only considered terrorism or militia groups. A foreign government initiating the Acacia Avenue Protocol would be tantamount to declaring war."

"You think if Kim Jong-un had a magic ERASE THE USA button, he wouldn't press it?" Koenig said. "Of course he would. So would Putin. Even our allies would think about it."

"We aren't short of enemies," Draper agreed. She knew better than anyone how unpopular the US was in some parts of the world. "Koenig's right. If they could do this without leaving fingerprints, they absolutely would."

Carlyle put her head in her hands. "Why, Margaret?" she said. "Why do this? Was it money?"

"It wasn't money."

"I know it's not ideological. You believe in democracy just as much as I do."

"It's the worst form of government—"

"Except for all the other forms," Carlyle cut in, completing the Winston Churchill quote.

"It wasn't ideological, Elizabeth."

"Then what? Please, help me understand."

Margaret shrugged. "America had to be punished, dear," she said.

CHAPTER 96

"I've never really talked about my family, have I?" Margaret said.

"Not in any depth," Carlyle replied. "Your father was a hereditary peer; your mother was involved in charity work. You have an elder brother who worked in the city."

"*Two* elder brothers," she said. "Anthony, my eldest brother, inherited the estate. As was customary for our family, James and I received nothing."

"Bit cruel," Koenig said.

"It's how the British aristocracy has survived for so long. The firstborn inherits everything. Nothing is split. It's how generational wealth and power is built up. The family uses its influence to ensure the noninheriting siblings are given rewarding roles to stop them causing trouble. And as money was the altar at which my family worshipped, James was given a well-paid position in an investment bank."

"And you joined academia."

"I wasn't supposed to," Margaret said. "I was *supposed* to attend a Swiss finishing school. Their motto might as well have been 'It's better to learn from us than your mother-in-law.' As soon as I knew how to do silly things like interview for a gardener—you ask them about their preferred seed catalog, in case you're interested—I was scheduled to marry some weak-chinned country lord and knock out children like a brood hen."

"I can't see you accepting that, Margaret," Carlyle said. She looked sad.

The way people did when good friends did bad things. "In fact, I know you didn't."

"No, I enrolled at Oxford. Studied cultural anthropology."

Carlyle nodded.

"Except what you know is incomplete, Elizabeth," Margaret said. "There's a gap in my résumé." She picked up her cup and finished her coffee. "A nine-month gap."

"You were pregnant," Koenig said.

Margaret nodded. "If I might be permitted to use some vulgar American vernacular, my family had a stick up its ass. And that extended to our education. My brothers went to some ghastly boarding school in Scotland where sporting ability rather than academic achievement was celebrated. I was sent to the all-female equivalent. Imagine it. One hundred and fifty teenage girls all stuck in the middle of nowhere. Contact with boys was strictly forbidden. Some nights the air in the dormitory was so thick with pheromones you could barely breathe."

"Who was the father?"

"A local boy. Delivered the strawberries in summer and the sprouts in winter. He never knew, and he has no bearing on this sorry tale."

"Your family weren't happy?"

"I'd never seen my father so angry. I swear, if my aunt hadn't been there, he'd have thrown me in the moat."

"You had a moat?"

"It's an expression, dear."

"The nine-month gap in your résumé meant you had the child?"

"My mother and father told their friends and acquaintances that formal education wasn't for me, and that my needs would be best met by touring the Antipodes. My aunt would act as chaperone. She'd had a wild youth, full of indiscretion and scandal. Had had to tour the Antipodes herself at one point, she told me."

"Where did you really go?"

"A sanitorium in France, one that catered for the elite of Europe and their many self-inflicted ills. I stayed there for six months, my aunt at my side the whole time. I'd thought she was there for support, to make sure I was OK. Really, she was there to do her duty. Do you know what that meant?"

Koenig didn't hesitate. "She told you the baby died in childbirth."

"Indeed she did," Margaret said. "Something to do with the umbilical cord getting wrapped round the neck, blah blah blah. I had a day to recuperate, then it was all about showing them what the Wexmores are made of. The stiff-upper-lip, blessing-in-disguise speech."

"And the baby?"

She opened her arms wide.

"What happened to the baby is everything," she said.

CHAPTER 97

"My brother Anthony married a wretched woman," Margaret said. "A spiteful beast who saw everyone as a threat and no one as a friend. Little wonder she died alone. Not even her daughter, my niece Felicity, called upon her after Anthony finally succumbed to his gout."

"Gout's not fatal," Draper said.

"It is when your fingers get so swollen you can't call the emergency services after you've fallen into the cesspit."

"Where's Lassie when you need her?" Koenig muttered. He was getting impatient. They'd been in the air thirty minutes, and he still had nowhere near enough information to question Nash.

"Anyway, Felicity's a lovely woman. Madder than a beef-fed cow, but doesn't have a nasty bone in her body. When her mother died, the family solicitor asked Felicity to find some paperwork relating to inheritance tax. Now Felicity, God bless her stupid soul, had no idea what she was looking for, so she ended up looking everywhere. And guess what she found in a locked drawer in my mother's old roll-top writing bureau?"

No one replied. It was clearly a rhetorical question.

Margaret continued like they'd answered her anyway. "Exactly, she came across paperwork detailing what had happened to my daughter," she said. "What had *really* happened."

"Which was?" Koenig said.

"A childless couple in Oregon adopted her. Good people. It was all done legally, and my mother had kept all the paperwork. And not just the adoption papers. Emily's new parents sent photographs. Two a year—birthdays and Christmas. There were also papers detailing the trust fund my mother had set up. The medical bills she'd paid. The things she'd done to ensure my daughter had a head start in life. And because Felicity had never been told it was a secret, she didn't know not to give it all to me."

"That must have been quite a shock, Margaret," Carlyle said.

"To say the least."

"It sounds like you had a legitimate grievance against your late mother and father. Definitely your aunt. But for some reason it's the US you're blaming. Why is that, Margaret?"

Margaret smiled, but the humor didn't reach her eyes. "What do you know about America's dirty little secret?" she said.

CHAPTER 98

"My sister-in-law died six years ago," Margaret said. "Felicity sent me my daughter's paperwork shortly after that. As you might imagine, it was quite a shock. Disbelief, really. My first emotion was anger. No, *hatred*. A hatred of the people who had denied me my daughter for so many years. And yes, hatred toward myself. For accepting the explanation my aunt had given me. For not questioning it. For not realizing that as too-cool-for-school as she was, my aunt *always* put the family's name first. That she'd been sucking at the teat for too long to give it up."

Margaret held her cup toward Koenig. He refilled it. Her cancer diagnosis might have been a lie, but her age wasn't. She'd been talking for a while and the cabin was pressurized. Her throat would be popcorn dry.

"My second emotion was joy," she said after she'd blown on the coffee and taken a sip. "Pure, unadulterated joy. I'd worked in academia my entire life and had assumed maternal instincts were for others. That I was too intellectual to be burdened by the need to procreate." She smiled wistfully. "Turns out that was horseshit. As soon as I had discovered the truth, I loved my daughter like I'd been in her life since she drew her first breath. I then had a decision to make. To involve myself or not. And let me tell you, that wasn't as easy as you might think. I didn't even know if she knew she was adopted. She was an adult by then, of course, but even so, having your family history rewritten would shock anyone. And what about her parents? They deserved my consideration too. In the end I did what I thought best: I wrote her parents a letter and introduced myself. Explained a little of what had happened and why I hadn't been in touch before." She took another sip of her coffee. Traced a circle in a spill on the table. "And then I waited for a reply."

"How long did you have to wait?" Draper asked.

"Do you have access to the US military's database, dear?" Margaret asked Draper.

"Not officially."

"I'll take that as a yes. Be a good girl and look up Lieutenant Braddock. Emily Braddock. US Navy." She gave Draper a date of birth and a nine-digit service number. "She was a late entrant. Had a career as a teacher before she accepted her commission."

Draper held Margaret's gaze a beat, then opened her laptop. Her fingers danced over the keyboard. Touch-typing. She stared at the screen, then used the trackpad to navigate around whatever site she was on. She asked Margaret to repeat the service number. Koenig watched her type it into a boxed-off field on a US Navy personnel website. It was one he hadn't seen before. Draper obviously had a back door into something that wasn't in the public domain. A small egg timer loaded on the screen as they waited for the information to appear.

The screen changed, and Draper leaned in to read it. She frowned.

"It says here that Emily Braddock was court-martialed," she said. She read a bit more. "She was found guilty of making a false official statement and dishonorably discharged. It doesn't say what that statement was, which is odd. It looks like it's been deleted."

"She was raped, dear," Margaret said. "A fellow officer raped her. He went into her bunk and subjected her to an ordeal that should have got him a thirty-year prison sentence. Instead, the navy covered it up. He got thirty days confined to base for not being at his post. He was confined to base, and my daughter was dishonorably discharged. They said she'd made a malicious complaint after being passed over for a promotion. They cover them *all* up. The systemic rape of women serving their country—and the retaliations they face when they report it—is known as America's dirty little secret."

"Did Emily tell you this? It must have been hard to hear."

"No. I found this out independently. People were willing to talk. Statistically, female soldiers are more likely to be attacked by a fellow soldier than killed by the enemy. There's even a term for it: 'military sexual trauma.' It's now the leading cause of PTSD among female veterans."

Carlyle nodded. "Sexual assault–related health care now costs the VA almost a billion bucks a year," she said. "Military culture still sees war as the domain of men. Unfortunately, that means servicewomen can be viewed as little more than camp followers. It's improving, but not as fast as it should be."

Margaret took a drink. Wiped her lips with the back of her hand.

"The man who raped Emily was a fellow lieutenant called Marc Du Pont. He's the son of a vice admiral, and Emily's wasn't the first complaint made against him. The enlisted women in his unit even had laminated cards made up for new arrivals. It warned against accepting drinks from him. If he was in the building, they were to pair up when going to the bathroom. And on no account were they to attend a summons to his office, even if it meant disobeying a direct order."

"How did he keep getting away with it?" Koenig said. "Powerful daddy or not, a rapist is a rapist."

"That's what she'd thought," Margaret said. "When she finally made it to the sick bay, battered and bruised, she was admitted as an emergency. The doctor, a lieutenant commander, was administering a drip to stabilize her blood pressure when he got a phone call. Emily didn't know who it was he spoke to, or what he was threatened with, but when the call ended, he removed her drip and told her she was faking it. That her injuries were self-inflicted and superficial, and that he wanted nothing to do with her."

"The US is one of the few countries that still lets the military conduct its own rape investigations," Carlyle said. "It means command has an overwhelming say over what happens. If the base CO doesn't want a rape prosecuted, it isn't prosecuted. And in most cases, there are no upsides. They lose at least one man from their unit, and it demonstrates there's a problem with discipline. It doesn't surprise me in the slightest that Daddy Du Pont was able to pull strings and protect his son."

"You're going to prison, Margaret," Koenig said. "There's nothing I can do about that. But when this is all over, I'm going to talk to your daughter, and I'm shining a big light on what she went through. On what Du Pont did. You have my word."

"That's very kind of you, Benjamin," Margaret said. "But you won't be able to talk to Emily, I'm afraid. Eight years ago, she gave up her struggle for justice. She drove to the ocean she'd always loved, watched the sun come up, then blew her own brains out. *That's* why America must be punished."

CHAPTER 99

"OK," Koenig said. "That explains the why. It doesn't explain the how."

"And you won't get that from me," Margaret said. "Not willingly."

Koenig looked at Draper. Waterboarding an old lady who'd just disclosed that the daughter she thought had died at birth had actually been alive and thriving until she'd been thrown out of the job she'd loved because she'd had the audacity to complain about being raped by the son of a vice admiral seemed . . . distasteful. Draper would do it, though, Koenig knew that. She had the ability to compartmentalize her emotions. To take them out of her decision-making process. It was why he disliked her so much. Emotions were good. They were the starting point for everything wonderful about the human condition. Empathy. Sympathy. Compassion. Love. Their roots were *all* emotion. But right now, they needed to know what Margaret knew. And Draper was the only person who could make it happen.

"Drowning me won't change anything, Benjamin," Margaret said, reading to the end of the page. "After I'd told my sponsor what I wanted, they appointed someone who can best be described as a project manager. The aforementioned Jakob Tas. We only ever met over the phone, never *facie ad faciem*. We discussed the big picture, but never the finer details. Jakob wrote the small print, not me. There are several ways the Acacia Avenue Protocol can be executed; I have no way of knowing the route he chose. I'm in the dark too." She paused. Smiled, then added, "Exciting, isn't it?"

Koenig ignored her last remark. "Part of this 'big picture' you discussed was abducting the people who'd attended Bess's Future Threat meeting?" he said.

Margaret nodded. "I didn't know everything. Elizabeth was paranoid about uncovering something that might work. She kept us in silos. But there was only so much she could do. I knew some of the others who'd attended. Jakob questioned them about their input and who *they'd* met while they were there. Over the course of a few months we'd mapped out everything. The only thing we were missing was Elizabeth. I never believed she was dead. It was simply too convenient."

"If you knew everything, why did you need her?" Draper asked.

"Because the preparatory actions we took—"

"Please, have the balls to call it what it is. They were abductions and murders."

"Jolly good," Margaret said. "The *abductions and murders* were necessary, but they did leave a pattern. One that Elizabeth would see and act on. And I needed to understand what those actions might be. Maybe even steer them."

"You knew she would come out of hiding to watch over you."

"I was heavily involved in most of the protocol," Margaret said. "It made sense that I would be at risk too. So, I made myself look like an easy target. Vulnerable. Practiced my old-lady-with-cancer limp and hired some goons to approach me unawares at Speakers' Corner every Sunday. I knew she would turn up eventually, and I knew she would take robust measures if she thought there was a threat to my life."

"*Robust measures?*" Carlyle said. "I killed them, Margaret. I *murdered* them."

"You did what you thought was best, Elizabeth. And one of the things I've taken from having faked cancer for half a decade is that while the easiest people to con are the cheats and scoundrels, the easiest people to *manipulate* are the honest and decent. Take it as a compliment."

"Why not just kill her?" Draper said. Tactful.

"Because I needed to know the safeguards she had put in place. We got close during the Acacia Avenue week, but I knew there were parts she hadn't shared. That there were—"

The Gulfstream hit a patch of turbulence. It acted like a full stop. Gave Koenig time to catch up on what Margaret had told them. Now he'd recalibrated himself to challenge everything she said, her lies weren't difficult to see.

She was right; she *wasn't* a field agent. When she improvised, she got it wrong. She overcompensated. Said too much.

"Why did you kill Hobbs?" he said. "Because if you're as removed from the actual operation as you claim, killing him doesn't make a whole lot of sense. If you're as in the dark as we are, how can you help steer the investigation?"

Margaret said nothing.

"Who did you call to get those mercenaries to the airfield in Scotland? Who did you call to get them to Stillwell Hobbs's apartment?"

Margaret still said nothing.

"What's in San Diego?"

Margaret held his gaze for a full thirty seconds. Her breathing was steady. She looked calm. In control. "You really are very good, Benjamin," she said. "When this is over, please don't think ill of me."

She then picked up her cup by its base, smashed it against the table, and gouged a shard of bone china into her neck.

CHAPTER 100

"A little help here, Koenig!" Draper shouted.

She was holding a towel against the gaping hole in Margaret's neck. Pressing hard, trying to stem the tide of blood. She was on her second towel. It was already sodden. Koenig thought it was a wasted effort. Margaret had done her job well; the wound was fatal. The shard of china she'd used had been the size and shape of a fluting knife, and she hadn't hesitated. She hadn't warned them. She'd jammed it into the soft tissue underneath her jaw and twisted until Koenig had grabbed her hand. The blood pouring from her neck was dark red, like roasted beets. She'd severed one of the major veins in her neck. The external jugular, for sure. Maybe the internal jugular as well. Not the carotid artery. The blood wasn't light and frothy, and it wasn't coming out hard and fast like a busted fire hydrant. This was more like an overflowing storm drain. Slow and steady but equally powerful.

But not for long. After a minute it was little more than a trickle. And then it stopped completely. Margaret's eyes went glassy; her mouth hung open. She was dead.

Draper threw the towel to the floor in disgust. She glared at Koenig. "This is your fault," she said. "I wanted to cuff her, but you said not to."

"That's enough," Carlyle said. Her face was ashen. But it was also hard. Like tempered steel. "This was a collective mistake, Miss Draper. We should all have recognized Margaret's monologue for what it was—a death row confession. We need to regroup and refocus because turning on each other isn't going to get the eggs scrambled."

Draper sighed. "I know," she said. "It's just . . . it felt like we were about to get somewhere, you know? To get so close, only for it to . . ."

"We weren't close," Carlyle said. "Margaret didn't tell us anything; all she did was provide the context. Even if we'd forced the issue, she'd have had plausible misdirection ready to go. She'd have made us look at her right hand while her left was picking our pockets."

"We have to do some—"

A sound made them turn toward the back of the plane.

It was Nash. She was smiling.

And giggling.

Koenig looked at Draper. "You want to go and see if she'll let us in on the joke?"

CHAPTER 101

"You're laughing," Koenig said. "Why?"

"Because you guys are dumbasses," Nash replied. "That old lady was the key to everything, and you watched her kill herself. I'm laughing at your fuckwittery."

"You might want to rethink your predicament," Koenig said. "The music's stopped and you're the only one without a chair now."

Nash rolled her eyes. "I think I'm going to be fine," she said.

Koenig knelt. Stared into her eyes. Nash looked right back. She wasn't trying to alpha him. Wasn't playing mind games. It was as if she didn't recognize him as someone worth bothering with. Like he was the ant at her picnic. She might stomp on him; she might not. She certainly wasn't going to spend time thinking about it. Koenig wondered if she was a psychopath. If, now that her father was dead, she was looking forward to spreading her wings. Like a harpy, not an angel.

"How old are you? Twenty-one? Twenty-two?"

"If Stillwell was to be believed, I'm twenty."

"Don't you know?"

"I've never seen my birth certificate."

"You were adopted?"

"Fostered. Stillwell showed up when I was seven. Up until then, I'd lived in a kids' home in Albuquerque."

Koenig nodded. He thought it explained things. Hobbs had wanted an apprentice, and he'd wanted a child to give him cover. He would no longer be the loner people remembered after the cops had arrived; he would be the doting father on a road trip with his daughter. And over time she became someone he could mold into his own image. Similar to how the hitman had molded the orphan in one of Koenig's favorite movies, *Léon: The Professional*.

Koenig had no idea how Hobbs had managed to jump through the fostering hoops. Child protective services were supposed to have safeguard after safeguard to stop vulnerable kids being placed with predatory adults. Then again, he imagined their antenna was more attuned to pedophiles and the perma-angry. He doubted they had an "Are you, or have you ever been, a contract killer?" tick box. But Hobbs was, and the system had failed Nash. Big time.

And now there was a monster to deal with.

"Do you know who your birth parents were?" he asked.

"What part of 'I've never seen my birth certificate' didn't you understand?" she said. She paused a beat, then muttered, "Fucking dummy."

She giggled.

Koenig didn't respond. He'd been called a lot worse in his SOG days. Draper had called him a lot worse that morning. But he did have to rethink how he approached this. Nash was a killer, almost certainly a psychopath, but she was still, at heart, a damaged kid. Hobbs wouldn't have been interested in Nash's childhood development. He probably actively discouraged it. He was only interested in her for what she brought to his business. She was a prop. And yes, over time he'd developed strong paternal instincts, but they'd never been reciprocated. Nash was, and always would be, motivated by one thing: self-interest.

"I may be an effing dummy," Koenig said. "But I think you suffer from psychopathy."

Nash smiled. Like she was looking forward to what he would say next.

Patronizing.

"Thing is, being a psychopath isn't illegal," Koenig said. "It isn't even uncommon. At least one percent of the population has what is classed as severe psychopathy. One percent of three hundred and thirty million people. That's over three million psychopaths in the US alone. Most have jobs and families. They've learned to fit in. To laugh at jokes that aren't funny. To cry when someone dies. They're law-abiding. Lots are successful. Superficial charm and a lack of emotion are assets, not drawbacks, in some jobs. Now, let's imagine there's a subset of a subset in the broad umbrella of psychopathy—the one percent of the one percent of the one percent. The kind of psychopath who sees people as cattle, there to be used and discarded. *That's still not illegal.* The DA's office could no more convict you of being a psychopath than it could convict you of being a human being."

He waited for Nash to respond. Eventually she said, "Moo."

"Murder, of course, *is* illegal. And I'm sure when it all comes out in the wash, when the tallies are totaled, the FBI will find that you and Hobbs have killed more people than Jack Reacher. You don't get to own a loft on the Lower East Side without being extremely good at extremely lucrative work. But even though the pair of you were at the top of the murder-for-hire business, you couldn't be sure you hadn't left evidence behind somewhere. Not one hundred percent. Trace DNA. A partial print. Getting caught on a camera you didn't know about. Something that would culminate with a no-knock warrant. Indictments. Trials. Life-with-no-parole jail sentences."

He nodded at Draper. She went to the back of the Gulfstream and grabbed the medical kit. It was a molded plastic box, green with a white cross on the lid. Draper flipped the catches and opened it. She pulled out a pack of disposable gloves and ripped it open with her teeth. She snapped on a pair like a thirty-year robbery-homicide veteran.

Nash watched without concern.

"But getting caught doesn't concern you, does it?" Koenig continued. "Because if you *are* in that one percent of the one percent, yada yada yada, you've already thought of this. You've *planned* for this. Because in your mind, at least, a one-percenter like you should never have to face any consequences. Consequences are for the cattle. You'll have someone in place to take the fall. A patsy. A witless fool in a THE BUCK STOPS HERE T-shirt. Stillwell Hobbs, in other words. All these years, and he still thought of himself as the master manipulator. He had it back-to-front, though. He wasn't manipulating you; you were manipulating *him*. He was your insurance policy. Your circuit breaker. So, even if the FBI did find evidence, it would have been Hobbs who spent the rest of his life in a supermax. You'd have walked free. Another of his victims."

"Doesn't matter what you know, dummy, it only matters what you can prove," Nash said.

"Unfortunately, things have moved on."

Draper reached into her pocket and removed an envelope. She opened it and tilted it so Nash could see the single-point self-defense ring inside, the ring with the blade that looked like a raptor's beak. The one Nash had used to tear out the throats of her would-be rapists in New York. Draper had taken it from her index finger while Nash had been unconscious in the alley outside her apartment. Draper slipped the ring into a new envelope and sealed it. Wrote the date and time on the seal. Scrawled her signature across it.

"There we are, all nice and legal," she said. "All the evidence the DA will need to convict you. Your DNA, their DNA, and an eyewitness who saw everything."

Nash's eyes narrowed. "What eyewitness?"

"Me," Koenig said.

Nash looked mildly annoyed. Like she'd accidentally deleted her Netflix profile.

"I'm a twenty-year-old girl, dummy. There's no way a New York jury will find me guilty. The cameras will prove they dragged me into that alleyway. Even the stupidest public defender will be able to prove self-defense." She paused a beat. Added, "And I won't have the stupidest public defender."

"What cameras?" Koenig said. "We were there the best part of a week, and we didn't see any. And the reason we couldn't see any was because you and Hobbs had deliberately chosen to live somewhere *without* cameras."

"You have a choice to make," Draper said. "Tell us what you overheard Konstantin say in that Holiday Inn. You thought it was meaningless drivel, but Margaret killed Hobbs before he could tell us what it was. Tell us what you heard, and Koenig does you a favor."

"And what would that be?"

"He tells the NYPD he saw those men drag you into the alley. That he ran to help and saw you act in self-defense."

"Which is mostly true," Koenig said.

"And if I *don't* tell you what I overheard?"

"Then Koenig saw you lure those poor men into the alley. He witnessed you murder them in cold blood. No DA's office in the land will shy away from this. They have a ring that is essentially a weapon. That shows premeditation. They have a federal eyewitness—because, believe it or not, Koenig is *still* a US Marshal—and they'll have the attorney general herself leaning on them."

"She's our friend," Koenig said.

Nash pouted. "That's not fair."

"Call it paying it forward. You might not be guilty of these murders, but as sure as fish on Friday, you're guilty of a hundred others. I'll lie to the NYPD, then I'll sleep fine."

"It's a binary choice," Draper said. "You help us, or you go to prison for thirty years."

"Our interests are aligned, Miss Nash," Koenig said. "I'm no astrologist, but it's as if the stars themselves want you to help us."

CHAPTER 102

"A waterbed!" Draper shouted. "The only thing she overheard Konstantin say was 'waterbed'? That's what Margaret killed Hobbs for? That's the big secret?"

Koenig didn't respond.

After a while Draper got control of herself. "Do we believe her?" she asked.

Nash had told them that when she'd checked out Jakob Tas, the big Russian, and an unnamed female, prior to them meeting with Hobbs, she'd overheard a snippet of conversation. Konstantin had said "waterbed" and Tas had shushed him. And that was it. She hadn't heard the start of his sentence, and Tas stopped it before it ended. She'd overheard the middle. A concrete noun. One word. Two if Konstantin meant the bottom of a pond rather than a sciatica-causing mattress. Nash had told Hobbs on the ride home and he hadn't responded. She'd put it out of her mind. Hadn't thought about it since.

That's what she claimed.

And Koenig *did* believe her. If it had been anyone else, Koenig's default position would have been that they were lying. Hiding something. But Nash was driven entirely by self-interest. It was her only concern. She had no reason to lie, every reason to tell the truth.

"I think if she'd wanted to lie, she'd have been more inventive," he said.

"That's what I think as well," Draper said. "I think Hobbs played us. He dangled a worm in front of us, one he knew we'd bite. And it worked. His foster daughter is alive."

Her phone buzzed in her jacket pocket. She grabbed it and checked the screen.

She accepted the call.

She listened.

Then she said, "Smerconish has found something."

"Is it a waterbed?" Koenig said.

CHAPTER 103

Smerconish hadn't found a waterbed.

But he had found the truck that had collected the NorseBoat in Maine. He'd also found a bunch of dead guys. They were in a paint wholesaler's abandoned warehouse in Logan Heights, one of the oldest neighborhoods in San Diego. The warehouse was a stone's throw from the I-5, the route Smerconish now knew Jakob Tas had taken. Whoever had killed them had made no effort to move their bodies. They hadn't been hidden. No one was in a rolled-up carpet. They were lying where they'd died. The killer hadn't even bothered pulling the warehouse's roller door all the way down.

A portable fingerprint scanner and access to every database in the world confirmed the dead guys' identities. Cora Pearl was an ex-paramedic, ex–bounty hunter, and ex-MMA champion. She was now ex-alive. She'd had her throat slashed. The wounds were clean and neat. Even depth. Looked like they had been done by a surgeon. Smerconish said he doubted this had been the first throat the killer had cut. The second person was Konstantin. The waterbed guy. Hobbs had called him a monosyllabic brute. And maybe he had been. Or maybe he didn't have good English. Didn't matter now, though. Not with a bullet hole in the back of his head. Smerconish said the entry wound showed muzzle imprint. Konstantin had been shot at point-blank range, the end of the muzzle pressed against his skull before the trigger had been pulled.

The last dead guy was an Australian called Jenkins. He had a string of smuggling offenses. He'd almost made it out of the old paint warehouse, but a bullet in the back of his knee had taken him down and a bullet in the brain finished him off.

There was no sign of Jakob Tas.

Koenig didn't need Smerconish to tell him what had happened. Tas had killed Konstantin first. Walked up to him and put a gun to the back of his head. Probably a silenced weapon, probably controlled his fall. He'd then slit Pearl's throat. They were the threat and had to be taken care of first. They were fighters. Hardened mercenaries. The Australian had been shot while attempting to flee.

Koenig figured there was no one left. That Tas had killed his entire team. That was an all-in play. You couldn't leave a couple alive and tell them they were going to be OK. That they definitely weren't going to be killed later. It didn't work that way.

The truck was still in the warehouse, but the boat and the trailer were gone.

"He's switched vehicles," Koenig said.

"He has," Draper confirmed. "And the warehouse was in a run-down part of Logan Heights. There are no cameras and plenty of major roads he could have taken. Smerconish has lost him."

"He must be furious."

"Actually, he's not."

"He isn't? Why?"

"Because Smerconish thinks he knows why Jakob Tas is in San Diego," she said.

CHAPTER 104

"Smerconish believes that because Jakob Tas smuggled a boat all the way from Maine, the threat is water-based," Draper said.

Koenig rolled his eyes. *Of course* the threat was water-based. It was such an obvious conclusion that no one on the Gulfstream had bothered to voice it. Tas had risked hauling the boat almost 3,500 miles, across multiple states and multiple time zones. He'd only done that because he'd had to. If it was something *inside* the boat, he'd have unloaded it somewhere quiet and scuttled the boat in a handy lake.

"Any specific water-based threat, or is that all he has?" Koenig said. "Because the way this is unfold—"

"Tas's target is Naval Base San Diego," Draper cut in. "He believes the boat is a bomb."

Koenig shook his head. "That doesn't make sense."

"He thinks it does."

"I agree it's a water-based threat, but it's not a bomb. He could have gotten explosives anywhere. He wouldn't have to smuggle them into the country."

"The target doesn't make sense either," Carlyle said. "Naval Base San Diego doesn't meet the objectives of the Acacia Avenue Protocol."

"Again, he thinks it does," Draper said. "HMS *Queen Elizabeth*, the Royal Navy's aircraft carrier, has just docked there. It's undertaking interoperability training with a Marine Corps F-35 squadron. Smerconish thinks it's the British ship that's the target, not one of ours. He says destroying the flagship of a major ally won't only damage our reputation, it'll impact on our military capability."

Koenig looked at Carlyle. "Bess?"

"Not being able to protect our allies' ships during peacetime *would* be a major embarrassment," she said. "But it doesn't meet the objectives of the Acacia Avenue Protocol."

"And blowing up an aircraft carrier doesn't need a bunch of mercenaries," Koenig said. "It doesn't need Margaret getting close to Bess. And what about the people Hobbs and Nash killed? And Carlyle's missing academics? How does all that fit? All a naval base attack needs is a man in a canoe with an oil drum full of fertilizer and a death wish. But that's why Smerconish isn't worried. Naval bases have more protection than people realize. A *lot* more. Tas wouldn't be able to paddle alongside the *Queen Elizabeth* unnoticed. That would be foolhardy, and I don't think Tas is foolhardy."

"He's hardly a genius, though," Draper said. "If he were, we wouldn't have been able to track him to San Diego."

"If that's what really happened."

Draper didn't respond.

"Think about it," Koenig continued. "Tas was in constant contact with Margaret, so he knew we were onto him. But instead of getting rid of his cell phone in the middle of nowhere, he's observed throwing it into the sea. Why was that?"

"You said he'd made a mistake."

"And now I don't think he did. I think that was somewhere for us to start. The first breadcrumb. A trail that would lead to three dead bodies in an old paint warehouse in San Diego. And HMS *Queen Elizabeth*'s visit isn't a secret."

"It's misdirection?"

"I think that's exactly what this is. I think he wants us putting our resources into bulking up security at the naval base. And while we do, he'll be somewhere else with a boat that's rigged with something a lot more exotic than C-4."

"What, though?"

"I have no idea."

"Bess?" Draper said.

Carlyle shrugged. "I don't know what he's up to, but I agree with Ben; the naval base is misdirection."

"And you still won't tell us what this master plan of yours is?"

"If I thought it would help, I would. But I don't, so I won't."

Draper shook her head in frustration. "Got to say, Bess, I'm getting mighty fucking tired of that answer."

"I won't compromise national security to assuage your curiosity," she said, calm as a toad in the sun.

"Tell him then!" Draper snapped, pointing at Koenig. "I don't like not being trusted, but I'll accept the compromise."

"How is that different?"

"Because you're right. I *would* be a risk. I've completed my resistance to interrogation training, and I know my limits. I would hold out for as long as I could, but I would talk eventually. I wouldn't be able to help myself; my pain would overrule my patriotism. I've watched zealots being tortured, men and women who would have happily died for their cause, and not one of them held out indefinitely. They all talked in the end. Everyone does." She paused a beat, then pointed at Koenig. "He won't, though," she said. "I don't think there are any circumstances in which Koenig would talk."

"He's not invincible, Miss Draper," Carlyle said.

"He's better," Draper said. "He's stubborn."

"Stubbornness isn't a substitute for—"

"Do you want to know how he's able to do all that stupid shit? Walking toward men in body armor like he's invincible. Throwing bodies down oily stairs like he's at a bowling alley. Taking out a bunch of corrupt cops with a credit card. A hundred other things you don't know about?"

"I assumed he—"

"It's because the asshole can't feel fear, Bess!" Draper cut in. "And I don't mean in a heroic, overcoming-what-you're-scared-of way. I mean, he literally can't feel fear. His brain's all fucked up. The bit that regulates his fight-or-flight response has calcified harder than a dinosaur turd."

Carlyle looked at Koenig thoughtfully. Looked like she was evaluating him.

"And torture is all about fear," Draper continued. "That's how it works. It's the *fear* of pain, not the pain itself. If the person applying pain understands the psychology of torture, they should ensure the pain is noticeably worse than the time before. The victim not only has the memory of the pain they've just experienced, they also have the fear of the pain to come. No one talks *during* the pain. It's always before the next lot is applied."

"That may be so, Miss Draper," Carlyle said. "Maybe Ben won't be the national security risk I was. But I don't see how a problem shared is a problem halved. Not in this case. I know the Acacia Avenue Protocol better than anyone, and I can make neither head nor tail of what's happening. I can see the individual pieces, but the bigger picture eludes me. I can't see how they connect. And I know what I'm looking for. Ben wouldn't. I'm sorry, but I don't see how this helps."

"That's the thing, Bess," Draper said. "He *can* help. If you let him, he's the best chance you have."

"How?"

"Because Koenig happens to be the best lateral thinker I've ever met. If anyone can make sense of these disparate pieces, it's him." She stood. "Now, I'm going to give Nash a drink of water. I'm knocking off all internal communication devices. Please, please, *please*, tell Koenig what the Acacia Avenue Protocol is."

She left the front of the Gulfstream and shut the door behind her. It closed with an expensive-sounding *snick*. Carlyle held Koenig's gaze for a full minute. Didn't say anything. Just stared and scrutinized.

"You have to trust someone, Bess," he said. "If not me, who?"

Still nothing.

"I know part of it anyway," he added.

"Oh?"

"Like Jen says, I'm a lateral thinker. I think the Acacia Avenue Protocol is an attack on our infrastructure. It has to be. It's the only thing that joins up all the dots."

"What makes you say that?"

"Because of who Hobbs and Nash were killing. They weren't random. Not if you ignore who they were and concentrate on what they *did*. Louise Durose was a landfill-management expert. Hank Reynolds worked for the Environmental Protection Agency, something to do with wastewater systems, and Michael Gibbs had designed software that was supposed to increase deepwater port productivity. They're infrastructure jobs. We don't yet have the bios of the sixteen others that Hobbs and Nash killed, but I'm sure they'll have worked in infrastructure too. And I bet not one of them headed up their department."

"Why?"

"Because of the Peter principle."

"Go on."

"It's the management theory that people rise to positions of incompetence. They get promoted out of jobs they're good at but eventually get a job they're *not* good at. In some hierarchical organizations the entire management structure is staffed by the incompetent."

"And why would this be relevant to an attack on our infrastructure?"

"Because the people Hobbs and Nash killed were the ones who got things done. The ones who understood how everything worked. And how to fix it when it broke. The people above them are the Peters in the Peter principle. And the Peters aren't just the incompetents. They're the policy wonks. The political appointments. The dumb lucky and the nepotists. But because most organizations don't take continuity planning seriously, if you take out the level below the Peters, the organization grinds to a halt." He paused, then added, "Have I passed?"

Carlyle slumped in her seat. Seemed to go back into her shell. But just when he thought she was going to take Acacia Avenue to her grave, she decided not to. She decided to trust him.

"What do you know about the Partition of India, Ben?"

CHAPTER 105

"Out of left field": baseball terminology for the base runner sprinting to home plate being surprised by a throw from left field.

It now means unexpected.

The East Coast Sweeney had been unexpected. So had Margaret using her hairpin to murder Hobbs and a shard of bone china to slash her own throat.

And now Elizabeth Carlyle had asked Koenig what he knew about the Partition of India. She had come out of left field.

Because when he'd figured out the Acacia Avenue Protocol was an attack on the US's critical infrastructure, he'd expected Carlyle to reel off one of the greatest hits. The transportation network is always vulnerable, particularly bridges and tunnels. The infrastructure-reliant Global Positioning System—GPS—can be disrupted. The power grid is susceptible to acts of men, like terrorism, and acts of God, like solar storms. A successful cyberattack on the financial markets would have generational consequences. And these were the risks he'd known about a decade ago. Things would have moved on. The more advanced infrastructure became, the more susceptible it became to bad actors. It was the price of advancement.

But Carlyle hadn't reeled off one of the greatest hits. She'd asked him about the Partition of India. What he knew about it. Which wasn't much. Other than the headlines. That it was when Britain split one country into two: India and Pakistan. It was probably on the British curriculum, but it wasn't taught in American schools.

"I know it didn't go as planned," Koenig said.

"That's like saying the *Challenger* launch didn't go as planned," Carlyle said. "It was an unmitigated disaster. I can't even say it was an unmitigated disaster from start to finish, as the consequences are still being felt today."

"This is important?"

Naval Base San Diego was sealed tighter than a frog's ass. SEALs in the water, eyes in the sky. A dozen other security measures, some so secret they wouldn't even be written down. It was secure. Koenig knew that. He also didn't care. Naval Base San Diego wasn't the target. It was chicanery. Smoke and mirrors. Tas had his eyes on a much bigger prize. He'd also pulled the time-to-murder-your-team-and-go-it-alone trigger. That meant they didn't have long. Maybe not even long enough for a history lesson. Carlyle knew this. Yet she still thought he'd benefit from the context.

So instead of insisting she get to the point, he said, "Tell me what I need to know."

Carlyle nodded. Like she understood the mental gymnastics he'd gone through. An unspoken acknowledgment that she thought the same.

"A little history," she said. "The East India Company gained a foothold in India in the early seventeenth century. They took effective control in 1757 following the Battle of Plassey in Bengal. The company's principal aim was to plunder through taxation and one-sided trade treaties. They acted on behalf of the British government until the Indian Uprising of 1857. That's when the British Crown stepped in and instituted direct imperial rule. This period, lasting until Indian independence in 1947, is known as the Raj."

"I worked with a guy whose grandfather was a colonel out there," Koenig said. "He showed me photographs. The Brits lived like kings. Massive houses, servants, cooks, gardeners, chauffeurs, the lot."

"They did," Carlyle agreed. "And it's why it ultimately failed. The powerlessness of Indians to decide their own future led to an increasingly inflexible independence movement. The British had always managed rebellions with brutal suppression, but after the Second World War their economy couldn't cope with an overextended empire. It was agreed that they would exit India and split the country into two independent nation states: the Hindu-majority India and the Muslim-majority Pakistan. But instead of managing Partition carefully, the British rushed it. A civil servant called Cyril Radcliffe, a man who hated India from the moment he disembarked to the moment he set sail back to Britain, headed up the boundary committee. The process should have taken three years. Radcliffe did it in five weeks. He used out-of-date maps and census reports and then drew an arbitrary demarcation line. The *Radcliffe* Line. It came into effect in August 1947. The British then left and washed their hands of the whole thing."

"Five weeks to decide the fate of a continent?" Koenig said. "No wonder they screwed it up."

"What followed was one of the greatest human tragedies of the twentieth century," Carlyle agreed. "All along the Radcliffe Line, communities that had coexisted for a millennium turned on each other overnight. There were mass killings and mass abductions. There were forced conversions. Villages were set ablaze. Men, women, and children were hacked to death. Rape was commonplace. British soldiers who'd seen Nazi death camps said Partition was worse."

Koenig didn't respond. Anything he said would have seemed pedestrian. Too small.

"But the think tank didn't study the Partition of India because of the sectarian violence," Carlyle continued. "Despite what you might read, the United States takes the First Amendment seriously. The freedom to practice your religion is constitutionally guaranteed. Our country will never tear itself apart on religious grounds."

"What *did* you study it for, Bess?" Koenig said gently.

"Mass migration," she replied. "The Acacia Avenue think tank studied the Partition of India because it led to the greatest mass migration in human history."

CHAPTER 106

"Partition led to twelve million people being displaced in the Punjab alone," Carlyle said. "Overnight, Muslims found themselves in India, Sikhs and Hindus found themselves in Pakistan. People whose identities had been rooted in geography, not religion, found themselves mixed up in the biggest population exchange in history. An unprecedented number of refugees poured across the Radcliffe Line to regions completely foreign to them."

"And I guess these new countries weren't expecting it?" Koenig said.

"Weren't expecting it, weren't ready for it," Carlyle confirmed. "How could they be? They'd had five weeks' warning. The Brits drew a line on an out-of-date map, then left the subcontinent so quickly they only lost seven soldiers. But in the short period that followed their withdrawal, two million people died. There was an incredible amount of bloodshed at the border. Hundreds of thousands never even made it across. And those who did found themselves in a country that simply didn't have the resources to feed or house them. This caused conflict with the people who already lived there, which led to even *more* migration."

"You looked at how a mass migration event would impact the US?" Koenig said.

"We already study mass migration. We have to. It's rarely contained to one country. An event in Bangladesh will spill over to India, which leads to tension at the Chinese border, and so on. And although it wasn't technically a future threat—there have been two mass migration events in recent US history, the

California Gold Rush and the Great Migration—it's what the Acacia Avenue think tank landed on. We thought about what might cause millions of Americans to flee one part of the country and seek refuge in another part."

"War is the obvious one," Koenig said.

"But war doesn't happen overnight. There's a buildup. Attempts at diplomacy. There are skirmishes and a whole bunch of other things that happen before we declare war. Ultimately, war is predictable unpredictability. We ignored climate change for the same reason. Whether it's drought in the Southwest, tropical storms in the Southeast, or flooding in Louisiana, it doesn't happen overnight. We'd have time to adapt. To find room for the displaced and make them our neighbors."

"A Chernobyl-type event?"

"Certainly. Whether it's a catastrophic system failure or a terrorist attack, a nuclear incident would be sudden, devastating, and long-lasting. But it's not a *future* threat. We know our nuclear plants are high-value targets. Measures are in place to protect them, and drills are well practiced should a plant go into meltdown. It would be serious. It might even trigger mass migration, but it wouldn't be a surprise. We were looking for that one thing we hadn't thought of. The thing we *didn't* have contingencies for."

Koenig considered it from the think tank's point of view. He reckoned they'd have focused on the basics. What did humans need? Not want, *need*. They probably used Maslow's hierarchy of needs as a starting point. It was something her academics would have been familiar with. Maslow's five-tier model was often depicted as a pyramid. The bottom tier were physiological needs. Food and water. Clean air. Clothing and shelter. The next tiers were psychological needs like friendship, employment, and intimacy. Important, but nothing that would cause a stampede.

"The food chain can be vulnerable," he said. "If a well-resourced group managed to simultaneously introduce mad cow disease, foot-and-mouth, swine fever, and avian flu into our farms, most food animals would have to be culled." He stopped to think through what he'd said. "But although that would cause untold economic and logistical problems, it wouldn't cause a mass migration event."

"No, it wouldn't," Carlyle said. "Food can be imported. For the eighty percent of Americans who live in urban areas, it *is* imported. There would be no reason for anyone to move. Certainly not in the numbers we were looking for. But you *are* on the right lines."

"Air, then," he said. "If something happened to the air. Say it went bad. That would cause a migration event."

Carlyle nodded. "Bad air *would* cause a mass migration event. What else?"

"Water," Koenig said. "Water's not like food. Sure, we provide water trucks and bottles in severe droughts, but they're temporary measures. If the water dries up, or if something leaches into it, the population has to move. Look at what happened in Flint. The population is less than half what it used to be, and a large part of that is due to water crisis."

"Good. What else?"

"I can't think of anything."

"That's because there *isn't* anything," Carlyle said. "Not really. We considered air and we considered water. And after much discussion, we discounted water. While some parts of the country *are* reliant on a small number of sources, these lakes, springs, and rivers are so vast, there's nothing practical that could contaminate them. Even if you dropped a shipping container full of poison into the Mississippi, the effect would be negligible and short-lived. Even the Deepwater Horizon spill got cleaned up."

"You focused on air."

"We concluded the only viable way to trigger mass migration would be a biological attack on a geographically close group of major cities."

"Something like smallpox?"

"Not smallpox. All that would trigger is a mass vaccination program and a local lockdown. We wanted panic. We wanted people running for the hills."

"What then?"

"We decided one of the mycotoxins would work best. They're naturally occurring in fungi, they can cause death and cancers and a whole bunch of horrible stuff, but mostly you get very sick."

Koenig nodded. He could see how that would work. Stay-at-home mom wasn't going to stay at home for long when her little darlings were breathing in deadly spores. She was going to load up the station wagon and drive to her sister's. Or to her BFF from college. Anywhere the funky mushrooms weren't. Koenig hadn't studied the psychology of mass hysteria, but he figured it wouldn't take too many people upping sticks before *everyone* was upping sticks. Sure, there'd be the contrary whack jobs who'd enjoy the attention they got from staying put. And you couldn't move the "back in my day, things were much worse" crowd from their prefabs with a block and tackle. But most people *would* move.

Then Koenig thought about who they had strapped to a table in the back of the Gulfstream. Nash hadn't been involved in a plot to poison the air with funky fungi. She'd been paid to kill people with very specific jobs.

"You didn't stop there, though, did you, Bess?" he said. "Triggering a mass migration event was the start, not the finish."

And Carlyle said, "Do you know how to make a fruit salad, Ben?"

Out of left field.

CHAPTER 107

Koenig frowned. "I'm more of a chocolate-milkshake guy," he said. "But . . . if the choice was between making a fruit salad or watching *Police Academy 4: Citizens on Patrol*, I suppose I could peel some grapes." He paused half a heartbeat. "But the fruit salad is rhetorical. What you're *really* asking is if I understand how supply chains work."

"I am," Carlyle said. "Take New York. The magnitude and scope of the infrastructure that keeps a city like New York running is beyond most people's comprehension. Interdependent systems like sewerage, power, telecoms, water, road, rail, marine traffic, are piled on top of each other like a giant bowl of spaghetti. But here's the thing—it's efficient, integrated, and synchronized. Finely tuned chaos theory, it's been called. Unpredictable behavior governed by deterministic laws. Getting the ingredients for a fruit salad to the New York delis, markets, and grocery stores is nothing short of a miracle, yet it happens every single day."

"I guess I've never really thought about it," Koenig admitted.

"We did," Carlyle said. "We thought about it a lot. Nine million people live in New York. Then we thought about what might happen if there were mass migration events in Philly, Baltimore, and DC."

"Nine million becomes *nineteen* million."

"And now New York's infrastructure is stretched beyond breaking point. It's overloaded with little to no warning. The city's reserves are quickly used up. People are panic buying. The just-in-time supply chain becomes the *three-weeks-too-late* supply chain. Now what happens?"

"There's a period of readjustment. It's not pleasant, but with outside help New York begins to cope. The city manages sixty million tourists a year, so it has the capacity to expand when it needs to."

"Exactly," she said. "A mass migration event on its own might not achieve the effect we wanted. The country would be lopsided, like a badly loaded washing machine, but it wouldn't last forever."

She stopped talking. Let Koenig finish.

"That's where Hobbs and Nash came in," he said. "You don't let your enemy regroup when they're vulnerable. You stomp on their throats. Hobbs and Nash weren't involved in the mass migration event; their role was about amplifying the aftereffects. They killed the type of people who'd be essential in the event you describe. The damage-limitation guys, the ones with institutional memory."

"We identified the people that cities and states would need when it came to mounting effective crisis management," Carlyle confirmed. "The ones who could steady the ship before it passed the event horizon. The protocol dictated they were killed in the lead-up to the trigger event. Quietly, nothing that would arouse suspicion."

There was also something Carlyle wasn't telling him. Koenig thought their deaths had served a dual purpose. Their expertise in crisis management wasn't the primary reason; it was the *secondary* reason. He didn't know whether to be impressed or appalled. He kept his face neutral. Carlyle was a good woman, and she did what she thought best. Who was he to second-guess her actions?

"The Acacia Avenue Protocol was a three-stage attack on the infrastructure of the United States," Carlyle continued. "Step one was removing the people who could limit the damage after a mass migration event."

"Which Hobbs and Nash have now done. Their contract was complete."

"Step two is *triggering* the mass migration event."

"Which, as unlikely as it seems, Tas seems to think he can do," Koenig said.

"And step three was a coordinated attack on key infrastructure. Nothing massive, and most of it will look like it was due to an overload on the system. A tunnel fire cuts off a critical supply route. A train derails. A ship sinks in a deepwater port. A cyberattack shuts down the city's waste management system.

The protocol designed a whack-a-mole attack. One incident after another. Relentless. Too many to contain. Eventually the whole system would collapse. We calculated we would go from 'everything is normal' to a National Guard–enforced curfew within three weeks."

"That quickly?"

"That's a conservative estimate," she said.

"It wouldn't take that much seed money," Koenig said. "Mycotoxins already exist in weaponized form. Assholes like Tas and Hobbs need paying, but otherwise there'd be no other significant costs."

"We calculated one hundred million dollars," Carlyle said. "And there are almost one thousand billionaires in the US alone. They could fund it with the money they keep under their mattress."

Mattress.

Carlyle's analogy shone a light on what Nash had overheard Konstantin say. Helped Koenig see it properly. *Waterbed.* A waterbed was a mattress. It hadn't made sense. Except now it did. Now he had the missing context. Konstantin hadn't said "waterbed." He was Russian. Russians didn't talk like that. Konstantin had said something different. Something lost in translation.

"Konstantin didn't say 'waterbed,'" Koenig said. "I trained with the Russian SOBR, their special forces police unit, and I know how they speak English. The open and long æ doesn't exist in the Russian language. The vowels *A* and *E* end up being pronounced the same way—as an 'eh' sound. So 'fad' becomes 'fed'—"

Carlyle swallowed hard. "And 'bad' becomes 'bed' . . ."

"Exactly. Nash didn't overhear Konstantin say 'water*bed*,' she overheard him say 'water *bad*.'"

He took a moment. Let it sink in.

"Tas isn't using mycotoxins," Koenig said. "He's found a way to poison the water."

CHAPTER 108

"It can't be done," Carlyle said. "Attacking the water at its source was the first thing we considered and the first thing we dismissed. The logistics are insurmountable. Tas would need a significant and steady supply of toxins. A barrel of acid dumped in the Colorado won't cut off the water supply to forty million people. That's not how it works. It would dissipate. The best he could hope for is a small problem. Maybe a day. There's nothing he can do to cause a mass migration event."

"He's found a way," Koenig repeated.

Carlyle was adamant he hadn't but agreed that Draper should be told anyway. Not all of it, but enough to use her influence on Smerconish. Koenig calling the DIA spook to tell him he was wrong about an attack on HMS *Queen Elizabeth* would be dismissed. An ex-CIA agent telling him the same thing would be taken more seriously. He hoped.

Koenig briefed her as quickly as he could.

When he'd finished, she said, "Would this fulfill the objectives of the Acacia Avenue Protocol?"

Carlyle said, "If he's successful, yes."

"*If* he's successful?"

"I don't believe it's possible to poison the water. The best brains in the country studied this from hundreds of angles. Considered every possible scenario."

"Underestimating Margaret would be a catastrophic mistake," Koenig said. "She had access to your data and she had time to think. Time to refine your plans."

"I'll ask Smerconish to retask some of the surveillance drones he has covering the naval base."

"California is the most hydrologically altered land mass on the planet," Carlyle said. "It gets its water from a limited number of sources. Tell him to start with the Colorado, Sacramento, and San Joaquin Rivers. They all supply California. Lake Mead, obviously. The Mono Basin, maybe."

Draper scrolled through her contacts, then pressed the green call icon.

"Sir, we have a problem," she said.

CHAPTER 109

One person who didn't have a problem was Jakob Tas. Everything was on schedule. Koenig had been a thorn in his side, but ultimately he'd changed nothing. He'd *achieved* nothing. Yes, Tas had lost men in New York and in Scotland, men he'd fought wars with, but they'd taken his money; they understood the risk. Letting go of Pearl and Konstantin had been more of a wrench. He'd spilled blood with Konstantin in the Central African Republic, and Pearl had saved his life in Mali. He hadn't cared about the Australian. He'd been like a single-shot anti-tank weapon. Used once, then discarded.

Tas smiled to himself. He'd been listening to the police scanner app on his second cell phone. It wasn't illegal to listen to the cops in America. Weird country. San Diego PD had found the bodies in the paint warehouse, right when he'd needed them to. He'd have been annoyed if they hadn't. He'd left enough clues. That bowlegged idiot in New Silloth had watched as he threw the team's cell phones into the sea, he hadn't changed registration plates on the truck, and he'd made no attempt to disguise the NorseBoat. SDPD finding the bodies was part of the plan. Temporary misdirection. He'd known what their response would be.

What he needed it to be . . .

He checked his watch. Seven hours until the sun disappeared over the horizon. They hadn't found him yet, but they would.

Even if he had to make the call himself.

A stab of pain ripped through his stomach, bad enough to wipe the smile from his face. He grimaced and reached for his fentanyl. He shook the box.

One patch left. Seventy-two hours of pain relief. He wasn't worried. One patch was all he would need. He peeled off the liner and pressed the sticky side to his upper arm. He held it there until the pain ebbed away.

He smiled again.

Then he dropped anchor and waited.

CHAPTER 110

"Smerconish isn't convinced," Draper said. "But he *has* reassigned some of his drones."

"How many?" Koenig said.

"One."

"One? That's nowhere near enough."

"One's all we're getting," Draper said.

"He's humoring us," Koenig said.

"He is. He still thinks Tas plans to attack the British aircraft carrier."

"How long until we land in San Diego?"

Draper checked her watch. "A little over an hour. The pilot will be starting his approach soon."

"I'm going to sleep then."

"You're going to *sleep*?" Carlyle said.

"Sure, why not?" Koenig said.

"How can you even think of sleep right now?"

"Don't worry about it, Bess," Draper said, tapping the side of her head. "I don't think there's much going on in there. Just the *Spider-Man* theme tune on a continuous loop."

Koenig ignored her. "I haven't slept for twenty-four hours. That means I'm cognitively impaired."

"You can say that again," Draper muttered.

"My memory and hand-eye coordination are compromised. So is my hearing. My pain receptors are more sensitive. Sleep isn't a luxury, Bess; it's a necessity."

"Jeez, Koenig," Draper said. "You're such a dork."

CHAPTER 111

Koenig woke forty-five minutes older. Draper was shaking him by the shoulder. She wasn't being gentle.

"We're about to land," she said. "And you've been drooling on my cushions."

He felt groggy. Worse than before he'd gone to sleep. He reached for a bottle of water and swilled some around his mouth. Pushed it between his teeth. Sucked it back in. It didn't help. His throat was dry, like he'd swallowed dust. He needed a shower and a shave. A change of clothes. Definitely some mouthwash.

"Nothing from Smerconish?" he said.

Draper shook her head. "Not yet."

"He should have used more drones."

"You'd better put your seat belt on." The cell phone she was holding buzzed. She looked at the screen. "Speaking of the drone Nazi," she said. She tapped the green phone icon. "Sir?"

Smerconish talked; Draper listened. She said, "Five minutes," and ended the call.

"Courtesy call?" Koenig said.

"Seems Smerconish knows more about drone surveillance than we do," she said.

"He's found Tas?"

"He has."

"Where?"

"Lake Mead."

Koenig shared a glance with Carlyle. She shrugged. Koenig understood why. Making Lake Mead's water undrinkable *could* trigger a mass migration; she just didn't think it could be done.

"That seemed a bit too easy," he said.

"Smerconish says Tas isn't exactly hiding. He's not skulking in an inlet. He's made no attempt to change the NorseBoat's appearance. And get this, there was a guy at the lake who told Tas he couldn't leave his vehicle on the shore after he'd gotten the boat into the water. Said it was against regulations. Tas threw him the keys and told him he could keep it. A brand-new Lincoln Navigator. Less than a thousand miles on the clock. Worth a hundred grand of anyone's money."

"He wants us to know where he is."

"Smerconish doesn't think that. He thinks Tas doesn't realize we're onto him."

"No, that's what we're supposed to think," Koenig said. "It's misdirection again. Everything has been misdirection. *Everything.* The breadcrumbs he left in New Silloth, the bodies he dropped in San Diego—everything has been about getting that boat onto Lake Mead. And making sure we found him."

"No argument from me. He's acting like he *wants* to be noticed."

"What's he doing now?"

"Nothing," Draper said. "Looks like he's dropped anchor."

Koenig didn't answer. He shared another glance with Carlyle. She seemed as confused as he was. If Tas had found a way to poison the lake, why hadn't he already done it? Unless he wanted to do a spot of fishing, there was no reason for him to wait. And once again, Koenig felt he was missing something. Like he was playing chess against a child prodigy. Each time he thought he had a shot at the king, he was put back in check. And when he thought he was winning, he was exactly where he was supposed to be. Koenig didn't think Tas had gotten complacent. He thought Tas knew exactly what he was doing. That meant if Tas was chilling in the middle of Lake Mead, he wanted to be *seen* chilling in the middle of Lake Mead.

"Smerconish says the NorseBoat's lying low in the water," Draper continued. "That it seems heavier than it should be. His advisers think it's because it's packed with explosives."

"Don't tell me; they think he's going dynamite fishing?"

"Not exactly," Draper said. "They think Tas is waiting until it's dark."

"Then?"

"Then he's going to make a run at the Hoover Dam."

Not out of left field.

Not even close.

CHAPTER 112

"I've never heard anything so ridiculous in my life," Carlyle said.

"Really?" Draper said. "Because from my point of view, the Hoover Dam is an impressive target. The symbolism alone is huge, never mind the carnage destroying it would cause."

"Destroying the Hoover Dam doesn't meet the protocol's objectives."

"It's the only theory Smerconish has."

"He's wrong," Carlyle said.

"What's he planning to do?" Koenig asked.

"He's sending in a SEAL team when it's dark. They'll board the boat and take Tas alive. He wants to know who bankrolled Margaret."

"And if Tas gets bored? Makes a run on the dam before it gets dark?"

"He already has F-35s in the air. If Tas makes a run on the dam before the SEALs get to him, they'll blow him out of the water."

"Which Tas will be very much aware of," Koenig said.

"Aware or not," Draper said. "A dead terrorist poses no threat."

Koenig said nothing. Not until the clunk of the Gulfstream's landing gear kicked his brain into gear.

"We can't land then," he said. "We need to stay in the air."

Draper didn't hesitate. She didn't ask why. She grabbed the Gulfstream's internal phone and said, "Abort landing."

The plane lurched. Koenig felt it in his stomach, as if they'd driven over a humpback bridge.

CHAPTER 113

"F-35s in the air means everything else gets grounded," Koenig said. "That includes us."

"Smerconish has already done it," Draper said, nodding. "The entire West Coast is on the ground. It's so the F-35s have maneuverability. He can't cancel attack runs because some asshole in Vegas is flying his I HATE FOUNTAINS blimp over the Bellagio."

"Which is why we can't land."

"Why is that, Ben?" Carlyle asked. "I think the best thing we can do is try to talk sense into whoever is in charge down there."

"We can't land because Tas is exactly where he planned to be, and right now, Smerconish is doing exactly what he wants him to. Grounding flights is an entirely predictable move. Tas has anticipated it. And if he's anticipated it, it means he wants it. If we bench ourselves, we become irrelevant. Smerconish will never allow us to take off again."

"What do you suggest?" Draper asked.

"We *don't* bench ourselves," Koenig said. "We stay in the air. Become a variable. Something Tas hasn't planned for."

"We need to land somewhere, though. We can't keep circling the airport like a fly buzzing a turd."

"How long to Lake Mead?"

"An hour, give or take," she said. "But there isn't a runway we could use at

Mead. Smerconish has instructed the FAA to close *all* airfields, not just the major ones. We're only authorized to land at Harry Reid."

Koenig looked blankly at her.

"It's what McCarran is called now. Flights scheduled to arrive in the next thirty minutes can still land, everything else has been turned around. And it doesn't matter where we land, we have no way of getting to Lake Mead. Even the Grand Canyon choppers have been grounded. And yes, we can hire a car, but we wouldn't get within ten miles of the lake. Smerconish is locking it down."

Koenig's brow furrowed. Draper was right. It didn't matter where they landed; Smerconish wasn't going to let them anywhere near where they needed to be. Maybe the best thing would be to force a landing in San Diego. Find Smerconish. Make him understand the Hoover Dam didn't work as a target. Explain the whole thing was a game of chess. And Tas wasn't just controlling the board; he was the only one who knew how the pieces moved. Which reminded Koenig of a famous quote: *The best chess move is the one your opponent least wants you to make.* And right now, Tas was in the middle of a lake where everyone could see him. Smerconish thought he had him in check. Didn't realize Tas was ten moves ahead. That he was about to spring an elaborate trap.

And when he did . . . checkmate.

Carlyle was right: Convincing Smerconish he was wrong about Tas was the best move. But was it the move Tas least wanted him to play? Koenig didn't think so. He thought Tas wanted him grounded. Tas didn't want to worry about Koenig being the specter at his feast. He didn't want him out there, somewhere. Still in play. Planning something . . . *unorthodox.* Something he hadn't thought of.

But Tas and Margaret had been planning this for years. They'd thought of everything.

Hadn't they?

It didn't matter where they landed; Smerconish wasn't going to let them anywhere near Lake Mead . . . That was the key. Getting to the lake without Smerconish stopping them. If Koenig could get out onto the water, they were in the game. They had a chance.

"Hey, assholes," Nash shouted. "Any chance of getting some service over here? I haven't had my peanuts yet."

Nash had lost blood. She'd been waterboarded. She had a bullet in her ankle and her fingers were broken. She'd be dehydrated. Koenig bet she was bored too. She wasn't the center of attention. Probably wasn't used to that.

"I'll go," Koenig said. He got out of his seat and grabbed a bottle of water from the fridge. He twisted the cap as he approached her.

"How you doing?"

"Great," she said. "I've never been on a private plane before."

"Want some water?"

She rolled her eyes. "No, I want you to throw me out of the window," she said. "Of course I want a drink."

Koenig took a seat and put the bottle to her mouth. She slurped at it greedily.

"It's not very cold," she said.

"Everyone's a critic."

"I'll come for you, you know. I'll come for all of you."

Petulant.

Koenig smiled. "Maybe I *should* throw you out of the window."

"Maybe you should throw yourself out. Save yourself the pain that's coming."

Which gave Koenig an idea.

Something Tas wouldn't expect.

Out of left field.

CHAPTER 114

"You want to jump out of the plane?" Draper said, like she'd been told the first line of a joke and was waiting for the punchline.

"I have problems with the word 'want,'" Koenig replied. "But essentially, yes."

"Without a parachute?" Draper continued.

"It's not as stupid as it sounds."

"Really? Because I have to say, it sounds pretty fucking stupid."

"When I was in Russia, I—"

"I swear to God, if you say you once trained with some weird unit no one's ever heard of so you can justify more of your bullshit, I won't be responsible for my actions."

"When I was—"

"Let me guess, some Russian assholes jumped out of planes without parachutes?"

"Not exactly."

"Well, *what* exactly?"

"They told me about some soldiers who had."

"Oh, they *told* you."

"During the Second World War a Serbian regiment jumped from planes to attack a German tank column advancing on Moscow. They didn't have parachutes. The plane flew low and slow to make it as safe as possible."

"Why didn't they use parachutes, Ben?" Carlyle said.

"They didn't have any. The Soviets were in dire straits at the time."

"What percentage survived this jump?"

"It depends on who you believe."

Draper opened her laptop and tapped something into her search engine. She stared at her screen, expanding the occasional article. "Thirty percent, it says here," she said eventually. "One in three survived to fight. Two-thirds broke their legs or their backs or both." She read some more, then added, "Also, there's anecdotal evidence it never happened. That it was Soviet propaganda. A way to shore up morale. To demonstrate resolve. Show what their troops were willing to do in defense of the Motherland."

"Doesn't matter," Koenig said. "The theory is sound. And don't forget, skydivers are always surviving parachute malfunctions."

"'Always' implies it happens *frequently*," she said. "Whereas I would suggest that surviving a parachute malfunction happens so rarely it becomes a global news event when it does. It's suicide, Koenig. And while your death would undoubtedly make my life a hell of a lot easier, Smerconish will find a way to blame me."

She slammed her laptop closed. A bit of plastic snapped off. Shoddy.

"Full disclosure," Koenig said. "The Soviets were jumping into snow. Water's worse."

"It is?" Carlyle said. "How?"

"Because snow compresses; water doesn't. After a certain height, hitting water is the same as hitting concrete. I'd need to be low enough to avoid terminal velocity, but not so low I couldn't get into the right position. Too low and I'd hit the water like a bug splatting against a windshield. I'd break every bone in my body. I figure fifty meters will give me enough time to get into position but not so high I'll reach terminal velocity."

Draper said nothing. Just glared.

"I'll need a knifelike entry into the water," Koenig continued. "One that offers the smallest surface area. That means I have to go in feetfirst." He paused a beat. "I'll need to break my ankles."

"Your ankles?" Carlyle said.

"I need them to absorb the worst of the impact. The same way the crumple zone on a car protects the passenger compartment. I'll be all shook up, but if I enter the water at the right angle, I should survive."

"And that doesn't sound like a problem to you," Draper said. "Going against Jakob Tas with kindling legs?"

"With any luck he won't see me. I'll breaststroke my way to the boat and put ten rounds in him before he even knows I'm there."

"How's he not going to see you?"

"Doesn't matter if he does. I'll shoot him anyway."

"Bess, please talk some sense into this asshole. Tell him we won't sacrifice him just because we're out of ideas."

Carlyle said nothing. Looked down, began wringing her hands.

"Bess will be fine with it," Koenig said.

"She won't."

"Sure she will," Koenig said.

"How can you possibly know that?"

"Because she's done it before," Koenig said. He paused. Let it linger, like a bad smell. "Isn't that right, Bess?"

Carlyle looked up. Her eyes were wet.

"How long have you known?" she said.

CHAPTER 115

"I didn't know," Koenig said. "I suspected. Thanks for confirming."

"I had no choice," Carlyle said.

"I know."

"What the hell are you two talking about?" Draper said.

"The Acacia Avenue Protocol is an attack on our infrastructure," Koenig said.

"That much I'd worked out for myself."

"And to amplify the effect, the protocol called for certain people in certain roles to be eliminated before it went live."

"The people Hobbs and Nash killed?"

"Exactly," Koenig said. "Louise Durose had an innovative way of managing landfills, Michael Gibbs was an expert in deepwater ports. Everyone on Hobbs's list will have held similar positions."

"Makes sense, I suppose. You want to hamper the recovery efforts."

"Except it *doesn't* make sense. Three hundred and thirty million people live in this country. In a national emergency, we'd *find* the experts. Other countries would send us theirs. People have transferable skills. Killing nineteen people who happen to work in infrastructure would make no difference whatsoever."

"So why bother?"

"Because after the protocol was put together, Bess added a safeguard. Something only she knew about. A Trojan horse. She told some of her think tank that for the protocol to work certain people in certain jobs had to die. She even dictated in what order they were to be murdered. But the real reason had nothing to do with amplifying the effect of the trigger event. It was because she needed a trip wire. She knew that if her security arrangements failed, her Trojan horse would get fed into the protocol alongside everything else. And when these people began to die, she'd know the protocol had been initiated and how far along it was. Now, I know Bess to be a good person. A moral woman. Yet she was willing to sacrifice nineteen people so she had a heads-up." He paused. "That's why I know she'll let me jump out of the plane."

"Her willingness to sacrifice innocent people aside, it changes nothing. Because you jumping out of the plane *achieves* nothing. You won't get anywhere near Tas."

"I can't defend what I did," Carlyle said. "And one day I will answer for my actions. I've lived with it for too long anyway. But trust me when I say if Jakob Tas achieves the impossible and turns Lake Mead toxic, it will be the starting pistol on a chain of catastrophic events the like of which this country has never seen. I'm not exaggerating when I say that successfully initiating the Acacia Avenue Protocol will set the US back thirty, forty, even *fifty* years. So yes, with one small adjustment, I am willing to sacrifice him."

"Yay," Koenig said.

CHAPTER 116

"You want to jump out of the plane too now?" Draper said to Carlyle.

"You said it yourself, Tas will see Ben jump into the lake," Carlyle replied. "And if he *does* break his ankles, he won't be able to swim. Certainly not fast enough to avoid being shot."

"So?"

"So we do as Ben suggests. He jumps into the water and he starts shooting at Tas. He might get lucky, he probably won't."

Koenig nodded. He knew where Carlyle was going. "But while he has eyes on me, he won't have eyes on the Gulfstream," he said. "I'll be shooting at him. He'll be shooting at me. And he won't be expecting this, so he won't have hearing protection. The moment he returns fire is the moment his ears start ringing. If you were to drop in on his blindside, he won't see you. He certainly won't *hear* you. You can definitely get close enough to put two in the back of his head."

"And I'm a good shot and an excellent swimmer," Carlyle confirmed. "If I can get in close, I won't miss."

"You won't get in close, though," Draper said. "Because you'll have broken ankles as well."

"Broken ankles can be fixed!" Carlyle snapped. "A curated mass migration event can't be. And I'll wear one of the Gulfstream's life jackets. And as Ben has just said, you can still breaststroke with damaged legs. We used to do arms-only breaststroke swimming drills in college. It helps develop a stronger catch phase."

Draper shook her head in disgust.

Eventually Carlyle said, "I have to try. I *need* to try."

Draper shook her head. "I won't let you."

"Do it! Do it! Do it!" Nash chanted.

CHAPTER 117

"It won't work," Draper said. "Tas will see you. He'll see you both, and he'll kill you both."

"Not when I'm shooting at him he won't," Koenig said. "He'll be one hundred percent focused on me. He'll be in a firefight with someone who won't take cover. He won't be able to lay down suppressing fire, as I won't react to effective enemy fire the way he'll expect. It'll be like it was on that airfield. His confusion will turn to panic. He won't see anything but me."

Draper shook her head in disbelief. "This is utter madness," she said.

Her cell phone rang again. She tilted the screen so Koenig could see who was calling. It was Smerconish. She sighed. "He's no doubt calling to find out why we aborted the landing." She accepted the call. "Sir?" She listened for around two minutes, then said, "Sorry, sir, you're breaking up. I'll call when we're on the ground." She powered off her cell phone. Threw it on the table. "Boy, is *he* cross. Says if we fly within ten miles of Mead, he'll treat us as hostile and order an F-35 to turn us into air debris."

"He won't."

"Of course he won't," she said. "And I'm kinda insulted he thought he could bully me." She thumped the table. Angry. The cell phone bounced in the air. "I hate being ordered around by stupid people," she muttered. She stood, the change in her demeanor evident. "I'm going to see my pilot."

She was back in a minute.

"I'm surrounded by lunatics," she said, taking her seat and brushing the hair out of her eyes.

"He'll do it?" Koenig said.

"Not only will he do it, he thinks he knows *how* to do it. He says he'll reduce the airspeed until we stall. And after you've jumped, he'll try to restart the engine."

"You don't employ fools, do you?"

"It's why I've never offered you a job," she said, although Koenig could tell her heart wasn't really in the insult.

"Are we on?" he said.

"We are. But you're wearing a life jacket as well."

"I can't. I'll stand out like a fishing float. Plus, I'll need to reload underwater. That will be the only time Tas will feel safe enough to return fire. I might as well make it difficult for him."

She didn't respond for several moments. Finally, she sighed, "I guess the two of you are jumping out of my fucking airplane."

CHAPTER 118

Koenig felt rather than heard the Gulfstream's airspeed slow. He thought it was probably the pilot applying the air brakes. Draper had gone into what he thought of as her CIA mode. Her emotionless, take-charge, take-no-shit-from-anyone mode. Smerconish had tried contacting her through the pilot. She'd ignored him. He'd sent an F-35 to escort the Gulfstream back to San Diego. She instructed her pilot to fly right at it. The F-35 blinked first. It was now following them at a respectable distance.

The Gulfstream's internal phone rang. The call tone seemed especially shrill in the quietening cabin. Draper answered it. "How long?" she said. She listened, then placed the phone back in its cradle. "Ten minutes."

They made their way to the rear cabin.

"Hi, guys," Nash said. "I was only joking about being thrown out of the plane. No sense of humor, that's your problem."

Draper stared at her, a small frown forming. It looked like she was trying to figure something out.

Nash said, "Why don't you take a picture, it'll last longer."

Childish.

"Ready?" Draper asked them.

"As I can be," Koenig replied.

"I'm ready," Carlyle said.

"Tie yourself to something. We're low, so we won't need masks, but it's going to get windy."

Koenig did. He tied a seat belt around his left wrist. Used a reef knot. Right over left and under; left over right and under. It was the only thing he remembered from his time with the Boy Scouts. That and he was supposed to do a good turn daily. Carlyle did the same. She was wearing a life jacket. Bright orange.

Draper reached up and removed a long, flat panel above the over-wing porthole. It exposed a red toggle.

"As soon as we've located the NorseBoat, the pilot will climb, then slow as rapidly as he can," Draper said. "When the engine stalls, he'll bank right. The second he does, you step out of the emergency hatch like it's a hangman's trapdoor, Koenig. He thinks it'll be safer that way. But he can't hold the banking position for long. Not with a dead engine. You'll need to go immediately as he'll need to recircle the boat so I can heave out Bess when you're shooting at Tas."

"He's done this before."

"No, Koenig. No one's done this before. We're all improvising here. But like you said, I don't employ fools."

"Won't banking after he's stalled the engine make it harder for him to restart it?"

"Let him worry about that."

"But—"

"But nothing. Have you both got everything you need?"

Carlyle had her Makarov. It was underneath her life jacket, in a shoulder holster. Wasn't going anywhere.

Koenig held up his SIG and his Fairbairn-Sykes.

"You're taking your knife?" Draper said. "Isn't that like running with scissors?"

"Of course."

Koenig holstered the SIG. He'd had a choice between a shoulder holster and a drop-leg holster. He didn't like either. He'd have preferred an inside-the-waistband holster. An IWB would have been ideal. They were uncomfortable to wear, but it would have kept the SIG secure. He chose the drop-leg holster in the end. Shoulder holsters were impractical when jumping out of a plane. The gun would flap about when he was in the air. Might hit him in the face. It was why paratroopers didn't use them. And he would be landing hard. Much harder than paratroopers landed. Carlyle was using a shoulder holster but that was fine; she had it under her life jacket. The drop-leg holster was the marginally better option. It hung from his belt and was strapped to the thigh. He adjusted it so the SIG was within his grasp when his arms were at rest. The holster wasn't perfect. It had Velcro fasteners instead of a strap and buckle. Velcro came undone during intensive movement. It was noisy. They could turn, end up on the inside of the thigh. And when you moved, the holster moved, making it an unpredictable draw. Particularly when running. Plus, they were a little too macho for Koenig's liking. Like they'd been designed by someone who'd played too much *Call of Duty.*

He didn't know what to do with the Fairbairn-Sykes. He didn't want to leave it behind, but he had no real way of securing it during an uncontrolled fall. He'd either stab himself in the leg or, worse, lose it. He decided to take it anyway. He grabbed a field dressing from the medicine box and wrapped the knife in as much padding as he could. He then slipped it into the back of his pants. Fiddled with it until it was snug against the base of his spine.

He raised his shirt and said to Draper, "Tape me up?"

"Er, hello?" Nash said, screwing up her face. "Can you *please* do this someplace else? I don't want to see your gross old-man ass."

Draper ignored her. She grabbed a roll of medical tape, the non-stretch porous kind used to secure dressings to flesh. She tore off a dozen strips and began taping the Fairbairn-Sykes to his back.

While she did, Koenig mentally rehearsed what he needed to do after exiting the plane. The first thing would be stabilizing himself. To halt the unavoidable uncontrolled spin. He would tuck his arms and legs in, like a kid cannonballing into a swimming pool. The kind of move that got you whistle-checked by the jerk in the lifeguard chair. He figured he'd need two seconds. He'd then fold out his legs and raise his arms. Like he was surrendering. Logically, this was the most aerodynamic position. It would reduce the drag force, which would increase his velocity, but it would get him to the water in the right position. Two moves. The cannonball, then the surrender. Two seconds for the first move, one for the second. Three seconds in total.

Then he'd either hit Lake Mead gracefully and streamlined, like a gannet, or spinning wildly like an out-of-control helicopter. If it were the former, he'd come up shooting. Be the diversion Carlyle needed him to be.

The cabin phone chirped. Draper answered it.

"We're over Mead now," she said after she'd hung up.

"Has the pilot found Tas?"

"He's in the middle of the Boulder Basin."

"No wonder Smerconish thinks the dam is the target," Koenig said. The Boulder Basin was the large open part of Lake Mead, just north of the Hoover Dam. "With a strong wind he could be there within minutes."

"You still think it's misdirection? Because if you aren't sure, it's not too late to call this off."

"I'm sure."

"I guess we're doing this then," Draper said. Resigned. She reached up and pulled the red toggle. Koenig heard the click of the emergency exit unlocking. It wasn't big, about the size of the top half of a stable door. Draper pulled. Koenig assumed it would come out, then up. Or to the side. That it would stay attached to the cabin. But it didn't; it came out completely. Like Draper was removing a storm panel after a hurricane. The cold air rushed in. Faster than a wind tunnel. It stung Koenig's face. Draper wedged the emergency exit between a seat and the cabin wall.

She grabbed Koenig's head and shouted directly into his ear, "He's going to put you within two hundred yards if he can. Remember, banking right is your green light. And the moment you get in the water, you start fucking shooting. Give Bess a fighting chance."

Koenig formed a circle with his thumb and forefinger. *OK*. He moved to the open emergency exit. The wind battered his face. Rippled his cheeks like an astronaut during high-g training. He couldn't breathe. He turned away from the wind and sucked in a lungful.

The engine sputtered, caught again, then stopped completely. The Gulfstream stopped being a sleek private jet and became a poorly designed glider. The pilot banked to the right.

"Go!" Draper shouted.

"I hope you get eaten by a shark!" Nash yelled.

Koenig smiled and nodded. Then he stepped out of the airplane.

And fell into the lake faster than a cannonball.

PART FOUR

THE SPECTER AT THE FEAST

CHAPTER 119

Jakob Tas had expected the F-35s and he'd expected the surveillance drones. But he hadn't expected the Gulfstream. He watched it with mild curiosity. He initially thought it was a Vegas whale on a comped trip to see the Grand Canyon. An overweight, overindulged lard-ass. The kind the casinos manipulated with free shit so they didn't feel bad when they lost a quarter mil at the baccarat tables.

But then the Gulfstream started circling the NorseBoat. He *definitely* hadn't expected that. It was out of place. An anomaly. Something he and Margaret hadn't planned for.

And then the Gulfstream began to lose altitude. Tas wondered if it was in trouble. That the pilot was considering an emergency landing on the lake. Which would be stupid. Gulfstreams weren't seaplanes. They couldn't land on water. Their hulls were aerodynamic; seaplane hulls were *hydro*dynamic. Seaplanes were designed to land on water. To float on water. To take off from water. They had more in common with boats than with airplanes. If the sleek-as-a-falcon Gulfstream attempted a water landing, it would break on impact. Everyone would die. No miracle on the Hudson for this wannabe Sully.

He reached for his 10×50 tactical binoculars. They'd cost over $2,000 but had been worth every cent. They had good magnification, a large depth of field, and image stabilization. Made the F-35s appear so close he felt he could reach out and touch them. He brought the binoculars to his eyes and cast around until he found the Gulfstream.

The pilot *was* in trouble. Tas could see the open emergency exit. Just above the wing. Looked like the passengers were getting ready to bail. Suicide. The water would be like granite at that height. He figured they had no choice. Maybe there was a fire onboard. Or a lunatic.

The Gulfstream was about one hundred meters above him now. Low enough for Tas to no longer need the binoculars. He kept them glued to his eyes anyway. Something wasn't right. The Gulfstream was now circling the NorseBoat. Tighter and tighter. Clockwise, like an emptying sink. Tas felt like the axle in a wheel. He was getting dizzy.

The Gulfstream had now lost so much airspeed it was in danger of stalling. Right on cue, Tas heard the engine sputter, then catch again. It made another complete circle. Dropped maybe another fifty meters.

Then it did exactly what Tas thought it would do. It stalled. The engines quit and died. Silence instead of noise. The Gulfstream should have plummeted. And it did. Kind of. Except first it banked so sharply the wings were almost in the six o'clock position.

Tas blinked in surprise. Someone had fallen out of the emergency exit. A man. His arms and legs were flapping like a rag doll. Stayed that way for maybe a second before he tucked his legs and hands into his torso. Looked like he was going to hit the water like a mortar shell. Tas held his breath, fascinated. Then, right at the last second, literally, the man's legs shot down and his arms shot up. He hit the water. Hard. Despite it happening two hundred yards from the NorseBoat, Tas heard the crack of the man's legs breaking. Sounded like a gunshot. Tas winced.

He trained the binoculars on where the man had hit the water, at the epicenter of an expanding series of ripples. The man hadn't entered the water like an Olympic diver. He'd made quite the splash.

The man bobbed up. It didn't mean he was alive, though. Unless bodies were weighted down, they floated. For a while, anyway. Tas knew that for certain. He'd been involved in a job in Vienna where a body hadn't been weighted down right. Someone got a punch-dagger in the spleen over that mistake.

Tas figured the Gulfstream guy was dead or dying. He certainly wasn't moving. He adjusted the magnification so he could see the man's face. He gasped.

"I don't believe it." He said it out loud. Couldn't help himself. There *had* been a lunatic on board the Gulfstream. It was Koenig. Miss Wexmore had sneaked a picture and emailed it. The crazy asshole had jumped without a parachute. And now he was in the water. Facedown. Lifeless. Broken legs, probably a broken back. If he wasn't dead, he would be in a minute.

Then, to Tas's astonishment, Koenig lifted his head. He treaded water with his arms and turned his body so he was facing the NorseBoat. He then began to breaststroke toward him.

Slowly.

A noise behind him made him turn away from Koenig. Another splash. A louder one. Someone else had jumped from the Gulfstream. Whoever this guy was, they'd made a better landing than Koenig. He reached for his binoculars, then grinned. It was Margaret's friend Elizabeth. She was wearing an orange life jacket and was about one hundred yards away. Tas didn't know what was happening, but he knew a gun when he saw one. Elizabeth had just found hers. Tas let muscle memory take over. He raised his Heckler & Koch G11 and snapped off a couple of rounds. The first missed; the second didn't. He saw the puff of blood and watched as Carlyle slumped in the water, motionless.

He nodded, pleased with himself. A kill shot at one hundred yards, fired from an unstable platform, was good shooting. He turned back to Koenig.

The crazy fool was still swimming toward the boat. The blood in his wake looked like an oil slick. Some people didn't know when they were beaten. Tas raised his gun, although he didn't think he'd need it. Koenig looked half dead. Like he had nothing left to give. The only thing left in his tank was stubbornness.

And then it all got too much. Koenig stopped. Hung limply in the water, head down. Not moving at all. Like a Rolling Stone in a swimming pool. Tas raised his gun and aimed for the top of Koenig's spine. His fingers tightened on the trigger.

And then he eased off. He shook his head in admiration.

"Ah, what the hell," he said. "A man shouldn't have to die alone."

He put the gun down and started the engine.

CHAPTER 120

FIVE MINUTES EARLIER.

Koenig hit the water way too hard, way harder than he'd anticipated. The impact sent a shock wave through his entire body. One of his shin bones bent, then snapped. Like a bamboo stick. He felt the jaggy splinters push through ligaments and muscles, flesh and skin. The bone was on the outside of his body now. His ankles felt like they were full of broken glass.

The pain wasn't bad, but he knew that was because adrenaline had flooded his body. Nature's anesthetic. It numbed everything. Made it manageable. It wouldn't last long. He hung in the water, facedown for a moment. Gathered his thoughts. He resurfaced, spat out some water and took a moment to check which limbs were working and which weren't. He didn't have long; Carlyle would be in the water soon. His arms seemed fine. His legs weren't. He could feel his feet, so he wasn't paralyzed. He could move his head.

Koenig used small arm movements to turn himself in the water. He'd taken note of where Tas was before he'd jumped, but he needed to reorientate himself, then start shooting. Tas wasn't hard to find. His boat was the only one on the water. He was about two hundred yards away. Tas was watching him through a pair of binoculars.

Koenig could see the Gulfstream behind Tas. He reached for his SIG. Time to make some noise.

His holster was empty.

He checked it again. Still empty. It hadn't magically reappeared. The violent impact had torn open the Velcro straps. He could feel them moving in the water. Like kelp. The SIG was at the bottom of Lake Mead now. He groaned. He couldn't cause a distraction without a distraction-causing weapon.

He reached for his Fairbairn-Sykes. Felt the reassuring bundle Draper had taped to his back. At least the knife had survived the fall. It was better than nothing. Koenig needed to start moving. Bobbing up and down like a rubber duck in the bath made him an easy target. Like shooting fish in a barrel. Something Tas probably did on the weekends. If he could just keep Tas's attention, Carlyle still had a chance.

There was something else to consider. He was losing blood, but he had no way to tell how much or how fast. He was alert, so he hadn't ruptured a major artery. But it would get him in the end. While he was in the water, his blood couldn't clot. His heart would keep pumping it out until there was nothing left. If he didn't get out of the lake, he would bleed to death.

So Koenig ignored the pain in his legs and, figuratively, kicked off toward the NorseBoat. Breaststroke. Upper body only. No leg propulsion.

Tas watched him with interest. The Gulfstream carried on banking. When it was directly behind Tas, Carlyle jumped out. She entered the water vertically. The splash drew Tas's attention. It wasn't supposed to. Koenig was supposed to have his undivided attention by now. Tas turned his back on Koenig and faced Carlyle. Koenig stopped swimming and watched in horror as Tas raised a weapon. He fired a short burst. Two rounds, not three.

After a moment, Tas turned to face Koenig. Which was when he knew Carlyle was dead. She had to be. Tas had shot her in the water. Koenig hoped it was quick.

He wasn't sure what to do next. It seemed hopeless. Tas had a gun and Koenig had a knife. Tas was on a boat and Koenig was still in the water. Koenig was injured and Tas wasn't.

"To hell with this," he said.

He started swimming again. Tas lowered his weapon and watched.

Koenig quickly realized not securing the SIG hadn't been his only mistake. He was wearing denim jeans and a thick cotton shirt. Woolen socks and sturdy boots. They were waterlogged and heavy. Dragging. He should have stripped down to his undershorts. Gotten naked even. Each stroke was ten times harder than it ought to have been.

Koenig was naturally wiry. A greyhound, not a mastiff. But he was no endurance athlete. He wasn't capable of Herculean feats of strength. A two-hundred-yard swim with no legs, low blood pressure, and waterlogged clothing was beyond his capabilities.

He kept going anyway, expecting to take a bullet to the head any second. He wondered if he'd just die, or whether there'd be pain first. He got to within a hundred yards before his battery went flat. He was spent. He kept going some more, lungs heaving like bellows. Used reserves he didn't know he had.

It wasn't enough.

His head began to drop below the water. For seconds, then bunches of seconds. Soon he couldn't raise it long enough to draw breath. He swallowed water; then he swallowed some more. There was a burning sensation as it entered his lungs. He coughed and inhaled. Like Nash had when she'd been waterboarded.

He stopped moving. Concentrated on coughing out water. On staying afloat. On staying alive. Until even that became too much effort. It seemed easier to die. His clothes were simply too heavy, like he was wearing a lead overcoat. His arms spasmed, then cramped. Game over for any swimmer.

Koenig closed his eyes and relaxed into death. There was nothing left to do. He wished he could have seen it through until the end, but it wasn't to be. Tranquility stole over him like a shot of morphine. He knew it was part of drowning, but he embraced it anyway. He'd done all he could. Left nothing on the playing field. All anyone could have asked of him.

He was vaguely aware of his body going through hypoxia, hypoxemia, and anoxia: low oxygen, *abnormally* low oxygen, then absence of oxygen; the process accelerated because of his injuries and recent exertions.

And then he passed out.

CHAPTER 121

Koenig didn't so much as wake as begin sensing pain. He was alive. He didn't understand why. He didn't understand *how*. The last thing he remembered was drowning. He should be dead. But he wasn't. He was on a boat. He could feel the rocking motion. Hear the grumble of an idling engine. Water lapping against the hull. Which seemed unlikely. Whose boat was it? And how had he gotten on board? He certainly hadn't clambered on under his own steam. He'd been steam-free. Still was. His armpits felt bruised, which meant he'd been hauled on board.

He opened his eyes. He had binocular vision, dark around the edges. Blurry. A sure sign he'd been unconscious. He waited for them to clear, then took stock. The boat was modern but kinda old-fashioned at the same time. It smelled of the sea and of gasoline. The deck was wooden, polished but stained with blood. *His* blood. There were no seats. The interior had been stripped bare. Like cargo space had trumped comfort. He was sitting on the deck, his back against the cabin door. Where the wheelhouse would have been in a boat with an inboard engine. Someone stood at the stern-end of the boat. A tall man. He was wearing a vest and baggy shorts. Looked like a lake bum. He had his back to Koenig. He was fiddling with a pair of outboard engines. Adjusting them. Koenig was about to shout his thanks but didn't. His brain fog cleared. The only boat anywhere near where he'd landed was the NorseBoat.

Logically, the man with his back to him was Jakob Tas. Which was non-sensical. They'd never met, but they were kind of sworn enemies. Tas must have known Koenig was there to kill him. He'd saved his life anyway. Perhaps he was a nice man after all. Misunderstood.

Then he remembered Tas had shot Carlyle. She *wasn't* on the boat. Seemed Tas had only fished out the living. Koenig screwed his eyes shut. He'd lost men and women before, but this felt worse. Carlyle had sacrificed her freedom when she disappeared, and now she'd sacrificed her life. It didn't seem fair. *He* was supposed to be the diversion.

Koenig wasn't restrained. He looked at his legs and understood why. He'd felt a bone snap when he landed in the water, but he had no idea how serious his injuries were. His right fibula, the smaller of the two shinbones, had exploded through his skin. A burst fracture, when bones break in multiple directions. Happens in severe falls. Which sounded about right. It was sticking out of his shin at ninety degrees. Looked like a chopstick in rice. His legs and ankles were swollen and purple. They looked broken. They *felt* broken. But bad sprains looked like that too. Hard to tell. Now he could see his injuries, the pain kicked in. The *real* pain. It flowed into his legs like electricity. Pulsating. Stabbing. Searing. A marine drill instructor had once told him that pain was weakness leaving the body. Koenig sucked in a mouthful of warm desert air and buttoned it down. Tried to act like a marine.

The next surprise was that Tas had treated the burst fracture. As best he could, given what was to hand. His right leg had a torniquet. Above the knee. It had stemmed the blood loss. Tas had used Koenig's belt.

The third surprise was that he was naked. Not down-to-his-shorts naked. Butt naked. Splinters-in-his-ass naked. Hope-Draper-wasn't-watching naked.

Koenig cleared his throat and only half stifled a groan of pain. "I'd be lying if I said I wasn't flattered, Jakob."

CHAPTER 122

Jakob Tas turned at the sound of Koenig's voice. He leaned against the stern.

"You're awake?" he said.

Koenig didn't answer the question. It seemed rhetorical. Instead, he said, "Is Bess dead?"

"She is. I didn't want to kill her, but you two left me no choice. I couldn't leave her where she was."

"*I'm* not dead, Jakob. Why is that?"

Tas chuckled. "I thought you *were* dead, Koenig. I thought you'd drowned, but it seems some people just don't know when it's time to die."

"That doesn't answer my question."

"Because we're the same, you and I." He held up his hand before Koenig could protest. "Yes, we are. We're both singularly focused on achieving our goals. I sacrificed my friends in San Diego, you sacrificed Miss Carlyle not twenty minutes ago."

Koenig didn't bother correcting him. Instead, he said, "Can I have my clothes back, please?"

"I threw your clothes overboard," Tas said.

"Even my boots?"

"*Especially* your boots."

"May I ask why?"

Tas picked up something small. He showed Koenig. It was a punch-dagger, all shiny and dreadful. "This fits neatly into my belt buckle," he said. "The craftsmanship is so good, not even airport scanners can tell it's a weapon."

"I'm not Rosa Klebb, and this isn't *From Russia with Love*. I don't have a boot knife."

"But you *are* a resourceful guy," Tas said. "You killed my team in Scotland—"

"They were wearing stupid armor. They had stupid guns."

"And New York? Those guys knew what they were doing."

"What can I say?" Koenig said. "I like to get my retaliation in early."

"They were the best at my disposal," Tas continued. "Been together for years. They had you outnumbered and they had better weapons. Yet you still beat them. So, forgive me, the only way I could be sure you hadn't secreted a weapon in your clothing was to throw it overboard."

"I liked those boots," Koenig said. "Bought them in Texas last year. The leather was as soft as silk."

"Sorry."

Koenig looked over Tas's shoulder. They were still in the Boulder Basin. He recognized the layered rock formation. It was coffee-colored, from the darkest French roast to the milkiest latte. Looked like one of those Bavarian cakes. It was called the law of superposition. Meant that in layers of sedimentary rock, the oldest layer is at the base, with each layer above getting progressively younger. It was all relative, though, Koenig thought. The top layer was still millions of years old.

"We're in the Boulder Basin," Koenig said. "Exactly where you wanted to be found."

Tas didn't answer. Instead, a great hacking cough rattled through him. It wasn't gentle. Wasn't restricted to his lungs. This was a full body tremor. Didn't seem like a pepper-up-the-nose cough. Sounded like an end-of-life cough. The kind heard on palliative care wards the world over. And Tas *did* look pale. Pallid. His skin glistened like warm cheese.

Koenig put two and two together. Came up with terminal illness. A real one this time. Tas was dying. Which solved the exit-plan puzzle. Tas didn't need one. He planned to die on Lake Mead.

Kamikaze-style.

CHAPTER 123

Tas took a time-out after his coughing fit. He sipped some water and threw a handful of pills down his neck. Crunched them. Winced as he swallowed. Looked as though he was in even more pain than Koenig. Tas noticed him watching. "Are you hoping I'll die before I finish?" he said.

"That would be *great*."

"I'll live long enough."

"Long enough for me to kill you?"

"Do you believe that is likely?" Tas glanced at Koenig's legs. "Because from this end of the boat, it looks like the only thing keeping you alive is the tourniquet."

"I don't suppose I could loosen it for a bit?" Koenig said. "My right ankle has gone numb. I'll get sepsis if I don't get the blood circulating again."

"That will be incredibly painful," Tas said. "Maybe you shouldn't worry about sepsis, Mr. Koenig. Perhaps you shouldn't worry about anything anymore."

Koenig tilted his head. Looked up at the sky. It was as blue as a robin's egg. Beautiful. "That really deserved a roll of thunder," he said. He nodded at the tourniquet. "May I?"

Tas nodded his permission.

Koenig leaned forward and grabbed the belt. He gritted his teeth. Wished he had a bit. Something to bite down on. Tas wasn't lying; loosening the tourniquet *was* going to be painful. And because it was a belt, it had to be pulled tighter first. He had to get the prong out of the punch hole before he could loosen it. He figured quicker would be better than slower. Like ripping off a Band-Aid. He took a deep breath and closed his eyes.

He pulled the belt tighter. The burst of pain was as sudden and as shocking as a lightning strike. He snorted. Loud, like an angry bull. He kept pulling. Eventually the prong fell out of the hole. He let go and the belt loosened. Blood crept back into his leg. It felt like acid. He snorted again, louder this time. He hadn't known he had a pain threshold. He'd certainly never reached it before. Now he had.

It was too much.

Far too much.

The lights went out again.

CHAPTER 124

Koenig woke quicker this time. Surer of his surroundings. The torniquet was back on his right leg. Fresh blood covered his shins and ankles. The deck was wet with it. Like he was sitting in a puddle. Tas had allowed the blood to flow, then tightened the belt again. Good wound management. The pain was horrific, but better than when he'd passed out. Even the memory was nauseating.

Tas was back at the stern. In complete control. Koenig wanted to change that. Try to, anyway.

"How long do you have left, Jakob?" he asked.

Tas checked his watch. "Soon," he said.

"Not *we*, you. You're dying, right?"

He offered a wan smile. "Is it that obvious?"

"You're paler than a snail's foot, you're coughing like a barking dog, and I can see the fentanyl patch on your arm. And unless this boat has a trapdoor, you're about to go down with your ship."

"You see a lot, Mr. Koenig."

"Looking is all I have right now," Koenig said, pointing at his leg. "You're terminally ill. It's why Margaret chose you for this job. Like M only choosing orphans for the Double-0 program. Less to lose."

"It's why I *volunteered* for this job," he said. "I have stage four stomach cancer. I also have a young family. Now my wife won't have to make difficult decisions about schools and health care after I've died."

"You know Margaret faked her cancer, right?" Koenig said. "She was pretending to have cancer the same way you've no doubt been pretending you *don't* have cancer. She used you, Jakob."

Tas frowned. "You're lying," he said.

"Am I? You look like you need a five-pint blood transfusion. She looked like she needed a spa day. Your cough sounds like a death rattle. She didn't even have one. But mainly I know she didn't have cancer because she told me. It was part of her cover. Made it acceptable for her to have extended time off."

"I don't believe you," he said. "Miss Wexmore is a principled woman."

"*Was* a principled woman. She's dead."

Tas pushed himself off the stern. Picked up his punch-dagger.

"Relax, Jakob," Koenig said. "I didn't kill her."

"How?"

"She stuck something very sharp into something very soft."

"She killed herself? Why?"

"The same reason she killed Stillwell Hobbs," Koenig said. "To protect the plan."

"When?"

Koenig gestured toward the sky. "Up there, not two hours ago. Right after we'd figured out *she* was the organ grinder and *you* were the monkey. She didn't want to give up anything." He took a silent moment. "Which is ironic considering we now know everything."

"Everything?"

"Almost. We know she did this to avenge her daughter's death. We know she planned to open Pandora's box. We know she planned to trigger a mass migration event by attacking a body of water. '*Bad* water.' Wasn't that what Konstantin said to you before you met with Stillwell Hobbs?"

Tas stared into space. "The server was his daughter?"

Koenig nodded.

Tas shook his head in admiration. He whistled. "I didn't like Hobbs, but he came highly recommended. I'm told his daughter is even worse. I hope you didn't annoy her. She isn't the kind of person you want holding a grudge."

"No, I think she really likes me," Koenig said.

Tas smiled. "I think that is a small lie?"

Koenig pinched his fingers together. "A teeny-tiny one. However, Bess Carlyle told Margaret a whopper."

"A whop . . . I'm not familiar—"

"A lie, Jakob. A big one. Margaret told you certain people had to die to maximize the impact of the mass migration."

Tas nodded. "Miss Wexmore said it would be like the controlled demolition of a skyscraper. A substantial explosion followed by a series of coordinated precision explosions. Bring the skyscraper down exactly where you want it."

"This boat is the substantial explosion?"

Tas nodded.

"And the people Hobbs and Nash killed were the precision explosions?"

Tas nodded again.

Koenig shook his head. "Wrong. Carlyle put those people into the plan for one reason, and one reason only: to act as a ticking clock. The same way rock bands play the same preshow music over the PA so the stage crew know how close they are to curtains up. Carlyle sacrificed nineteen people so she'd know how close we were to the trigger event. So maybe you're not as in control as you thought."

"I'm where I need to be, when I need to be, and the people trying to stop me are where *they* need to be."

"Your trail? The one so obvious even the stupidest federal agents could follow it? That bullshit with the phones in New Silloth. The bodies you left in the paint warehouse. Giving the guy at the marina the keys to your Lincoln Navigator. Making everyone think the Hoover Dam is the target."

Tas patted his jacket. "If they hadn't found me, I would have made an anonymous call."

"We saw through it, Jakob. We saw through everything. Whatever you think is about to happen *isn't.*"

"Is that so?"

"It's over. They plan to leave you out here until you turn into air-dried meat."

Tas laughed. A big belly buster. Probably hurt like a bitch given what else was going on down there. But he laughed anyway. "Miss Wexmore said you were funny. But I thought she meant quick or witty." He stopped laughing, got all serious. "I didn't think she meant like a clown. Because if it *is* all over like you claim, Mr. Koenig, why the hell did you jump out of the Gulfstream? Why did Miss Carlyle? Why are you bleeding all over my deck?"

Koenig didn't have an answer. He wished he did. They fell into an uneasy silence. Watched an osprey silhouette above them, waiting for an unwary green sunfish to get too close to the surface. It obviously hadn't gotten the memo about flights being grounded.

Koenig wondered what Smerconish was doing. Was he watching them? Were there drones in the air right now? F-35s? Had Draper managed to get hold of him? Would it make any difference if she had? He thought not. Smerconish would listen to her as a courtesy, but ultimately dismiss her misgivings. Or maybe he'd even think she was lying. An ill-advised attempt to save her prized asset. He imagined Smerconish found it difficult to trust anyone. When you dealt in lies, that was all you saw. And there'd been far too many recently. Too many secrets. Too many people telling lies and too many people keeping secrets. Draper and Smerconish. Margaret and Carlyle. Secrets and lies. As ridiculous as it sounded, Tas was the only person Koenig could trust right now. He was the only one without a hidden agenda. Which made Koenig think: *Why not just ask him?*

"OK," Koenig said. "I get it. You've had some setbacks, admittedly mainly caused by me, but you claim you're exactly where you want to be. In a boat on Lake Mead with the authorities believing you plan to destroy the Hoover Dam. I don't think it's possible, but the idiots in charge won't take the risk. They'll blow you out of the water before you get anywhere near it. I think you know this."

"You have a point?"

"More of an observation. Why the grandstanding? Why not do whatever it is you plan to do and get it over with? Why risk the SEALs and the F-35s? When you catch James Bond, you don't gloat. You don't stick him in an over-complicated death trap, then walk off like it's a done deal. You shoot him in the head, and you keep shooting until there are no more bullets in your gun."

Tas reached into his jacket, pulled out a cigar case. He turned it upside down and tapped the end. A red-brown stogie slid out. It was eight inches long and thicker than his thumb. Looked like a double corona. He pinched the end, then sliced it off with his punch-dagger. Stuck it in his mouth, then lit a Zippo under it. He sucked until the end glowed brighter than the heart of a furnace, then offered Koenig one.

Koenig shook his head.

Tas took a deep draw. Held it, then blew out a thick blue-gray plume of smoke. He sighed in pleasure, coughed, then went silent. Seemed to be enjoying the cigar and the peace of the moment. "I'm no James Bond villain, Mr. Koenig," he said. "But it's funny you used a movie reference."

"It was? Why?"

"Because I was about to use one myself," he said. "Tell me, have you ever seen *Die Hard*?"

CHAPTER 125

"*Die Hard*?" Koenig said.

"It's an action movie," Tas said.

"I *know* it's an action movie, Jakob. Everyone knows it's an action movie. There are uncontacted tribes in the Peruvian jungle who know it's an action movie."

"But have you seen it?"

In his pre-drifter days, Koenig had a bunch of 35-millimeter *Die Hard* film cells mounted on the wall of his home office. Cost him ninety bucks on eBay. Came with a certificate of authenticity and Bruce Willis's supposed autograph. Looked like it had been signed by a toddler. Which, admittedly, didn't rule out anything.

"I've seen it," he said. "But unless you want to debate whether or not it's a Christmas movie, I suggest you tell me what's on your mind."

Tas chuckled. "You understand the basic premise?"

"*Die Hard* isn't big on allegory. There are no hidden messages. Hans Gruber, arguably the greatest movie villain of all time, takes a bunch of corporate types hostage under the guise of terrorism. John McClane gate-crashes his party when he tries to save his wife. Eventually McClane figures out the terrorism angle was bullshit. Gruber was after the bearer bonds in Nakatomi Plaza's safe. He wasn't a freedom fighter; he was just a thief."

"Wrong, Mr. Koenig," Tas said. "Hans Gruber wasn't just a thief; he was an *exceptional* thief. Do you want to know why?"

"Because that's how he describes himself throughout the movie?"

"No, the reason he was an exceptional thief was because of the way he constructed the heist. The bearer bonds he wanted were inside a state-of-the-art, high-security vault. You'll remember it was protected by seven levels of security. Seven locks."

"Gruber's whiz kid was able to bypass the first six, but the last was outside of his control," Koenig said, wondering where Tas was going with this. "The electromagnetically sealed seventh lock was powered by circuits that couldn't be cut locally."

"That's right. But Gruber, being an *exceptional* thief, had planned for that. By posing as a terrorist from the beginning, he was able to manipulate the FBI into shutting off the building's power. That deactivated the last lock and opened the vault. He used the FBI's predictability against them."

Koenig nodded. Gruber's master plan was riddled with plot holes, but when a movie was as entertaining as *Die Hard*, you went along with it.

And then he caught up with Tas's subtext. A feeling of dread crept up his spine. Because Tas hadn't just been ahead of them the entire time. He was *still* ahead of them. Nothing had been left to chance. He and Margaret had considered everything, and they had planned for everything. Right down to the minutiae. Being observed ditching his cell phone in New Silloth. Choosing a date that coincided with a visiting British aircraft carrier. Leaving dead bodies in downtown San Diego. Giving away his Lincoln Navigator on the shores of the lake. Everything led to Lake Mead with F-35s in the air and a trigger-happy DoD spook.

And the plan had worked flawlessly, like an expensive Swiss watch.

There was one thing *outside* Tas's control, though. Something outside his sphere of influence. But that didn't matter. Not when you were as skilled at manipulating people as Tas was. He didn't need to be in control of the final piece of the Acacia Avenue Protocol. He had people for that. People who didn't even know they were doing exactly as he wanted.

Koenig shuddered. He understood the *Die Hard* reference now.

CHAPTER 126

"You *want* the F-35s to attack," Koenig said. A statement, not a question.

Tas smiled. Then he coughed. Then he smiled again.

"Because in this real-life remake of *Die Hard*, the F-35s are the FBI and the boat is the electromagnetically sealed vault at the Nakatomi Plaza," Koenig continued. "You can't blow up the boat yourself, so you need them to do it for you."

"Is it not a beautiful way to end this movie?"

"And I guess right here, right now, I'm John McClane to your Hans Gruber?" He paused a second. "I should have worn a white vest."

Tas chuckled. Genuine amusement. It reached his eyes. They crinkled. "I've not thought of it like that," he said. "But I suppose there *was* a sense of inevitability that we would end up together like this. Of course, in this version, there is no Beretta 92 secured to your back with Christmas tape." He picked up something. It was long and tapered and deadly. Koenig's Fairbairn-Sykes. The one Draper had taped to the small of his back. "Although I appreciate the effort you went into providing such an authentic experience."

Koenig didn't respond.

"This is elegant," Tas said. "Original?"

"Far as I can tell, it saw service in Normandy."

"I like knives. Guns are so impersonal. There is something intimate about ending a life with a knife. I think it's the bodily contact. You're close enough to watch the light in their eyes dim. To witness the absolute shock when they realize the unthinkable is happening."

"Knives are a tool, Jakob," Koenig said. "A weapon of last resort."

"Not for me," Tas said. "There's a history to knives you don't get with other weapons. A shared link with our ancestors. Ever since Paleolithic man defended what was his with pieces of chipped stone, men have been killing each other with bladed weapons. Knives are perfect in their simplicity. They don't jam. They don't run out of ammunition. They don't stop working because it's wet. Or too hot. Or too cold."

"Paleolithic man?" Koenig said.

Tas nodded. "It's the period of human technological development characterized by the use of rudimentary stone tools."

"I know what it is," Koenig said. "I'm just surprised a chump like you knows that too."

"I haven't always been in this profession," Tas said, ignoring the insult. "I studied ancient history at Constantine the Philosopher University in Nitra. Although even as a child I had a fascination with knives. Read everything I could on the subject. I even studied the convergent evolution of bladed weapons. Do you know what that is, Mr. Koenig?"

"It's where species occupying similar ecological niches adapt in similar ways."

Tas nodded. "And did you know that no matter where our ancient ancestors lived, the very first tool they developed was a chipped-stone blade?"

Koenig didn't respond. He couldn't. A wave of pain was coursing through him. It was traveling up his body, from the tips of his toes to his hair. It felt like he was being lowered feetfirst into lava. He let out a low growl.

Pain is just weakness leaving the body. He tamped it down. Did his best to ignore it.

"Has anyone ever told you that you're a very boring man, Jakob?"

"Not twice," Tas replied.

He smiled, but it didn't reach his eyes this time. They were crinkle-free. Koenig thought that was interesting. Tas was manipulating everyone and everything around him, but he was still vulnerable to manipulation himself. He had an ego and he liked it stroked.

"Tell me, Mr. *Interesting*," Tas said, "what do *you* want to talk about?"

Koenig shrugged. Wished he hadn't. "We're at the point in the movie when Gruber shared his plan with John McClane," he said. "You fished me out of the water so you didn't have to die alone. I get that. But should we not die like men? And men talk. *Real* men."

Ego stroked.

"So, how about we talk about how you've managed to do what I'm assured isn't possible?" Koenig continued. "Bess says you can't permanently contaminate Lake Mead. I say you've found a way. Something to do with the F-35s."

Tas checked his watch. "Sure, why not," he said. "We still have a few minutes to kill. The optimum time for an attack on the dam would be at dusk, during the park rangers' shift change. That's what would seem most believable to the eye in the sky." He checked his watch again. Nodded once, little more than a head bow. "Why don't you try to work out exactly what it is you're sitting on?"

"Can I phone a friend?"

Tas grinned.

Koenig added the *Die Hard* information to what he already knew. The boat was low in the water. It had landed in Maine and been driven across the country. That meant Tas hadn't been able to use any old boat. He'd had to use *this* boat. Koenig had never studied marine engineering, but he understood the physics. Boats floated when the amount of water they displaced was heavier than the boat itself. The primary way to displace water was to create space. Space that could be filled with drugs, guns, wine, cigarettes, even people.

"It's not explosives," he said. "You could have picked that up anywhere. There was no need to smuggle it into the country."

"It's not explosives."

"A virus?"

"Why would I need a boat for a virus? Surely a test tube would do?"

"A poison or a chemical the think tank hadn't considered? One with longevity."

"No. Miss Carlyle is quite correct. Poison would be inconvenient. It wouldn't indefinitely render the water undrinkable."

"Bess thought the most likely way to intentionally cause a mass migration event was to poison the air with weaponized fungi," Koenig said. "One of the mycotoxins. Causes severe illness, enough to displace the population. But we're on water. That would make a mycotoxin release *less* effective, not more effective."

"It's not fungi," Tas said.

Koenig was fresh out of ideas. He was almost fresh out of blood. "I have no idea, Jakob. We know there aren't any nuclear bombs in play."

"I'll give you a clue," Tas said. "You're getting warmer."

"There *are* no missing nukes, Jakob. When there's a threat like this, everyone checks their stockpile. No country wants suitcase bombs in play."

"You're not listening, Mr. Koenig," he said. "I said you're getting *warmer*."

He emphasized warmer. Like he was being literal, not figurative. And when Koenig thought about it, he *was* warm. And he should have been cold. The body compensated for blood loss by restricting the blood vessels in the limbs and extremities. It concentrated on vital organs like the heart and the lungs and the liver. The skin and the arms and the legs got a much-reduced amount. The less blood you had, the colder you became.

But Koenig was warm, as if he were leaning against a radiator. Which meant the heat was coming from an external source. In the last ten minutes the deck had gone from feeling like wood warmed by the sun to wood that hadn't long been out of the fire.

He could think of only one thing that generated heat like this.

Despite the heat, Koenig shivered. Like he'd stepped out of a sauna and into the snow. He understood everything. He understood why the boat had been smuggled into the country. And he understood why Tas needed Smerconish to close the deal.

Koenig had failed.

He had failed and Tas had won.

Margaret had won.

Because as sure as bacon for breakfast, Lake Mead was about to become toxic. And there wasn't a thing he could do to stop it.

"The boat isn't packed with explosives, is it, Jakob?" he said. "It's packed with something much worse."

"You've worked it out, Mr. Koenig!" Tas said, grinning from ear to ear. Proud. "Well done! The boat *isn't* packed with explosives; it's packed with spent nuclear fuel rods."

CHAPTER 127

Koenig had once been involved in the hunt for an embittered, mid-level nuclear scientist called Oscar Sands. Sands had somehow been included on an interdepartmental email chain, one of those rambling ones where the most recent email had little to do with the originating email. Sands had joined the chain near the end. He'd been asked for his input on something Koenig hadn't understood. Unfortunately for the person who'd cc'd him, the originating email was way above Sands's security level. And Sands wasn't the kind of guy to ignore that. Sands was the kind of guy who would print out the entire email chain, then go shopping for a buyer.

He was a clumsy criminal, though. Hadn't realized that all departmental printers kept a record of who printed what and when. A warrant was issued for his arrest, and because it was time sensitive, Koenig's team got the call.

So, Koenig knew a bit about how nuclear power plants worked. He knew uranium was processed into small pellets, which are then stacked together in sealed metal tubes called fuel rods. A bunch of these rods are bundled together to form a fuel assembly. Individually, fuel assemblies aren't enough to sustain a nuclear reaction, but when they are lowered into the reactor core with around two hundred others, fission takes place. This causes heat. This heat turns water into steam, which nuclear power plants use to spin the turbines that produce carbon-free electricity. After eighteen months, the fuel assemblies no longer produce enough heat to spin the turbines. They are then classified as "spent." Although no longer useful in providing electricity, spent assemblies keep producing heat for decades. They are kept in cooling ponds until they are safe enough for dry storage vaults—usually a geologically stable bunker miles from populated areas—where they remain dangerously radioactive for ten thousand years.

Spent nuclear fuel rods are extremely well guarded. They are all accounted for. If one goes missing, it's a huge deal. In 2023 an eight-millimeter-long radioactive capsule fell off a truck in the Australian outback. It sparked a national alert and a search involving thousands of people. That's how seriously missing nuclear material is taken.

Yet Tas had gotten hold of some complete rods anyway. They were probably fitted to the inside of the boat's hull. Along with gallons and gallons of coolant. It was why the boat was sitting so low in the water. It hardly seemed possible. Smerconish would have known if any were missing. He would have been briefed. Not knowing about missing fuel rods didn't seem like a ball Smerconish would drop.

Even so, having a bunch of spent fuel rods wasn't enough. Tas couldn't just dump them into Lake Mead. That wouldn't work. It wouldn't achieve the objectives of the Acacia Avenue Protocol. The rods would leak too slowly. They'd be recovered before any lasting damage had been done. Tas needed to blow them up. To turn a few fuel rods into ten million pieces of radioactive hell. Leaching foul poison into Lake Mead for the next ten thousand years. But Tas couldn't do that himself. He couldn't risk bringing his own explosives on board. The heat of the fuel rods might set off the detonators prematurely.

Which was where Smerconish came in. Because blowing things into ten million pieces was what the US Air Force did best. It was their raison d'être. So when one of Smerconish's F-35s fired an air-to-surface missile into Tas's boat, the water for millions of people would immediately be rendered undrinkable. It couldn't be fixed. It couldn't be neutralized. "Lake Mead" would become synonymous with "Chernobyl." An updated byword for nuclear disaster.

Koenig thought he could detect Margaret's hand in this last part. She'd have wanted the US military to be the author of America's demise. A final screw-you to the institution that had let down her daughter.

But then he thought about Carlyle. Considered how thorough she was and how adamant she'd been that a significant body of water couldn't be rendered toxic. Not for any length of time. Koenig doubted Carlyle would have overlooked spent nuclear fuel if a small amount could get the job done. That didn't seem plausible.

Again, Koenig felt he'd been put in check. That there was still something he wasn't seeing.

He shook his head and took a flier. "You don't have enough of the nasty stuff, Jakob. Nowhere near enough. If you could get enough on a boat this size, Bess Carlyle would have thought of it."

"You're quite right, Mr. Koenig," Tas said. "There isn't enough spent fuel on this boat to cause long-lasting damage." He smiled. Humoring him.

"But?"

"Do you know what the fastest growing branch of anthropology is?"

Koenig didn't. He said as much.

"Margaret did," Tas said. "She was a cultural anthropologist. And although she was almost retired, she kept up to date with all new developments."

"Enlighten me," Koenig said.

"*Digital* anthropology."

And there it was. The vital ingredient Carlyle hadn't considered. She believed destroying a body of water was impossible. And she was right. It *was* impossible. But she was also wrong. She hadn't made a mistake. The vital ingredient hadn't existed then. Not in the toxic form it existed now.

Social media.

And social media had been weaponized. It could move mountains. Fewer and fewer Americans were getting their news from traditional outlets these days. They were getting it from TikTok and Instagram. From Facebook and the artist formerly known as Twitter. From YouTube. A hundred other platforms. And the phenomenon of fake news had exploded *after* Carlyle's think tank. They hadn't considered it because it hadn't existed. Not like it did now.

Tas dumping spent fuel rods in Lake Mead would cause a mid-level toxic event. Big, not huge. Disastrous but manageable. Government advice would be to stay calm. To use bottled water until told otherwise. But what about when the Russians got involved? The Chinese and the Iranians. The North Koreans. They had whole departments dedicated to sowing discord in the American population. Bot factories. Dividing opinions and people. What would happen when they got going on social media? And in the comments section of websites. Posting links to "real" science. *Do your own research, people!* Drip-feeding their audience disinformation. *It's in the groundwater, people!* If Margaret had known what she was doing, and Koenig had to accept she had, she'd have held back some radioactive material. And each time the government said the water was clean, another dirty sample would be found. *It's a cover-up, people!*

No one cares which cow started the stampede.

Within days people would begin fleeing the immediate area. And the ones who didn't? The ones who trusted the government? *Sheeple!* Within weeks, Los Angeles and Las Vegas and San Diego and a dozen other towns that relied on Lake Mead for drinking water would empty. Vast numbers of the West Coast population would migrate east and north. To towns and cities ill-equipped to deal with them. Just like it had after Partition, the infrastructure would collapse.

Chaos.

The richest country on earth turned on its ass.

CHAPTER 128

Koenig thought Tas had played a perfect game. He'd pitched nine innings without a single batter reaching first base. No hits, no walks. Twenty-seven up, twenty-seven down. In 140 years of baseball, it's only happened twenty-four times. Just once for the Red Sox. Cy Young threw a perfect game in 1904, back when they were called the Boston Americans.

Jakob Tas wasn't going to be largely unknown. Margaret Wexmore wasn't going to be a footnote in history. When they wrote the books on how the Lake Mead incident changed the landscape of the United States, Tas and Margaret were going to be infamous. Forever remembered. Like Sid and Nancy. Hitler and Eva Braun.

"Is what we're sitting on the reason you killed your colleagues?" Koenig said. "You could have left the one body in that paint warehouse. We'd still have ended up where we are."

He didn't really care. He was buying time now. It was his only hope. Hope that someone would figure out what was *really* in the boat. Because if things played out like they were supposed to, Tas would make a run at the Hoover Dam, and Smerconish would make the biggest mistake in US history. Draper would object, but hers would be the only dissenting voice. Blowing up the boat would seem the logical choice to Smerconish. Oxymoronically, the *only* choice. The safe option.

"I would have killed the Australian anyway," Tas said. "The man never shut up. Kept going on about how wonderful Australia was, despite having lived in Poland for twenty years."

Koenig grunted. Australians were weird like that. Spent their entire lives bragging about a country they seemed desperate to escape. He figured it was something to do with the water going down the toilet the wrong way.

"But you're right, I killed Konstantin and Cora because I didn't want them to suffer. They didn't know what it was we'd brought into the country. They thought it was a nerve agent. Only Miss Wexmore and I knew it was nuclear rods. By the time we got to San Diego, they'd had too much exposure to the rods."

"I'm sure they'll write folk songs about you," Koenig said.

"They *will* write folk songs about me. Half the world will feign sympathy, but the other half will call a public holiday. No more bully in the playground."

Koenig didn't respond. The biggest dog in the pound was never popular.

"This is suicide," he said. Weak response.

"I'm already dead."

"Not for you. I mean for whoever provided you with the spent fuel rods. That stuff has a signature. It'll take our guys twelve hours to identify the nuclear plant they came from. We'll be at war with that country twenty-four hours later. A month after that it'll only exist on historical maps."

"Speak softly and carry a big stick?"

"It's not a joke, Jakob. The US will *have* to retaliate."

"Against whom?" Tas said. "The theft of the fuel rods has been reported. The relevant authorities have been notified. In two hours, Reuters will have it. Soon *all* the news agencies will have it. The accusations will fly, but ultimately everything will lead back to me. The bank accounts are all in my name."

"You had seed money, though," Koenig said. "You and Margaret needed a float to get this done. Someone funded this."

"Eighty million. Chump change for one of the world's three thousand billionaires."

"It can still be traced."

"It *will* be traced, Mr. Koenig. All the way to an American citizen. Driven by greed, not ideology. He thought he was buying influence. A favorable ruling on some strip-mining laws. Over the next few months, the details of my transgressions will be leaked. Your government won't be able to control the narrative.

The world will believe the story we've put out. They'll believe America was attacked by a lone wolf funded by one of their own. There'll be no country to retaliate against."

He threw back his head and howled.

Koenig recognized it for what it was. The final scream before you went over the top. An adrenaline-fueled way of steadying the nerves.

It was time.

Tas was making his run at the Hoover Dam.

CHAPTER 129

Tas hauled in the anchor. He took one of the outboard engines out of neutral and into forward. He rotated the tiller. The engine went from grumble to growl. Koenig felt the deck vibrate. Like he was sitting on a massage chair. He was too low to see anything other than the sky, but he knew the boat was sailing toward the dam. The clouds were moving. Koenig wondered if there would be any warning. He wasn't expecting the *kooouuuueeee* of a World War II bomb. Those bombs had whistles attached to weaken enemy morale. As they dropped and accelerated toward the ground, the pitch changed due to the Doppler effect. Civilians on the ground could hear the bombs, but they didn't know if that was their last moment on earth. It was a way of terrorizing the people you didn't manage to hit. As if war weren't cruel enough. The missiles the F-35s fired were state-of-the-art. They wouldn't whistle. Koenig thought he'd just go from being alive to being dead. No big bang. No flash of light. From flesh and bone to red mist.

What a pedestrian way to die, he thought. Waiting. Helpless, like a rabbit in headlights. And there wasn't anything he could do to change it. Nothing out of left field. No oil-filled Coca-Cola bottles. He was naked and he was immobile. He was weak with blood loss. He was unarmed and he was unlegged.

He'd hoped either he or Carlyle would shoot Tas from the water; in his wildest dreams he hadn't thought Tas would drag him on board, unconscious. Strip him naked. Take his Fairbairn-Sykes. He should have concealed a weapon. The suture needle from the Gulfstream's first aid box could have been hidden in his hair. It could have been pushed into his skin, all the way up to the needle's eye. He'd seen prisoners do it with paperclips. Used them later to open their restraints.

He thought back to his training. Multiple instructors from multiple countries and multiple backgrounds—kind of like the convergent evolution of the chipped-stone blade Tas had been babbling about earlier—had told him that the only difference between an object and a weapon was intent. But Tas hadn't even given him that chance. He kept a clean deck; there wasn't anything to hand. Nothing he could use as a weapon. No anchors. No boat hooks. Not even rope. He pressed backward against the cabin door, but it didn't budge.

Tas had done his job well.

Unbidden and unwelcome, part of Reinhold Niebuhr's Serenity Prayer popped into Koenig's mind. *Grant me the serenity to accept the things I cannot change.* Alcoholics Anonymous used it. It seemed apt. It anchored AA's core message: You cannot control everything. And *trying* to was the reason you were addicted to mood-altering substances. Which was ironic, as Koenig wouldn't have minded a drink. A cold bottle of Sam Adams. Maybe two. He'd have to settle for the next best thing.

"I'll have that cigar now, Jakob," he said.

Maybe he could send up a smoke signal.

Tas didn't respond. It seemed like he was concentrating. He was looking forward with his hand resting lightly on the tiller. Nothing but small adjustments. Appeared they were headed in the right direction. Koenig thought Tas would want to attract the F-35s before the boat reached the canyon that led to the dam. Ecological-disaster-wise, it made sense to blow up his spent nuclear fuel rods where the water was deepest. Koenig figured Tas was five minutes away from going full throttle.

Koenig tried again.

"We're about to see the business end of an F-35 strike," he said. "If that doesn't deserve a Cuban, I don't know what does."

Without taking his eyes off the horizon, Tas picked up his case and tapped out a cigar. He threw it toward Koenig. It flipped over in the air, like the bone the hominid throws in *2001: A Space Odyssey*'s opening sequence. The one he'd just used to beat a rival to death. It implied the invention of the first tool was the beginning of the hominid transition to human. It was the dawn of man. Stanley Kubrick was Koenig's favorite director, but although he liked *2001*, he didn't love it. He thought it was disjointed. Segments of the movie weren't connected. The final scene was flawed. And if he was being hypercritical, parts were a bit boring. It hadn't stopped him from having an original poster hanging in his hallway, though. It *was* a Stanley Kubrick film.

The cigar landed in Koenig's lap. He made no attempt to pick it up. He stared at it. His mouth went dry. He knew what he had to do. It was the only play he had left. He felt a prickle of something. He was so surprised he didn't immediately recognize it.

It was fear. Or maybe it wasn't. Maybe it was just the *memory* of fear.

Koenig didn't care. It was inconsequential.

So he did what he'd almost forgotten to do after all these years without it. He leaned into his fear and embraced it like an old friend.

CHAPTER 130

Tas had been concentrating so much on steering the NorseBoat, he'd neglected his cigar. Cigars weren't like cigarettes; they were living things. They needed constant supervision. Leave a cigarette unattended and it burns down to the filter. Leave a cigar alone and it goes out. After he'd thrown Koenig a cigar, Tas took a draw of his own. Got nothing in return. He plucked it from his mouth and studied the end. It was dead.

He took his Zippo from his pocket and relit his Cuban, rotating the tip to get an even burn. He closed the Zippo with a practiced flick, then threw it to Koenig. Koenig caught it with his right hand, and Tas went back to staring at the horizon. It seemed like he was going through the motions now. The way suicide bombers go into a semi-trance before they meet their maker.

Koenig tried to light his cigar, but the blood on his hands made the Zippo too slippery to hold. It shot from his grip like a bar of soap. Clattered along the deck, ended up back at Tas's feet.

Whoopsie-daisy.

Koenig held up his hands to show how bloodied they were. He said, "Sorry." His eyes were half shut. The blood loss finally taking its toll.

He watched Tas pick up the Zippo. He saw him frown and look at Koenig. Suspicious. Like he was being pranked.

"Worried you can't take an unarmed man, Jakob?"

Ego. The bedrock of all bad decisions.

Tas scowled and made his way to the bow. He flicked the Zippo's flint wheel. It sparked and lit the wick. A rolling, gentle flame. Like a candle. Koenig held out his cigar to warm up the end. He'd seen people do that on TV. It made the cigar easier to light. Tas reached down and held the flame underneath the end of the cigar.

"You were wrong before, you know?" Koenig said.

"Oh?"

"You said the first blade on every continent was made from stone. That it was an example of convergent evolution."

Tas nodded.

"But that's not quite accurate," Koenig continued. "There's archaeological evidence to suggest that the first blades to come out of Morocco weren't made of stone."

"You have me at a disadvantage then," Tas said. "What *were* they made of?"

"Bone," he said.

Koenig's left arm shot out. He grabbed Tas by the collar. He bunched it up and pulled toward him. Threw his head forward and butted him. A weak blow from a sitting position but enough to water Tas's eyes. Tas responded by smashing his fist into the side of Koenig's head. He felt his ear pop. His vision blurred.

Tas panted.

Koenig panted.

"Now what?" Tas said.

"This," Koenig replied.

He reached down with his right hand and grabbed his exposed fibula. It was wet. He gritted his teeth and pulled Tas toward him with his left. By the time Tas realized what he was doing, the tip of the bone was already under Tas's shorts and pressed against the inside of his thigh. As soon as Koenig was sure it was in the right place, he grabbed the back of Tas's shirt with both hands. And started pulling Tas toward him.

Onto his fibula.

The pain was worse than anything Koenig had ever felt. He ignored it. Ignored everything but the bone in his hand. He ignored the punches Tas was hammering into his torso, and he ignored the headbutts smashing into his nose and cheekbones. He ignored the bites and hair-pulling. He closed his eyes and concentrated on not passing out.

And then Tas understood what Koenig was doing. He saw the danger. Tried to push himself off Koenig. It was futile. Koenig was using his biceps to pull Tas toward him. Tas was using his deltoids to push himself away. Tas was fighting a losing battle. All things being equal, the biceps generate double the amount of force of the deltoid.

Slowly, inevitably, like a knife going into fridge-cold butter, the bone punctured the skin and entered Jakob Tas's groin.

Koenig kicked with his leg. Made the wound bigger.

Game over.

CHAPTER 131

Not quite game over.

Tas was a dead man. He knew it. Koenig knew it. The blood was leaving his groin faster than steam out of a kettle. Spewing from his shorts onto the already slippery deck. Tas remained calm. Like getting stabbed in the femoral artery with a fibula was an everyday occurrence. He didn't even look annoyed.

Instead, he looked at the outboard motor's tiller.

Koenig hadn't stopped anything yet. The boat was *still* headed toward the Hoover Dam. Smerconish was *still* going to blow it out of the water. The spent fuel rods were *still* going to end up at the bottom of the lake. All Tas had to do was reach the outboard motor before he did. If he managed to twist the tiller, give it full throttle, he'd win.

And now the race was on.

Koenig let go of Tas's shirt and bear-hugged him instead. Held on for dear life. Tas punched and he bit and he butted. Koenig hung on, but he knew he couldn't keep it up. The blood from Tas's femoral artery was spraying the air like a power shower. It was like fighting in a Jell-O pool. Tas's face was completely red. The blood rolled down his nose and dripped into Koenig's open mouth. It tasted coppery. Koenig spat it into Tas's eyes. Followed it up with another headbutt. Weak. Nothing in it.

Tas grinned. His teeth were pink from where Koenig had busted his lip. Time was on his side. Even if he didn't manage to reach the tiller, the boat was still chugging along to the Hoover Dam. Smerconish wouldn't risk it getting within five hundred yards.

Koenig let go and pushed Tas off him as hard as he could. Tas fell backward. Slid along the blood-soaked deck like he was on ice. Before Tas could get to his feet, Koenig used his arms and began crawling toward the stern. Like a drunk trying to get back into the bar. He'd only made it a yard when his exposed fibula caught on the wooden deck. Dug in like a fishhook. The pain seared into his memory. He knew he'd never forget it. He lifted his leg until he was able to move forward again.

Koenig raised himself into the half-press-up position. Kept his fibula away from the deck. He thought it might be faster to crawl like a baby. He'd barely made it a yard before his hands slipped on Tas's blood. He fell forward, just as Tas swung his right foot where his head had been. Tas lost his balance and fell. Like he was Charlie Brown and Lucy had pulled the ball away. And now they were grappling with each other again. Cats in a sack. Trench warfare. Lots of blood; small, incremental gains on both sides. No one winning.

Tas's eyes fluttered, then closed. He loosened his grip. Blood loss—it did that to you. He should have used a tourniquet. Koenig punched him. A weak jab, but it was all he had left. It had the wrong effect. It didn't finish him off. Woke him up instead. His eyes opened and he started fighting again. Weaker than before, but so was Koenig.

Koenig knew Tas couldn't beat him. But he didn't have to. All Tas had to do was not lose. Smerconish's F-35 was Tas's MVP right now. And then Tas looked at the sky. He smiled.

He could see the F-35.

Koenig had seconds now.

Tas had all the time in the world.

Koenig had to change that. He stopped fighting and reached down and hooked an index finger into Tas's wound. He yanked down. Hard as he could. It was like skinning a rabbit. Once it went, it went. Koenig tore Tas's femoral artery wide open. He fell back on the deck, exhausted. Watched as Tas's blood left his body like a burst water balloon.

"Ah, Koenig," Tas sighed. "You really are one crazy son of a bitch."

Then he died.

Koenig looked up. The F-35 was almost on him. He couldn't hear anything. You didn't with modern fighter jets. Not until they'd passed you and the sound had caught up. He gathered every ounce of energy he had. He pushed himself onto his elbows and slithered across the blood-wet deck.

He reached the stern. Pulled himself up. He grabbed the tiller and twisted it. The boat slowed.

The F-35 screamed over his head. Faster than a bullet. Louder than a banshee. Low enough that Koenig felt the heat of the afterburners.

Koenig laughed. Hysterical. He shouted, "Yippee ki-yay, motherfu—"

Then everything went dark.

PART FIVE

HANNIBAL LECTER IN A RAMONES T-SHIRT

CHAPTER 132

NINE MONTHS LATER.

Draper arrived first. She was on time. Wouldn't have mattered if she hadn't been. Smerconish always made her wait. She'd once watched him circle the block so he could arrive second. Underlings waited on their boss. It was never the other way round. She'd forgotten how much stock the intelligence community placed in who had the more powerful position. It was a game she hadn't missed.

Exactly five minutes later, Smerconish slid into the booth. Took the opposite side to her. Picked up the menu, even though they both knew he wouldn't be there long enough to order anything. Another power play.

Yawn.

"How's the patient?" he said.

Draper stifled a sigh. She picked up her mug of coffee and took a drink. Smerconish rarely asked a question he didn't already know the answer to. She played the game anyway. "Discharged himself a week ago," she said.

"Prognosis?"

"The infection's cleared up."

"The leg?"

"He had his last operation a month ago," she said.

"And?"

"He'll limp for a while, but there were no life-changing injuries."

When the F-35 pilot had aborted his missile strike, the recovery teams rushed in. Koenig and Carlyle were airlifted to Boulder City Hospital, where they were both stabilized. Tas's bullet had entered Carlyle's neck but hadn't punctured a major blood vessel. She'd lost blood and consciousness, but the life jacket she was wearing was designed to keep the head above water. Koenig was transferred to Walter Reed, where a specialist in leg trauma was flown in from Germany.

"And the radiation?" Smerconish asked.

"Our guys will keep him under observation, but they don't think he was on the boat long enough. Guess we'll find out."

"You took him out of Walter Reed," Smerconish said.

"I did."

"Why?"

"I wanted the best physiotherapy for him. Walter Reed's good, but Koenig needed one-on-one attention. Plus, you know what he's like. He was making the others uneasy. The way a jungle goes silent when a puma walks through it."

"Where did you put him?"

Draper told him.

"You like him, don't you?" Smerconish said. "That place isn't cheap."

"He's a self-centered, arrogant asshole."

"A description that would have fitted you, fifteen years ago."

She shrugged. It was probably true.

"Do you have what I asked for?" he said.

She pulled a manila file from her briefcase. It was thin. She placed her hand on it. "The guy who funded it?"

"The money man Ms. Wexmore approached—"

"*Miss* Wexmore. She didn't run a bordello."

"As you wish," he said. "He was just another sad billionaire. Used to getting his own way. Didn't like the word 'no.' Miss Wexmore convinced him she could fix some mining permits for him. He'll be convicted of something unrelated."

"Koenig won't like it."

Smerconish shrugged. Unconcerned. "You're his handler. Handle him."

"And Bess Carlyle? Will she have to disappear again?"

"That's the thing with Pandora's box," Smerconish said. "You can only open it once. Lieutenant Commander Carlyle has been welcomed back to the fold. The protocol is out in the open. There is no reason for her to hide any-more."

Draper lifted her hand from the file. Smerconish made no move to take it.

"Did you hear about Admiral Du Pont's son?" he said.

Draper picked up the menu. Studied it. Said nothing.

"He was murdered last night," Smerconish continued. "Someone shot him five times in the head."

"What a shame."

"Not really. The evidence found on his phone suggested he was a serial sex offender."

Draper kept studying the menu.

"Yes, it looks like he filmed some of his rapes, including of Miss Wex-more's daughter, Lieutenant Emily Braddock."

"Seems careless of him to leave evidence like that behind."

"Doesn't it? Although to be fair, he'd kept everything in a highly encrypted app. But whoever killed him knew how to break into it anyway. Almost like they'd had special training in that kind of thing. Access to proprietary soft-ware."

Draper looked up. "Any suspects?"

"No DNA, no fingerprints. One witness might have seen a blonde woman getting into Du Pont's car, but that's the only lead NCIS have."

"I guess Admiral Du Pont won't need to cover up any more rapes then," Draper said carefully.

"Never a truer word said," Smerconish said. "Because Admiral Du Pont was also murdered last night. Someone disabled the marine guard outside his quarters, broke into his home, and stuck a knife in his heart. Thin blade. Like the kind the commandos used on D-Day."

"Lots of those about," Draper said. "Do base security have anything?"

"A blurry shot of a guy with a limp."

Draper paused before saying, "They have nothing then."

Smerconish paused before saying, "Admiral Du Pont was a good officer, Miss Draper."

Draper put down her mug. Wiped up some spilled coffee. "No, sir," she said. "He really wasn't."

Smerconish smiled. "No, I don't suppose he was." He picked up the file and said, "Why did this take so long?"

"You wanted it done on the Q.T. That takes time. And anyway, her story wasn't straightforward. It took a while to trace the mother."

"And?"

"Died giving birth."

"The rest of her story checks out?"

Draper nodded. "Seems so. Nash grew up in care in Albuquerque. Frequently ran away. Stillwell Hobbs somehow managed to cheat the system. He fostered her when she was seven. Used her as cover while he traveled the country murdering people for money. Eventually she was old enough to learn the family trade. Turned out she was much better at it than he was. Not surprising really."

"And there's no doubt?"

"None whatsoever. We took a sample of her DNA from the self-defense ring she wore. Matched it against what we already had in our database. Harper Nash *is* Koenig's daughter."

"And he doesn't know?"

"No. As far as I can tell, Koenig and Rebecca Nash's paths only ever crossed the once. She visited Koenig's college with her lacrosse team. We figure they hooked up then."

"Does she have the same condition as him?"

"She does. We scanned her when she was under a general anesthetic for the bullet in her ankle. It's not as advanced as Koenig's, but she *is* on the same track. She *is* heading for the same station."

"Koenig doesn't know about her Urbach-Wiethe either?"

"No."

"He doesn't suspect."

"I don't think so," Draper said. "He's not dumb, though; he knew something wasn't right. She didn't react to the waterboarding as we'd expected. I think he put it down to psychopathy. But I've been watching Koenig for years, and I could see they shared similar traits. Urbach-Wiethe is so rare I thought it was at least worth checking. If only to rule it out."

"No wonder she's so dangerous."

"She's worse than dangerous, Andrew," Draper said. "At least Koenig has a moral compass. She doesn't. She's Hannibal Lecter in a Ramones T-shirt. And she has no fear. Whatever happens, she can never go free. You understand that, right?"

Smerconish didn't answer. Draper had known he wouldn't. He wouldn't be able to see past what could be achieved with *two* Urbach-Wiethe-compromised assets. Draper thought it was a mistake. Recruiting Harper Nash would backfire. Smerconish would have to find that out for himself, though. He wouldn't listen to her.

He never did.

He said, "Are you going to tell Koenig?"

"That Nash is his daughter?"

Smerconish nodded. Interested. Draper suspected this was the only question that mattered to him. The reason they were meeting face-to-face.

"Am I hell," she said. "Who needs that kind of emotional baggage?"

"Do you think he'll find out on his own?"

"He's Koenig. Of course he'll find out. It's a miracle he hasn't already. Two people like that, operating the way they do. I'm amazed they didn't enter each other's orbits earlier."

Smerconish pushed the file back across the table. It remained unopened.

"Something to ponder then," he said. "And now I must leave you, Miss Draper." He stood and offered his hand. They shook. "Until next time."

He walked toward the door. A car pulled up outside. He stopped and turned. "One last thing," he said. "Do we know where Mr. Koenig is now?"

"I have no idea," Draper said. "He said he might head to Nebraska."

"So?"

"So that's the last place he'll be."

Smerconish smiled. "I'll keep an eye on the news."

ACKNOWLEDGMENTS

I would like to thank my agent, David Headley; my wife, Joanne; my editors Christine Kopprasch and Krystyna Green; and the editorial, production, publicity, marketing, and sales teams at both Flatiron Books and Little, Brown. Readers, librarians, booksellers, reviewers, and bloggers, thank you for your continued support.

And thank you for reading this book; I hope you enjoyed it.

Blimey, that was a short one.

ABOUT THE AUTHOR

M. W. Craven is an English crime writer. He is the author of the Washington Poe series and *Fearless*, the first in the Ben Koenig series. His novels have won the Crime Writers' Association Gold Dagger, the CWA Ian Fleming Steel Dagger, and the Theakston Old Peculier Crime Novel of the Year.